'Cyprus!' Maddy said dreamily, a[...] his shoulder. 'Oh Stephen, I can hardly wait to be there with you. It's going to be so wonderful – all that warm sunshine and those lovely beaches, and all our friends ...'

'Steady on!' he laughed. 'We're not going on holiday, you know. I'm a serving RAF officer – I'll have work to do.'

'I know.' Her face sobered. 'And it could be dangerous, I realise that. But we'll be together most of the time. That's the important thing. And maybe I'll be able to grow up at last, and learn not to trample on other people's feelings.'

Stephen smiled. 'You're quite grown up enough for me, my darling. Now, shall we finish this champagne and then go to bed? We've got a busy couple of days in front of us before we go back to the air station. There are a lot of people to say goodbye to – it'll be a long time before we're back in Burracombe again.'

Lilian Harry's grandfather hailed from Devon and Lilian always longed to return to her roots, so moving from Hampshire to a small Dartmoor town in her early twenties was a dream come true. She quickly absorbed herself in local life, learning the fascinating folklore and history of the moors, joining the church bell-ringers and a country dance club, and meeting people who are still her friends today. Although she later moved north, living first in Herefordshire and then in the Lake District, she returned in the 1990s and now lives on the edge of the moor with her ginger cat and two miniature schnauzers. She is still an active bell-ringer and member of the local drama group, and loves to walk on the moors. Her daughter and two grandchildren live nearby. Visit her website at www.lilianharry.co.uk or you can follow her on Twitter @LilianHarry

Celebrations in Burracombe

LILIAN HARRY

An Orion paperback

First published in Great Britain in 2014
by Orion Books
This paperback edition published in 2015
by Orion Books,
an imprint of The Orion Publishing Group Ltd,
Orion House, 5 Upper St Martin's Lane,
London WC2H 9EA

An Hachette UK company

3 5 7 9 10 8 6 4

A CIP catalogue record for this book
is available from the British Library.

ISBN 978-1-4091-2823-6

Typeset by Deltatype Ltd, Birkenhead, Merseyside

Printed and bound in Great Britain by Clays Ltd, St Ives plc

The Orion Publishing Group's policy is to use papers that
are natural, renewable and recyclable products and
made from wood grown in sustainable forests. The logging
and manufacturing processes are expected to conform to
the environmental regulations of the country of origin.

www.orionbooks.co.uk

For Vivienne

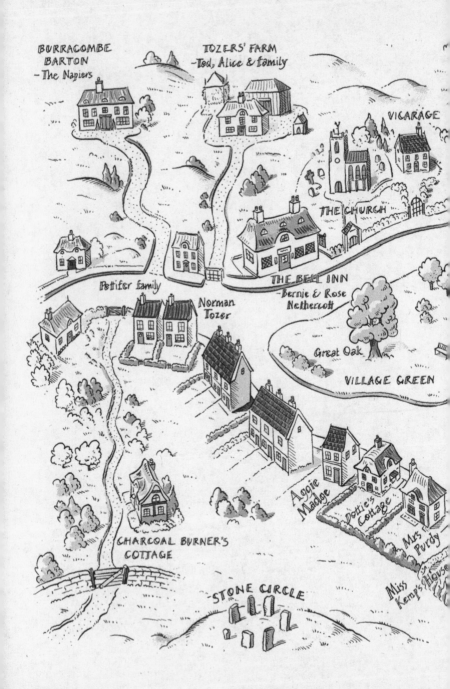

BURRACOMBE
BARTON
– The Napiers

TOZERS' FARM
– Ted, Alice & family

VICARAGE

THE CHURCH

Pettifer family

Norman
Tozer

THE BELL INN
– Bernie & Rose
Nethercott

Great Oak

VILLAGE GREEN

Aggie
Madge

Dottie's
Cottage

Mrs
Purdy

CHARCOAL BURNER'S
COTTAGE

Miss Kemp's House

STONE CIRCLE

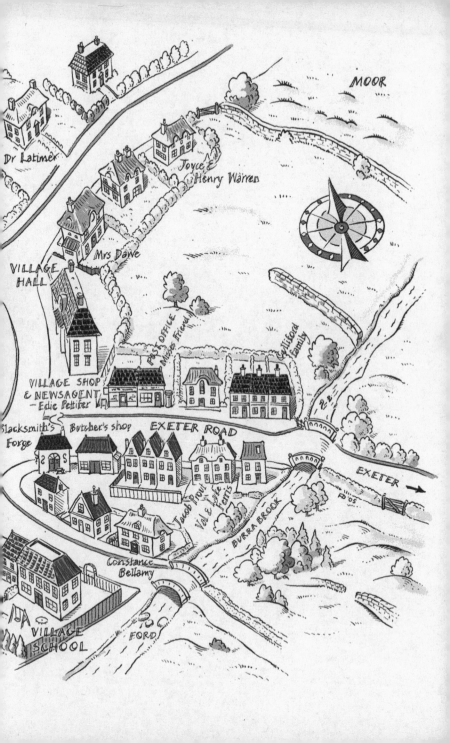

MOOR

Dr Latimer

Joyce &
Henry Warren

VILLAGE
HALL

Mrs Dawe

POST OFFICE
Miss Friend

Clifford
family

VILLAGE SHOP
& NEWSAGENT
— Edie Pettifer

Blacksmith's
Forge

Butcher's shop

EXETER ROAD

EXETER →

Jacob Prout

Val & Kyle Janis

BURRA BROOK

Constance
Bellamy

VILLAGE
SCHOOL

FORD

Chapter One

Sybil has died ...

Hilary put down the phone and stood, shaking, beside the hall table. David had said more than that, much more, but those were the words that stayed in her mind, overshadowing all others. *Sybil has died* ...

Slowly, stiffly, she turned and made her way into the drawing room. She closed the door behind her and crossed to the window to stand gazing out across the gardens of Burracombe Barton, her home for all her life, and past the fields and woods to the rising moor beyond, green and gold with the colours of June, dimming to purple in the distance.

It was all utterly familiar. And it was as if she stared at an alien landscape.

Sybil has died ...

Hilary had never met David's wife, yet Sybil's influence over her life had been immense. Without her, the unexpected reunion between Hilary and David, the man she had loved in Egypt during the war, yet had been forced to part from because both were already engaged, would have been very different. Their relationship could have been innocent and joyous, without the need for secret meetings and the fear of discovery; without the anguish of knowing that they might never be able to be truly together.

Faithless, spiteful and possessive as Sybil had been, David could not contemplate leaving her – or, rather, Hilary could not allow him to. Sybil herself had demanded a divorce, so that she could marry her latest lover, but to be cited as the guilty partner would have ruined David's career as a doctor. And the scandal would have devastated Hilary's ailing father, Gilbert Napier, and the village of Burracombe, where he was squire. With apparently no way out of their dilemma, they had finally agreed to part, not realising just how impossible that would be.

'I have to know I can hear your voice,' David had said despairingly in one of his phone calls. 'I have to be able to see you sometimes, even if that's all there can ever be.'

It had, indeed, seemed that that was all there ever could be – until Sybil had suffered her stroke.

Helpless from the start, with her own lover abandoning her, she now relied utterly on her husband, and David had had no choice but to stay with her, to care for her for as long as need be. Which might, Hilary knew, be for years.

Their love had seemed more hopeless than ever. But now ...

Sybil had died.

Did we wish this on her? Hilary wondered as she gazed out across the land that her father owned, that would be hers and her brother Stephen's one day – the land for which she had taken responsibility since Gilbert's two heart attacks. Did I wish her dead? I tried not to, but it was hard not to imagine what might happen if she had another stroke. And now she has ... Was it our fault, mine and David's?

No. Neither of them had ever wished her dead, even though it had seemed certain that she would never recover, that her life was in truth a living death. People did sometimes recover, David had said, especially young people like Sybil, only in her early thirties. The body could be surprisingly resilient.

And if she had, he would still have had to stay with her, for her recovery could never have been complete. But I didn't wish her dead, Hilary told herself fiercely. I *didn't* ...

In any case, it was no good wondering. Sybil had died, in what many people would have considered a 'happy release', and the world had shifted a little on its axis. And who could tell now what the future would be?

Already it seemed that the happy wedding she had just attended was in a different world. It was hard to imagine that the reception was still going on at the Bedford Hotel in Tavistock, where

2

Felix Copley's large family of clergymen had settled in with their whiskies to hold their own family reunion, and that half the village would be at the Bell Inn, where Bernie and Rose Nethercott were offering a spread of Dottie Friend's sausage rolls, cheese straws and other savouries. Here at the Barton, all was quiet. Hilary felt flat and restless, unable to settle. Exhausted after all the preparations and now wrenched back to her own problems by David's phone call, she wanted nothing more than to rest, but when she forced herself to sink on to the big sofa it was no more than a few moments before she was on her feet again, staring out of the window and wondering whether to go round to the stables and saddle up Beau for an evening gallop.

But that would mean changing all my clothes, she thought, catching a glimpse of herself in the mirror, still wearing the silk dress and jacket that she had bought for Stella's wedding. And by the time I've done that, I probably won't want to go any more.

Still, she ought to take off the wedding outfit. Perhaps a bath would help her to relax. She climbed the stairs and went to the bathroom, leaving the water running as she went into her bedroom to undress.

'Coo-ee!' called a voice from downstairs. 'Hilary – are you there? It's us.'

Hilary, just stepping out of her dress, paused in surprise and went to the door. 'Maddy? Is that you?'

'Yes, where are you?' Maddy was at the foot of the stairs, peering up. 'Oh, look at you, half undressed. Never a moment's peace, is there! Sorry – were you going to bed?'

'No, I was just changing. Don't worry, I'll be down in a minute.' She returned to her room, then remembered the running tap and dashed across the landing to find the bath half full of hot water. Bother, she thought, I was looking forward to that bath! With a sigh, she left it, then went back and pulled on the first skirt and blouse that came to hand.

Maddy and Stephen were in the drawing room. Stephen was holding a bottle of champagne, while Maddy ferreted in the cabinet for glasses. She emerged triumphant and laughing, holding up three flutes. Hilary recognised them as antique engraved glasses belonging to her mother, that she had never known used. She opened her mouth, then closed it again. What did it matter? It was what they had been made for, after all.

'What's all this?' she asked instead. 'I thought we'd been celebrating all day.'

'It's not over yet,' her brother told her. 'We knew you'd brought Dad home early and we didn't see why you should be here on your own when everyone else was having fun. So we decided to bring some fun to you. Hold out the glasses, darling.'

'No, let's take it out on the terrace,' Maddy suggested, going over to the long French windows. 'It's much too nice to be indoors.'

Hilary followed them out, feeling as if she'd wandered into a dream. How was it, she wondered, that one person could be so bemused, and nobody else notice? She took the chair that Stephen offered her and watched as Maddy set out the three glasses and held one out for the first explosion of champagne.

'There!' the younger girl said, handing Hilary a fizzing glass. 'Here's to more happy times – and more weddings! *Lots* more weddings!' Her laughing blue eyes met Hilary's before Hilary looked swiftly away. 'I love them. Especially mine. And now you've got to have one, Hilary. Honestly, they're the best thing in the world.'

There was a sudden silence. Stephen glanced quickly at his sister, then back at his wife. 'I think perhaps you've had enough champagne, darling.'

'Why? What have I said?' Maddy looked at Hilary again and added, uncertainly, 'I haven't upset you, have I? I only meant—'

'No, it's all right,' Hilary reassured her, but her voice cracked on the words and to her horror she felt tears in her eyes. They spilled over before she could stop them and she brushed hastily at her cheeks with her wrist. 'I'm sorry, I ... Look, I don't think I'll have any champagne, if you don't mind. It's a lovely idea, but ... Actually, I was just going to have a bath ... I think I'll do that anyway if the water's still hot, and just go to bed. It's been a long day ...'

With a quick, brittle smile, she got up and almost ran into the house. She heard Maddy's little cry of dismay and the scrape of her chair, as if she were just about to follow, but ignored it. In the safety of the bathroom, she turned on the hot tap again, stripped off her clothes and sank with a sigh of relief into the water, where

4

she lay back, closed her eyes and felt the hot flow of tears seep from beneath her lids and down her cheeks.

Everybody wants me to get married, she thought. Father, with all his talk of taking whatever chances life offers me, and now Maddy, and probably Stephen too, if I'd given him half a chance. And if only they knew about David. If only they knew the truth ...

But only two other people knew that. Her friend Val Tozer, who had been with her in Egypt, and Charles Latimer, the family doctor here in Burracombe. And neither of them could help her now.

Down on the terrace, twirling her glass between her fingers, Maddy bit her upper lip and looked ruefully at her husband.

'I really didn't mean to upset her. I just meant it would be lovely to see her married and happy. Like us.'

Stephen sat down beside her and took her hand. 'I know, darling. But poor old Hil, I think she's a bit sensitive about the subject. She's turned thirty, after all – she must think it will never happen. I think she found it rather hard today, watching Stella and Felix getting married and looking so happy.'

'But she surely couldn't begrudge them their happiness, after they've been through so much – that awful accident, and Stella thinking she'd never be able to walk again and that she shouldn't marry Felix after all.'

'No, of course she wouldn't begrudge it. But she still might not be able to help feeling rather lonely, especially when she had to come home early with Dad and make sure he was OK. She worries a lot about his health, you know.'

Maddy looked remorseful. 'Of course. There I go again – putting my big foot in it, never thinking how other people might be feeling. Should I go up and apologise?'

Stephen shook his head. 'Hilary's best left to cope in her own way. But I'll try to have a word with her before we leave. I've thought for some time there's a bit more to what's been troubling her. I'd like to get to the bottom of it before we go to Cyprus.'

'Cyprus!' Maddy said dreamily, and leaned her head against his shoulder. 'Oh Stephen, I can hardly wait to be there with you. It's going to be so wonderful – all that warm sunshine and those lovely beaches, and all our friends ...'

5

'Steady on!' he laughed. 'We're not going on holiday, you know. I'm a serving RAF officer – I'll have work to do.'

'I know.' Her face sobered. 'And it could be dangerous, I realise that. But we'll be together most of the time. That's the important thing. And maybe I'll be able to grow up at last, and learn not to trample on other people's feelings.'

Stephen smiled. 'You're quite grown up enough for me, my darling. Now, shall we finish this champagne and then go to bed? We've got a busy couple of days in front of us before we go back to the air station. There are a lot of people to say goodbye to – it'll be a long time before we're back in Burracombe again.'

Chapter Two

At the Bell Inn, the party was in full swing. Leaving the Bedford Hotel in Tavistock to Felix's family, many of the guests and most of the villagers had arrived by eight o'clock and were now enjoying Dottie's sausage rolls and some local ale. Felix had insisted on paying for the party, and some of those present were intent on taking full advantage of his generosity.

'I reckon you've had enough now, Josiah Hannaford,' Bernie told an elderly stockman who was holding out his pewter tankard for a refill. 'Vicar's not made of money, and I don't suppose he've seen you in church much above three times since he first came to Burracombe.'

'That don't mean I don't wish him well,' the old man said righteously. 'Always had a good word to say to me if us ever met round the village. And that young Miss Simmons he've wed today have been real good to my little great-niece, Janice, having her as bridesmaid, so I reckon I got as much right to be here as anyone. More than some I might mention,' he added, letting his eyes rove around the bar parlour and come to rest on Arthur Culliford's face.

Arthur coloured up immediately. 'If you'm making insinuations—' he began dangerously, but Bernie intervened.

'That's enough, Arthur. This ain't the time for argufying, so I'll be grateful if you don't take umbrage. 'Tis meant to be a happy occasion.'

'And I'll be all the happier if you fill up my tankard,' Josiah said, and Bernie sighed.

'Once more, and that's all. And if you needs to be carried home, don't ask me to do it.'

'Have another of my sausage rolls, Josiah,' Dottie suggested. 'That'll stick your feet to the ground.'

'Weigh 'em down, more like,' Ivy Sweet commented. Her face was nearly as red as her hair and her voice was louder than usual. 'Don't know what you think, Dottie, but seems to me your pastry's a bit on the heavy side since you came back from America.'

Dottie flushed. 'I won't lower meself to answer that, Ivy, not while I'm Bernie's side of the bar. But if your husband's got any complaints about my baking, I hope he'll tell me himself.'

'Of course I don't have no complaints,' cut in George Sweet, the village baker, for whom Dottie often produced extra cakes and scones for sale in the shop. 'It's as good as ever, as Ivy well knows. You'm not too proud to serve me one of Dottie's pies for my dinner,' he told his wife sharply, 'so keep your remarks to yourself. And you'd better take your time finishing that port and lemon, because it'll be just lemonade next time.'

'Might be a good idea to keep her on lemonade all the time,' Jacob Prout suggested. 'I never did know a ginger-haired woman that could hold her drink. That's when it's proper ginger, of course,' he added, not quite under his breath.

Ivy tossed her head and there was a brief, awkward silence. Everybody knew that Ivy's hair had been more brown than red until the last year of the war; she had started to dye it not long before her Barry was born. It was common knowledge too that the Sweet marriage was an uneasy one, although the couple rarely disputed in public. Bernie glanced at Dottie, then rapped on the bar and called out, 'Last orders for the Vicar's round! After this one, you all pay for yourselves. And some of you have had enough anyway. I'm looking at you too, Bob Pettifer. You've had three pints of cider to my certain knowledge.'

'He's hoping it'll make him look pretty,' said Bob's friend Reg, and everyone laughed while Bob pulled one of his gargoyle faces. 'Take more'n a drop of cider to do that!'

'Let's have a bit of music,' Norman Tozer suggested. 'Can't let the party end without a sing-song. Alf Coker's brought his fiddle along – I saw it behind the door.'

8

The blacksmith fetched his instrument and began to play, starting off with a few jigs and then going on to songs they could all join in. 'Widecombe Fair' had them going at once, with its list of names and special emphasis on ''Arry *'Awke*'. They sang all the verses, right down to the ghoulish-voiced 'skirlings and moans' of Tom Pearce's old mare, 'a-rattlin' 'er bones'. Then Norman and the other bell-ringers held court with 'The Bell-Ringers' Song' – 'But the bells of Northlew rang so steady and true, there never was better in Devon, I hold', with Ted Tozer cutting in as usual with, 'Only because Burracombe couldn't be there that day, us was too busy with harvest.' After that, the singing became a free-for-all, with one old tune following another – 'Tavern in the Town', 'Henery the Eighth', 'Waiting at the Church' (hardly appropriate on the day of the Vicar's wedding, Dottie commented) and 'Clementine'. Tom Tozer, who had a pleasant tenor voice, sang 'The Ash Grove', and Alf Coker laid down his fiddle and gave a rendition of 'Ol' Man River' that they all agreed was as good as Paul Robeson any day. That led naturally on to 'Old Father Thames', and they finished with a full-throated chorus of 'Rule Britannia', after which Bernie struck the bell that hung above the bar and called time.

'It's been a good party,' Ted Tozer announced, holding up his hand for silence, 'and I'm sure all of us wishes the Vicar and his new wife well, even though they'm now Little Burracombers. Well, none of us is perfect, after all ...' He paused for the laughter that followed this remark. 'I reckon both he and young Stella will be sorely missed in the village, but he says they'll be pleased to see any of us any time us cares to cross the Burra Brook to look 'em up. And I for one means to do so. Three cheers for young Vicar and Mrs Copley! Hip-hip ...'

The cheers almost raised the thatched roof of the Bell Inn, and then the revellers dispersed and made their way, some more rowdily than others, to their homes in the village. Josiah did not, after all, have to be carried, but he leaned heavily on Bob Pettifer and Reg until they deposited him at his cottage door to be hauled in by his diminutive wife, and after that the two young men leaned on each other.

'How's your Terry liking married life, then, Bob?' Reg enquired

9

as they staggered towards the Pettifer cottage. 'I noticed he weren't in the pub.'

'He's not old enough, is he.' Bob said. 'Old enough to get a girl in the family way, old enough to marry her, but not old enough to drink a pint or two in the village inn. Anyway, he can't afford it. Him and Patsy are saving up for cots and things.'

'Cots at his age!' Reg exclaimed. 'My stars, that's a warning to us, isn't it! I don't mean to be saving up for baby gear for a good few years yet. Nor do you, if you got any sense. We'm not twenty-five yet – got a few wild oats to sow first.'

'And that's what starts it all,' Bob said. 'Sow wild oats and you get a harvest at home. Best not to take the chance, Reg.'

'As if we even get much chance anyway,' Reg said gloomily. 'Tell you what, though, there's a hop over Meavy way next Saturday night. Square-dancing and that. I thought we might go along.'

'Square-dancing? That's country dancing, isn't it?'

'Yes, only more American. The music's sort of hillbilly. Roy Nethercott's been talking about getting up a band to play something like that. I reckon us could be in it.' They arrived at Bob's gate and let go of each other. 'You all right to get up the path?'

'I'm all right. You all right to get on to your place?'

'I'm all right.' Reg stepped carefully away and Bob watched him weave along the village street. Then he opened the gate and went round to the back of the cottage where he lived with his parents, his brother Terry and now Terry's young wife Patsy.

It had been a good evening, he thought, and the best wedding of the three that had taken place so far this year. First, that of Stephen Napier and Maddy Simmons, whom Bob had known as a child; then, under a bit of a shadow, his brother and Patsy, who had embarked on a pregnancy solely so that her father would allow them to marry; and now the schoolteacher Stella Simmons and Felix Copley, who had been curate in Burracombe until the previous vicar of Little Burracombe had died.

Three weddings, and only halfway through the year. Three celebrations in Burracombe. What would come next?

Stella and Felix, the latest of the newly-weds, were on their way to Tenby, in South Wales. Felix had booked a hotel in Bristol for their first night and they arrived in time for dinner.

'I don't really want a big meal,' Stella said as they put their suitcases down in their room. 'We had that nice lunch at the Bedford, and then tea on the train. And Dottie insisted on giving me a huge cooked breakfast. I seem to have been eating all day.'

'Well, you did fit in a wedding as well,' Felix said, taking her in his arms. 'And quite honestly, I'm starving. I find getting married very hunger-making.'

'You find everything hunger-making,' Stella told him. 'All right, I suppose we'd better go down. I'm surprised Dottie didn't pack us a few sandwiches and some cake to keep us going on the journey.' She caught his look and exclaimed, 'She didn't, did she? Oh, Felix!'

'Only a few of her home-made biscuits and a slice or two of fruit cake,' he said defensively. 'You never know, the train could have been held up. I'm sure we'll be glad of them at some point.'

Stella laughed and punched him on the arm. Then she looked up into his face and her expression grew serious. 'Felix, I do love you.'

'And I love you,' he said, bending his head to kiss her. 'And if you really don't want to go down to dinner, I'm sure I can manage on a few biscuits and some fruit cake ...'

Stella smiled. 'I'm not. You need regular feeding, and Dottie will be very cross with me if she thinks you've lost weight when we get home. Let's go down now.'

'All right.' He kissed her again. 'But I don't want to tire you out. You're still not as strong as you were, and it's been a long day.' He hesitated. 'Darling, I know this is our wedding night, but if you are too tired, you only have to say. If you just want to go to sleep ... I shan't mind. We've got all the time in the world now, to love each other.'

'I know.' She leaned her head on his shoulder and he rubbed his face against her dark curls. 'All our lives ahead of us. I'm so very happy, Felix.'

He wrapped his arms about her and held her close, rocking gently. They stood together for a few moments, then slowly, reluctantly, drew apart. Stella knew that they had both been thinking how nearly this moment had never come about, how close she had been to throwing away this love that had always been so precious to them both. But there was no need to say so. It was in the past now, and could safely be left there. The future lay before them, and she felt sure it was going to be a happy one.

'Let's go down to dinner,' she said quietly, and hand in hand they left the room.

Chapter Three

'Everyone wishes dear Stella well, of course, and no one more than I,' Miss Kemp said when the school governors met a day or two after the wedding. 'But it does leave us still needing a new assistant teacher.'

'It's not really Stella's wedding that's done that,' Constance Bellamy pointed out in her gruff, well-bred voice. 'Nor even her accident – she was leaving us at Christmas anyway. It's our bad luck in appointing that dreadful Miss Watkins to take her place. Who could have thought she'd turn out to be a liar and a thief?'

'We'll certainly have to be careful whom we appoint now,' Basil Harvey agreed. 'The children must have been very unsettled by it all, especially the little ones in her class. As for poor little Billy Culliford ...'

'Yes, he's been much maligned,' Miss Kemp said. 'I cannot comprehend how a woman who is supposed to care for and teach little children can make a scapegoat out of an innocent child – and one who's only four years old! It's wicked.'

'She'll never get another chance,' Colonel Napier said grimly. 'Now that the education authority has decided to prosecute her, she'll have a prison record and never be able to work in a school again. Now then, Basil, tell us about the new applicants.'

'There are only two,' the vicar said, ferreting about amongst a pile of papers. His white hair stood out around his head like a halo. 'One is a Scottish lady who sounded very nice on the telephone, but her accent is dreadfully strong – I'm not sure the children would understand her, or she they. And the other is – well, he's a man.'

He looked at them almost apologetically. 'I'm afraid it's a bad time of year to be looking for a new teacher.'

'A man,' Constance said thoughtfully. 'Well, it's not unheard of in primary schools – male teachers are quite common for the older classes. But for the infants ...' She lifted her eyebrows at the headmistress. 'What do you think, Miss Kemp?'

'I've no objection in principle. I've known some very good male teachers. But as you say, for the babies ... I suppose there's no real reason why not. It depends very much on what he's like, of course. Is he a young man, Basil?'

'He's in his fifties. He worked in London – a stockbroker, I believe – before the war, and enlisted as soon as hostilities broke out. He only went into teaching afterwards and has been working in a private prep school, but the post is rather strenuous and he's looking for something quieter. He was wounded in the war, apparently. In fact, he lost a leg.'

'A *leg*?' Miss Bellamy exclaimed, as if that were the last thing anyone could be expected to lose. 'But doesn't that put him at rather a disadvantage?'

'I imagine it does,' Basil said mildly. 'But if he's been teaching successfully for the past six or seven years, it seems he's managed to overcome it quite well.'

Constance looked a little abashed. 'I didn't mean to imply ...'

'Of course you didn't. And he does say quite specifically that he's looking for a quieter post than his present one. He probably considers that teaching in a village school like ours, where the children all go home in the afternoon, is somewhat less onerous than a boys' prep school, with boarders having to be looked after.'

'Which service was he in?' Gilbert Napier asked abruptly, and Basil turned to him with some relief.

'The army. He was a major when he was discharged.'

'Sounds a decent sort of fellow,' Gilbert said. 'I think we should have him in, see what he's got to say for himself.'

'But an army major ...' Miss Kemp said doubtfully. 'He sounds so different from Stella. She was so gentle with the little ones.'

'I don't suppose he'll have 'em marching up and down the playground and presenting arms,' Gilbert said testily. 'The feller should be given a chance. He's served his country, after all – shouldn't be thrown on the scrapheap.'

'I never suggested—'

'The Colonel's right,' Basil intervened quickly. 'It will do no harm to see the man. But shouldn't we see Miss MacAllister as well?'

'Miss ...? Oh, the Scotswoman,' Gilbert said dismissively. 'Well, I suppose so, but didn't you say her accent was difficult? And what's she doing applying for a post down here in south Devon? Doesn't she want to be in Scotland?'

'I don't think that's for us to say,' Miss Kemp countered. 'Presumably she has her own reasons. She may have lived in the south for years. Is she a younger person?' she asked Basil.

'In her forties. We'd probably have to wait until September to get a younger teacher. If you'd rather have one fresh out of college and be able to train her to your own ways, we could look at a locum instead. Or even ask Mrs Warren to help out, as she did before.'

'What about your wife?' Gilbert asked. 'She and Mrs Warren did a very good job between them before Christmas, when Stella had her accident.'

Basil shook his head. 'That was only for a short time. I don't think she'd be able to take it on from now until the end of term. Summer is so busy. And Mrs Warren would probably say the same. It really was an emergency – neither of them had taught for years and the county might not approve of our using them now.'

They all sighed. Then Miss Kemp said, with obvious reluctance, 'I suppose we'd better see them both since they're our only applicants, although I have to say, neither sounds entirely suitable to me. How soon could they come for interview, Basil?'

'Almost at once,' he said, consulting his papers again. 'Major Raynor has actually left his post at the prep school and can come at any time – he lives in Somerset – and Miss MacAllister is in London but is prepared to make the journey whenever it suits us.'

'Ask them to come at their earliest convenience, then,' Colonel Napier said. 'The sooner we have a new teacher in place, the better. Miss Kemp has soldiered on alone for quite long enough.'

'I'll telephone them both this evening,' Basil replied. 'Is there any day this week or next when we can't meet?'

'Why not telephone them now?' Constance Bellamy suggested. 'If they're in, we can arrange an interview straight away.'

Basil nodded, and picked up the phone. Within a few minutes he had organised an interview with Miss MacAllister on Thursday afternoon and one with the Major on Friday. He put the phone down again and they looked at each other.

'Well, there it is,' Miss Kemp said. 'Neither of them in the least like Stella – or, thank heavens, the dreadful Miss Watkins. Things are going to be very different in Burracombe school, whichever we appoint.'

'And we might not appoint either,' Constance Bellamy said, rising to her feet and stumping across to the door. 'We're not so desperate we'll take just anyone. We've been down that road before.'

'Things are going to be different anyway,' Basil said. 'Our children's teacher has a considerable influence on village life. We must never, ever forget that.'

Ted Tozer was also considering the changes that might be coming to Burracombe.

Leaning over his farm gate that evening, watching the cows graze the lush June grass, he reflected on the events of the past few months and the questions that had been brought up by his son Brian during his stay on the farm earlier in the year.

Brian had been discharged from the army and the family had assumed he was simply in Burracombe on a visit with his German-born wife Margret, before moving on to take up a career in engineering. It had come as a surprise to find that he had other ideas – ideas that concerned the future of Tozer's Farm far more than either Ted or his younger son Tom liked. If Brian had been allowed his way, Ted thought, chewing on a piece of straw, there wouldn't have been much of a farm left – just a factory turning out agricultural equipment in barns that had once housed cows and sheep, and the noise of machinery where once the air had been filled with the sounds of animals and the clip-clop of horses' hooves.

'We got to move with the times, I know that,' he'd said. 'But in farming, not manufacturing. Making a bit of shearing equipment, stuff us understands and works with ourselves, that might not be a bad idea, and us could use that old barn for it. But turning ourselves into a factory – no, Burracombe's not the right place for that and it'll never happen while I'm in charge.'

'Nor while I'm here,' Tom had agreed. But it had been Brian's idea that he himself would be in charge, and if that had happened, Tom and his wife Joanna would have had to leave. The two brothers had never got on, and sharing the farm would have been impossible. Nor were the rest of the family any more enamoured of the idea – Brian had made himself unpopular with all of them and had finally been taken to task by his grandmother Minnie, Ted's mother. After that, he'd announced he was moving away to team up with an army friend and start a manufacturing business in the Midlands.

'You'll be buying machinery from us in five years' time,' he'd told them, but Tom had shrugged.

'Maybe we shall – if it's decent quality. I'm not averse to moving on, as you ought to know. It's got to be done. But we shan't be turning Burracombe into an industrial site, that's the important thing.'

Tom was right, Ted reflected now. They did have to move on, and had already done so, buying their first tractor just before the war began. Shortages of fuel had meant the horses had continued to work, and none of the family wanted to see them go. But Barley was getting on now, and Ted knew that when he went, he would not be replaced. The sight of a big shire horse drawing a plough through the fields would soon be a thing of the past.

Ted heaved a sigh. That would be a part of his heritage – a part of his memories of farming from when he was a babe in arms, carried round the fields by his father – gone for ever. No longer would he and Alice look out of their bedroom window of a morning to see old Barley's head peering over his stable door; no longer would the great horse be brought in from the fields after a day's work to be rubbed down, fed and watered, talked to and even, sometimes (he thought with a grin) consulted. No longer would the children, Robin, Heather and Christopher, come running with an apple to hold under his velvety nose as a treat, or be lifted up on to his broad back to ride around the yard.

The tractor was a handy piece of equipment, it couldn't be denied, and now that fuel was easier to come by, it was getting more and more use. It made sense to own one and get as much out of it as you could. But Ted felt dimly that this was about more than replacing one piece of equipment with another, more modern and more efficient. When the horses went, farming itself would change, and things would never be quite the same again.

He became aware of someone else beside him at the gate and looked round to see his daughter, Val. She smiled. 'You look deep in thought, Dad.'

'Just chewing things over in my mind. Things are changing, Val. Things on the farm, things in the village. Things all over the world, I suppose. I'm trying to sort out whether I like it or not.'

'You'll like some things, and you won't like others. That's what usually happens. But why are you thinking about it now? Nothing looks all that different to me.' She turned her head and gazed out over the fields and the moors that rose behind them. 'Burracombe never seems to change much.'

'It do, though. Think of all that's happened in the past few years. You and Luke getting married and having young Christopher. My brother Joe coming over from America for a visit and taking our Jackie back with him. Our Brian leaving the army and setting the cat among the pigeons ... yes, that's what started me off thinking about the changes on the farm. But it don't stop there, maid. I reckon the wedding yesterday got a part in it too. We've all been sort of treading water, waiting for that, and now it's over, us have got to start looking forward again. And that means changes. Vicar's looking for a new curate, school'll be getting a new teacher. It's more outsiders coming in, isn't it?'

'Burracombe has always welcomed new people,' Val said. 'We're a friendly place.'

'I'm not saying we're not. But newcomers are bound to have an effect, especially when they've got a position in the village. Look at the trouble that Miss Watkins caused.'

'She was a bad egg,' Val agreed. 'But the governors will be careful to make sure the next teacher isn't like that.'

She hesitated for a moment and Ted gave her a sharp glance.

'Something on your mind, maid? Or are you just enjoying a bit of a stroll?'

'Yes, that's all,' she said quickly. 'Luke's busy with some letters, so he's looking after Christopher. I decided I might as well take the chance. It's such a lovely evening.'

'Best time of the day,' her father said. 'And best time of the year, too. Have you been in to see your mother?'

'I thought I'd go now.' They turned away from the gate together and walked back towards the farmhouse. The evening sun, dropping towards the horizon behind them, cast a warm glow on the cream-washed walls, and hollyhocks, evening primrose and foxgloves stood tall in Alice's garden, intermingled with rows of peas and beans now coming to their peak. Ted's mother, Minnie, was sitting outside on the old wooden bench, her back against the sun-warmed wall and her face lifted to catch the evening warmth.

'Doesn't she look peaceful?' Val said softly. 'So content just to sit there and enjoy the sun, and not worry about where life is taking her.'

There was a wistful note in her voice that caused Ted to look at her again, his eyes narrowed a little. But all he said was, 'I hope it's not taking her anywhere for a while. Us can't do without Mother. She've been the mainstay of this farm since before I was born.'

'Goodness, I didn't mean that!' Val said, horrified. 'She's not ill or anything, is she?'

'No, her's as spry as ever. But us got to remember her age, Val. None of us goes on for ever.'

He opened the gate from the yard to the garden and they walked up the narrow path. Minnie opened her eyes as they approached and smiled sleepily.

'Time you was in bed, Mother,' Ted told her. 'I don't reckon you've got over all the excitement of the wedding yet. Look at you, half asleep there.'

'And where better to be half asleep?' the old woman demanded. 'Outside in the fresh air watching the sunset and smelling God's good flowers? I'll go to bed when I'm good and ready, thank you Ted, and I don't need telling to go by someone I used to bath in front of the fire of an evening!'

Val laughed and Ted grinned. 'I don't suppose I'd have got away with back-answering you that way, though. Had to mind our Ps and Qs,' he said to Val. 'Her and Father wouldn't put up with no lip from Joe and me. Us had to do as us was told, preferably before us was told it.'

'Quite right too,' his mother agreed. 'Tackers like those two were brought up to respect their elders and betters. Not like today.'

'Christopher respects Luke and me,' Val said mildly, and her father laughed.

'He'm only eight months old! You wait till he's growed a bit. Anyway, Mother, Val and me are going inside for a cup of tea, so come on – sun's going down now and it'll be getting cool out here.'

Minnie sighed and nodded. He helped her to her feet and they went in through the low doorway to the big farmhouse kitchen, where Alice was just putting the kettle on the range. She turned and smiled.

'Val! Good to see you, my dear. Come and sit down – move the cat off that chair. Mother, your cocoa's nearly ready for you, and there's one of Joanna's flapjacks to go with it. Ted, I was thinking of doing you some cheese on toast for your supper if you fancy it.'

Val sat down at the table, taking the cat on her lap as an apology for disturbing him, and the door opened to admit Tom and Joanna. Jackie, who had come home from America for the wedding, ran down the stairs and waved at her from across the room.

It still struck Val, every time she saw her, how a few months away had changed her young sister. She had always been the rebellious one, wanting to tread a different path from the others and making it plain that Burracombe would not be enough to hold her, but she seemed now to have stepped even further from the family. She had had her hair cut in a sharper, more modern style, and she wore more stylish clothes. And wore them well, too, Val thought, even though she knew their parents didn't approve. Trousers were all right for working in, Alice stated, but you didn't go out and about in them. Her lips tightened every time Jackie appeared in a pair of slacks with a shirt or jumper, and as for those awful things they called 'blue jeans' – why, they were no more than what a fisherman might wear, and that nasty stiff denim they were made of couldn't be comfortable. And they had a *fly front*, just like a man's! It wasn't decent.

Apart from their thankfulness at having their youngest child home again, Ted and Alice had found a lot to disturb them about Jackie's return. There was this so-called engagement, for one thing, to one of the bosses at the glass-making factory in Corning where she'd found herself a job while staying with Ted's brother Joe and his family. She was sporting a ring, true enough, and a big flashy thing it was too, in Alice's opinion – she herself had always been more than satisfied with the tiny five-diamond half-hoop that Ted had given her years ago – but she didn't seem to have made any plans to marry. She just shrugged off any questions, saying airily that there was plenty of time; she wanted to have some fun first and see a bit more of America.

'Fun!' Alice had exclaimed when they first heard this. 'A young girl getting married shouldn't be thinking of fun! You ought to be making plans – getting your trousseau together, and your bottom drawer. I dare say you haven't even thought about that.'

'I didn't think you wanted me getting married yet,' Jackie said, all innocence and wide eyes. 'You ought to be pleased I'm not rushing into it.'

'Well, of course we are. We never wanted you getting engaged over in America, to someone we've never even met. But since you have, you ought to take it seriously. You shouldn't be thinking about "fun", and as for wanting to see more of America ...' Alice shook her head. 'Seems to me all you want is a ring on your finger. And you tell me this young man's been married before, too.'

'Yes, and widowed. It's very sad. And I *am* taking it seriously. I want to make him happy again.'

'Which gadding off round America without him isn't going to do,' Ted said sternly. 'What does he have to say about that? I know what I'd be thinking, if it was me.'

'Well, it isn't you,' Jackie said rudely. 'It's him and me, and we'll do what suits us. You don't know him, so you can't say. And you won't have to worry about me for much longer, because I'll be going back in a couple of weeks.'

'Yes, and that's another thing,' Ted began. 'How are you going to pay your fare? It cost me and Joe a pretty penny to send you over there this last time, and I've wished every minute of my life since that we never done it. You needn't think me and your mother's going to shell out again.'

'You won't have to. It's booked and paid for already. My *fiancé* has paid it.' She looked at them defiantly. 'You don't need to look so surprised. You knew I'd be going back.'

There had been little more to say after that. Alice buttoned her lip every time Jackie appeared in her slacks ('Katharine Hepburn

21

wears them'), and Ted held his tongue when she talked about rock and roll and some new American singer called Elvis Presley that nobody had heard of but who she reckoned was going to be famous, or played her record of Bill Haley and his Comets singing (except that Ted couldn't see how anyone could by any stretch of the imagination call it 'singing') 'Rock Around the Clock'.

'She's changed,' he said to Alice when they were alone. 'And not for the better.'

'I know, my dear, but there don't seem to be anything us can do about it. Don't let's spoil the rest of her time at home with any more argufying. It's not going to do any good.'

Since then, there had been an uneasy truce at the farm, and Jackie now seemed perfectly at ease as she helped her mother prepare supper, slicing the bread for the toast and making cocoa. The family settled down as they had done so often before, sharing their food and their news, and by the time Val left to walk back to the cottage where she lived with her husband and baby Christopher, the sky had darkened to indigo, smudged with a deep, burning orange.

Ted and Alice accompanied her down the lane to say goodbye. Val had been unaccustomedly silent during the family chatter, and as she walked away, they looked at each other.

'Are you thinking what I'm thinking?' Ted asked, and his wife nodded slowly.

'There's something bothering her. Something her's not telling us. I thought once or twice her might, but then her held back again. I wonder what it can be.'

'Whatever it is,' Ted said, 'she won't tell us until she's ready. I just hope ...'

'What?' Alice asked, and he sighed.

'I hope she'm not expecting again, that's what. After all the trouble she had with Christopher, and him only eight months old ... It's far too soon, Alice, and I don't know as she should ever risk it again. We nearly lost her then. I don't reckon any of us wants to go through that again.'

Chapter Four

'I've *told* you,' Hilary said. 'There's no need to worry about me. I'm as fit as a fiddle. You and Maddy go off to Cyprus and concentrate on being married. And take care of her – and yourself. I know it's not going to be any picnic for you.'

They were in the drawing room. The sun had gone behind some clouds and it had turned cooler out on the terrace. Stephen had carried the tea tray in through the French windows and they dropped into easy chairs, looking out across the gardens towards the moor.

'It's my job,' Stephen said. 'I know I'm only on National Service, but going into the RAF for five years has turned it into a career for me. I've had a marvellous training and I'm glad to be able to put it to good use. And we're only there as a peacekeeping exercise – we're not a fighting force.'

'All the same, it'll be a bit different from the RAF station at White Cheriton. I hope Maddy realises that.'

'Maddy knows quite well what it will be like. And don't try to change the subject, Hil. We're both concerned about you and I don't want to go away for maybe two years without knowing you're all right. So come on – out with it. I know there's something. You've been twitchy for months.'

'Twitchy!' she exclaimed, trying to be indignant. Then she sighed and said, 'All right, Steve. You win. There is something on my mind.' She stopped, and he waited expectantly. When she continued, her voice was trembling. 'It's not easy to talk about it.'

'Hil!' he exclaimed, and moved towards her. 'You're really upset.'

'I know.' She took a deep breath and tried to continue, but to her dismay, tears brimmed from her eyes. Impatiently she brushed them away. 'Oh, damn! I didn't mean to do this. I was hoping you wouldn't ask me.'

'Well I have, and I'm not going until I've had an answer,' he said firmly. 'You've got to tell me now. Look, I'll go and ask Patsy for some more tea . . .'

'No, it's all right. There's still some in the pot.' She waited while he poured milk and tea into her cup. 'Thanks. Where's Maddy, anyway?'

'She's gone to say goodbye to Dottie. I said I'd go along later, to give them some time together first. And Dad's safely over at the Vicarage, interviewing this army major they're thinking of appointing as the new teacher. So nobody's going to disturb us. You can let your hair down as much as you like.'

Hilary sighed. 'I can see you're not going to move until I do. All right.' She took another deep breath and stirred her tea. 'You may as well know. It's a man.'

'Yes, I thought it might be,' he said after a moment. 'Well, don't look so surprised, Hilary. It had to be either that, or the estate or Dad, and if it were either of those you'd have told me. And you're not so old that you're past having man trouble.'

'Man trouble!' she exclaimed. 'That's an odd way of putting it.'

'Is it? Why?'

'Well, it makes it sound so – so commonplace. So . . .' She stopped, the colour deepening in her cheeks.

'So what?' he asked quietly, and she answered in a tone almost too low to hear.

'So *sordid* . . .'

Stephen reached across quickly and laid his hand on hers. 'Nothing you do could ever be sordid, Hil. That word never even occurred to me.'

'It might,' she said in the same low tone, 'if you knew all about it.'

'I think you'd better tell me, just the same,' he said, keeping his hand on hers. 'After all, you know quite a bit about me that might be called sordid.'

'Marianne? Yes, maybe I did think that when it first happened – that morning I saw you coming out of her room. But that was

24

before – well, before I realised just how strong such feelings can be and how they can make everything look different.'

'Not in that case,' he said ruefully. 'I hated her and hated myself, even while I couldn't resist her. And she never had any real feeling for me – she was simply out to feather her own nest. But it's not like that for you, is it?'

'No, it isn't.' She raised her eyes to his face. 'But how do I know it isn't just – just *lust*? Or infatuation? How does anyone ever know, when it feels so real?'

'Hilary,' he said, shifting a little closer, 'you're not a young girl. You're thirty years old. You've been engaged, and lost your fiancé in the war. You've gone all these years since without anyone else. You're not going to be bowled over by infatuation.'

'Don't you think I'm just the sort of person who *would* be bowled over by infatuation?' she asked wryly. 'An ageing spinster, getting desperate.'

'For Pete's sake!' he exclaimed. 'You're not ageing! You're thirty – that's all. And I don't think you've been bowled over – not really. Now come on, stop hedging and tell me all about him. What's he called?'

'David.' Speaking his name brought a strange mixture of relief and dismay. For so long, she had been unable to say it aloud to anyone, except for Charles Latimer and Val; now that she could, it was almost a joy to hear it on her own lips. At the same time, there was a kind of horror, as if the genie had been let out of the bottle and could never be crammed back in. 'David Hunter.'

'Solid, upright sort of name,' Stephen observed, and she laughed with sudden surprise. 'What's so funny about that?'

'Nothing. Only you sound just like Dad, making a judgement about someone simply on the basis of his name. But he is, as it happens – a solid, upright sort of man. He's a doctor.'

'And where did you meet?' Stephen enquired. 'Come on, let's hear it all now you've started. So far, it's been like drawing teeth.'

Hilary smiled. 'All right. Here goes.' She told him how she and David had met again at the reunion last November of those in the regiment who had served in Egypt during the war; how they had known and loved each other then, under the desert stars, but parted because they were both already engaged; how David had married

25

Sybil but found her faithless and a social climber; how they had snatched a few meetings in London until Sybil had suffered her stroke; and how she had died only a few days ago, leaving Hilary in a strange, uneasy limbo.

'Good Lord,' Stephen said when she had finished. 'That's quite a saga. No longer you've been looking so pinched and worn out.'

'Have I? I've tried hard not to let it show.'

'I don't see you could prevent it. Not that anyone else would have seen it,' he added hastily. 'Only people who know you well.'

'I've wondered a few times if Dad has noticed. He's been saying some odd things lately – like the night of Stella's wedding, when he made a real point of telling me to make the most of my life, take the chances that come my way. But it sounded more as if – as if ...'

'As if?' Stephen prompted gently, and she looked down at her hands. He had removed his at some point during her narrative and leaned back in his chair. Now he came forward again.

'As if he didn't think he had much time left,' she said in a low voice; and then, the words bursting from her, 'Oh Steve, there's been so much to think about! You and Maddy, Dad, Stella's wedding – I've hardly had time to think about David and me, and now Sybil's died I don't know *what* to think! It's all so confusing.'

'It does leave the way clear for you,' he ventured after a pause.

'I know! But it seems so awful even to think that way – and in some ways it almost seems to make everything even *more* difficult. I mean, where do we go from here? Do I leave Burracombe to be with him? And if I don't, where can David go? He can't just up sticks from his father's practice – I don't even know that he wants to. I'm not sure *what* he wants. In a funny sort of way, while it was all impossible, *anything* was possible. Can you understand that? We could dream. But now ...'

'Now the dreaming's got to stop. You've got to make real decisions.'

'Yes,' she said. 'Yes. And yet we can't, can we? Not yet. It's far too soon. I feel as if I'm swinging in space. I don't know what David wants; I don't even know what I want myself. I certainly don't know if either of us can have what we want.'

Stephen was silent for a few minutes. Then he said, 'I'm younger than you, Hilary, and I've had a lot to learn. I've probably got a lot more to learn yet. But I think I've learned this, over the past two or three years. Nothing stays the same. Things change, and if you don't know what to do at this moment, it's best to wait a while. The moment will come when you *do* know what to do, and when that happens, you'll be able to make it possible.' He grinned, suddenly self-conscious, and ran his fingers through his fair hair. 'That's the sum total of my wisdom so far!'

'It sounds wise enough to me,' Hilary said. 'I hope you're right. I hope the time will come when I – when David and I know what we want to do and can make it possible. Just at present, it all seems very far away.'

He took her hand again and squeezed it. 'It will come, Hil, I'm sure of it. But I really ought to go now and say goodbye to Dottie myself, or Maddy will have eaten all her scones!' He stood up, then bent and kissed Hilary's head. 'Don't worry too much, sis. I'm sure things are going to come right for you. And you will keep me posted, won't you, while I'm in Cyprus?'

'Yes, of course I will. And – you can tell Maddy if you like. I'm not going to ask you to keep secrets from her.'

He nodded and let himself out through the French windows. Hilary watched him run down the terrace steps and stride away down the drive. He looked very carefree, she thought, and yet he'd had more than enough sadness in his young life. Perhaps she should try to emulate his blithe attitude.

She piled the tea things on to the tray and carried it out to the kitchen, where Patsy Pettifer, now nearly five months pregnant, was peeling vegetables for the evening meal and the new housekeeper, Mrs Curnow, was making pastry for a strawberry flan. They both turned and smiled as she came in, and she felt warmed by their presence. They too had had their troubles, yet they could still find a smile. It's the same for all of us, she thought, and smiled back.

'It's lovely in here,' she said. 'The heart of the home, my mother always used to say. If the kitchen's a happy place, the rest of the house will be happy too.'

David rang again late that evening. He sounded tired, and Hilary ached to hold him in her arms. Why do we have to live so far apart? she thought yearningly.

27

'How are you, David? What's the news?'

'Things are much as might be expected. I've been organising the funeral.' His voice cracked a little. 'It's such a strange time. I don't even know how I feel about it all. I loved her once – or thought I did. We shared our lives for nearly ten years. And now ...' He seemed unable to go on. Then he said, very quietly, 'You know, Hilary, there was a moment – a short time, when she had the first stroke – when she was almost lucid for a while. And just for that time ...' He paused, then went on. 'Just for that time, it was almost like it had been, in the very early days, before we got married. Before I went to Egypt. When I – when I ...'

'When you loved each other,' Hilary said, her throat dry and aching.

'Yes.'

'So you loved her again.'

'Just for that time. At least, I think so. It doesn't make things any different between you and me,' he said quickly, urgently. 'It was more like reliving a memory. And then she slipped back into unconsciousness and I – I'm not even sure now that it happened. Perhaps I just thought – perhaps I dreamed ...'

'Perhaps you wanted it to happen.' She was dimly surprised, even shocked, by the coolness of her tone, and she knew at once that David had heard it.

'No! Darling Hilary, no! You mustn't think that. I tell you, it makes no difference to us. It was – it was just a passing sensation. And if it gave her some comfort ...'

'Yes, of course. I'm being selfish.' She stopped, unable to think of anything else to say, and there was a brief silence.

'Hilary? Are you still there?'

'Yes, I'm here.' She had never had such a stilted conversation with him. She spoke more briskly. 'So what's happening? Have you arranged the funeral?'

'Yes.' He sounded deflated and miserable. 'Yes, it's next Tuesday morning. We're doing ham sandwiches and so on back here afterwards. And then I suppose there'll be things to sort out. Her clothes, jewellery, various possessions. You know the sort of thing.'

'Of course.'

'And after that ...'

'Yes?' she said, after a moment. 'After that?'

'Hilary, what's the matter? You sound different. Have I upset you?'

'No, of course not.' But you have, she thought, and she knew that she must be honest with him. 'I'm sorry, David. It's as you said just now – all rather strange. You're nearly three hundred miles away, and heaven knows when we'll see each other again. And even then – oh, I don't know. It all seems so impossible!' Her voice broke.

'Darling, don't say that! Of course it's not impossible. Nothing's impossible.' His voice was urgent, pleading. 'We love each other. We've got to hold on to that. Yes, it's difficult, but no more than – than before. How can it be?'

'I don't know,' she said drearily. 'It just seems to be, that's all. I'm sorry, David, I don't know what we're going to do. I don't know what to think. I feel – I feel as if I'm in a sort of limbo. And you're so far away.'

'I'm with you in my heart,' he said quietly. 'You must believe that, my darling. I'm always with you in my heart.'

But are you? she thought as she replaced the receiver a few minutes later. How can you be, after you shared those few moments with Sybil, loving her again as if nothing else had happened, and then watching her die?

How can you ever turn away from Sybil now?

29

Chapter Five

Major Raynor was everything you expected a major to be, Miss Kemp thought. A little younger than herself, in his early fifties, and tall, with broad shoulders and dark hair that swept back in a deep silver-streaked wave from a square face with a forehead as corrugated as the iron roof on an old air-raid shelter. His eyes were dark too, under strong brows, and his mouth was firm. He looked what the Colonel would probably call 'a good type' – but was he the type to teach small children? Miss Kemp, meeting that straight gaze, thought he was more likely to frighten them. And they'd already had quite enough of being frightened, by the unpleasant Miss Watkins.

'Do sit down,' Basil said, directing the visitor to a chair. They had discussed this before he came in, wondering just how much his leg incommoded him and Gilbert Napier had decreed that it should be a hard chair with a good strong back and arms. 'The captain's chair you've got in your dining room,' he told Basil. 'That'll be just the ticket. High enough so that he won't have any trouble getting in and out of it, and the arms will help too. Bring that into your study.'

Basil had done so, and now the Major came across the room and sat down, one leg held slightly stiffly in front of him. His gait was slightly stiff too, but not so much that it caused him to lurch or look ungainly. Really, Miss Kemp thought, it was no more than a limp. You wouldn't know he had an artificial leg.

Basil opened the interview.

'You're Major James Raynor, retired from Her Majesty's Army?

Thank you for coming – we're very pleased to meet you. I'm Basil Harvey, vicar of Burracombe and chairman of the board of governors. This is Miss Kemp, our headmistress, the lady by her side is Miss Bellamy, from one of Burracombe's oldest families, and this is Colonel Napier, our local squire. Now, we understand that until recently you've been teaching at a boys' prep school ...'

The interview proceeded smoothly. The Major explained that he had enjoyed teaching the boys, aged from eight to thirteen, but that they were extremely lively, and that with boarders you were on duty almost all the time.

'I was also assistant housemaster,' he said. 'I enjoyed it very much. It had never originally been my ambition to teach, but after I'd been invalided out of the army, I didn't want to go back to my old occupation as a stockbroker, so once I was mobile again I took a training course and started work in 1948.'

'You went to Oxford and have degrees in English and history,' Miss Bellamy said, looking at the sheet of paper Basil had handed her. 'Aren't your qualifications rather high for a small village primary school? I'd have thought any prep school, or even a public school like Kelly College, would be pleased to have you on their staff.'

'Not to mention a grammar school,' observed Miss Kemp, who was always keen to promote the education provided by state schools, to which most of her pupils would go.

Miss Bellamy inclined her head. 'Certainly. The principle is just the same. Is there any particular reason why you have chosen to apply to us, Major Raynor?'

The Major smiled. 'First of all, I'd rather like to drop the term "Major". It's all very well for a private school, but I think it might be slightly intimidating in a village. I'd prefer to be plain Mister.'

Colonel Napier's thick eyebrows rose. 'Drop your army rank? Surely it's something to be proud of?'

'And I am indeed proud of it. But I was never a career soldier. I missed serving in the First World War, so when hostilities broke out again in 1939, I felt I ought to do my bit and enlisted. I was just under forty, or they probably wouldn't have taken me. It was only by luck – the bad luck of other poor wretches who would have been promoted if they'd lived – that I found myself becoming a major. Simply a case of being in the right place at the right time.'

'You were mentioned in dispatches.'

'So were many others.' There was a slight pause, then he went on. 'The war is over now and many people want to forget it. I became a major by chance. Now I want to return to my civilian life, and that means reverting to my proper title.' He hesitated again. 'You see, I don't come from the class who would have sent their children to private schools. My father was a greengrocer. He owned several shops in Brighton, where I grew up, and I went to the local primary and boys' grammar school – I won a scholarship to go there, but there was still a fee, which he could afford to pay. I was very fortunate to be able to go on to university, but it was due to my parents' belief in education rather than any privilege or wealth.'

'But the respect due to your rank,' Gilbert protested. 'You've earned that.'

'And now I'd like to earn the respect due to my own self.'

Gilbert lifted both hands and let them fall back on his knees.

Miss Kemp said, 'Your first post was in a prep school. Was it your wish to teach younger children?'

'Yes, it was. I enjoy their company and the sense of being able to help form their developing minds. And I think it's important that children from ordinary working families should have a good education. They have just as much potential as the more privileged. I want to help them make the most of themselves – to rise just as high as they are able. To become teachers and doctors, if that's where their talents lie, or to take pride in being farm workers, bricklayers or bus drivers like their fathers, knowing that they play just as important a part in society.'

Gilbert stared at him. 'Are you telling us you're a communist?'

'No, but I like to think I am a true socialist, and will endeavour to see that every child leaves the school knowing that they are valued for their own selves.'

'Don't see much wrong with that,' Constance Bellamy said in her gruff voice, and Miss Kemp nodded her agreement.

'In any case,' she said, 'Major – *Mr* Raynor's politics are no concern of ours.'

'Provided he doesn't indoctrinate the children with them,' the Colonel said brusquely.

'I imagine their own parents will do that,' Basil said mildly. 'And some of them may even learn to think for themselves.'

'That,' James Raynor said with a smile, 'is exactly what I would hope to teach them.'

There was a short pause.

'English and history,' Miss Kemp said thoughtfully. 'The finest of all subjects for young children – their language and an understanding of the past. What about the others, Mr Raynor? Geography, arithmetic and so on?'

He smiled at her. 'No problems with those, or any of the other general subjects required.'

'What about craft works?' Constance enquired. 'Miss Simmons was very keen on things like painting and learning poetry. She taught the girls embroidery and crochet, too.'

'I'm not sure I would be up to her standard with those,' he admitted with another smile. 'But what were the boys doing while this was going on?'

'Jacob Prout, our village handyman, used to come in and teach them simple woodwork,' Miss Kemp said. 'Not that they could do very much, at their age.'

'Well, I could do that, unless you'd prefer that Mr Prout continues. And maybe there's a woman in the village who could take over the girls' handicrafts for us.'

'No problem there,' Gilbert declared. 'Dottie Friend ... Joyce Warren ... Perhaps even your own wife, Basil. We can't expect any teacher to have all the talents at his fingertips.'

'There's still singing and country dancing,' Constance said doubtfully. 'I know Stella instigated some of those herself and they're not an essential part of the curriculum, but the children do enjoy them.'

'And can continue to do so,' their applicant declared. 'I've a passable voice myself – I might even ask if I can join your church choir, Mr Harvey – and I play the piano. And if, as I understand it, your former teacher is only moving to the next village, it might be possible to prevail upon her to come back occasionally to run country dancing classes.'

'I'm sure Stella would love to do that,' Miss Kemp said. 'She's mentioned it to me herself. She's thinking of starting an actual club, as soon as she and Felix are properly settled into the Little Burracombe vicarage, for both villages. I'm sure she'd be pleased to run a class for the children too.'

The interview continued. Major Raynor had been widowed during the Blitz, he told them, when his wife was killed while volunteering at a large air-raid shelter. His parents, who were already in their eighties, had died within a year of each other, shortly before the war ended.

'And you have no other ties?' Basil asked diplomatically. 'No other relatives?'

'Apart from a few distant cousins in Hampshire and a relative in Australia, none. I lost touch with most of them during the war, and we were never a very close family. My parents were in their forties when I was born, so all my first cousins were older than me and I never really had much contact with them. Just weddings and funerals, that kind of thing.'

'And you don't want to make your life in Brighton? It's your home town, after all.'

He shook his head. 'I left there at eighteen to go to Oxford, and apart from visits to my parents, I never lived there again. I started work in London when I came down and stayed there until the war. We had a home in Hampstead, but after my wife died, I sold it.' He paused, then went on. 'My grandfather – my mother's father – came from Beer, on the south Devon coast, but I felt I had a rapport with the whole county. I looked around that area for a post, but there were none available. In any case, although I may have very distant relatives there, I don't know them and they wouldn't be interested in me. It's better to start somewhere completely new.'

There was a short silence. Colonel Napier looked at the others. 'I think we've covered everything now. Unless any of you have any more questions?' They all shook their heads and he nodded at the major. 'Perhaps you'd like to wait outside for a few minutes while we have a chat? Although I can't promise a final decision today, of course.'

'Use our sitting room,' Basil said, and showed the major through, leaving him with a copy of *The Times* to browse. He returned to find the others deliberating.

'He seems a very good sort,' Gilbert was saying. 'Must say, I was a bit taken aback when he said he didn't want to use his rank, but I suppose it will be easier for the children. What do you think, Constance?'

'Well, we all agreed yesterday that Miss MacAllister was not really suitable,' the little woman said, referring to the teacher they had interviewed the previous day. 'My only concern is that he might not stay with us very long. He's fifty-two now – only a few years from retirement age.'

'I agree,' Gilbert said. 'And I think you're right about his qualifications, too. With degrees such as those, why does he want to confine himself to teaching small children to read and write? All you need for that is a year or two at a teacher training college.'

'Reading and writing are the basic building blocks of education,' Miss Kemp pointed out mildly. 'They shouldn't be dismissed too lightly.'

'I'm not saying they should. I completely understand that he may be a very fine teacher and would do a good job with our children. I just wonder if it will be satisfying enough for him – whether he will find sufficient stimulation in the task. Sufficient *challenge*.'

'I think some of our children are quite challenging enough, even for an army major,' Miss Kemp remarked drily. 'The Crocker twins, for example.'

Basil smiled, but his voice was serious. 'It strikes me that the major – Mr Raynor, I mean – has had a good many challenges in his life already and might be looking for something more peaceful. It must be very difficult for a man who never sought a military career to find himself spending six years of his life at war, with growing responsibilities all the time. Especially when he lost his wife in such a tragic way.' He paused, then went on. 'I have a suggestion. We're halfway through the summer term, without a second teacher, and Mr Raynor is free immediately. Why not ask if he would accept the post on a probationary basis, perhaps until half-term? It would only take a week or two for Miss Kemp to get a good idea as to whether he is suitable, and if she has any doubts, we can start to look around again.'

'It might be the best we can do,' Constance said. 'Our only objection to Mr Raynor seems to be that his qualifications are rather high.'

'And that we don't know how he would get along with girls,' Miss Kemp added. 'He's only taught boys so far, remember. Suppose one of the little girls has a problem he can't deal with.'

'Presumably he'd come to you,' Basil said. 'You're only on the other side of the partition, after all.'

Colonel Napier looked around. 'Is that agreed, then? We call him back and offer him the post on a probationary basis? It can apply on both sides, after all – he may decide that a village primary school isn't right for him, once he's had a taste of it.'

'There's one point we haven't considered,' Miss Kemp added. 'Where is he to live? I'm not sure that Dottie Friend will feel comfortable having a male lodger, and her stairs might be a problem for him. There's Aggie Madge, of course – Felix Copley always seemed happy enough there. But Mr Raynor may be looking for something rather different.'

'That's up to him,' Gilbert declared. 'We can give him their addresses and he can see what he thinks. He may decide to take lodgings in Tavistock and come in by bus, as Miss Watkins did.'

But when they put the point to the new teacher, after giving him the news of their decision, it seemed that he had other ideas.

'If I'm going to settle down here, I'll want my own place,' he said. 'Once we've completed the probationary period to our mutual satisfaction – which I hope we will – I'll look around for something to buy. It's a settled home I want, not lodgings. Preferably in Burracombe, but if not, I'll look in one of the nearby villages, or Tavistock.' He smiled round at them, and Miss Kemp thought what a strong, attractive face he had. 'Thank you very much for giving me the opportunity. I'll do my best to see that you won't regret it.'

'I don't think we will, either,' Colonel Napier declared when the visitor had been shown out to catch his bus back to Tavistock. 'He seems a very good, well-set-up type to me, and obviously acquitted himself with some distinction during the war, even if he didn't set out to be a military man. Considerable loss to the service, I'd say.'

'We must just hope that the army's loss is Burracombe's gain,' Basil observed. 'And he has a very kindly look about him – quite fatherly, in fact. Pity he had no children of his own. You may find him a great help in dealing with some of the more unruly boys, Miss Kemp.'

'The Crocker twins,' she agreed ruefully, and they all laughed.

Chapter Six

D inner at the Barton that evening was a poignant affair. Everyone was conscious that this was Stephen and Maddy's last meal at home before leaving for Cyprus, and Gilbert had decreed that Charles and Mary Latimer and Basil and Grace Harvey should be invited, although Hilary would rather have had her brother and new sister-in-law to herself. It would have been nice if Felix and Stella could have come, she thought wistfully, but they were still on their brief honeymoon. They would be back next day, just in time to wave goodbye to the departing pair.

In the event, she was rather glad to have the two older couples there. There was a tension in the air that she knew came entirely from herself and her anxiety over David. Now that Stephen knew – and presumably, by now, Maddy – she wanted to avoid any further discussion; there was nothing more to say, after all. Charles Latimer, too, knew of the situation between herself and David, although she hadn't yet told him of Sybil's death. The air seemed full of secrets, of unasked questions and unspoken answers. She caught Basil Harvey's eyes on her once or twice and wondered what he was thinking. He might look and behave like Alice's White Rabbit, but he was always sensitive to a troubled soul. Even her father, impervious to atmosphere as he normally was, seemed aware of a strain between them all.

Typically, though, and not unreasonably, he put it down to his son's impending departure. Whatever he said, Hilary knew that he was not looking forward to an absence of nearly two years. He masked his feelings with gruffness, which softened whenever he spoke to Maddy, and when the meal was over he proposed a toast.

'To Madeleine and Stephen. To Stephen because he's turned out to be a son I can be truly proud of, and because he's brought me the sweetest daughter-in-law I could wish to have; and to Maddy because she's just that, and because one day she'll be the mother of my grandchildren. Some of my grandchildren, I mean,' he amended, and Hilary knew he was thinking of his other grandson, the half-French Rob, and not of any that she herself might produce. He's like me, she thought, given up all hope of that.

'To Maddy and Stephen,' she echoed, pushing such thoughts firmly from her mind and lifting her glass. 'You needn't blush, Maddy. It's quite normal for people to have children when they're married.'

'And we probably will,' Stephen answered. 'But in our own time, if you don't mind. We want to enjoy being married for a while first.'

'And so you will,' Hilary said warmly, and realised that she felt nothing but warmth and deep affection for this pair who were clearly so happy together. No envy, no comparison with her own situation – just straightforward, honest-to-goodness affection, and thankfulness that life was treating them kindly at last. They had come a long way to be sitting at this table tonight, at the beginning of their life's journey together, and she wished them well from the bottom of her heart.

Afterwards, as their guests were leaving, Charles Latimer turned to her in the bustle of sorting out hats and coats and said quietly, 'And how are you, my dear? I know you haven't had much time lately, but if you need to talk, you know where to find me. Or Basil, of course. Either of us has your well-being at heart.'

'I know. Thank you, Charles.' She hesitated. 'Actually, there has been a – a development. Something rather serious. I'd like to talk to you about it. Perhaps I could drop in after surgery one day.'

'Of course.' His grey eyes rested on her face for a moment, then his wife Mary appeared behind him with a light raincoat over her arm and he turned away to help her into it.

Hilary watched the two couples depart into the dusk of the summer evening, then closed the front door. She turned back to find her brother waiting for her.

'Are you going to be all right, Hil?' he asked quietly. 'While we're away, I mean. Two years is a long time. I don't think I quite realised it until now.'

'Yes, I'll be all right. I'll talk to Charles – and probably to Basil as well. And Val, of course. I've got plenty of people to confide in. Not that that will make any difference really,' she added with a sigh.

'It will help you to cope, though,' he said. 'And you know Maddy and I will be thinking of you. You can write to us. You could even fly out to see us sometime!'

'I suppose I could.' She smiled at him. 'I'll think about that. But now I'm going to bed, and so are you. You're going back to the air base tomorrow, as soon as you've seen Stella and Felix, and you'll have a lot to do before you leave for Cyprus next week. So you don't need to waste your time worrying about me, OK? I'll be all right.'

'I know you will,' he said. 'You're strong – you always have been. But I want you to be more than all right. I want you to be happy.' He kissed her cheek. 'Good night, Hil, and thanks.'

'Thanks? For what?'

'For being my sister,' he said, and grinned. 'And being a right pain in the neck sometimes, too! I probably deserved it, most of the time.'

Hilary laughed and gave his arm a slap. 'You *always* deserved it! Good night, Steve. Sweet dreams.'

She watched him run up the stairs, and then went round turning off lamps before going up to her own room. Her heart was lighter than it had been for some months. The situation between herself and David was no easier than before, yet she felt surrounded by love and affection. By people who cared about her. She felt suddenly lucky.

Am I really strong? she wondered. I don't always feel it. I feel as if I'm buffeted about in all directions, by whatever wind happens to blow. But maybe I will be all right. One way or another.

She stood at her bedroom window and gazed out into the gathering darkness. Stars were beginning to prick the deepening blue of the sky, and she wondered if David might be gazing at them too.

I love you, my darling, she said in her heart. And somehow, some day, we *will* be all right.

*

'We had a lovely time,' Stella said, as she and Felix sat in Dottie's cottage the next afternoon, enjoying the inevitable scones and rock buns. 'Tenby's such a pretty little town, and the sea was gorgeous. We swam every day. Felix got sunburned. We took a boat out to the islands. They're absolutely crammed with seabirds and they were all nesting – little bundles of fluff everywhere. Oh, and we've brought back some Welsh cakes and bara brith for you to try, *and* the recipe.'

'Welsh cakes? Look like drop scones to me, with a few currants in,' Dottie said. 'And this other – what did you call it? – why, it's just fruit loaf. But I dare say they do their best. I'll cut a few slices now anyway, since you've brought them.'

Stella smiled. She and Felix had anticipated just this reaction, and doubted they would ever see Welsh cakes or bara brith on her tea table again. She jumped up as the back door opened and her sister came in, with Stephen close behind.

'Maddy! I was hoping we'd catch you before you went.' The two hugged, and then Maddy stood back, holding Stella at arm's length and inspecting her. She nodded approvingly at Felix.

'I can see you're looking after her.' She turned back to Stella. 'As if I could possibly go off to Cyprus for two years without making sure you were all right! It's just a shame we haven't got time to come and see you in your vicarage. We couldn't just pop in on the way past, could we, Stephen?' she asked her husband coaxingly.

'Little Burracombe's not on the way past to anywhere,' he answered with a grin, 'but I dare say we could manage ten minutes or so. As long as Felix doesn't spend too long here filling himself with those little pancake things.'

'They're Welsh cakes,' Felix said. 'All the way from Welsh Wales. You must try one. How soon do you have to leave?' he asked his newly acquired sister-in-law.

'In about half an hour,' Stephen answered for her. 'Not a minute longer, or I'll be in jankers and Maddy will be spending a week on her own. We'll just have time to look at you in your new home if we go now. You don't mind, do you, Dottie? I'm sorry it's such a rush.'

'Bless you, of course not. I can see these two any time.' The little woman gave them both a hug and then dashed the back of her hand

41

across her eyes. 'You go off now, and take these scones and buns with you. Heaven knows when you'll see proper home cooking again, unless Maddy remembers all I taught her when she was a little maid, standing on a chair at this very table while I was baking. You'd better have some too, Stella. Now, you take good care of your wife, Mr Stephen, and Maddy, you make sure and don't sit out in that hot sun too long. You know it gives you freckles.'

Maddy laughed and hugged Dottie fiercely, but her eyes were wet and her voice quivered a little. 'I'll be back before you know it, Dottie darling. And I *will* make Stephen scones and cakes, just as you taught me.' She turned to her sister and they clung together silently for a moment, then she broke away and Felix put his arms around her. 'Thank you,' she said in a muffled voice. 'Thank you for all you did for me when I was sad over Sammy, and when I was being so silly and selfish. And it's lovely to have you for a brother at last. There were times when I thought it was never going to happen!'

'Me too,' he said, kissing her cheek. 'And of course, Stella knows perfectly well that I only married her so that I could have you as a sister.' He let her go and shook hands with Stephen. 'Good luck, old man. Although I don't know why we're saying all this now, when we'll have to go through it all over again at the vicarage in half an hour's time!'

'We won't,' Maddy said, bending to stroke the big cat Alfred, slumbering as usual on his cushion. 'We'll just say goodbye as if it was an ordinary day. These sorts of things are bad enough done just once.' She gave Dottie a final hug and then turned and swept out of the door, and they all knew that if she had stayed another second, she would have broken down in tears.

'Come on,' Stella said to Felix. 'We ought at least to try to get there at roughly the same time as them, even if we can't be at the door like proper hosts. We'll see you tomorrow,' she added to Dottie. 'We're coming to lunch with Basil and Grace, so we'll pop in during the afternoon, before going home for Evensong. And thank you for the buns and scones, but after this I'm going to have to try to make my own.'

'Dottie will never stop giving us cakes,' Felix said as he started the little Austin that Hilary had insisted he have on permanent loan when Stella was in hospital. 'It's not in her nature.'

42

'It seems funny to be leaving Burracombe to go home,' she said as they proceeded at a stately pace along the village street, waving at passers-by. 'I wonder if we'll ever feel quite so fond of Little Burracombe.'

'It will be home to us, just as anywhere we are together will be home,' he said. 'But Burracombe will always have a very special place in our hearts, because it's where we met.'

'And because it's a very special place,' Stella said. 'There can't be anywhere on earth that's quite like Burracombe.'

Val was using almost exactly the same words to her husband Luke as she finished feeding baby Christopher and laid him in his cot for his afternoon sleep. 'It's our *home*, Luke. We're so happy here. Why should we want to leave it?'

'I *don't* want to leave it. Not really. But this is such an opportunity, Val. I can't pass it up.' Luke sat at the table and picked up the letter that had arrived a few days ago, staring at it as if he didn't already know every word off by heart. 'It's an important gallery, Val, and they want to feature *my* paintings. It could lead to so much – maybe even to exhibiting at the Royal Academy. But I need to be able to show them more paintings than I've got, and I need time to do them. And I really need to be in London a lot of the time. It would mean staying there, and that means accommodation. And giving up my teaching job. I can't do that *and* stay in Burracombe, and we can't afford two homes – not just yet, anyway. Once I start to make a decent income from my work—'

'But how can you be sure that will happen? I know enough about the art world to know that it's all very uncertain, especially just now. The country is only just getting back on its feet after the war. Are people really going to start spending a lot of money on pictures?'

'I don't see why not,' Luke said, a little stiffly. 'A lot of people are getting their homes together now, building new ones and decorating them in new styles. They'll want good pictures.'

'It just seems too much of a chance. We've got Christopher to think about now, and without my earnings ...'

'I never wanted to depend on your earnings anyway. I'd prefer to support my wife and family myself.'

'But *can* you?' Val cried. 'It seems to me we'd always be waiting

43

for someone to buy a picture. Suppose nobody does for weeks – even months? How are we going to live? And in London, too, where we don't know anybody and there's no one to help us. I just can't do it, Luke.'

'I keep telling you, it won't be like that. The gallery—'

'I know, I know. The gallery will show your pictures and people with lots of money will flock to buy them, and we shall be rich ... but suppose it doesn't happen, Luke? Suppose you give up your job and nothing comes of it? What do we do then? We won't even have a home to come back to here, because Jennifer will let the cottage to someone else. It's too much of a risk. I don't know how you can even think of it.' She rubbed one hand over her forehead. 'I'm sorry. You know I've always believed in your painting, but this ...'

'Have you?' he asked. 'Or were you just saying that? Because it seems to me that if you really believed in it, you'd be as excited as I am about this opportunity. As I *was*,' he added a little bitterly.

Val looked at him. His thin face was unhappy, his dark eyes shadowed. She felt a pang of guilt.

'I feel as though I'm holding you back. Perhaps you shouldn't have married me.' But her tone came out wrong and she saw the hurt in his eyes and reached out a quick hand. 'I didn't mean that! Not the way it sounded. Luke ...'

'Are you sure?' he demanded. 'I think perhaps you did. You usually do say what you mean, after all. Or maybe it's you who thinks we shouldn't have got married.'

'No! Luke, please – we're getting muddled up. Of course I don't think we shouldn't have got married. I love you.' She gazed at him anxiously. 'It's just that – well, I thought we were so settled. You said you were happy teaching art in Tavistock and painting in your spare time. You have the whole of the school holidays. And your paintings sell. Why throw it all up – a steady income, and a growing reputation as well – and move to London, of all places?' She looked down at the baby, already falling asleep. 'I wanted to bring up our family *here*.'

'I know. So did I. I still do. But I want to be able to support you – all of us – in the way I'm meant to. As an *artist*. That's what I am, Val. Not a teacher.'

'But what's wrong with teaching?'

44

'Nothing, if that's what you're cut out for.' He came across the small room and took her hands. 'Look, I've always believed that we each have our own talents, and we have a – a sort of *duty* to make use of them. We shouldn't waste them or fritter them away doing something else. Well, not unless we've absolutely got to. Your father and Tom – they're farmers. They'd be miserable doing any other kind of job. You're a nurse, or were until you had Chris. You wouldn't have wanted to do anything else, would you?'

'I don't know,' she said doubtfully. 'I really only went into nursing because of the war. I'd always thought I'd like it, but ...'

'There you are, then. It's what we always wanted to do that tells us where our talents are. If we burn to do something, we probably can.'

'I don't think I did burn to do it. If anything, I burn to be a mother.'

'And you're a wonderful one. And I burn to paint. Don't you see?'

'But you *do* paint!' she cried. 'You just teach as well. Isn't that even better?'

'No,' he said quietly. 'It doesn't seem as if it is.'

There was a silence. They looked at each other miserably.

'I thought you understood,' Luke said at last. 'You always seemed to want to support me and my painting. I thought you knew what it meant to me.'

There was another silence. They looked at each other helplessly, neither knowing what to say next. At last Val drew in a deep, shaky breath.

'We've never, ever quarrelled before. Not since you came to Burracombe and found me again, after all those years apart. It frightens me, Luke.'

'Val – darling – there's nothing to be frightened of.' He took her in his arms, but she could feel him shaking and knew that he was as disturbed as she. 'And we're not quarrelling. What we have to do is sit down together and talk it over properly. Look at all the pros and cons. It really is a great chance for me, and I don't want to throw it away without at least having a proper discussion.' He looked seriously into her eyes. 'I won't do anything unless we both agree on it. I promise you that.'

45

Val looked at him and nodded. But her eyes were full of tears and she was biting her lip, and he knew that she was having difficulty believing him.

'I know you won't,' she said at last, in a quivering voice. 'But you'll try to persuade me all the same, won't you? I *know* you'll try to persuade me.'

Chapter Seven

'It were a lovely wedding,' Edie Pettifer said sentimentally, wrapping the sugar she had just weighed out in a cone of blue paper. 'Prettiest I ever saw. Even the Queen herself never thought of a rainbow wedding, and she had enough bridesmaids.'

'Sweet pea wedding, I call it,' said Ivy Sweet, who always had to have a different opinion. 'Bit gaudy, to my mind – not what I'd say was suitable for a vicar's wedding. I'll have a quarter of liquorice toffees, please.'

'The bridesmaids aren't the groom's choice, though, are they?' Edie countered. 'It's the bride's prerogative to decide on them, and Stella told me herself she thought seven girls all in one colour would be just too much. Although she did tell me a rainbow had been his suggestion, come to think of it. Anyway, rainbow or sweet peas, I thought it was a really pretty idea. And having all those wild flowers in the church instead of smart bouquets made it all seem so natural, just like Stella herself. She's going to be really missed in Burracombe.' She reached up to a high shelf for the jar containing liquorice toffees and tipped some out on to the scales.

Ivy nodded. 'I hope they make a better job of finding a new teacher this time, after that hatchet-faced old harridan they got after Christmas. My Barry hated her. Could have caused no end of trouble, she could.'

'She did. Stealing all those bits and pieces and accusing little Billy Culliford of being a thief. Nasty piece of work.' Edie lowered her voice, although there was nobody else in the shop. 'I did hear they've appointed a man this time. In fact, I've seen him.'

'Seen him? You?' Ivy stared at her jealously. 'When?'

'Yesterday afternoon. Came out from Tavi on the afternoon bus. I just happened to be putting some new tins of fancy biscuits in the window and I saw Mr Harvey meet him. Took him straight down to the school, he did, so I reckoned it must be the new teacher.'

'A *man*?' Ivy said wonderingly. 'For the little ones? What sort of a man was he? Old? Young?'

'Well, I didn't get much of a look at him then,' Edie said virtuously. 'I couldn't stare, could I? But they came back not long after – I was changing the tins round to make a better display – and went into the vicarage. And Miss Bellamy had come along only a few minutes earlier, so I reckon that's what 'twas.'

'I don't suppose you know how long he was there?'

'I do, as it happens, because while I was altering the display around I noticed the window needed cleaning, so I popped out an hour or so later to give it a wipe, and he was just coming out then, in time to catch the bus back to Tavi.'

'So what was he like?' Ivy asked a little impatiently. 'You must have had a pretty good idea by then.'

'I don't know what you'm insinuating by that,' Edie said huffily. 'I was busy working all afternoon. I only *happened* to see him those times. And I never got a really good look. But from what I could see, he's an older man. About Miss Kemp's age, I should think. Strong-looking sort, only he's got a limp – favours his left leg. Not the sort of man I'd have expected to see teaching the babies' class.'

'Well maybe they won't appoint him, then,' Ivy said. 'They're bound to be careful this time.' She consulted her list. 'Have you got any of that cheese you had in last week? Cheddar, with a bit of bite to it.'

Edie turned away and Jacob Prout came in. He said a brief good afternoon to Edie, glanced at Ivy without smiling and began to examine the glass-topped tins of tea, biscuits and other dry groceries in front of the counter.

'Edie was just telling me about the new teacher,' Ivy said. 'I don't suppose you've heard anything up at the vicarage, have you?'

'If I had, I wouldn't be spreading it round the village. It'd be confidential, same as anything else the vicar sees fit to tell me in my duty as churchwarden.'

48

'I don't see as that would be confidential,' Ivy retorted. 'Everyone's going to know who the new teacher is, soon as he starts.'

'And that'll be soon enough to start talking about him,' Jacob said. 'That's if you got to make him a subject of gossip at all. If you've time to pass me a packet of Woodbines, Edie, I've got the right money in my hand.'

Edie gave him the cigarettes with no comment and he handed over a shilling and a threepenny bit before grunting his thanks and departing, without even looking at Ivy Sweet again. The ginger-haired woman rolled her eyes.

'He's in a bit of a mood.'

Edie said nothing. It was well known that Jacob and Ivy didn't get on, and although Edie hadn't been in the Bell Inn on Monday evening, she'd heard about their 'words'. It was unlike Jacob to pass nasty remarks, but the feeling was that he'd been annoyed by the aspersions Ivy had cast on Dottie's baking. Jacob had always had a soft spot for Dottie.

'Is there anything else you'll be wanting?' she enquired. 'Only it's getting on for four o'clock and you know I like to close early on Saturdays. I don't know why I don't close at twelve, like Jessie Friend does. I've often thought of it.'

'There wouldn't be anywhere in the village to do a bit of shopping then.' The baker's wife looked at her list again. 'No, that's all. Oh, I'll take a bar of that Fry's sandwich chocolate. My George likes that on a Saturday evening, and now it's off ration us can let go a bit. It's like the advert says, if you can't decide whether to have milk or plain, why not have both in a sandwich!'

She packed her purchases into her basket and left the shop. Edie sighed with relief, locked the door and turned the Closed sign round. As she did so, Jessie Friend's brother Billy peered through the glass, his wide, flattened face beaming. Edie smiled and unlocked the door again. When he looked as happy as that – and he nearly always did – you forgot his differences and just enjoyed his simple cheerfulness. It was a pity that people who didn't have his disadvantages couldn't be as contented with their lot.

'What have you been doing, Billy?'

'I've been helping Mr Foster with the meat.' Bert Foster, the village butcher, who was a particular friend of Edie's, not only allowed

49

Billy to help with the carcasses, he paid him a small wage for doing so. 'He gave me my wages.' He opened his palm and showed Edie two half-crowns and a ten-shilling note. 'I want to buy some sweets. Can I?'

'Yes, of course you can. You'll save some of it, though, won't you? In your post office savings book?'

'Yes, I'll save five shillings.' He set the two half-crowns aside. 'I'll be able to buy a new coat for winter. I give Jessie five shillings for my dinners' – it never occurred to Billy that his money paid for more than his dinner each day – 'and that leaves five shillings for me. So I can buy sweets and go to the pictures.'

'That's right.' The little family – Jessie, her sister Jeanie and Billy himself – went to the Carlton cinema in Tavistock for the teatime showing nearly every Saturday afternoon, after they had closed the village post office. 'And what are you going to see today?'

'Mickey Mouse,' he said with satisfaction. There was usually a cartoon to accompany the big picture, the small one and the Pathé Pictorial news, but to Billy they were all Mickey Mouse and he enjoyed them all equally. Once again, Edie envied him his simple pleasures.

She served him a bag of assorted toffees and closed the door again before any more late customers could arrive. Bert was coming in for his supper, as he did every Saturday, and they would probably play cards. She wanted to get the cottage pie in the oven in good time and wash her hair.

As she locked the door for the second time, she saw her sister-in-law Nancy's boy Terry coming down the street with his arm around young Patsy's waist. She paused to watch them, wondering just what had gone on in old Percy Shillabeer's farmhouse over in Little Burracombe when he'd discovered that his eldest daughter was in the family way and wanting to marry Terry. Done it deliberately, too, Nancy had told her. Percy had given her an ultimatum – either go away to have the baby quietly and get it adopted, and no one in either of the Burracombes any the wiser; or marry young Terry and never see her own family again. No daughter of his would she be, he'd threatened, nor of her mother.

'Cruel, I call it,' Nancy had said. 'And Jack feels the same. Gave our Terry the rough side of his tongue for doing it, of course he

50

did – that's no way to start married life, specially when they'm both hardly more than children themselves – but there was never no doubt in either of our minds that we'd give them a home. To start with, anyway. They'll have to think of something else when Terry finishes his apprenticeship, but he ought to be able to get a good job then.'

All the same, Edie thought it was kind of Nancy and Jack to give the young couple a home. They had little enough space in that cottage of theirs, and their actions had found no favour with Percy Shillabeer, who had expected them to support him. He'd looked like thunder at the wedding, Nancy had said, and she wouldn't have been surprised to see him raise his fists at both Jack and Terry afterwards, but Felix Copley, who had conducted the service, had been unusually stern and given him a straight talk about Christian charity and love, ending with a reminder that Patsy was Mrs Pettifer now, and out of his jurisdiction.

'Ah, so she is, and I wish her joy of it,' Percy had growled, and taken his wife Ann's arm in an ungentle grip. 'Come on, we're going home. We've got other children waiting for us, children who might show a bit more gratitude. Young Mary's our eldest now, after today's piece of work.'

'You must just let me say goodbye,' Ann had begged, and at a glance from Felix, the farmer had shrugged. 'All right, then, but make it quick. I got cows to milk.' He'd waited impatiently while mother and daughter hugged each other, both with tears streaming down their cheeks, and then pulled her away. Terry had put his arm around his young wife's shoulders and, with Nancy on her other side and Jack and Bob Pettifer following, they'd walked down the church path and across the green in the direction of the Pettifers' cottage.

It had been a sad sort of wedding day, Edie thought. Yet a lot of parents would have taken the same view as Percy Shillabeer. They would have made their daughter go away to endure her pregnancy and give birth at a mother-and-baby home, concocting some tale about going to stay with a relative or having taken a job; and although most people would have had their suspicions about the truth, it would never be mentioned. It wasn't that unusual a story, after all.

But that was when the young man wouldn't or couldn't stand by the girl and marry her. If he could, the girl's parents would get the wedding done with as soon as decently possible, and even though there would be sideways looks at the 'seven-month baby', there would be no more than a short burst of gossip, and it would be forgotten soon enough. In a village, there was always something new to talk about.

For Patsy Shillabeer, it had been a different story. She had been forced to make a choice no young woman should have to make, and she had chosen her sweetheart and her baby. It was a tragedy, but the person who was going to suffer most was Patsy's own mother, deprived of both her daughter and her first grandchild.

He's a cruel, hard man, Edie thought, watching the young couple pass, and felt sorry for poor, downtrodden Ann Shillabeer who had to live with him. Why did she ever marry him in the first place?

Patsy and Terry were going for a walk up to the Standing Stones, the ancient circle of granite blocks that stood on the hill above the village. It was a favourite walk amongst the villagers, with a strange kind of serenity to be found in the grassy circle amidst the brooding stones. Nobody knew how long they had been there or why they had been erected. Nobody knew who had hauled such massive slabs to this place and struggled – for it must have been a struggle – to heave them upright, burying enough underground to ensure that they would never fall. Why had they chosen this spot, and what did it represent for them? Nobody knew.

Whatever their reasons, they must have been peaceful ones, for the air of calm never left this grassy knoll, not quite at the top of the hill; and the people themselves must surely have been the ancestors of many of the families who lived in Burracombe to this day, who all felt a sense of kinship with those who had populated the valley so long ago. Tozers, they might have been, and Pettifers and Friends and Nethercotts. Prouts, Endacotts and even a Culliford, letting his hut or whatever they lived in then go to rack and ruin, much as Arthur Culliford did today. So if you could go back to that time and walk on these moors, you would meet faces as familiar to you as those you met today. Family resemblances, handed down through the generations.

But you would see no Napiers, not that far back – the Napiers were fond of saying that they'd come over with William the Conqueror, so they were mere incomers, late arrivals compared with those whose forefathers had put up these stones. It made you wonder, Norman Tozer said sometimes (he was a bit inclined to the left, was Norman), how they came to be up at the Barton, owning most of the land hereabouts and lording it over the rest of them who'd always lived in these parts.

Whoever it was who'd been responsible for the Standing Stones, they'd known more about building stone circles than good solid houses. There was a ruined village not far away, little more than a tumble of old walls that gave you some idea of the tiny rooms they'd crammed themselves into and what it must have been like with no proper fireplace or chimney. Most of the stones had been removed to build decent cottages down in Burracombe, where it was more sheltered – who would want to live up on the moor anyway, unless the weather was better back then? – and the old village was used only by children for dens, where they could light small fires to cook a few bits of bacon and hide treasures amongst the roughly hewn lumps of granite. Sometimes other people would come to look at the place – learned men who would put up in Tavistock and spend their days measuring the walls and the spaces between them and discussing how the ancient families had lived, and even writing books about it. But mostly it was deserted; some even believed it to be haunted.

Terry and Patsy took the path up through the woods, past the charcoal burner's cottage where Luke Ferris had once lived and which he still used as a studio, and out on to the open hillside, where the gorse blazed golden in the sunshine and gave off a smell of coconuts as its pods cracked open, shooting seeds away as if firing tiny guns. The late-afternoon sun, so close to midsummer, was still hot and high in the sky, and Patsy needed no coat thrown on the grass when she and Terry sat down, their backs against the warm granite of the broadest stone. She lifted her face to the warmth and settled herself against him.

'You're not too tired?' he asked. 'It's a bit of a climb up here.'

'Go on, 'tis no distance at all. I'm not ill, you know – 'tis just a babby on the way. And he's only a little tiddler anyway. I'm hardly showing yet.'

'You will soon, though, won't you?'

'Oh yes – now we're at five months, I'll pop up like a balloon.' She slanted a glance at him. 'I can't do my skirt up properly as it is, hadn't you noticed? I had to ask your mum for a big safety pin yesterday. I'll need to start wearing those maternity clothes Mrs Ferris has lent me soon.'

'I still can't believe we'm going to have a babby,' Terry said. 'You and me, Patsy, being a mother and father. D'you really think we'll be able to manage?'

'Of course we will. Babbies are easy to look after – you just feed them when they're hungry and change them when they're dirty and cuddle them when they cry. That's all there is to it.'

'I suppose you know a lot about them, having all those brothers and sisters and being the oldest. You've had to help look after them all your life.'

'And now I'll have my own to look after.' She looked at him again. 'You're not sorry, are you, Terry? I know it wasn't the way you wanted us to be, and I sort of talked you into it, but you don't really mind, do you?'

'I'm not sorry we're married,' he said. 'And I'm not sorry we're having a babby. I just wish it hadn't made such bad blood between us and your dad. I wish you could see your mother whenever you want. It's not right, you being shut out of your own home.'

Patsy was silent for a few moments.

'I wouldn't care if it was just him,' she said at last. 'I wouldn't care if I never saw him again in my life. It's Mother and the little'ns I care about.' She turned to him and her face, which had been so happy, crumpled with misery. 'I miss them so much,' she wept, and he drew her close against him, shocked by her sudden distress. 'I didn't know it would be like this, Terry. I didn't know I'd feel so bad about it.'

'Oh Patsy,' he said, helpless. 'Sweetheart … don't cry. It'll come right in the end. Babies bring their own love – that's what my mother says. He won't stop you seeing her for ever.'

'He will. You don't know what he's like, Terry. Once he makes up his mind to something, he never changes it. Especially when he drags God into it,' she added bitterly.

'But you said you'd be able to visit on cattle market days, when

54

he goes to Tavistock. He can't be round the farm all the time.'

'He'll know. He'll ask her who's been at the house while he's been out, and she'll tell him. She can't lie to him, Terry, she's too frightened of him. He can tell straight away. And then he'll – he'll ...'

'Hit her?' Terry said quietly. 'Is that what he'll do?'

Patsy nodded miserably. 'He says it's God's will – his punishment. Everything awful he says is God's will. Then it's not his fault, see? He says if you go to church on a Sunday, like we all had to, and listen to the preacher, you'll walk in the path of the righteous, and that anyone who doesn't must be punished according to God's law.' She spoke as if quoting something that had been said to her many times.

'But Mr Copley wouldn't ever say that,' Terry said. 'I've been in church when he was curate here and listened to his sermons, and he's never said that God wants people to hit their wives. He'd never hit Miss Simmons – I mean, Mrs Copley. And my dad would never hit my mother.'

'She'd hit him back if he did!' Patsy said with a wavering grin. 'I saw her do it the other day.'

'Yes, but that's just friendly,' Terry said. 'Playful, like. Your father's got it all twisted up, that's what it is.'

'Well, whether he has or not, it's the way he is and nothing's going to change that,' she said gloomily. 'And nothing's going to make him let Mother see me or the babby. And that's the worst of it.' Her tears began to flow again. 'We *ought* to be able to see each other. Nothing I've done – nothing we've done – is so bad us shouldn't be allowed to see each other like normal families do.'

'Are *you* sorry you did it?' he asked after a minute or so. 'He did say, didn't he – he did give you the choice. Do you wish you'd done what he really wanted?'

'And lost you *and* our babby?' she asked, raising her wet face towards him. 'Because that's what would have happened. If I'd gone away and let our babby go to strangers, would you have still wanted me when I came back? Would you?'

There was a small silence.

'I don't know,' he said at last. 'I don't know if I would. I love you, Patsy, you know that. I'd lay down my life for you. But—'

'But if I'd done that,' she said, 'I wouldn't be the Patsy you loved. I'd be someone else. And anyway, it never even entered my head. We knew what we were doing, Terry – it wasn't an accident. We wanted to get married, and we have. I'm not sorry about that, not one bit. But ...' Her voice quavered again. 'I just never knew it would hurt this bad, not being able to see Mother and the little'ns —

He held her close and they rocked together. Patsy felt the damp seeping through her hair and looked up to see that Terry's eyes were wet too. At this, she broke down completely and a storm of weeping overtook her, so that he began to be afraid that it really would harm her. He drew in a deep breath, controlled his own sadness and stroked her hair, kissing her streaming face and murmuring every word of comfort he could think of. At last her crying began to subside and she lay more quietly against him, shuddering now and then with a deep, racking sob but otherwise calm.

'We've used up all our handkerchiefs,' Terry said. 'And my shirt's soaked. Mother will think us got caught in a storm.'

'The sun's still warm. It'll dry soon enough.' She glanced at him. 'I'm sorry, Terry. It just all seemed too much for me. I'm better now.'

'Let's think of something else for a bit,' he said. 'Names. What are we going to call our babby?'

'We'll have to have two lists,' she said, making a determined effort to turn her mind to this new game. 'One for a boy and one for a girl. Which would you rather have, Terry?'

'I don't know.' His mind grappled with the question. 'I haven't got used to the idea of a babby yet. I can't seem to picture it as a boy or a girl.'

Patsy laughed, a rather trembling little laugh but one of real amusement. 'It's got to be one or the other!'

'I know, but ...' He gave up trying to understand his own feelings, let alone explain them. 'Let's just make the lists, shall we? I expect us'll change our minds a dozen times in the next few months anyway.'

Patsy nodded, and began to rise to her feet. 'And what about this walk we were supposed to be going for? It'll be supper time before we know it, and Dr Latimer said I ought to have proper exercise. I don't think he'd call walking up to the stones and lolling about on the grass all afternoon proper exercise.'

Terry came to his feet too and they walked on to the ridge, hand in hand. He glanced down at her once or twice, relieved that the storm seemed to have abated but aware that it would not be the last. Patsy's distress over the separation from her family, especially her mother, was very real, and wasn't going to go away.

'Edward,' she said, counting names off on her fingers. 'George. William. John. Or if it's a girl ... Susan. Linda. Carol ...'

What a surly old bully Percy Shillabeer was, thought Terry. Like Edie Pettifer, now getting supper ready for Bert Foster, he felt a wave of pity for the woman who had married him. She couldn't have known what her life was to be like. And surely it must be even worse now that she had to bear the brunt of his fury against Patsy.

He looked down at Patsy's silvery hair, so fair it was almost white, lying loose about her slender neck, and was washed with tenderness. I'll never treat you like that, he promised her silently. I'll look after you all my life.

'Catherine,' Patsy murmured, still ticking off names. 'Angela ... Judy ... Michael ... Keith ...'

Chapter Eight

'Yes, I see,' Charles Latimer said thoughtfully, after Monday afternoon surgery. 'It hasn't made things any easier for you, has it?'

Hilary looked at him wryly, grateful for his understanding. 'It hasn't. And I feel guilty for even thinking that way. The poor woman has *died*, and she was no age at all. A year or two older than me – in her early thirties – that's all. I didn't know people could have strokes at that age.'

'It's not so common, certainly, but by no means unknown.' He looked at her compassionately. 'You mustn't blame yourself for thinking what it means for your own situation. It's only natural that you should. Have they had the funeral yet?'

'It's tomorrow morning. At eleven o'clock.'

'Find yourself something do,' he advised and she nodded.

'I'll take Beau for a ride, up on the moor, away from everyone. I don't honestly know how I'm going to feel, you see. I might suddenly break down and start howling like a baby, and nobody would know why. Or I might feel as if I've turned to stone. I'll be better by myself.'

'Don't try too hard,' he said. 'To be brave, I mean. You must allow yourself your own feelings or you'll be ill.'

'I feel so ashamed of them,' she said in a low voice.

'You don't need to. Your feelings are your right. They're nothing to do with anyone else.'

Hilary met his eyes and then looked down, twining her fingers together.

58

'But they are, aren't they? I mean, if David and I hadn't met again and – and given way to our feelings ... if we hadn't gone on meeting, when we knew it was wrong ... if we hadn't lied to people about it – if I hadn't lied to Father ...'

'Are you trying to say that Sybil wouldn't have had her stroke?' he asked, and she nodded, unable to look up again. 'My dear Hilary, you know that's nonsense. Nothing that you or David – or even Sybil herself – did brought that about. It was a physical event, a bleeding into the brain – nothing to do with anyone else. How could you have caused that? You do know it's nonsense, don't you?'

'Yes ... I suppose I do.'

'Of course you do. And it's even more nonsensical to torment yourself with it. You are not to blame, Hilary. The situation you got into was difficult and probably regrettable, but entirely human, particularly as the marriage seems to have been no marriage at all. Sybil's stroke was not your fault.'

'I wonder if Basil would think that,' she said ruefully. 'Some people might say I'd got my comeuppance, at her expense.'

'If all you say is true,' he said, 'and that was really the way things work, it would seem more likely that Sybil has had her own comeuppance. And I'm sure Basil *wouldn't* think that!'

She laughed a little, then looked up at last and met his kindly gaze again. 'Thank you, Charles. It's helped to talk to you – although I still don't know what's going to happen next.'

'This is not the moment for decisions,' he said. 'You have to let things settle first. It's a difficult time for David, too.' He paused, as if weighing something in his mind, then said, 'I believe I know his father, by the way.'

Hilary stared at him. 'David's father? But – how?'

'We're both doctors,' he reminded her. 'I thought his name sounded familiar when you came to talk to me before, so I looked him up. James Hunter. We trained together. We were quite friendly – stayed in contact for a while after we finished our training, but life was so hectic then, working all hours in hospitals for the first year, there was no time for keeping in real touch, and gradually it stopped. Pity – he's a nice fellow. If your David takes after him, I'm not surprised you think so much of him. You'd be well matched.'

Hilary looked down again, aware of the warm flush spreading up

59

to her cheeks. 'I believe we are. But I don't see how we can ever be together – even now.' She stood up. 'I'll have to go now. Thank you, Charles. It helps to have someone to talk to.'

'You're very welcome, Hilary, my dear, at any time. I haven't told Mary any of this, by the way, but if you felt you wanted to talk to a woman ...'

'Oh, you can tell Mary,' Hilary said, surprising herself; it wasn't so long since she hadn't wanted anyone at all to know. 'I don't mind her knowing. Especially as you knew David's father.'

She went out and set off along the village street, back towards the Barton. As she neared the end of the drive, she saw Patsy Pettifer coming out, having finished her day's work, and stopped to exchange a few words with her. The girl was blooming, she thought as they parted, her pale cheeks coloured a delicate pink and her eyes bright. She was happy, despite the ordeal she had been through with her father, even despite the sadness that Hilary knew was still in her heart over his harshness. She was married to the boy she loved, she was expecting a baby, and nothing, not even Percy Shillabeer's despotic cruelty, could alter that.

Will I ever look like that? Hilary wondered as she went on up the drive. Will people look at me and think, *She's happy*?

And then she thought of how Patsy's happiness had been achieved. She had seen the way forward and taken it, determined to win whatever the consequences. She might be happy, but she was paying for her happiness, and so were others – most of all, her mother. Patsy was, in some ways, very much her father's daughter – strong-minded and ruthless.

Could I ever be so ruthless? Hilary thought. Am I really prepared to pay, whatever the consequences?

By ten thirty the next morning, Hilary was high on the moor, galloping Beau along the ridge above the village. She paused, gazing down at the blue waters of the reservoir. There was no wind, and the sky was reflected so perfectly that you could almost believe there was no water at all, that the sides of the valley sloped down for ever into the depths of the earth. But somewhere down there, she knew, were the ruined cottages, the ancient bridge and the tiny church of the drowned village from which, years ago, farmers and their families had been moved out of to make way for the little river to fill the steep-sided valley, so that Burracombe and the other villages around could be supplied with fresh, clean water.

Beau flicked his ears and she patted his neck and then walked him slowly along the ridge. They were out of sight of Burracombe now, with the sloping whaleback of Sheepstor before them and the shimmering waters of Plymouth Sound far beyond. Looking west, she could see the old mine workings on the nearest hills of Cornwall – Kit Hill, between Gunnislake and Callington, and Caradon Hill beyond that, with the jagged outline of Bodmin Moor in the distance. To the north and east, she could name every tor within view – Pew Tor, Cox Tor, Staple Tor and Great Mis Tor. They were as familiar to her as her own garden and she had walked or ridden up them all at one time or another.

The moor was her home, she thought. It was a part of her, bred into her flesh and bones, and to leave it would be like tearing herself apart.

And yet she knew that if it came to it, if David asked her to leave, she would do so, because he was a greater part of her even than this, and she could think of no better future than one shared with him.

She glanced at her watch. It was five minutes to eleven. They would be gathering at the church now, friends and family already inside. David and his father and mother and Sybil's own family would be at the door, watching as Sybil's coffin was unloaded, carefully and with respect, from the hearse. The undertaker's men would bow their heads and step forward to take the burden on their shoulders and carry it up the aisle.

Hilary wondered suddenly if it were the same church where they'd been married. Had David stood at the head of the aisle, waiting as Sybil walked towards him on her father's arm, dressed in white? Had he waited with joy in his heart, still in love with her even though by then he had met Hilary herself? Had he believed that their marriage would be a success, that they would make each other happy?

And what was he feeling now, knowing the truth? There must, surely, be sadness and regret. It would be wrong to suppose otherwise. Wrong to suppose that he even spared Hilary a fleeting thought at this time.

I don't want you to be thinking of me now, my darling, she thought, but I send you all my love just the same. If it can help at all, if it can give you even a little strength, that's all I ask.

She slipped from the horse's back and looped his reins around a hawthorn branch, then sat down on a rock and gazed down at the serene blue waters of the reservoir. She stayed there for the full half-hour that she expected the funeral service to take. What her thoughts were during that time she could never remember, but at eleven thirty she stood up, patted Beau's neck again, unlooped his reins and swung herself into the saddle. She turned her back on the wide blue valley and let the horse walk for a few minutes before setting him to a gallop along the length of the ridge on their way back to Burracombe.

Chapter Nine

James Raynor came to Burracombe the following week. He had little to clear up in Somerset, he said – he'd been in lodgings there since leaving his post at the prep school – and he was happy to stay at Aggie Madge's cottage for the time being. There were only four weeks to go before the end of term, and she would be having holiday visitors then, but by that time both he and the school governors would know if he was suited to the position of primary school teacher.

'I can put up somewhere else – probably in Tavistock – and look for a place of my own during the holidays,' he said to Miss Kemp when he came to the school house the evening before his first day. 'Ideally I'd like to be in the village, but I don't suppose cottages come up for sale here very often.'

'They don't, I'm afraid. I'm lucky, of course, to have the school house, but I'll have to look for somewhere else myself when I retire, and I doubt if it will be in Burracombe. Nobody ever wants to move away.'

'I can understand that.' They were sitting in the garden, on the scrap of lawn under a gnarled pear tree. A blackbird was serenading them with his evening song from the top of the roof, and a busy twittering came from the bushes, where small birds were preparing to roost. Miss Kemp's garden was sheltered by azaleas, their vibrant pink, red and yellow blooms lit to a fiery blaze by the sun as it dipped lower in the western sky, and in her borders, tall foxgloves rose above the acid green of clumped euphorbia and a foam of old English roses.

'What a pleasant spot,' James observed. He had brought a bottle of sherry, and Miss Kemp, somewhat surprised by this, had found two small glasses and brought them out on a tray, with some of Dottie's biscuits. 'This garden is a credit to you. Do you do it all yourself?'

'Mostly. Jacob Prout helps me sometimes, but I enjoy pottering about out here when it's quiet, with the children all gone. Do you like gardening, Mr Raynor?'

'I've never had much chance. We only had a tiny courtyard in London and I never seemed to have the time anyway. I worked long hours at the Stock Exchange. Dorothy grew geraniums in pots to brighten it up, but that's all. She would have loved a garden like this.'

Miss Kemp glanced at him. 'The war changed a great many people's lives.'

'It certainly did.' He put a hand on his left knee. 'Not that this is much of a burden, compared with what other people suffered.'

'You lost your wife.'

'Yes.' He was silent for a moment, and Miss Kemp wondered if she had said too much, even though he had himself mentioned his wife only a few moments earlier. Then he smiled at her and said, 'She died a heroine's death, though, looking after bombed-out families during the Blitz. I always tell people she was in an air-raid shelter, but she wasn't – she was outside in the thick of it all, helping to rescue mothers and children from houses that had been destroyed by enemy attack, some of them on fire. She had just gone into one where she thought children were trapped when it was hit again and completely flattened. Nobody came out alive.'

Miss Kemp stared at him, appalled. 'How do you know this?'

'One of the other volunteers told me. She'd been working eight hours with hardly a break, but she insisted on carrying on. Someone tried to stop her going into the house, but she'd been told there were small children inside and nothing would stop her.' He paused again. 'Dorothy loved children. We'd planned to have a family of at least four.'

Miss Kemp felt her eyes fill with tears. She brushed them away and said quietly, 'You must be very proud of her.'

'Oh yes. Very proud.' He glanced up and met her eye. 'I'd still rather have her with me, though.'

There seemed to be little to say after that. He poured more sherry and they went on to talk of the school and how he would plan his first week of teaching. Miss Kemp gave him a brief resumé of the children in his class and talked about the traditions that had built up over the years, as well as some of the newer events, such as the pageant they'd held two or three years ago, the performance of *A Midsummer Night's Dream* that Joyce Warren had organised, and the Nativity play that had wound its way through the village last Christmas, ending up, as one of the boys had said, at the pub.

'The children sound a lively bunch,' he said. 'And Burracombe a lively village. I'm looking forward to working here – and, I hope, living here too.'

He stood up to go and Miss Kemp rose from her garden chair. She gave him her hand to shake and said, 'I hope you will, too. I think you and Burracombe will suit each other very well.'

As she carried the tray back into the school house, Miss Kemp thought over the sad little story that she had just been told. Two young people, just beginning their lives together, caught up in a savage war that was none of their doing, and one of them lost for ever in the most brutal way. What must it have been like for the young soldier, far away from home, to be given such news? You heard so much about those at home receiving that fateful telegram that told them their loved one was 'missing, presumed dead' or had 'died of wounds' in some unimaginable battle overseas, but not about those who were away being informed that their families had been torn apart by enemy action.

This was the first war that had done that, on any great scale, she thought. In the First World War – still called, by some, the Great War – there had been a certain amount of bombing, mostly on the east coast, by Zeppelins and early bomber aircraft, but nothing on the scale of the Blitz over London and other major cities. Stories were still told in Burracombe of the way the sky had been lit by the destruction of Plymouth, and how even out here on the edge of Dartmoor, you could have read a newspaper in the glow of the flames. So many of those killed must have had relatives in the armed forces, and so many of those relatives must have received the news – if they had been alive to receive it.

Washing up the glasses and plate, she thought again of that other war – the Great War, the one that was supposed to end all wars and make a country fit for heroes to live in. Cynically – but with more than a grain of truth – some people would comment that you needed to be a hero to live in it. And that applied even more now, with the slow and painful process of rebuilding barely started in some of the bombed cities, with meat still rationed, with a greyness still hanging over so many aspects of life. People who had lived through the fear and destruction, staunchly refusing to give in, were tired now and disheartened, and more and more of them were looking elsewhere to carry on their lives. Australia, New Zealand, Canada ... all of which were holding out their hands, offering a welcome, a home, work – and better weather!

Miss Kemp finished tidying her small kitchen and went upstairs to bed. The school house boasted a bathroom that had been put into what had once been a tiny third bedroom, and she washed and cleaned her teeth before going into her own room, made pretty by flowery curtains and a colourful patchwork bedspread, which she had inherited from her mother. She put on her nightdress and then, as she did every night, paused to look at a photograph of a young man in army uniform that stood on her dressing table.

'Good night, my dear,' she said softly, touching the smooth young face with her fingertips. 'Sleep well.'

The new teacher was greeted next morning by the children with a certain degree of caution.

'He was a soldier in the war,' they told each other as they assembled in the playground. 'Got medals for being a hero. He've only got one leg.'

'That's not true,' Shirley Culliford asserted. 'My mum saw him going into Mrs Madge's yesterday and he had two then or she'd have said.'

'One of them's made of tin,' Edward Crocker explained. 'It's a false leg. It's because he were a soldier and got blown up.'

'Was he a tin soldier, then, like in that story?' Billy Culliford enquired, and they all laughed. George Crocker aimed a friendly blow at the four-year-old's head, Betty Culliford pummelled both twins with her fists and a chase ensued all around the playground.

James Raynor, coming through the gate at that point, was almost knocked over by a hurtling mass of children.

'Children!' Miss Kemp emerged from the school door, ringing the bell vigorously. 'What in heaven's name are you doing? Form lines at once!'

Still giggling, the children hastily organised themselves into four rather straggly lines, facing the school. Miss Kemp stepped up on to the stone dais by the door and regarded them.

'That's better. I know you all like to run about and enjoy yourselves in the playground, but you really must be careful not to knock people over. We don't want our new teacher to spend his first week in hospital, do we!' The children glanced at each other, unsure whether this was meant as a joke or not, and decided it was best taken seriously.

'No, Miss Kemp,' they chorused.

'I should think not. Now, since you are all here and quiet for once, I'd like to introduce you to the brave man who has agreed to take Miss Simmons's place and try to teach you all that sensible children need to know. I want you to show him just how much you have learned and just how willing you are to learn even more. You already know what a good teacher Miss Simmons was, so remember that if you don't behave as she would expect you to, you'll be letting her down just as much as you'll be letting me, our school, Burracombe and your own selves down. But I'm sure you won't do that, will you?'

'No, Miss Kemp,' they chorused again.

'That's good. Now, it's time to start school, so let Mr Raynor see how well you can file into your classrooms and go to your places. Infants first.'

The line of five- and six-year-olds, led by Joey Culliford, marched solemnly past the two teachers and into the big classroom, divided as usual by the folding partition. James Raynor followed them in and took his place behind the big desk at the front. He let his eyes move slowly over the small faces looking up at him, and then he smiled.

'Good morning, children. I'm very pleased to meet you all. Now, you all know my name, don't you? What is it?'

'Mr Raynor,' they replied in a rather uncertain, ragged chorus.

'That's right. Mr Raynor. You may hear people call me Major Raynor, because I was in the army during the war, but I would rather be called Mister.'

'My dad says a major is important,' one of the Crocker twins said. 'Why don't you want us to say it?'

James looked at him seriously. 'Because I'm not in the army now. I only went in because of the war, and now that all that's over, I'd rather be a proper civilian instead. Do you know what "civilian" means?'

'Someone who's not in the army?' Janice Ruddicombe said, a little doubtfully.

'Or in the navy,' Billy Madge said more forcefully. 'Or the RAF.'

'Yes, that's more or less right. Someone who doesn't wear a uniform, perhaps. And since teachers don't wear uniforms, that's what I am now.'

There was a brief silence as they considered this. Then the other Crocker twin, bold enough to ask the question that was on all their minds, said loudly, 'Please, sir, is it true you've got a tin leg?'

The others gasped at his effrontery and those in front turned to stare at him, but James smiled again. 'Yes, it is true, although it's not exactly tin. Would you like to see it?'

A second gasp ran round the room. Some of the girls hung back, but the boys, led by the Crocker twins and Billy Madge, were already half out of their seats. James stood up and waved them back before rolling up one trouser leg.

'There. Nothing to be frightened of.'

'How does it stay on?' Robin Tozer asked.

'It's like a kind of glove. My own bit of leg fits into it, you see, and these straps hold it in place. Now look at the ankle. The foot moves a bit, so that I can walk much the same as you do yourselves. And I still have my knee, which helps a lot. Imagine how hard it would be to walk if you didn't have a knee to bend. Try it.'

The children stood up and began to strut stiff-legged round the classroom. After a few minutes they started to giggle. Joey Culliford said, 'It makes you walk all funny. I have to swing my leg out sideways.'

'Like I do,' Janice said, indicating her heavy built-up boot, and they stopped and looked at her in surprise.

'Yes, but you've got a proper leg, not a tin one.'

'The calipers make me walk like that,' she explained, and some of them came over to examine them and compare them with their new teacher's artificial leg.

'I've never really noticed before,' Jenny Coker said. 'We'm all so used to you, we never think about it.'

'And that's how I want you to think of me,' James said, thankful for the opportunity to say what he'd been wanting to lead up to. 'Someone who has a different leg from the rest of you, but that you get so used to you don't even notice it any more.' He rolled down his trouser leg. 'And now that you've all had a good look at it, you won't have to wonder and you'll just think of me as your teacher. Now, what lesson would you like to do this morning?'

The children blinked.

'Miss Simmons never asked us that,' Janice said. As one of the oldest in the infants' class, she had appointed herself spokesperson. 'She always *told* us what lessons we'd do.'

'And so shall I. But because this is our first morning together, I thought I'd let you choose. Reading? Writing? Arithmetic?'

'Could us draw?' Billy Culliford asked, a little nervously. 'I like drawing.'

There was an immediate outburst from the others. 'Yes, can us draw, please, sir? Can us make cards for our mothers? They likes us to make cards.'

'I don't see why not. Let's see – you need an occasion for making a card. What about Midsummer's Day? A summer card, with things that make you think of summer.'

An excited buzz of conversation indicated that this was a popular idea, and the two Culliford sisters came to show their new teacher where the paints, brushes and fish paste jars, for water, were kept. Fortunately, there was also enough paper to go round, and soon the class was working busily, brushes clenched in fingers, tongues poking from the corners of mouths, and an array of summer-related pictures taking shape. Before anyone knew it, the bell was clanging for playtime, and as the children threw down their brushes and raced for the door, Miss Kemp looked in from the other side of the partition.

'How are you getting on? Oh – they're drawing.'

James Raynor's corrugated face creased even more in a broad grin. 'I gave them a choice for our first lesson. Don't worry, it won't happen every day.'

'I don't imagine it will,' she responded drily. 'A good idea, though. And have you found a way to tell the Crocker twins apart yet?'

'I haven't actually tried. But I'm sure inspiration will strike soon. Now, would you like me to take playground duty, so that your class can have a good look at me too?' He gave her an unaccustomedly cautious glance. 'I showed them my leg, by the way. The artificial one, I mean.'

Miss Kemp's eyebrows rose. 'Did you indeed?'

'Yes, I thought it best to nip any speculation or other distraction in the bud. They've all had a good look, and now that their curiosity is satisfied, we can forget about it. I hope you don't object. Perhaps I should have mentioned it to you first.'

'To tell you the truth,' she confessed, 'I'm quite glad you didn't. I'm not sure what I would have said.'

James laughed. 'Then all's well that ends well. And now I'll go outside and make sure nobody's murdering anyone. Some of those little girls are quite frightening!'

He departed, and Miss Kemp went into the school kitchen, where Mrs Dawe, the cook, had just handed out the small bottles of milk and was now making a large pot of tea in between preparing vegetables for the dinners for those children who lived too far away to go home for their midday meal. She poured out two mugs, and Miss Kemp took one out to the new teacher, then returned for her own.

'How be he getting on, then?' the cook enquired. 'Bit of a surprise, taking on a man for the little ones. I'm not sure everyone thinks it's a good idea, if you don't mind me saying so.'

'I don't mind at all, and I'm not surprised that everyone doesn't agree. But the governors were very careful about this appointment and he seems a very nice man. I think some of the boys in particular will respond well to having a male teacher.'

To avoid further discussion, she took her tea back to her own classroom and sat at her desk, sipping reflectively. It was early days yet, but so far the new teacher seemed to be coping very successfully. She wondered how many other wounded soldiers would have allowed a cluster of five- and six-year-olds to examine an artificial limb.

She thought again of what he had told her the previous evening. A happy marriage to a brave woman; a large family planned. Yet now he was widowed and childless.

Was his decision to go into teaching a compensation for that childlessness? Did he see these little ones as the family he had never had? But it was not too late for him, she thought. He was not too old to marry and have a family.

Unlike herself. For Frances Kemp, that hope had gone for ever.

Chapter Ten

July 4th began as a day of celebration in Burracombe. Not because it was America's Independence Day, nor even because it happened to be Val Ferris's birthday, but because at last – after years and years of restrictions – meat had come off ration.

Unfortunately, because it was a Sunday, nobody could rush into Bert Foster's shop, and their Sunday dinners could be no more lavish than the previous week's. Nevertheless, Bert hung bunting all around the outside of the shop. He stretched a big Union Jack across the top of the window and made as fine a display as he could inside. As a manufacturing butcher, registered to make pies and sausages, he had become famous in the village for his 'Cokers' – sausages so thick they were like the blacksmith Alf Coker's huge fingers – and a long string of them wound their way like a pink snake in and out of the other cuts. An entire pig took pride of place, surrounded by joints of lamb and beef, and set off by artificial grass of a brighter green than any grass seen anywhere else in Burracombe. He and Edie Pettifer had spent all the previous evening doing it, he told his customers, helped by Billy Friend, who was always pleased to earn a shilling or two hefting the carcasses on to his shoulders.

'You must have been saving all this up for months!' Aggie Madge said, surveying the display with wonder. 'I haven't seen so much meat since before the war.'

'Abe Endacott sent the pig down and Ted Tozer let me have the lamb special. 'Tis all good local produce. And the sausages got more meat in 'em now, too – I had to bulk they out with bread before.' He came outside to admire his window, which had looked so sparse for so long. 'I'll have to put it all in the cold store later on, to keep fresh for tomorrow, but I couldn't let the day go by without making some sort of show. Who'd have thought, when they first brought the rationing in, back in 1940, that it would last so long! I think if I'd known that, I'd have shut up shop in the beginning.'

'I don't know what else you'd have done if you had,' George Sweet commented. 'Just about everything was rationed. I had a struggle to make enough bread to go round, and not being able to sell it till it was a day old didn't make it any easier. As for cakes ... well, you all remember those wedding cakes I made, with everyone chipping in their dried fruit and sugar rations, and cardboard put round instead of icing.'

'Why couldn't you sell bread till it was a day old?' asked Janice Ruddicombe, who had come down with her mother to see the display. At just seven years old, she hadn't even been born until the war was over, yet rationing had always been part of her life. In fact, there were children of fourteen or fifteen who couldn't remember a time without it.

George smiled at her. He had a soft spot for most of the children, but especially Janice. 'Why, because everyone likes new bread best, so the high-ups reckoned they'd eat more if they could buy it newly baked! And it's harder to slice thin, too. Keep it a day, and you can cut thinner slices and won't eat more than you should.'

'Not that anyone wanted to, by then,' Aggie Madge observed. 'That awful grey colour! I didn't fancy it at all.'

'That weren't my fault—' George began defensively, but he was interrupted by Bert, who didn't want his moment of glory diverted by the baker's problems.

'Anyway, that's all over now. Meat's the last thing to come off ration and we can make a bonfire of our ration books and forget about it. You can all have whatever you want from tomorrow, no matter what it costs.'

'Us burned them up when sugar came off,' George Sweet said. Unlike most other food rationing, which had been allocated according to weight, meat had been rationed by price. It meant that if you couldn't afford expensive joints, you could eat reasonably well on cheaper cuts or sausages, while those who wanted better cuts got much less for their money. One shilling and twopence per person per week by the end of the war, and still only two shillings now, wouldn't buy much of a leg of pork. No more than the trotters, Jacob Prout had said once, though you could make a good enough stew out of them.

'It was just a figure of speech,' the butcher said in a nettled tone. George was getting on his nerves a bit this morning, he thought; just because he'd been free to use any baking ingredients he wanted since last September, when sugar came off. 'And you needn't think it's going to make a lot of difference straight away. There'll still be a lot of shortages before it gets properly sorted out.'

'I think what upset me most,' Aggie Madge said, obviously in reminiscent mood, 'was the rationing that came in after the war was over. Like bread and potatoes, after that awful winter in 1947. As if we hadn't had enough to put up with. It was like even the weather wanted to join in.'

'My stars, yes, that were a terrible time,' Mrs Ruddicombe agreed. 'It was the year I had my Janice. It was snowing the night I started labour, and when my John went for the midwife, the drifts were four feet high across our lane. He thought they'd never get back, and there was only my Doreen there to help me. And the cold was so bitter, us all lived in the kitchen for weeks, put mattresses down on the floor every night we did, because it was the only warm room in the house.'

'We had burst pipes,' said Jeanie Friend, who had come out of the cottage across the road, where she and her sister kept the post office, to join the group gathering round the window. 'I've never seen such a mess. And when they were mended, we were so afraid they'd go again that we drained all the water down every night before we went to bed, and turned it off. It was a real pantomime.'

'Well, I'm glad you all like my display so much,' Bert Foster said, annoyed to find the conversation drifting off again, and they turned quickly and hastened to reassure him.

'It's lovely, Bert' ... 'A real picture' ... 'It just brought back all the memories, that's all' ... 'You and Edie did real well. Pity we haven't got a camera to take a picture' ... 'It's a proper celebration, and so it should be.' And Jacob Prout, who had been standing at the back, stepped forward and held up his hand for silence.

'I think it warrants a bit of a speech,' he said. 'The last thing to

74

come off ration, as Bert says, and we've waited long enough for it to happen. It's a good day for us all. But what I think us ought to remember is how well Bert's done for us all this time, right through the war and up to today. There's never been as much in his shop as any of us would have liked, but he've managed to put food on our tables just the same, and he's always had a smile and a good word to cheer us on our way.' This wasn't strictly true, because Bert did have his off days and could be as grumpy as the next man when things got too much for him, but everyone nodded and murmured their agreement. 'And none of us is ever going to forget what a good supper a couple of Cokers made, so let's have three cheers for Bert Foster,' Jacob finished, and everyone cheered.

Bert looked pleased and mollified. He nodded at Jacob and said, 'Thank you for that, Jacob, and there'll be a couple of Cokers with your name on if you care to come in tomorrow. And I'd just like to say, 'tis been a pleasure to serve the village – well, most of the time, anyway. I won't mention the time two certain ladies threatened to scratch each other's eyes out over half a pound of liver, nor that couple of lamb chops that disappeared while I was out the back one time, *and* I know who took 'em, too, though I'll never be able to prove it … But on the whole, though it's not been easy, us've got through it together, and I'll be pleased to welcome you in first thing tomorrow, to buy whatever you want. Only don't ask for too much,' he added, 'because I don't want to run out and start rationing it all over again.'

The group laughed and began to disperse. Jacob called out that he'd look in for his sausages first thing in the morning – 'not that you got to pay me for saying what I did, mind' – and went on his way along the village street to the church, where he was going to see if there was any cutting and tidying to do between the gravestones before joining the other bell-ringers. He wouldn't actually do any work, of course, since it was Sunday, but he could see where to make a start next morning.

Basil Harvey was just coming out of the church as Jacob walked up the path. He stopped for a chat and the two men surveyed the churchyard.

'It's looking very good,' Basil complimented him. 'I do think it was a nice idea to let the primroses and bluebells grow in the top part. It looked so natural and pretty. I sometimes think we try to be a little too tidy.'

Jacob's head tilted back a little, as if affronted. 'If you don't like the way I does the churchyard, Vicar ...'

'No, no, I didn't mean that at all,' Basil said hastily. 'Simply that in letting the top corner stay natural, we're allowing God to grow His own flowers – it's His garden, after all, in a way.'

Jacob snorted. 'Without meaning any criticism, Vicar, I don't think God got the same ideas about gardens as we have. I reckon if us let He have too much of His own way, the place'd be nothing but weeds. Why, I'll be on my way up to that corner first thing tomorrow morning, to cut down all that long growth the bluebells left – that's if you and God got no objection.'

'No, none at all,' Basil said, deciding to beat a retreat before he got further embroiled in theological discussion. 'I'm in a hurry anyway – there's a man coming to see the organ after the service. We really are going to have to do something about raising money for its refurbishment.'

'We bin talking about it for years,' Jacob agreed. 'Reckon it'll cost a pretty penny, though. Had nothing done to it since before the war.'

'I know. I've been looking through the parish records. The last proper attention it had was in the early thirties, and I don't think that was much more than a patching-up. I'd like to see it working as it should.'

'So would us all. That squeak it makes halfway through every hymn's bad enough, but the groan it lets out during the prayers sounds like a soul in torment. And it makes the youngsters snigger, too,' Jacob added disapprovingly.

The groan often made Basil want to chuckle too, but he dared not say so. Jacob was in one of his forthright moods (or, as others might have put it, downright grumpy), and it was best not to be too contentious. He glanced at his watch, murmured something about having things to do before the service, and hurried off. Jacob gave him a nod and proceeded up the path to the little shed where he kept his tools. It wouldn't hurt to make sure they were all sharp and ready for use next day.

Coming out again with his sickle, which he'd picked up to feel the blade and forgotten to put down again, he noticed Joanna Tozer

76

kneeling by one of the graves. He hesitated, knowing why she was there and not wanting to disturb her, but she glanced up at that moment and got to her feet.

'Hello, Jacob. I'm glad you're here – I've been wanting to say thank you for looking after Suzanne's grave so well. I come every week and do what I can, but you obviously keep it nice in between.'

''Tis no trouble, maid. It's not as if it's any size, poor little scrap.' They stood together looking down at the tiny mound with its small white headstone. 'Cruel hard, losing a babby like that, and her not even ill.'

'Dr Latimer still can't say why it happened,' she said sadly. 'Just dying so suddenly in her pram in the middle of the day … Easter will never be the same for me again, you know.'

'I can't see how it could be. And you still got to make it happy for the other little one, whatever you feel yourself. It's not easy. But 'twasn't nothing you done wrong yourself, Joanna, you knows that.'

'So the doctor says, but it's hard to believe. I watch Heather every minute, you know, afraid that it might happen to her too and wishing I knew how to prevent it. It's worse that they were twins. I can't help remembering what people say – that if one twin dies, the other will follow. I couldn't bear to lose Heather as well.'

'That's just an old wives' tale,' he said robustly. 'You don't want to take no notice of that. Little Heather's as bonny a babby as ever I saw. Her's going to grow into a fine young woman, and then you'll have another set of things to worry about!'

Joanna laughed and turned to walk back to the farm. Jacob continued up to the wild corner and stood for a moment looking at the lush green leaves left behind by the bluebells, and thinking.

'I reckon it's right, what they says about You,' he said aloud after a while. 'You moves in mysterious ways, Your wonders to perform. But there ain't nothing much more mysterious to my mind than taking a little babby that's hardly had a chance to live yet. So don't You go taking that other little maid as well, see? You just leave her be. Or You'll have *me* to reckon with.'

Val Ferris didn't celebrate her birthday with flags, either British or American. Instead, she had breakfast in bed, brought to her by Luke, and cuddled baby Christopher to her as he had his.

77

'Here are your cards,' Luke said, putting Christopher in his cot and producing a little pile of envelopes. 'There's one from America, look. That'll be your Uncle Joe and Russ. And some more came by post yesterday, so I hid them, and there might even be more today.'

'I shouldn't think so.' Val began to open the cards, laughing at the funny ones and smiling over pictures of kittens or country cottages. 'I can't think who else would send me one. Oh, here's one from you. Oh, *Luke* ... That's really lovely.'

Luke's card was rather bigger than the others, and was an original painting of their own cottage, with Christopher's pram in the garden. You could just see his face, peeping out. Val stared at it and her eyes filled with tears. 'Can it be framed?'

'Of course. I hoped you'd say that, so I've got a frame all ready for it. And here's my present.' He handed her a small parcel.

'A present as well! Most people would be pleased just to have one of your paintings.'

'You're not most people.' He watched as she unwrapped the little box and opened it, after which she gave a cry of delight as she took out a silver locket. 'It's got Chris's picture inside.'

'You painted that too! Oh, Luke, it's beautiful. Thank you *so* much.' She threw her arms around his neck and kissed him. 'I shall never have anything I like as much as this. I'll wear it all the time.'

'Well, not in the bath. Or in bed. Or when you go swimming. Or—'

'You know what I mean. I'll put it on as soon as I get dressed.' She opened the little case and gazed at the picture inside. 'It's a lovely idea.'

'I wanted you to have something special, darling. To show you how special you are to me.'

Val looked at the locket a moment longer, then raised her eyes to meet his. 'And to help persuade me to move to London with you?'

'No!' He stared at her in shock. 'Nothing like that! How can you accuse me of such a thing?'

'I don't know.' Slowly, she put the locket back into its box. 'It just came into my mind. I know how much you want to go.'

'Not so much that I'd try to bribe you with birthday presents,' he said in a cool tone. 'Especially with pictures of our son.' He got up off the bed and picked up her breakfast tray. 'I'll take this out of the way – I expect you'll want to be getting up now. Are you going to church?'

'I hadn't decided,' Val said. 'I thought we might go out somewhere for the day. We could put Christopher in his pushchair and walk over to the reservoir. Or go out to Windy Post. We could take a picnic.'

'Whatever you like,' he said in a remote tone, going out of the door. 'It's your birthday.'

'Luke! Please – don't go like that. I'm sorry for what I said. I didn't mean it.' But he was already halfway down the stairs, and Val slumped back against the pillows, all joy in her birthday and Luke's presents gone. She glanced at the baby, sitting up in his cot and playing with a string of plastic teething rings, and tears came to her eyes.

She knew that Luke wouldn't really have tried to bribe her with his present. I don't know why I said it, she thought sadly. Perhaps it's because we still haven't talked about it properly, so it's growing in my mind. We said we'd forget it, but we can't. It's too serious for that. We need to have a proper, honest conversation.

Perhaps today, if they went out somewhere away from the cottage, away from Burracombe, they would be able to do so. Val sat up straighter, then swung her legs out of bed. She went to the cupboard and took out a pair of dark blue slacks and a short-sleeved white shirt. Then she went downstairs to wash in the kitchen.

Luke was just finishing the washing-up. He didn't turn as she came in, so she stood behind him and wound her arms around his waist, laying her head against his back.

'I'm sorry. I shouldn't have said that. It was horrible and I really didn't mean it.'

For a moment, he didn't move. Then he turned and took her in his arms.

'I'm sorry I snapped at you. I knew you couldn't really think I'd do that. It was just—'

'I know.' She lifted her head and looked at him. 'But we do need to talk about it, don't we? We've got to make a decision.'

The thought of leaving Burracombe for London was like a heavy weight dragging on her shoulders.

79

Chapter Eleven

Maggie Culliford did not go to see Bert Foster's display, nor did she feel much like celebrating. She woke to an aching back, and when she heaved herself out of bed and stood for a moment with her hand on the old chest of drawers, she felt a rush of water between her legs and knew that her twins were on their way.

'Arthur!' In sudden panic, she turned and leaned over her slumbering husband, poking him in the back. 'Arthur, wake up! I've started. Me waters have broken. You'll have to get the nurse.'

'What?' He rolled over, reluctantly opening his eyes. 'What d'you say?'

'I said, I've *started*. The baby – *babbies*. They'm coming. And you know what the doctor said, he said we got to get the nurse straight off and not wait. They could come quick.' She sat down heavily on the bed, groaning. 'Oh my God ... Arthur, get a *move* on, for pity's sake. And you might ask Aggie Madge to look in too; the nurse is going to have enough on her hands and Aggie's helped at enough births ...' She lay back on her thin pillows, moaning.

Arthur gave her a quick look and scrambled up, dragging on his trousers and a shirt. He pulled the door open and thumped on the other two. 'Brenda! Get up and come and see to your mother while I go for the nurse. Jim, you go up and knock on Aggie Madge's door and tell her the babies are coming. Come on, don't just lay there staring. I'll be as quick as I can, my bird ...' He was at the bottom of the stairs before he finished, and shouted the last words up behind him, but they were drowned out by Maggie's sudden cry of pain. This was too quick, he thought, racing through the village, too quick even for one, and with two of them … He passed Bert Foster's display without even noticing it, or being noticed by the little group admiring it, and scurried down the side lane leading to the midwife's cottage. If she wasn't already up, it wouldn't take her long to get dressed.

But when he knocked on the door, there was no reply. He banged again, so loudly that he almost broke the knocker. An upstairs window opened in the cottage next door and a tousled head poked out.

'Whatever's all that racket? Oh, it's you, Arthur. Your missus started, has she? Well, Lucy's not in. Got called out just after midnight, her did, to Bess Hannaford . You'd better try phoning Tavi hospital, see if they can send someone.'

'There ain't time for that.' Arthur was already on his way back down the path. 'I'll get the doctor. Our Jim's fetching Aggie over …' He sprinted back to the main street and headed for the doctor's house.

Charles Latimer was at the breakfast table, spreading home-made marmalade on his second piece of toast. At the thunderous hammering on the front door he almost dropped it, and Mary, who was just pouring more coffee, spilled some on the cloth. She put the pot down quickly, but Charles was already on his feet.

'Sounds like an emergency. I hope to God it's not Gilbert …' But even before he could reach the door, they could hear Arthur's voice, bellowing outside, and while Charles pulled at the bolts, Mary went quickly to fetch his bag.

'Doctor, her've started,' Arthur began as soon as the door was open. 'The waters went soon as her woke up, and she've got the pains as well – I went for the midwife but she'm out with Bess Hannaford and her fourth. Can you come, Doctor, can you come now, only with two of them and it starting so quick I'm feared – I don't want nothing to go wrong. I dunno what I'd do without my Maggie, I don't really, and there's all the other tackers too, so—'

'It's all right, Arthur,' the doctor said, taking him firmly by the shoulder. 'Just take a deep breath and calm down. I'm coming at once. I'll bring the car. Maggie will be all right, you'll see, and so will the babies. Perhaps you could send one of the children for Mrs Madge.'

'My Jim's already gone for she. But it'll be just as quick to walk, won't it?'

'I'll bring the car,' Charles repeated, not wishing to add that it might be needed if things were not all right after all. 'You go on foot. You can run faster than I can. I'll be there in a minute.' He turned to his wife as Arthur, after an agonised moment of indecision, set off again down the drive. 'I may need to get her to hospital. Will you be ready to telephone if I do? I'll send one of the boys back with a message.'

'Of course. I do hope there'll be no complications. That poor woman ...' She watched as her husband unlocked the garage and backed the car out, then went back inside. The toast and the coffee were both cold, and she began to clear the breakfast table.

The crowd around Bert's window display had dispersed by the time Charles drove past, and Aggie Madge, caught by Jim Culliford just as she was going up her path, was already hurrying along to the ramshackle cottage at the end of the village. She'd gone indoors only to throw off her Sunday coat and snatch up a large pinafore, and followed Jim back past Bert's shop, arriving breathless as Maggie's voice called out in fear and pain from the bedroom.

Brenda appeared white-faced at the door as Aggie came up the stairs.

'Oh, thank goodness you've come, Mrs Madge. Mum's real bad. I didn't know what to do.'

'You've done well, my pretty. Now go down and get the kettle on. Us'll need plenty of hot water. And keep the little ones downstairs.' They were already clustered by the bedroom door, anxious, the girls in tears. 'Betty and Shirley, you'm sensible maids. Give the others some breakfast and then take them for a walk. Everything's all right here, but us don't need a lot of children underfoot.' As she spoke, she was bustling through the door, tying her pinafore around her thin, wiry body and surveying the groaning heap on the bed. 'Now then, Maggie, let's have a look at you. Waters gone already, I see.'

'Soon as I stood up.' Maggie was ashen, her features grimacing with pain. 'Where's Lucy?'

'Out on a call,' Arthur said, bursting into the room. 'I've been for the doctor. He's here now, came in his car. She's up here,' he called down as Charles pushed open the front door. 'You'll be all right now, maid.'

'I hope to God you'm right,' Maggie groaned. 'I don't never remember it being like this before.' She turned her head as the doctor came into the small, crowded room. 'I'm going to lose 'em, ain't I?'

'Of course not.' He gave her a quick, reassuring smile, then bent to examine her. 'Arthur, go downstairs. This room's too small for all of us.'

Arthur nodded and clumped back to the kitchen, where Brenda was boiling a kettle on the hastily lit range, and Betty and Shirley were pouring cornflakes into a variety of chipped bowls. The smaller children, subdued and anxious, looked wide-eyed at their father as he sank heavily into his chair, leaned his elbows on the table and rested his head in his hands.

Jeanie put down her spoon and reached across to him. She patted his arm to gain his attention, and after a few moments he raised his head and stared at her, almost as if he had never seen her before.

'Dad?' she said, uncertainly. 'Dad?'

'What is it, my bird?'

'Is Mum ...?' She swallowed and started again, her eyes huge with the tears that had begun to roll down her cheeks. 'Is Mummy going to die?'

Arthur stared at her, trying to quell the fear surging inside him. 'No! No, of course she's not. Doctor won't let her. She's just having a babby, that's all.'

'Two babbies,' Billy said. 'Brenda says there's two. Twins, like George and Edward Crocker. Will they have the same face, like George and Edward, and have to wear jumpers with their names on them and always be naughty?'

Christ, I hope so, Arthur thought. Anything rather than this ... 'It's a bit soon to know all that, Billy. They might be girls. Or one of each.'

'*Can* you have twins that are one of each?'

'Where are they going to sleep?' Jeanie asked. 'Only there's no space in our room for a cot, and if they'm girls or one of each they can't be in the boys' room either. And they'll need two cots anyway. And two beds when they get bigger, and—'

'For God's sake stop asking so many questions,' Arthur began, his head spinning, but before he could say more, Aggie clattered down the stairs and he jumped up. 'What's happening? Aggie ...'

'She've got to go to the hospital,' Aggie said breathlessly. 'Doctor says you're to telephone Mrs Latimer and she'll arrange it. We got to have an ambulance.'

'An ambulance? How long's that going to take, for pity's sake?'

'It'll come out from Tavi,' she said impatiently. 'Go on, Arthur. Get a move on. Have you got money for the phone?'

'I dunno.' He searched his pockets and Aggie snatched up her bag, found her purse and held out two pennies. Without pausing to thank her, he dashed out of the door and down the street to the telephone kiosk that stood outside the post office.

'I'll telephone straight away,' Mary Latimer said. 'I'll be able to explain better than you, Arthur. Put your phone down now so that I can ring them, and go back to your wife. They'll be with you as soon as possible.'

He went back, his heart thumping. Jeanie's question came back into his mind. *Is Mummy going to die?* Oh God, please no, he thought. Please don't let her die. I can't get on without my Maggie. He felt sick. It was all his fault. All those nights when he'd got drunk on money she needed to buy food for the kiddies. All those times he'd gone out poaching, risking being sent to jail – as he had been two or three times, leaving Mag to manage as best she could without him and with no money coming in. That last time had nearly done for them. She'd been as sure as God made little green apples that they'd all end up in the workhouse, and if it hadn't been for Dottie Friend getting everyone together to help them out and titivate the cottage up a bit, they could have. And the Squire, too, he'd done his bit, buying the cottage and letting them have it at a peppercorn rent and making that farm manager give him work ... But what good would any of it be if he lost her now? He could never cope with all the children on his own. Specially if the new babies lived. It would be the workhouse then for all of them, and he'd be lucky if he ever saw them again. He couldn't imagine that. Living on his own, no family, no Maggie. He might as well be dead too.

At the cottage door, he paused and braced himself, wondering if she might have gone already. But a scream from upstairs, painful though it was to hear, reassured him. She was still alive, and as

Dottie Friend might have said, while there's life, there's hope. He hoped now. He hoped to God it was true.

The ambulance seemed to take an eternity but arrived at last, ringing its bell through the village and bringing everyone who wasn't in church to their doors. Maggie was taken to Freedom Fields hospital in Plymouth. Arthur went with her, leaving Aggie Madge and other neighbours to look after the children, and Charles Latimer made his way wearily back home to his wife.

'It's going to be touch and go,' he told her as he sank into a chair at the kitchen table and gratefully accepted a cup of coffee. 'One of the babies is in breech position and they're struggling to be born. And as big as Maggie was, I don't think they're very large. They're a month early, by my reckoning, although with Maggie you can never tell. After so many children, she's never regular enough for proper dates.'

'How terrible,' Mary said, setting a plate of toast on the table. 'You'd better have this; you never finished your breakfast and I've hardly started preparations for lunch. What about Maggie herself? Is she going to be all right?'

'I don't know. I really don't know.' He took a slice of toast and began to butter it, hardly noticing what he was doing. 'I just hope she can hold out until she reaches the hospital. I thought of sending her to Tavistock – to the Chollacott maternity hospital – but they don't have the facilities for such an emergency. They'll probably do a caesarean in Freedom Fields, if it's not too late, and she'll almost certainly need blood.' Suddenly savage, he almost flattened the toast with his knife as he spread it with marmalade. 'That man has a lot to answer for! I just hope this'll teach him a lesson.'

'I'm sure it will. He's changed since he came out of prison this time. Jacob Prout told me he's actually a good worker when he puts his mind to it, and I think he had a shock when he found how desperate Maggie was. He seems to have turned over a new leaf.'

'Well I hope he extends it to looking after his wife and not giving her any more children,' Charles said forcefully. 'That's if she gets through this in one piece. Or if she gets through it at all . . .'

*

85

Val and Luke, almost ready for their outing, were amongst those who heard the ambulance arrive. They came to their door, just across the road from the Cullifords' cottage, in time to see Maggie brought out on a stretcher and driven away. Val went over immediately and Aggie Madge turned to her in relief.

'Oh, Val. I thought about coming over for you, but Doctor said there was no more anyone else can do. Maggie's real bad. They've took her to hospital – Plymouth.'

'Plymouth?' Val stared at her in dismay. 'But where's Arthur?'

'He's gone with her. They didn't want to let him, but Maggie carried on so, and he didn't know how he could get into Plymouth otherwise. So they've left me with all the children.'

'Oh, we'll take some of them with us,' Val said instantly. 'We're going for a picnic. We thought we might walk over to the reservoir. Shirley and Betty and Joe can come, if you can manage Billy, Freddie and Jeanie. Brenda and Jimmy will be all right here, if they don't want to come. I'll make some more sandwiches.'

'Well, if you're sure you don't mind,' Aggie said gratefully. 'I was wondering how I was going to manage them all. And don't you worry about sandwiches, I can put up a few with some fish paste or a bit of jam, and I've got a batch of rock buns I made yesterday, you can have those too. Now, you heard what Mrs Ferris said.' She addressed the children. 'You three are going on a picnic, and Billy, Freddy and Jeanie are stopping with me for the day. No, you can't go, Jeanie – you'd never walk that far on your little legs, and anyway I'll need you to help me with Freddy. And you two big ones, Brenda and Jimmy, you can sort things out here. There's this kitchen to be tidied up and the washing-up to be done, and you can make up the bed for your dad when he comes home. I'll take the sheets in and wash them myself, Sunday or no Sunday.'

Val and Luke set off with their straggling entourage, while the three smallest children went with Aggie, and the older two, much subdued, did the best they could in the cottage. The news of Maggie's sudden departure went round the village like wildfire, so that when the churchgoers emerged from the service eager to discover why they had heard the ambulance bell as they knelt to their prayers, the rumours had had time to spread as many tentacles as an octopus. But the basis of them all was that Maggie Culliford had been taken to Plymouth to have her babies, and was in a bad way, and Arthur had gone with her because none of them might survive.

'I'm afraid that's more or less true,' Charles Latimer said when Basil Harvey hurried round to find out the truth. 'I'm waiting for news now. They said they'd ring me as soon as – oh! There's the telephone now.' He hurried to pick it up and listened, his face grave, while Basil, Grace and Mary stood anxiously by. 'Yes. Yes, I see. I'm very sorry. Thank you for letting me know. Tell him that someone will come and fetch him home whenever he wants to come ...'

He put down the phone and looked at them. 'It's as I feared. The second baby was born dead and the first is expected to live no more than an hour or two. And Maggie's own life is in the balance ...'

Chapter Twelve

Arthur Culliford had finally arrived home late on the Sunday evening. Charles Latimer had gone himself to fetch him and to visit Maggie, who was lying white-faced and barely conscious in her hospital bed. She had lost a lot of blood and it was still touch and go, but if she got through the night she had a good chance, the hospital doctor said.

Arthur begged to be allowed to stay with her, but was told to go home. There was nothing he could do. She didn't know he was there, and there was no point in wearing himself out when he might be needed the next day. Either way, you'll need your strength, the doctor had told him rather brusquely, and Arthur had allowed Charles to take his arm and lead him away.

'He said they'd let me know if I was needed,' he said, bewildered. 'How are they going to do that? Does he think I got a telephone? And how am I going to get back in if I'm needed quick? We only has two buses a day and they only go into Tavi. I'd have to walk out to the main road for the Plymouth bus, or wait for the train. Don't these doctors have any idea what it's like to live in a place like Burracombe?'

'I've told them to ring me if anything happens,' Charles said, guiding him out to the car. 'And I'll collect you and bring you in straight away. Or if I can't, someone else will. I've already talked to the Tozers, and Ted said one of them will do it. You can be here in half an hour or so.'

'Half an hour? My Maggie could be dead in that time.' He turned to Charles, now getting into the driving seat beside him. 'She's not going to die, is she, Doctor? I'm not going to lose my Mag as well as the two babbies, am I?' His voice was shaking with panic.

'They'll do their very best for her,' Charles said, wishing he could lie, just to take the dread from the man's eyes. 'And Maggie's will to live will help her.'

'Her will to live?' Arthur gave a hollow laugh. 'I don't reckon that can be much now. What she got to live for? Lost the two little ones, and nothing to come back to but a poor wretch of a man who can't even look after her proper. And a jailbird, on top of it. Nothing but a life of worry and living from hand to mouth, and always frightened of a knock on the door and a copper standing outside. That's all she got to look forward to, Doctor. I don't reckon many women'd have much will to live, if that's all there were for them.'

'You're not to talk like that,' Charles said sternly, heading out towards the Tavistock road. 'You and Maggie have your share of difficulties, I can't deny that, and a lot of them are due to you, but you still have plenty to be thankful for. A home, a family, and neighbours who care about you. Plenty of people have less. I don't think Maggie would like to hear you talking like that.' He waited, but Arthur said nothing, and after a minute or two he said more gently, 'And you do have the chance to put things right, you know.'

'Do I?' Arthur said gloomily and without much conviction.

'Of course you do. Look how much better off you are now than when you went into prison not long ago. Your friends in Burracombe have all rallied round and made your cottage nice for you, Colonel Napier has made sure you'll never be evicted *and* given you work, and Dottie's been giving Maggie cooking lessons. All you have to do is stick to your job, stop drinking your wages away and look after your family. It can't be that hard.'

'Not when you says it like that. But suppose Maggie don't want me no more when her comes out of hospital? Suppose she bears a grudge against me for what's happened? I wouldn't blame her. She didn't want no more little'ns, you know, she asked me to use a French letter, but I wouldn't do it. Not every time, anyway. It's like going to bed with your overcoat on. And those things cost money, you know. I didn't mind sometimes, but not *every* time.'

Charles sighed. 'Don't you see, Arthur, it *has* to be every time … And there are other ways, you know.'

'Pulling out, you mean? That never suited Maggie and me.' He was silent for a moment, then said, 'The thing is, Doctor, me and Mags *likes* that side of life. Always have. I hopes us always will.'

Charles glanced sideways at him. He spoke carefully. 'I'm afraid you may find you have to adapt yourselves to a few changes there. This birth was very bad for Maggie. It may have done some damage.'

'Inside her, you mean? Bad enough to stop us ...?'

'Not necessarily,' the doctor said hastily, thinking that the man had endured enough bad news for one day. 'I didn't examine her, so I can't say, and it's probably too soon to know anyway. But it may take a while for her to recover, and I think you should make very sure from now on that there are no more accidents. It really must mean *every* time.'

They drove almost all the rest of the way home in silence. Just before they turned off the main road for Burracombe, Arthur drew in a deep, sighing breath. Charles glanced at him again and saw that he was staring straight ahead, his face set.

'I'll remember what you said, Doctor. If my Maggie gets through this, I'll look after her as I should. Her and the other tackers. And there won't be no more accidents. I swear that. I'll do whatever I have to, to make sure her has a better life from now on.'

The Culliford children seemed to be scattered all over the village when Arthur arrived home, and after finding out where they all were, he was glad to be able to leave them there. He was so tired, he felt almost drunk as he stood swaying at Aggie Madge's door, mumbling out his news. She looked at him with compassion and, although she would never have thought in all her days that she'd let him over her doorstep, invited him inside and offered him a cup of tea.

'I've got a bit of cold meat left over from dinner, too, if you fancy it,' she said. 'Now that it's not on ration any more, we can be a bit more free with it. There's some veg, too; I could fry up a pan of bubble and squeak. Seems to me you need something hot and tasty inside you.'

'I don't know that I can eat anything,' he said, sitting down heavily at her table. 'I've gone past being hungry. I just wanted to know where all the little'ns were, and Dottie Friend told me they're with you.'

'That's right. Some of them, anyway. The girls are over with Val Tozer as was, and Jimmy's down at Alf Coker's. I got the boys head to tail in the big bed my grandma and grandad used to sleep in.' She was busy getting out the frying pan as she talked, knowing that once food was placed in front of him, Arthur would be able to eat it. There was nothing for visitors to eat in the hospital. And the poor man probably hadn't had a bite past his lips all day.

Like most of Burracombe, Aggie had never had much time for Arthur Culliford, but her heart had been touched by Maggie's plight when he had been sent to prison for a month for poaching, leaving his wife and children almost penniless and on the brink of being sent to the workhouse. This latest blow seemed the cruellest of all, and Aggie's heart bled for them all.

The door opened and James Raynor came in. He'd helped Aggie settle the children in bed and gone out for a late evening walk down to the ford and along the Burra Brook. He hesitated, looking from Arthur to Aggie, and she said quietly, 'The poor little babbies have gone, and Maggie's none too clever neither.'

James came over to Arthur and laid his hand on the man's shoulder.

'I'm very sorry to hear that,' he said quietly. 'Life can be very harsh at times.'

Arthur nodded. 'I dare say you know about that too, being in the war like me. Took prisoner I was, at Dunkirk, so I never saw much of it after that, but I saw plenty of poor buggers coming in with legs and arms blowed off, if you'll pardon my French, Aggie.'

Aggie pretended not to hear. She sliced the leftover potatoes and other vegetables and piled them into the hot frying pan. While they sizzled, she made tea in her big brown pot and looked enquiringly at the Major.

'Cup of tea for you too, Mr Raynor? I dare say you'm thirsty after your walk.'

'Thank you, Mrs Madge, that would be most welcome. I'm very well looked after here,' he added to Arthur as he took another chair at the table. 'I shall find it very different when I'm living alone again.'

Arthur nodded vaguely. As he watched Aggie at the stove, he said, 'My Maggie makes good bubble and squeak. We has it on Mondays if there's a bit of meat to go with it, which there ain't often. The rations don't go far between us lot.'

'Well, it'll be better now it's off ration,' Aggie said comfortingly. 'And you got a regular wage coming in, too. Things'll be a bit easier for you and Maggie.'

'Only if her lives,' he said, and they stared at him in shock.

'Arthur! You mustn't say things like that. Of course her'll live.'

'Will her?' He shook his head, and to their consternation, tears came to his red-rimmed eyes and brimmed slowly over to roll down his stubbled cheeks. 'They don't seem all that sure about that down at the hospital. Lost a lot of blood, her did, and what with the shock of losing the babbies, her's in a poor way. I wanted to stop with her,' he went on, his voice rising in distress, 'but they wouldn't let me. My old girl dying and they wouldn't let me stop with her. What do you think of that? Cruel, that's what I call it – cruel.'

Aggie's face creased with sympathy, but it was James Raynor who moved quickly back to Arthur's side and gripped his shoulder again.

'I can't believe they would refuse you if they really believed that. They want her to rest and get a good night's sleep, that's all. It's a good sign.'

'Is it? I dunno.' Arthur shook his head again. 'She looked in a poor way to me, laying in that bed as white as a candle.' He looked up into James's face. 'I tell you, I seen some sights during the war, same as you did, but I never seen anything like what my Maggie went through having those two. Not that they'd let me in, of course, didn't want no men in there, not unless it was the doctor, but I could hear her and it went right through me.' He shuddered. 'Right through me. And all for the sake of buying a few French letters.' He threw Aggie an apologetic glance, which she pretended not to see as she scooped bubble and squeak out of the pan on to a plate. 'Too bloody selfish by half, that's me.'

'And too ready with your tongue, too,' she told him sharply. 'That's the second time you've used bad language in my kitchen, Arthur Culliford, and I've overlooked it till now, but I won't stand for a third. Now, you get that inside you and maybe you can talk like a respectable human being, about respectable subjects. I'm going in the front room, like I always do of a Sunday evening, to listen to the wireless. It's Tom Jenkins with *Grand Hotel*, halfway through by now, and then *Sunday Half Hour*, and that I never miss.'

She departed, leaving the two men alone. Arthur gave the Major a covert glance and James winked at him.

'It's all right, Mr Culliford. We're both old soldiers now and understand each other.' He stirred his tea and lifted the cup to his lips. 'But in many ways you're luckier than I am.'

Arthur stared at him. 'Me, luckier than you? How d'you make that out?'

'Why, you have a family. You have your troubles, I know, and just at present they're serious ones. But I think Mrs Madge is right. They wouldn't have sent you home if they hadn't believed Maggie would live through the night, and they know that you need some rest too. You wouldn't have got that if you'd stayed there. You'll probably go back tomorrow and find her on the road to recovery, and although you've lost the two little ones, you do still have all the others.' He hesitated, then said quietly, 'That's probably quite the wrong thing to say, but to me it seems that you still have much more than I do. Because my wife died in the Blitz, before we had a chance to start our family, and now I doubt I'll ever have children of my own.'

Basil Harvey called a meeting in his study next evening, while Arthur was at the hospital, attended by all those he thought had the Cullifords' interests at heart. In fact, it was attended by more people than he had actually invited, word having got round during the day, and even with all the dining chairs brought in, there were still a few of the men standing. The last person to arrive was Dr Latimer, and several of those with chairs stood up at once, but he waved them down and leaned against the door jamb.

'A few have sent apologies,' Basil said, after thanking them all for coming. 'Mrs Madge, of course, has some of the children, and can't leave them; Val Ferris sent a message to say that Christopher's teething but Luke will try to get along; and Dottie Friend is working in the pub because Rosie's got a summer cold and there are a lot of visitors around at this time of year.'

93

'And my father asked me to say that he would have liked to be here too,' Hilary said from one of the corners, 'but he has his lawyer down from Exeter for some business and can't get away.'

'That's a pity, but I'm sure you can speak for him, Hilary,' Basil said, and she nodded. 'Well, without further ado, let's start our discussion. We're all here because we want to help this unfortunate family, so perhaps first of all Dr Latimer could give us the latest news about Maggie.'

'I spoke to the doctor at the hospital just before I left,' Charles said from the doorway. 'He says she's doing better than he expected but she's not out of the woods yet. The births left her very weak, and she was not in good condition to start with. She was not well nourished – babies take what they need and the mother has what's left, and in this case it was less than enough on both sides – and not strong enough to cope with the shock. I'm afraid it will be a few days before we know for certain if she will recover.'

There was a sober silence. Then he added, 'I wouldn't normally be giving you such details about a patient's condition, but Arthur knows that the village is concerned about Maggie, and indeed the whole family, and he's given his permission.' In fact, Arthur had just shrugged and said, 'What's it matter who knows?' when Charles had asked him, but the doctor had taken this for assent.

'Well,' Basil said after a moment while they all thought about what they had heard, 'it's quite apparent that the Cullifords need even more help now. The village has done very well in looking after them over the past few months, but the situation now is really serious. It's up to us to rally round.' He looked at the doctor again. 'What's the best that can happen?' There was no need, he thought, to ask the worst – they all knew what that would be.

'The best outlook is complete recovery, of course, and that's not impossible. Maggie might never be quite as strong as she was before, but we have to remember that she has never really been completely healthy. She's never eaten properly – even after Dottie's cooking lessons, she would always give most to Arthur and the children. And I don't think her smoking did any good either. There's a definite opinion in medical circles now that it's bad for you. If she would consent to give up her cigarettes—'

94

'If she gave up cigarettes,' Joyce Warren interrupted, 'she'd have a bit more money to spend on food.'

'That's quite true, but smoking does seem to have given her some comfort. All of us who indulge know that it certainly calms the nerves.' Like several of the men present, the doctor smoked a pipe and found it very relaxing at the end of a long day. 'Be that as it may, and supposing she could just cut down, she still needs to build up her strength with better food. Now that Arthur is in regular work, thanks to Hilary and her father' – he glanced over at Hilary, who gave him a small smile – 'and Maggie knows how to make nourishing meals for the family, I don't think that is something we need to worry too much about. What we must concern ourselves with mostly this evening is the children. I have to say that I think it will be some weeks before Maggie is able to cope with having them all at home again. In fact, it will probably be a while before she comes home herself – she'll need at least a fortnight in hospital, as is normal after any birth, and then some convalescence. I'm hoping to find her a place in one of the convalescent homes around Tavistock, but they're all rather full, and she may have to go to one in Plymouth.'

'Plymouth?' Ted Tozer said. 'But that's going to be master hard for Arthur to get to every night. How's he going to manage with all they kiddies to look after? And nobody's given *he* cooking lessons.'

'That's just the point, Ted,' Basil said. 'Arthur *won't* be able to manage. We're looking at several weeks here until Maggie comes home. It seems to me that if the children all go back to the cottage, Arthur is going to be swamped by it and things will go from bad to worse.'

Again there was a silence while everyone absorbed this. Then Hilary said, 'What you're saying is that the children can't go home until Maggie is fit and well again. And they'll need to be looked after until then.'

'I'm afraid that does seem to be the position,' Basil agreed.

'But that's terrible!' Joyce Warren exclaimed. 'Where are they going to go? The people who've taken them in only expected it to be for a few days – we're talking about *weeks* now.' She looked towards the doctor. 'What would usually happen in a case like this? Would the authorities help in any way?'

95

He scratched the side of his neck and pursed his lips. 'I'm afraid they would take the children away to look after them. Either in foster homes or – well, to Bannawell Street, in Tavistock.'

'You mean the *workhouse?*' Joyce's horror was echoed by almost everyone present, and they all began to talk at once. 'Maggie'd go out of her mind if they was took there!' ... 'Her was scared out of her wits when her thought they'd have to go there when Arthur was in prison' ... 'It'd kill her, that's what it would do' ... 'Honestly, Charles, we can't allow that. We must be able to do *something*.'

It was Hilary who had spoken last, and everyone else fell silent. She went on, 'Foster homes might not be so bad, as long as we can be sure the children would all be brought back home as soon as Maggie is able to look after them herself. But I know that last time she was terrified of them being taken from her because she thought she *wouldn't* get them back. Once the authorities get to know you, she said, they're always coming round to keep an eye on things.'

'Snooping.' Jacob Prout nodded. 'That's what it is.'

'Well, to be fair,' Charles Latimer said, 'there are quite a few families who really do need to be overseen. And I have to say that I've sometimes thought the Cullifords were one of those families. But so far they've always managed to scrape through, and the village has been so good to them over the past few months that—'

'Us looks after our own,' Jacob asserted. 'That's what a village is for, and Burracombe's the best village there is. Us did it before and us'll do it again.' He turned his head to take in the crowded room. 'Isn't that right?'

There was a murmur of agreement. Then they all looked at each other as if waiting for someone to make the first move, and Basil once more took up the reins.

'I take it, then, that we wish to prevent the children from going into the workhouse, even for a short period, and also that we are not happy about their going to foster homes.'

'They'd be separated, wouldn't they?' Ted pointed out. 'Girls from boys in the workhouse, or else sent to different foster homes. They wouldn't be a family no more.'

'And they wouldn't be in Burracombe,' Jacob said.

'But if we want to keep them together, who would take in so many children?' Hilary asked. 'There are, what, eight of them? I've never been quite sure. There are only a few of us in the village with enough room, and they'd need to be looked after as well. It's not something to take on lightly.'

'Meals, washing their clothes, seeing that they gets to school on time – *and* looking after the littlest ones, that don't go to school,' Mabel Purdy said. 'And it's not just that – it'll be the school holidays before Maggie gets home, if you'm right about that convalescence, Doctor. That means they'll *all* be under our feet.'

'Well, we've got room,' Hilary said doubtfully. 'But I'm out a lot, and Patsy's nearly six months pregnant. Mrs Curnow will need more help as it is.'

'I don't see as you can have them,' Jacob said rather sternly. 'Not with Squire the way he is.'

'Oh, I don't think that would be a problem. He's quite fit again now. He does have to be careful, but we could keep the children out of his way most of the time.'

Travis Kellaway said, 'I'd offer to have a couple myself, but as you know, my wife's in the same position – we'll have our own baby in a month or two. I honestly don't think—'

'Of course you can't,' Hilary said. 'Well then, it looks as though it's up to me. After all, we do have the room, and perhaps I can get some extra help. The oldest girl – Brenda, isn't it? – is of an age to be quite useful, and I dare say she's used to helping with the younger ones. And—'

'There'll be no need for that,' Joyce Warren said abruptly. '*I'll* have them.'

For a moment or two, nobody spoke. Their faces, all turned towards the solicitor's wife, registered degrees of surprise that ranged from astonishment to outright disbelief. She returned their looks coolly, and spoke into the astounded silence.

'Henry and I have got plenty of bedrooms – we can put camp beds into some of them – and a big garden. We can easily take the whole family, and as you say, Brenda is old enough to help. Although I can't help feeling it would be better for her and Jimmy to stay in the cottage with their father. They'll be company for him when he gets back from seeing Maggie – I don't think it would be at all advisable for him to be returning to an empty house. Brenda can give him his meals and come and help me during the holidays. She seems quite a capable girl. I know Jimmy goes to work in Tavistock every morning, but he can give a hand too.'

'Isn't Brenda leaving school this term?' Hilary asked. 'She'll be looking for work.'

'Then she can work for me, helping around the house and with the other children,' Joyce said promptly. 'I'll pay her a small wage. It seems to me to be the ideal solution.'

They all looked at each other again. Mrs Warren was the last person they'd expected to volunteer to take in a family of children like the Cullifords. One or two rolled their eyes a bit.

'I did have evacuees during the war,' she pointed out, seeing their expressions. 'This won't be so very different.'

'It's very generous of you,' Basil said hastily, afraid that she was offended. 'And I'm sure we'll all help as much as possible, won't we? The children can be taken out for walks or picnics during the day, and those of us who grow vegetables or have our own hens can provide extra food. You mustn't be out of pocket, Mrs Warren.'

There was a general murmur of agreement at this. George Sweet said he was sure he could deliver a few extra loaves of bread at no charge. Ted Tozer offered butter when Alice or Joanna churned some, and Edie Pettifer said that her hens always produced more eggs than she could use herself and she'd be glad to send up a few. Miss Kemp, who had been sitting by the window with James Raynor, said that after a quick consultation they had agreed that the smallest children could join Billy and Betty in the infants' class two afternoons a week.

'We'll help in the holidays too,' she said. 'I'll be away for the first two weeks, but Mr Raynor has kindly offered to be on hand, and I'll be glad to do what I can after I come home.'

'Well!' Basil looked around at the assembled company, his pink face beaming. 'That's all very satisfactory, I must say. Mrs Warren has proved herself a real treasure, and I'm sure we'll all do what we can to make her task as easy as possible. I think the Cullifords will be most grateful.'

The meeting broke up then and everyone departed, discussing the new plans as they strolled home along the village street. Jacob Prout, walking with Hilary, said, 'If that don't beat the band! Whoever would have thought *she* would have give all they little

98

tackers, what hardly know a face flannel from a bale of hay, the run of her posh house? I just hope her knows what she'm taking on.'

'She did have evacuees,' Hilary reminded him. 'And she was very good with the children in the school when Stella was in hospital. I think she's been rather maligned in the village. I know she's sometimes been a little too eager to be in charge, but perhaps if she'd had a family of her own ... I think that may be what she's missed all her life, you know, Jacob. Children of her own to care for.'

'Ah, I can understand that,' he replied. 'I was always sorry me and my Sarah never had any, but there, 'twasn't to be. And then my Jennifer came into my life and now there's to be a family there, and I been told I'm to be called Grandad. Something I never thought to hear ... But you know, going back to Arthur and Maggie, there's summat us never did get round to talking about.' He drew in a deep breath and looked at her gravely. 'What about if her *don't* pull through? What if poor old Arthur finds hisself left on his own, with all they children? What'll happen to them all then?'

Chapter Thirteen

'I can't really think of the future at all yet,' David said. He and Hilary were sitting on a bench by the Serpentine, watching the ducks. There were so many different varieties that they made a kaleidoscope of colour, the patterns shifting every second with their movements. Some paddled quickly, darting flashes of brilliant feathers between the more sedately drifting white and brown birds, but when a woman in a brown coat approached with a bag of bread, the pattern was broken by a general flurry of wings and frantic splashing as each one battled to be first to be fed.

Hilary had come up for the day to meet him as he carried out various business tasks. When he had telephoned to ask her, she had almost said no, half afraid of what he might be going to say to her; the uncertainty she had been feeling over the past few weeks had grown darker in her mind and there had been some nights when she lay in bed convinced that it was all over. He was grieving more than he had expected for Sybil; he regretted their affair, and the days when he didn't ring were the beginning of a silence that would last all their lives.

'Are you sure you want me to come?' she'd asked doubtfully. 'Won't you be too busy?'

'Of course I won't. Hilary, we must see each other again. We need to talk properly, face to face. So much has happened.'

'I know.' And that was just the trouble. So much had happened that she hardly knew what was real any more and what was solely in her mind. But she knew that he was right. They must meet.

Whatever the outcome, whatever the truth, it needed to be said plainly and honestly, face to face.

He was staying two nights, Tuesday and Wednesday, but neither of them suggested that she should do so too, and to avoid temptation she had come on Thursday, when he would have finished whatever business he had to do and would be returning to Derby. It was too soon, she thought. And then, with a chilled heart: perhaps it will never happen again. Things had changed at the end, he'd said; there had been a sudden resurgence of the feelings he and Sybil had once had for each other. That emotion must affect his feelings for Hilary. Perhaps he had really loved Sybil all the time and had never realised it; perhaps that love, found too late, and the guilt he must now feel would overshadow everything else.

Perhaps he will never love me again, she thought sadly. Perhaps he never really did.

The worst of it was, she couldn't ask him. There seemed to be a barrier between them that neither could cross. They had met awkwardly at Paddington, Hilary coming off the train with a sudden, unexpected reluctance. She had been nervous all the way up, but had felt sure this would disappear the moment she saw him. Yet as she walked along the platform and caught sight of his tall figure waiting at the end, her nervousness increased. Her heart thudded and her skin prickled, and for a moment she almost turned and ran.

Her feet carried her forward, however, until she stood face to face with him, looking up into his serious eyes. They looked at each other, unsmiling, for a full minute, and then she said shakily, 'Hullo, David,' and stepped into his arms.

The kiss was almost tentative, like a first kiss, an exploration, each trying to assess the depth of the other's response. Her lips trembled against his and she felt tears come to her eyes. What is happening to us, she thought. Has it gone? Has it really all gone?

David stepped away and drew her arm through his. 'This isn't the place, is it? We need to be somewhere quieter than this.'

'Let's just walk,' she said, and he led her out of the bustling station, cutting through Sussex Gardens to Lancaster Gate and crossing the road into Hyde Park. Until reaching this bench by the water, blessedly far from other benches, they barely spoke. Hilary kept her hand through his arm, feeling the warmth and firmness of it, but when she glanced up at his face, it seemed shuttered and remote. I shouldn't have come, she thought. It's never going to be the same again. Whatever we had – if we ever really had anything at all – it's over.

They sat down and she stole another glance. This time, he was looking at her too, and her heart twisted as she caught a glimpse of torture in his eyes. Then the shutters came down again and her heart sank.

'What is it, David?' she asked quietly. 'What's troubling you? Are you wishing you hadn't come?'

His eyes widened. 'No! No, of course not. What makes you think that?'

Hilary paused, then took both his hands in hers and looked intently into his face. 'David, we must be honest with each other. Even if it hurts. If you – if you want this to end, if you feel differently about me now, you must say so. You mustn't pretend. Neither of us must pretend.'

'No,' he said after a moment. 'No, we mustn't. So ... are *you* wishing you hadn't come?'

Hilary gasped. She hadn't expected to find the ball thrown so squarely back into her court. She began to deny it, then remembered how only a few minutes ago she'd said they must both be honest.

'No, I don't wish that,' she said slowly. 'But I did wonder, as we were walking along, whether we'd been wise to meet again so soon. You seem – *seemed* – so different. I thought you were regretting it. I thought – I was afraid you were going to tell me it was all over.'

'All over!' he exclaimed, but she went on.

'Or that we'd try to continue without admitting it had changed, and that would have been worse.' Another brief pause. 'We won't do that, will we? We will say. We must. Because I couldn't bear it if we – if we ...' Her voice broke and the tears came at last, dripping on to their clasped hands.

'Hilary!' He twisted his fingers free and caught her in his arms, holding her close so that her face was pressed against his shoulder. 'Darling, don't cry. Of course it's not over. Of course I haven't changed. How could you ever think I might?'

It took Hilary a few minutes to recover herself. Dabbing her eyes and nose with her hanky, she said, 'I didn't know what to think. Of course I realise this has been a horribly difficult time for you, and you probably hardly knew what to think yourself, you've had so much to do and so much to worry about, and the funeral and everything, and Sybil's parents and ... and ...'

'And?' he asked quietly. 'None of that made any difference to my feelings for you, and you must know it. So what else is there?'

She looked up at him and searched his eyes for the truth. It had to be asked, and once asked it had to be answered.

'You said that at the end, you felt the same for her as you'd done at the very beginning,' she said quietly. 'You loved her again, and you believed that she loved you. That's what could have changed things, David, and I still don't really know if it did.'

His gaze flickered slightly but didn't move away. Instead, the darkness of his pupils seems to deepen, as if opening windows into his heart. His face was grave and his voice measured as he replied.

'That feeling was just a memory,' he said. 'It was like an emotion in a dream – real enough at the time, real even when recalled, but not lasting. I'm glad we had it, for the comfort it may have given her during those last hours of lucidity, but it's gone now. And even at the beginning, I can't say it was truly love. Youthful infatuation seems just as acute as real love, but when it's over you put it away from you. In mine and Sybil's case, it was over before we married, but custom, propriety, call it what you will, demanded otherwise.'

'It might have made you feel other things, though,' she said. 'Guilt, for instance.'

He looked back at the water, still splashed by the ducks as they scrambled for the bread the woman was throwing, and sighed. 'I've always felt that. We both have. But we can put it away now, can't we? We never really hurt Sybil. When she found out – little though she really discovered – it simply gave her the opportunity she wanted: a chance to divorce me as the guilty party.' He turned his head and looked into Hilary's eyes. 'Darling, we have to try to put it behind us. We have to look to the future.' And then he sighed and said, 'That's what really troubles me now. I just can't see what it is to be. I can't really think of the future at all yet.'

*

They got up after a while and walked by the lake, hand in hand. It didn't matter who saw them now. David could not be hauled through the divorce court nor struck from the medical register for walking with a woman who was not his wife. He was free – as free as Hilary. They could marry at any time. Tomorrow, if they wished. And yet …

'I don't feel as if anything's really changed,' she said eventually. 'I know we can't do anything yet – you've got to wait a reasonable time. But I feel like you – I can't see the future. It's as if a heavy fog lies between us and whatever is to happen next.'

'What do you want to happen next?' he asked quietly, and she stopped and faced him.

'You know what I want to happen. I want us to be married. A safe, secure couple, living a happy, normal life, part of our community.'

'Our community,' he repeated. 'You know, I think that's a large part of our problem. What *is* our community? Where are we to live this happy, normal life? In Derby, or in Devon? How do we reach that point?'

'That's where the fog comes down. I don't know, David. I've got the estate to think of, and my father, and you've got your practice – and your father. It's not easy for either of us to move away.'

'Easier for me than for you, perhaps. A partnership is easier to leave than an inheritance.'

She sighed. 'I'm beginning to wish Father had kept to his plan of leaving the estate to Rob. I could have walked away then.'

'I don't think you could. You'd have felt morally bound to stay until he was ready to take over. Another ten years at the very least. Hilary, I don't want to wait that long. I want us to have a family – to be that normal couple you dream of being. That *I* dream of being. We've waited too long already – and yet I can't see how we're to move on. We seem to be stuck where we are.'

'Maybe it's too early to be thinking about it now,' she said gently. 'Sybil's only been gone a few weeks. You're still working through your feelings. We have to give it time.'

'I suppose so,' he said disconsolately, and kicked at a small stone on the path. Hilary glanced at him and smiled despite her anxiety. For a moment he looked like a small boy, baulked of some childish desire – a bag of sweets, a whistle, a penknife. But her smile faded with the realisation that this was no boyish sulk but the misery of an adult who had suffered years of betrayal, yet could still see his longed-for prize dangling out of his reach like a carrot before a donkey. What a muddle, she thought. But what was it Stephen had said not long ago? Nothing stays the same. Things change. Paths become clear. Perhaps this will be true for us, sometime in the future.

'Let's try not to worry about it any more now,' she said. 'Let's just enjoy the time we have together today. We've only got a few hours – let's make the most of them.'

'All right,' he said. 'What would you like to do?'

'Hire a rowing boat,' she said promptly. 'And then have tea somewhere. A proper tea, with sandwiches and cake and pots of Earl Grey. Just be an ordinary couple, having an afternoon out. It will be something to remember when we're apart and everything seems dark.'

'All right,' he said. 'A boat and then tea at Harrods. We'll make it something special.' He stopped and took her hands in his, looking down seriously into her face. '*You're* very special to me, Hilary. You always have been. I love you very much. And we *will* be that happy couple, living a normal life. Where we'll live it, or when it will happen, I don't know. But it *will* happen. I promise you, it will happen.'

Hilary met his eyes and nodded. 'I know. We'll make it happen, David. But maybe not for a little while. We just need to pause and be patient first. And I love you too – very, *very* much.'

Chapter Fourteen

While Hilary was in London, Patsy Pettifer was pouring her heart out to Mrs Curnow.

'It was hearing about Maggie Culliford,' she said, the tears running down her cheeks not entirely due to the onion she was peeling. 'It's so awful – two babies, both dead, and Mrs Culliford nearly dying herself. They still don't know if she'll be all right, so I heard when I was in the shop. And I know it's selfish, but I can't help thinking – suppose it happens to me.'

'Dear Lord above, it won't happen to you,' the housekeeper said, rolling out pastry for the pasties they were making. 'You're young and healthy. I don't know her, only to pass in the village street, but Mrs Culliford was never well from the day she started those twins, and not much before that. And she'd had a lot of babies before. It takes its toll, especially if you live the way she did.'

'I know they never had much money, but then neither do Terry and me.'

'That's different. *You* get proper meals, here and at home. Your little one'll be a proper little bouncer, you'll see.'

Patsy finished slicing the onion and started on another one. 'People do die when they have babbies, though. And sometimes the babbies do. It could happen, Mrs Curnow, and I tell you what seems so cruel ...' Her voice broke suddenly and now no one could pretend the tears were because of the onion. She put both hands to her face, sobbing, and Mrs Curnow came quickly round the table and pushed her gently into a chair.

'Now then, my pretty, what's this all about? You're not really frightened you're going to die, surely? You got Dr Latimer looking after you, and that nice midwife, and you're booking into the maternity home in Tavistock when your time comes. What can go wrong for you? What are you really upset about?' She waited a moment as Patsy wept, and then said quietly, 'It's your mother, isn't it?'

Patsy nodded and fought to control her sobs. At last, mopping her eyes with the tea towel Mrs Curnow handed her, she choked out a few words.

'She'll never see her grandbaby. She'll never see me. He won't let her and it's so cruel, Mrs Curnow, I don't know how I'm going to stand it.'

The housekeeper nodded. 'I thought as much. And I dare say she's as upset about it as you are. Any mother would be. I've never had children myself, my man and I were never blessed, but if I had and my maid was expecting her first, I'd want to be with her. You're right, Patsy, 'tis cruel. I reckon it's time something was done about it.'

Patsy lifted her wet face. 'What *can* be done about it? He'll never let me over the step. I can only go in the evenings and he's there then. And Mother can't come to Burracombe. He'd know in a minute.'

'And is he there all the daytime?' Mrs Curnow demanded. 'There must be times when he has to leave the farm.'

'He goes into Tavi cattle market on a Wednesday sometimes.'

'Well, there's your chance. You can slip over then and see your mother. It won't take you more than half an hour to walk across the Clam, and you can spend an hour or so with her and then walk back in time for lunch.'

'But I'm supposed to be working then. I can't ask Miss Hilary to tell lies for me, if he asks her. And if he asks Mother, she'll have to tell him. He'd know straight away if she weren't telling the truth.'

'Miss Hilary don't need to know,' the housekeeper said robustly. 'I reckon she'd rather it was that way. You have a look in the *Tavistock Gazette* and see when the next market's on that he might go to, and you can slip over then. Your mother will be pleased to see you, and it'll make you feel better too. I don't suppose he'll ask her anyway. Why should he?'

Patsy gazed at her. 'Are you sure that will be all right? I don't want to cause any trouble.'

'Nor will you. I'll see to it that it's all right, and I won't tell lies for you either. If I read Miss Hilary right, a nod's as good as a wink to her, and she'll ask no questions. Least said, soonest mended. Anyway, she's not often here of a morning herself.' She looked down at Patsy's face, shining with fresh tears, and added, 'What you said is right. It's cruel, and I can't abide cruelty. You need to see your mother and she needs to see you, and your little one is going to need you both. And I wouldn't be surprised if your father himself don't come round in the end. There's not many men will turn away from their own grandchild.'

Patsy's face told her that she thought her father was one who would, but the girl said nothing. She mopped her face again, smiled rather shakily and got up to finish peeling her onion. The two of them worked in silence for a few moments, and then Patsy said, 'Thanks, Mrs Curnow. You'm a good friend to me. I won't forget this.'

Mrs Curnow sniffed and shrugged. 'There's not much I can do, my pretty, but we're all here to help one another, that's how I see it. And I tell you this.' She finished rolling the pastry and began to cut it into circles, ready for the meat, onion and turnips to be piled on top. 'If I had a girl of my own, I'd like her to be such a one as you. Fresh and pretty and loving. Only she'd never have to get married the way you did. I'd let her walk out with her young man open and above board, the way it ought to be, and I'd give her a proper wedding too when the time came. And I'd welcome all the little grandchildren she gave me, and think they were all God's blessing.' She looked suddenly fierce as she added, 'And if *my* man behaved the way your father's behaved, he'd find the door locked against *him*, that he would.'

Terry Pettifer was also finding the situation difficult. He confided in his brother as they worked together in an old farmhouse on the outskirts of Peter Tavy that was being wired for electricity for the first time. The house was to be redecorated as soon as the electrical work was finished, but there was nobody living there now, and he could speak freely.

'I dunno that we did the right thing at all,' he confessed. 'Patsy's missing her mother more than she ever thought she would. She cries about it in the night. I don't know what to do to make her feel better.'

'I'd have thought you'd have some idea by now,' Bob remarked with a grin, and Terry gave him a look.

'It's not funny, Bob. She's real upset. Mother says she got to look on the bright side and think happy thoughts, for the baby's sake, but her don't seem able to somehow. Sometimes I wish us'd never gone about it this way, but what else could us do?'

'What most other people do, I suppose – waited till old man Shillabeer come round in his own good time. Which he would have done in the end. This way, you've set him against you for life and I don't suppose he'll ever give way.'

'Patsy didn't think he'd come round. She said he'd keep her on the farm till her turned twenty-one and then find a whole lot of other reasons not to let her go. And she was afeared I'd have found someone else by then.'

'And would you?' Bob asked, cutting a length of cable.

Terry snorted. 'Course I wouldn't! I don't suppose anyone else would look at me anyway, with my ugly mug.'

'You'm right there,' Bob said cheerfully. 'It's a wonder to me any of us Pettifers keeps going, with the looks we got handed down to us. But we must have been around Burracombe for hundreds of years – look at they old gargoyles on the church tower. Spitting image of old Grandad, that one on the east corner is.'

'It'll be the spitting image of you too, then, when you gets to his age,' Terry observed. 'Gran says you look just like he did as a young chap. That's summat to look forward to! Anyway, like I was saying, I'd have waited years for Patsy if I'd had to, and sometimes I got to say I wish I'd never let her talk me into this.'

Bob, kneeling on the floor with a tangle of electrical wires around him, stared up at him. 'You don't really mean that, our Terry? You don't really wish you and Patsy hadn't got wed?'

'Not as such, no, of course I don't. I just wish it hadn't had to be this way, with her and her mother so upset, and old man Shillabeer going round telling folk I took advantage. I'd *never* have done that!'

he burst out. 'Not with *any* maid. I'd have waited till the right time – till our wedding night. Like us've always been told.'

Bob rubbed his long chin. 'I dunno what to say. I don't suppose Patsy wanted it to be this way either, but it seems to me you both got to stop thinking about that. You can't alter it. What's done is done, and you got to look forward now. You're wed and you got a little'n on the way, and that's what's most important. It's a shame about Patsy and her mother, but I reckon that'll sort itself out in time. They'll find ways round it, specially when the babby's here. Mrs Shillabeer's not going to let her first grandchild be born and live over the Burra and her never see it.'

Terry looked unconvinced, but there seemed to be nothing more to say. They worked in silence for a while. Then Bob asked, 'Have you thought of any names yet?'

'We've talked about a few, but there's a long time to go before us has to decide. Patsy fancies one of the names from *The Glenn Miller Story*.'

Bob stared at him. 'The picture, you mean?'

'Yes. It was the first one we went to see together. So that's Glenn or James for a boy, because James Stewart played Glenn Miller, and June or Helen for a girl – June Allyson played his wife and she was called Helen,' Terry explained. 'I don't mind, meself. Helen's a bit posh and she might get called Nellie, but June's all right. And I quite like Glenn. It's a bit unusual.'

'Glenn Pettifer,' Bob said consideringly. 'Well, 'tis your babby, Terry, and you can choose its name yourself, but I reckon there might be a few other people wanting to have a say too. Gran told me only last week that she've always wanted one of the family called after Grandad, so I dare say she'll be putting her oar in.'

'But Grandad's name was Ebenezer!' Terry exclaimed in horror, and Bob laughed.

'I know, and that's probably why nobody's ever used it since. You and me should think ourselves lucky neither of us got saddled with it.' He stood up and gave his brother a steady look. 'Now don't you worry too much about your Patsy,' he said, laying a hand on Terry's shoulder. 'From what I hear, young women are always a bit emotional when they'm expecting, and Patsy's had to stand up to a lot already. You just give her a cuddle when her gets a bit tearful, and tell her you love her and 'tis all for the best, and I dare say once the babby's born 'twill all come right after all. And you always got me and Mum and Dad to stand alongside you. Don't forget that.'

'I won't.' Terry was disconcerted to find that he felt a little tearful himself. Bob rarely talked so seriously or mentioned emotions of any sort. He rubbed a hand across his face and grinned a little waveringly. 'Thanks, Bob.'

'That's all right. And now us'd better crack on. Just because there's no one here to see what we'm doing, it don't mean us can slack on the job.' He bent and picked up his tools. 'You clear that lot up, Terry, and then come into the big bedroom. Us got a main lot of work to do there, and not too much time to do it.'

Chapter Fifteen

'So nothing's been decided, then?' Val asked as she brought a tray of tea through from her little kitchen.

Hilary shook her head. 'Nothing *can* be decided, can it? There's a lot for David to do – Sybil had money of her own, a legacy from her grandmother, apparently, and made a will, so that has to be dealt with, and then there are all her personal possessions to be sorted out. He's got her parents to take into account – they'll probably want some things, but her mother's an invalid and he has to wait until she can manage the journey. He said the funeral really took its toll on them both. And Sybil had other relatives – two sisters, a cousin she was fond of, and so on – as well as friends. She left them some items in her will, but there are plenty of other things and they all need to be distributed or disposed of in some way. He wants to give away as much as possible, but what does he do with anything that's left?'

'Sell it, I suppose.' Val poured the tea and offered Hilary a plate of home-made biscuits. 'Try one of these. They're melting moments – not entirely appropriate just now, come to think of it!'

Hilary gave her a wry smile. 'The moments at present seem to be as melting as Burra Tor! But I'll have one anyway – thanks. Yes, he says he'll send anything left over to auction, but it's all going to take time and he has his work as well. And that's another thing. His father's not been feeling too well lately and David's had to take on some of his patients as well as his own.'

'That's not so good. Is he really ill?'

'I'm not sure. He's getting near retirement age, so he may just be tired. But if he does decide to retire, David will have to find a new partner. It all seems to have come at once.'

'Things always do,' Val said, and something in her tone made Hilary look at her more carefully.

'Is something wrong? You've seemed a bit subdued just lately, but I've been so wrapped up in my own troubles …'

'Not really *wrong*, except – well, it's just that Luke and I have a bit of a dilemma.' She paused. 'I might as well tell you, but we haven't mentioned it to anyone else so keep it under your hat, won't you?'

'Of course I will. What is it?'

'Well, Luke's been offered an opportunity by a gallery in London. They want to feature his paintings on a regular basis. It would be almost like a permanent exhibition and he'd be sure to get sales from it. He says it's a wonderful chance and I believe him. The only thing is, he says he'd need more time to paint than he has now, and he'd need to be in London a lot of the time.'

'Oh.' Hilary digested this. 'So he'd have to give up teaching.'

Val nodded. 'And we'd have to move to London.'

'Val! Leave Burracombe? You can't do that!'

'I'll have to, if that's what he decides. A wife has to go where her husband takes her.'

'But you and Luke have always decided things together. Surely he'd never force you?'

'No, of course he wouldn't. But how can *I* force *him*? Because that's what it amounts to, if I refuse to go.'

Hilary nibbled her biscuit thoughtfully. 'I can see it's a problem. But there must be a way round it, surely. After all, Luke has the school holidays off – can't he get enough paintings done then?'

'He says not. He says he needs to paint at other times of the year, too, at different times of day, and term time is almost impossible. And he says teaching takes all his energy, and there's hardly any left over for painting; it takes him the first week or two of the holidays to feel he can do it again.'

'I see. But why do you all have to move to London? Surely he needs to be here to paint – on Dartmoor, not in the middle of the city. How is he going to produce enough there, if he can't do it here?'

'He can do other scenes as well. He likes the moors best, but he thinks he should widen his scope anyway. Not everyone wants to buy pictures of windswept landscapes.'

'But it will be so expensive, living in London. And *where* will you live? Why do you have to go at all? Can't Luke just stay there during the week and come home at weekends? Wouldn't that be better for you and the baby?'

'No, it wouldn't. I don't want that sort of life, Hilary. We're married – we want to be together. A proper family. And Luke feels the same. He likes us all to be together as much as possible.' She glanced over towards Christopher, who was sitting on the rug playing with a set of plastic beakers. 'Anyway, it would be far too expensive. Where would he stay – in a hotel, or lodgings somewhere? How could we afford that as well as this cottage?' She shook her head. 'It's got to be one way or the other. Luke is an artist, not a teacher – oh, he's a good one, they like him very much at the school, but it's not what he's *meant* for. And it's wrong to stop anyone doing what they're really meant to do.' She stopped and gave Hilary a rueful look. 'I seem to be talking myself into this and I don't want to at all, but I really am afraid that that's what's going to happen. I think we'll be leaving Burracombe, and going to live in London.'

They fell silent for a while, each contemplating a future that seemed too misty to see clearly. Then they turned to other village matters.

'Maggie Culliford's still hovering between life and death, by all accounts,' Val observed. 'Poor Arthur's going down to Plymouth every evening after work – Jennifer told me that Travis offered him time off to spend all day there if he needed to, but he says they won't let him in outside of visiting hours, and Dottie and Aggie and a few others have drawn up a rota for afternoons – but she doesn't seem to have improved much. She hasn't got worse either, so there's still plenty of hope, but it's really wearing him down. I saw him yesterday and he looked a shadow of his usual self.'

'It's dreadful,' Hilary said feelingly. 'I know we all think they've got too many children as it is, but to lose two babies ... it hardly bears thinking about. I mean, they would have loved them just as much as the others if they'd lived. They were *ready* to love them.'

'I know,' Val said quietly and Hilary remembered that Val herself had lost a baby, albeit in very different circumstances, and had had to suffer her grief almost entirely alone. The thought of Maggie and her twins must be bringing back many painful memories. There was a slight pause, and then Val went on, 'People think that a baby born dead, or not born at all, properly, isn't as bad as losing a child that's been alive, that's been a person you've got to know and love. But it is. You've been thinking of that child for months, you've carried it and talked to it and felt it kicking inside you, and it's just as much a person to you as it's going to be when it's out in the world and everyone else can see it. Almost more, in a way, because for those few months it's yours and nobody else's, as it never will be again. And then to lose it, just when it ought to be taking its first breath … never even to hear its little voice … never to look into its eyes and see them look back at you … There's nothing as bad as that, Hilary, nothing as bad as knowing it never even had a chance. Nothing.'

Hilary gazed at her. Although she was one of the few people who had known the story of Val and her little Johnny, as she'd called him, the baby who had never even gone to full term, who had been born months too soon on the voyage home from Egypt and given a secret burial at sea, she had never heard Val speak so heart-rendingly about what the experience had meant to her. She reached out a hand and laid it on Val's, wishing that she could offer more comfort, but she knew there was none to be had. This was Val's tragedy, to be acknowledged and lived with throughout her entire life, and although she could be happy, loved and loving, it would always be a part of her.

'And are the children still with Joyce Warren?' Hilary asked. Although she'd only been away from the village for two days, it seemed almost a lifetime, and she felt that anything could have happened during her absence.

'Oh yes. That woman really is amazing, you know. She's always seemed such a busybody, wanting to be in on everything and running it if she can, yet she's really turned up trumps here. Brenda and Jimmy are at home with Arthur, and Brenda's doing a good job of looking after him and having a proper meal ready for him when he comes home, but the rest are at the Warrens'. The older ones are at school, of course, which helps, but she seems to have them organised. I popped in yesterday afternoon and they were all sitting down to their tea, their hands and faces scrubbed, looking like little mice. And when they got down, she had them out in the garden playing rounders, laughing as if they hadn't a care in the world. They all go to bed between seven and eight, she told me, the older ones helping with the babies, and then she reads them a story. I had half a mind to ask if she'd have Christopher as well!'

Hilary laughed. 'They must be in a state of shock. I'm sure Maggie never had them as organised as that. As for reading them a story ...'

'I know. I think we've rather maligned Mrs Warren over the years. She obviously has a real way with children.'

'Missed her vocation,' Hilary said. 'I wonder if it was the First World War. She's of an age to have been caught up in that – maybe lost a sweetheart. Well, I don't suppose we'll ever know. I do hope Maggie pulls through, though. The whole thing is a tragedy as it is.' She stood up and stretched. 'I'd better go. Thanks for the tea and melting moments. And the chat. I hope things work out for you and Luke. I know you have to do what's best for the two of you, but it really would be a shame to lose you from Burracombe.'

'I know,' Val said soberly. 'And it's not just the two of us, either. It's Christopher as well. I *so* wanted to bring my family up here. Thinking of him growing up as a little Londoner – well, it just doesn't seem right.'

No matter what your own difficulties were, Hilary thought as she made her way back to the Barton, you never needed to look far to find someone whose troubles were worse. She'd always thought Val and Luke were so settled in their cottage, so content with their lives, yet in reality they were as torn by indecision as she and David. Considering that made her feel guilty for thinking she had problems at all.

Alice Tozer knew nothing, as yet, of the possibility of Val and Luke moving to London, and that was just as well, for her heart was filled with sadness at the prospect of losing Jackie all over again.

'You're not losing her, Mother,' Joanna said. 'She's going back to America for a while, that's all. She'll come home again.'

'Now and then, maybe, for a visit,' Alice said, wiping her eyes.

'But not to live. She's engaged to that American and he's not going to move to England, is he? He've got a good job over in Corning at the glass factory. He's not going to give that up.'

Privately Joanna thought she was right, but, still looking for comfort, she said, 'Well, that engagement may come to nothing. She's had her head turned by it all, but she's a sensible girl. She won't rush into anything. I'll bet you anything you like she'll be back in six months, and settle down like she's never been away.'

Alice shook her head. 'You know Jackie better than that, Joanna. Headstrong and wilful she've always been, and never satisfied to settle down like you and Val. Even as a little maid her would be looking at her grandad's old globe of the world and asking questions about all the different countries, when most other little girls would be playing with dolls. And then look at how she couldn't wait to get away and work at the big hotel in Plymouth. Ted and me knew then it would lead to trouble.'

Joanna paused to choose her words carefully. 'I know you're upset, but Jackie isn't in *trouble*. She just knows what she wants. That's not—'

'Yes, and that *is* the trouble!' Alice burst out. 'Like I said, she's as wilful as a monkey. Always wanted her own way, from the minute she was born, and never changed. Why, Brian and Val and Tom were never like that. They were biddable, all of them. You could reason with them. But not our Jackie. You might just as well talk to a brick wall as try to change her mind once her's made it up.'

'Well, perhaps it's just as well not to try,' Joanna said. 'You're only upsetting yourself. Jackie will do what she wants to do, and it seems to me you're right, nothing any of us says is going to make any difference.'

'I might have knowed you'd be on her side,' Alice said bitterly. 'But there, I can't expect no different – you're not Jackie's sister and you can't be expected to feel the same as we do about it all.'

Joanna bit her lip. 'I'm not on anyone's side, Mother. I do understand how you feel, but—'

'I don't think you do. You won't understand until your own daughter's putting you through the mill. Wait till your Heather's grown up and flouting everything you ever taught her – *then* you'll understand.'

Joanna stared at her. 'You make me feel as if I'm not one of the family after all.'

'Of course you'm one of the family,' Alice said irritably. 'I should have thought you'd been here enough years to know that.'

Joanna said no more. She murmured something about going to meet Robin from school, took Heather out to her pram and wheeled it away down the drive.

Jackie departed two days later. She refused to be taken to Southampton to catch the *Queen Elizabeth* and went by train instead. Alice and Ted saw her off in Tavistock and then Ted took his wife to have some dinner in the Bedford Hotel. It was meant to be a treat to cheer her up, but it failed miserably, as Alice had to keep dabbing her eyes throughout the meal and hardly touched her roast beef and Yorkshire pudding. She wouldn't have any plum crumble, saying it would just be a waste, and consequently Ted couldn't really enjoy his. They went home as soon as possible, and Alice went straight up to Jackie's room and stripped the bed.

'She's more upset now than she was the first time Jackie went,' Ted told his mother, who was sitting in the garden, under the gnarled old apple tree. 'I reckon we had some hope then that the maid would come home again, but now there don't seem to be any at all. Alice thinks us've lost her, and I don't mind telling you I think she might be right.'

Minnie's face was as creased and rosy as one of the apples themselves, when kept too long. She shook her head and said, 'You've not lost her, Ted. She might have gone back to America, she might stop there all her life, but you've not lost her. She'll still be your daughter, wherever she be.'

Ted gazed at her. 'I don't know as that's much comfort, Mother. It's her being our daughter at home, here in Burracombe, that Alice and me wants. And we both know what happens when folk go off to America – look at our Joe.'

'You don't have to remind me of Joe,' Minnie said, a little tartly. 'If anyone knows what 'tis like to have a son or daughter go off and live at the other side of the world, 'tis me. But it's what *happens*, Ted. Look at all the men and women who've gone off to other countries – all the Cornish miners, and the Devon ones too from hereabouts, gone to Australia and South America, and thousands of others too, seeking their fortune, looking for a better life.'

'Our Jackie didn't need to look for a better life!'

'That's your opinion,' Minnie said. 'The maid seems to think different.' She waited a moment, then said, 'It's no use you and Alice breaking your hearts over this, Ted. The way I see it, we has our children on loan. We do our best for them as children, and teach 'em the way they ought to go, and when they'm grown up they make up their own minds and us has to put up with it, and trust them to remember what they were told. There's nothing you can do about Jackie now, and you might as well get used to the idea.'

Ted stared at his mother and then folded his mouth and shook his head slowly, in reluctant acceptance. 'I suppose you'm right. You usually are. But I don't know how I'm going to make Alice see it that way.'

'She'll come to it,' Minnie said. ''Tis always harder for a mother to see her little ones fly away. But Jackie's a good girl, and when she grows up a bit more and loses her flighty ways, I reckon you'll have cause to be proud of her. But I tell you this, Ted, and it's summat nobody ever tells you when you'm young and just starting a family: from the day they're born, you never stop worrying about them. Never.'

Ted looked at her and raised his eyebrows, grinning a little. 'You're not telling me you still worry about me and Joe, Mother?'

'Oh don't I?' she said. 'You forget you're still my boy, Ted Tozer, and sometimes you seem to me to be just as much a babby as you ever were!'

Chapter Sixteen

It was on the Friday evening that Arthur finally received the news. The doctor came out to see him as he arrived at the ward door at visiting time and ushered him into a small office, and Arthur's heart plunged with fear. 'She've gone, haven't she?' he croaked in a suddenly hoarse, dry voice. 'I've lost her ...'

'Not at all,' the doctor said, smiling. 'I'm sorry to have alarmed you. Your wife is doing well, very well indeed. She sat up today and she's looking forward to seeing you. The danger's over and you'll have her back at home before you can say Jack Robinson.'

'Jack Robinson,' Arthur repeated wonderingly, and then grinned. 'I've always wondered who he was and why us had to say his name for anything happening a bit quick. But if he was here now, I'd shake him by the hand. So when d'you reckon her *will* be able to come home, Doctor?'

'Well, perhaps not that quickly. I want to keep her here for another week or so, and then she'll need some convalescence. Maybe another three or four weeks. What's the situation at home now? You've other children, haven't you? How are you managing?'

'It's the village that's managing for me. I got the oldest two at home, but the rest is all staying with old Bossyb— Mrs Warren, I mean. She've been real good to us, taking them all in and looking after them, and a lot of the others living in Burracombe are helping out too. They want their mother back, though, all the same.'

'That's very good to hear. The rest of the village must think a lot of you.'

Arthur shuffled uncomfortably. 'I don't reckon they think all that much of me, to be honest,' he muttered. ''Tis my Maggie and the little'ns they feel sorry for. I ain't much cop round the place, never have been.'

The doctor smiled and laid his hand on Arthur's shoulder. 'Well, your wife seems to think a lot of you, so I think you should go now and give her a kiss. She must think you're not coming and we don't want her having a relapse.'

'No, us don't,' Arthur agreed fervently. He stood up and took the doctor's hand, wringing it in his own. 'I got to say, you bin good to us both and us won't forget it. And I'll take good care of my Mag from now on. You won't see her in here no more.'

He hurried out into the corridor and through the swinging doors leading into the ward. Maggie's bed had been moved, and for a moment he couldn't see her. Then he spotted her arm waving from the end of the long room and hastened between the beds to reach her.

'Maggie!' he said, and found his eyes misting with tears. He dropped on to the chair beside the bed and took both her hands in his. 'Oh, Mag. The doctor says you'm going to be all right. You'll be coming home soon. That's the best bit of news I've had since – well, since they told us the war was over and we'd be leaving that blasted camp and coming home. And I tell you this, Mag, things is going to be different from now on. *I'm* going to be different. No more getting drunk of a Friday night. No more poaching and getting sent to jail. No more laying about when there's work to be done. You won't know me.'

Maggie laughed and reached out a thin hand to ruffle his hair. She was lying down again now, still pale and tired-looking, but with a life about her that had been pitifully absent since the birth. She said, 'I'll believe that when I see it! Anyway, Art, I don't know as I *want* you all that different. I might wonder where you've gone and who this strange chap is I've got living with me. What I really want is to be home again, with you and the little'ns, all of us together. That's all I need.'

'I need you too,' he said with some difficulty; he had never been one for soft speeches. 'But I mean what I say, Mag. I'm turning over a new leaf, and if you don't know me to start with, you'd better soon get used to me, because that's the way I'm staying!'

Failing in their original idea of starting up a folk dance band, Bob Pettifer and his mate Reg had decided on a skiffle group. They met in Jack Pettifer's shed, and Roy and Vic had joined them. They hadn't been sure what a skiffle group was to begin with, but Vic, whose cousin near Okehampton was in one, had explained.

'One of us plays a double bass, made out of an old tea chest, and one plays the washboard – I reckon all our mothers have got one of they – and there's all sorts of other instruments as well. You can use banjos or ukuleles or guitars, but if you don't have any of they you can use comb and paper, or a musical saw, or anything really. It's sort of folk music or country and western, jazzed up a bit. Jackie Tozer told me about it, but she reckons it'll be out of fashion soon because in America they're starting this new rock and roll.'

'Well, us had better get on with it, then. It's still OK here, isn't it?'

'Yes, it is,' Vic agreed, taking the position of authority. 'There's a bloke called Lonnie Donegan that plays in Ken Colyer's jazz band, and he does it in the intervals at the jazz club. Oh, you can play a mouth organ too. You've got one, haven't you, Bob?'

'Got it with me.' Bob took his mouth organ out of his pocket and started to play 'In the Mood'. Glenn Miller music was popular at the moment because of the film, and he'd learned 'Moonlight Serenade' and 'String of Pearls' as well. Encouraged by his audience, he played them all.

The others listened to his short concert and then Roy said critically, 'That's all right, Bob, but it's not skiffle. Is it, Vic?'

'No, skiffle's much more jazzy than that.'

'Glenn Miller played jazz,' Bob said with some indignation.

'No, he played swing,' Reg asserted. 'Like Ted Heath. Tell you what, he's got a smashing trombonist – Don Lusher, he's called. I've got his new record at home, playing 'Bone Idle' – just the trombone, nothing else. You can come round now and hear it if you like. We could have a trombone as well. And I've got 'Swinging Shepherd Blues', and—'

'We're talking about *skiffle*,' Vic said, trying to regain control. 'You don't get trombones in a skiffle group. Anyway, none of us have got one and we wouldn't be able to play it if we did.'

'I can play the spoons,' Bob offered. 'Not at the same time as the mouth organ, mind. That would be all right, wouldn't it? I mean, if you'm going to have a saw ...'

'Us might as well have a hammer and chisel as well and knock up a few tables and chairs while we're at it,' Reg said, still nettled by having his trombone record turned down. 'Who's going to come and listen to us, anyway?'

'We don't do it for people to listen to us. We does it for ourselves. Though we could be in the Christmas show that Mrs Warren's talking about doing instead of a pantomime,' Vic added consideringly. 'If we practise, we could be pretty good by then.'

'Us could jazz up a few Christmas carols,' Bob suggested, and played a few bars of 'The First Nowell', with odd spaces between some of the notes, to show how it could be done. He had to explain to the others that these weren't mistakes, but done deliberately. 'Jazz players always do it when they play old tunes.'

'Not real jazz musicians,' Roy argued. 'They make it up as they go along. It's not ever supposed to be the same twice.'

'Well that's all right, then,' Reg said, 'because Bob never plays any tune the same way twice.'

'I don't know as the vicar would be very keen on carols being jazzed up,' Roy said. 'They're sort of sacred music, aren't they? Anyway, you couldn't call them country and western. Here, shouldn't we wear cowboy outfits?'

'Check shirts are good,' Vic agreed. 'They wear those in my cousin's group, and he's got a Stetson he puts on sometimes. Well, it's not a real Stetson, more a sort of sunhat, but everything's a bit makeshift in a skiffle group so that don't matter. Anyway, let's decide what we're going to have in ours. We've got a mouth organ, and Bob can play the spoons as well as a sort of novelty. Anyone got a tea chest?'

There was a short silence, and it transpired that nobody quite knew what a tea chest was.

'It's that wooden box people pack stuff in when they move house,' Vic said impatiently, but since none of them had ever moved house, or even knew anyone who had done so, they were none the wiser.

'Why're they called tea chests, then?' Reg enquired, and Vic shrugged.

'I dunno. I suppose they're what tea comes in, from India and China.' A bright idea struck him. 'Creber's, in Tavi, might have them. I bet they'd let us have one – glad to get rid of them, I expect.'

'That's if all the people moving house haven't snapped 'em up first,' Reg observed, but Vic ignored him.

'I'll go in and ask on Saturday. I got to go to Tavi anyway. I can make it into a double bass over the weekend – you just need a long bit of wood and some wire for the strings. Who's going to do the washboard?'

'My mum got a new one last week,' Roy volunteered. 'She'll probably let me have the old one. I don't know how you're supposed to get a tune out of it, though.'

'You don't. You just sort of strum it with your fingernails, like a guitar. It's an accompaniment to the song.'

The other three stared at him open-mouthed. Reg found his voice first.

'*Song?* You mean we got to *sing*?'

'Well of *course* we got to sing,' Vic retorted. 'You can't expect people to sit and listen to a few blokes strumming on a washboard and an old tea chest and not know what the song's about.'

'If they got the choice between that and hearing old Bob here sing, I bet I know which they'd choose,' Reg said.

'I won't be able to sing anyway,' Bob objected. 'I'll be playing the mouth organ. Can't do both at once.'

'Go on,' Reg jeered. 'With a mouth the size of yours, you could play the *trombone* and sing at the same time. I still reckon us could make up a trombone somehow,' he added. 'All you need is a bit of pipe, bent round a bit. Alf Coker could knock one up in no time in his forge.'

'I've told you, we're not having a trombone. They just don't have them in skiffle groups. If you're so keen on making things, you can make a guitar.'

'A guitar? How the flipping heck d'you make one of those? It don't seem like there's anything left for me to play anyway. I might as well go home.' Reg began to get to his feet.

'Don't be daft.' Bob stretched out a long arm and pulled him back on to the old kitchen stool he'd been sitting on. 'Listen, I happen to know where we might be able to borrow a guitar. You could play that. It's dead easy – I saw a bloke playing one at the pictures last week. It's like Vic says, you just strum it in the background, and if you can pick out a bit of a tune, so much the better. I reckon you could do that easy as a wink.'

'Who's got a guitar in Burracombe?' Reg demanded. 'I've never seen anyone with one.'

'The vicar has. No, not Mr Harvey – Mr Copley, over in Little Burracombe. I helped him carry some of his stuff into Aggie Madge's when he first came to Burracombe. I bet he'd lend it to us. He'd probably show you how to play it, too.'

Reg considered it. The thought of playing a proper instrument, the only one in the band apart from Bob's mouth organ, was too much for him and he nodded. 'All right. But you got to ask him, mind. I haven't been in church since I left school.'

'Well, nor have I much.'

'You have. You were there for your Terry's wedding. At least he knows your face.'

'*Everybody* knows Bob's face.' Vic grinned. 'They've only got to look up at the gargoyles on the church tower. And the vicar can't say he never goes to church, because he's there all the time!'

'Oh, very funny,' Bob said, twisting his rubbery features into a fair imitation of a gargoyle. 'Don't it ever strike any of you that me and Terry might get a bit fed up with those jokes? All right, I'll ask Mr Copley if us can borrow his guitar. I'm doing a wiring job over to Little Burracombe, so I can drop in then. And if Vic can get a tea chest and Roy practises a bit on his mum's washboard, we could have a proper rehearsal sometime next week. Who's going to do the singing?'

'Well, all of us,' Roy said, but Vic shook his head.

'You got to have a lead singer – the one who does the verses. The rest of us joins in with the chorus.'

'Well, that's me out,' Bob said decisively. 'I got a voice like a crow.'

'You won't get me standing up in front of a lot of people making a fool of meself,' Reg agreed, and Roy too made it clear that he had no ambition to be a lead singer, even without an audience.

'What about you, Vic? You used to be in the church choir.'

'Only till my voice broke. Then Mr Harvey suggested I could

join the bell-ringers instead. Well, *someone's* got to sing the songs.' He hesitated, then said, 'A lot of bands have a girl for their lead singer.'

'A *girl*?' they echoed, in tones that ranged from outright disbelief to cautious interest. 'What girl?'

'I dunno. There must be someone we could ask. It'd be even better if she could play something too – another guitar, maybe.'

'Strewth, Vic, we don't even know if we've got one guitar yet, let alone two. Anyway, I don't know anyone round here who'd want to sing in a skiffle group with our ugly mugs.'

'You haven't thought about it yet.'

'I don't have to think. I know without thinking. Look,' Roy said in a final sort of tone, 'I think we got to make up our minds what this skiffle group's for. Is it just for us to meet in Bob's dad's shed a couple of nights a week and have a bit of fun, or are we going to be a bit more serious and practise properly so we can put on a show at Christmas?'

'I reckon that's what we ought to do,' Vic said. 'Otherwise I don't see much point. And if we're doing that, we ought to try and find a lead singer with a bit of a voice, and since a lot of bands have a girl for that, maybe that's what we ought to do too.'

'There's an awful lot of "ought to" there,' Reg said. 'I get enough of that at home from my mother – ought to keep my room tidy, ought to change my socks twice a week, ought to get up earlier on Sundays. It's like being back on National Service.'

'It's not that sort of "ought to",' Vic said, but before another dispute could break out, Bob said, '*I* know a girl who could come in with us.'

They all turned to look at him. 'Who?'

'Brenda Culliford. She've got a good voice. She sang that carol on her own when they did that Nativity play, remember? And we could make her a sort of banjo to play, with a bit of plywood. Or better still, there's an old clock in Alf Coker's forge, been waiting to be mended so long he's forgot whose it is. We could use that. It's just the right size. I reckon if us can make a double bass out of a tea chest, us can do that too, easy enough. And she don't have to play tunes on it. All she'd have to do is strum the notes.'

'Brenda Culliford? She's only fifteen.'

'What difference do that make? She's just about left school. She'll need something to do.'

'She'll need a *job*. Anyway, didn't someone say she's going up to work for Mrs Warren and help with all those other tackers? And she has to get supper ready for her old man every evening.'

'She'll still get a bit of time off,' Vic said. 'A couple of evenings a week, that's all we'd be asking. And the vicar said us all ought to rally round and help the Cullifords. I reckon having Brenda in our group'd count as helping.'

'How d'you make that out? We're not going to be paying her a wage.'

'No, but we'll be making her feel as if someone wants her,' Vic retorted. 'And you never know, she might get spotted by someone – in the Christmas show, perhaps – and get to be a proper singer, making records and being rich. We all might, come to that,' he added.

The others laughed. 'You been listening to too much of Jackie Tozer's talk about America! That sort of thing don't happen here. Still, I suppose us could ask Brenda along and see what she thinks.' Bob took his mouth organ out of his pocket and played a few bars of 'Take These Chains From My Heart'. 'That's the sort of thing I reckon us should be playing.'

'A bit,' Vic said. 'It's not really skiffle, but it's a start. We'll do that one and a couple of others, but what we really ought to do is write our own songs.' But at this suggestion, the others almost hurt their stomachs laughing, and when Reg suggested going to the Bell for a pint, they agreed they'd done enough planning for one evening. The main thing now was to get their instruments, practise a bit and then approach Brenda.

'It's not such a bad idea, at that,' Bob said to Reg as they made their way towards the inn. 'She's quite pretty when she tries to be. She'll have to get a check blouse from somewhere, mind. And us'll have to clear it with her old man.'

'He won't mind. He's too wrapped up in Mrs Culliford. He goes to see her every night, you know. He'll be only too pleased to think Brenda's got something to do.'

Bob thought Brenda probably had more than enough to do. But that was for her and her father to say, and she might not even want to join their group. He wasn't convinced that the skiffle would be a success anyway. Vic seemed to be the only one who knew anything about it, from his cousin in Okehampton. He said it had been around in America for years and was only just starting in England but was bound to be popular. Look at jive, he'd said, and how that had taken off. But Bob, whose long, gangling arms and legs had never been very suited to jive, or indeed any form of dancing, had shrugged. He didn't mind playing the music, and he quite liked country and western, but he couldn't really see Mrs Warren wanting a band consisting of a tea chest, an old washboard, a banjo made out of plywood and Reg's mouth organ in her Christmas show.

'It'll be a bit of fun, anyway,' he said at last, as they reached the door of the inn. 'Whose turn is it to buy the drinks tonight? Yours, I reckon, Reg.'

'It's always my turn,' Reg complained, but he fished a half-crown out of his pocket and put it on the bar. 'Two pints then, Bernie, please. And not so much water in it this time!'

Chapter Seventeen

Patsy Shillabeer slipped over to Little Burracombe to see her mother the very next Wednesday. She'd told Terry of her plan, and he consulted Bob, knowing that his brother would be working in the village all that week. Bob agreed to look out for old man Shillabeer setting out in the morning in his farm truck – 'Lucky I'm working handy to the road and can keep an eye open' – and to meet Patsy at the top of the footpath coming up from the Clam at dinner time.

'I'll make sure the coast is clear,' he told his brother. 'And if the old tyrant comes back while she's still at the farm I'll hold him up somehow.'

'I dunno how you'm going to do that,' Terry said doubtfully. 'You know he won't speak to none of us Pettifers now.'

'I'll smile at him,' Bob said, twisting his face into a terrifying expression. 'That'll frighten him off.'

In the event, there was no need for Bob to smile, although he found it hard not to, since he was normally cheery, as Percy Shillabeer left the farm at eleven o'clock and didn't come home until three. Patsy appeared at twelve and Bob went to meet her.

'It's all right, maid. He's safely out of the way.'

'Thanks, Bob. I'm ever so grateful.'

'You don't have to be.' He smiled at her kindly, without any of the fearsomeness he had threatened to offer Percy, and she thought what a nice sort of ugliness he and Terry shared. 'If a maid can't go and see her mother, specially when she'm expecting – well, it's a poor do, that's all. You go and have a nice time with your mum, and if I see him coming back, I'll nip up and warn you.'

Patsy nodded and went on along the lane. She passed the vicarage, where Stella was in the garden, weeding the flower beds. Stella caught sight of her and stood up.

'Patsy! How nice to see you. How are you keeping?'

'I'm all right, thank you, Mrs Copley. Beginning to show a bit.' She patted her stomach self-consciously. 'And I'm sure the babby's going to be a footballer. He's kicking like Stanley Matthews.'

'Or a boxer.' Stella smiled. 'Are you on your way to see your mother?'

'Yes.' Patsy hesitated. Stella hadn't asked, but she must be wondering, and Patsy didn't want to risk any unpleasantness with her father. 'Only Father don't know, you see, and I don't expect Mother will tell him, so ...'

'I won't mention it,' Stella promised, adding sympathetically, 'Things are no better, then? Not that it's any of my business – you don't have to tell me anything.'

'It's all right. I don't mind you knowing. After all, it was Mr Copley married us. Are you all right yourself, Mrs Copley? I mean, is your leg better?'

'Much better, thanks. I'm almost back to normal – just limping a bit. Well, you mustn't let me keep you. I'm sure your mother's looking forward to seeing you.'

'Oh, she don't know either – I couldn't be sure I'd manage it.' Patsy smiled awkwardly, not wanting to involve Stella in any subterfuge, and Stella, who understood perfectly, smiled back and went back to her weeding.

Patsy walked as fast as she could up the track to the farm. It was as rough as ever and there were large puddles left by the last rainfall. She could hear the clucking of hens before she arrived, and turned the last bend to see her mother moving slowly round the yard, scattering scraps of food from the apron she was holding out in front of her.

Patsy called out and Ann turned sharply. For a moment or two she stared as if unable to believe her eyes, then she dropped the corners of the apron and hurried to the gate, her face a mixture of smiles and tears.

'Patsy! Oh, my dear maid, whatever be you doing here? You'm all right, I hope? There's nothing wrong with you or the babby?'

'I'm all right, Mother.' Patsy was through the gate now and almost threw herself into her mother's arms. They clung together, both crying, until at last Ann drew back, catching up her apron again to mop her eyes.

'Oh, my dear bird. It's so good to see you. I've been half out of my mind with worry.'

'There's no need to worry, Mother. I'd have let you know if there was anything wrong.'

'I know, but only if 'twas something serious. There's all sorts of other things to worry about, like whether you've stopped feeling sick or if you're doing too much heavy work at the Barton, and if you'm eating right, and if – if ...' her voice trembled, 'if I'm ever going to see you again, or the little one. And I can't say anything to your father. As far as he'm concerned, you're not his daughter any more.' They were walking towards the house now, their arms around each other. 'I told him, you're still *my* daughter and always will be, but of course he didn't take no notice.'

'You told him that?' Patsy looked at her in surprise. 'Whatever did he say?'

'Oh, he ranted and raved for a bit, but I told him I wouldn't back down over that, and in the end he just slammed out of the house with the dog and I didn't see him again till next morning. He didn't stay out all night,' she added. 'He was there beside me in bed when I woke up, but I must have gone to sleep before he came in.'

'He didn't hit you, then? I don't want him hitting you because of me.'

'He thought about it. But I got round the other side of the table and picked up my rolling pin – I was making pasties at the time – and told him I wasn't afraid to use it and I reckon he believed me. Now, are you ready for a cup of tea after your walk?'

Patsy sat down, feeling slightly stunned. Her mother had never, in her experience, ever stood up to Percy before. She almost wished she'd been there to see it.

'You ought to be careful all the same,' she said. 'You know what he can be like.'

'Nobody knows that better than me. But he went too far when

he told you to choose between me and your babby, Patsy. Nobody ought to have to make that sort of choice. There wasn't nothing Christian about that, and I reckon he knows it.'

There was a new firmness in her voice and in her manner. She seemed to stand a little straighter and her eyes were steady. Even her hair, grey and scraped back as it was, looked different – thicker, with a bit of shine to it.

'I couldn't go no further than that, mind,' she added after a minute or so. 'I couldn't say I would go over to see you or have you over here. That would have been pushing him too far. But he won't stop me having that photo of you on the sideboard – the one we had took at the studio in Tavistock – nor the one with all the family together. And in time, maybe he'll come round to the rest and let me have you over here, open and above board.'

Patsy nodded. Her mother had not won quite so much ground as she'd hoped, but she'd made a start.

'I'll come over here on the days he's out,' she promised. 'And I'll bring the babby too, when he's born. Or she,' she added. 'And Terry'll get a message over to you the minute anything happens.'

'I ought to be with you then,' Ann said fretfully. 'A young woman wants her mother there when she'm having her first.'

She made tea and they settled down for a gossip. Patsy was hungry for news of the family, and heard all about what her younger brothers and sisters had been getting up to, about the farm workers she knew so well and the rest of the villagers of Little Burracombe. Until now, she hadn't realised how much she had missed the people she had grown up with. Little Burracombe was only just across the valley from Burracombe, but it seemed like a million miles away, and although news did of course get from one village to the other, it seemed generally as if each preferred to keep itself to itself.

'Don't forget the time,' Ann said after a while. 'Your father'll be back for his tea. He don't stop in the cattle market drinking and chinwagging like a lot of the farmers do.'

'It's all right – there's a good half-hour yet,' Patsy said comfortably, but hardly had she finished speaking when running footsteps sounded in the yard and someone hammered on the door. With a frightened look, Ann got up to open it and found Bob there, hopping with anxiety and impatience.

'He's coming,' he panted. 'I was up at the bedroom window wiring a lamp in, and I saw him turn the corner. He'll be here any minute.'

'Oh my stars!' Ann flew into a panic at once. 'Patsy, you must go! Go out the front way – you can get down to the Clam over Lower Field. Don't let him see you. Bob, you'd better get back too. He'll want to know why you'm here. Oh, the cups!' She darted round the kitchen, snatching up the teacups and piling them into the sink, gathering up any other signs that there had been another person present. Her earlier confidence had deserted her and Patsy, giving her a hurried kiss before slipping out of the front door and through the garden into the fields, realised that there was a long way to go before her father came round. As she scurried along, half sobbing, behind the high Devon bank, where nobody coming up the lane could see her, she heard the sound of her father's truck rattling towards the house. She hoped Bob had got out of the way in time, and that her mother had managed to conceal any signs of having had a visitor.

It's going to be years before I'll be able to bring my babby to see his granny, she thought, depressed. But that won't stop us coming over. There'll always be a market for Father to go to, and as long as us don't stop too long, he don't ever need to know. And Mother might learn to stand up to him even more. She really did look different this afternoon – stronger and more determined. I reckon she could surprise us all yet.

She caught sight of Bob, waving to her from the upstairs window of the cottage he was working in, and waved back to let him know that she was all right. She hoped to see Stella as well, working in the vicarage garden, but when she passed by, there was nobody there.

It had been a good afternoon none the less, she thought, crossing the narrow footbridge across the Burra Brook. And she would come again. She had been forced to make a choice, but it wasn't going to stop her seeing her mother. Not any more.

'The poor girl,' Stella said to Felix later as they ate their supper of tinned pilchards and salad. 'I could see she was terrified of her father finding her at the farm, and when I caught sight of the truck coming up the lane, I thought it was all up. But then I spotted her slipping through the fields and knew she'd got out in time. What a way to have to behave, just to see her mother.'

'It's a great pity,' he agreed, sprinkling mustard powder on his pilchards. 'I knew there was something badly wrong when I married them, but I wasn't sure what it was then. I wondered at first if it was a shotgun wedding, with Terry being forced into it, but he and Patsy were both emphatic that they wanted to be married. I couldn't imagine what the problem was until Percy made it quite clear at the wedding that he was washing his hands of her – and forcing his wife to do the same.' He shook his head. 'I shall never forget that poor woman's face as he took her away.'

'It's so cruel,' Stella said. 'I don't know how any father can treat his own child like that. And the baby, too – his first grandchild. It's not normal.'

'Percy Shillabeer *isn't* normal. He's a fanatic. He thinks he's a Christian and is strictly religious, but his religion is a world away from true Christianity. He believes in punishment and retribution – an eye for eye and all that sort of thing – and forgiveness, in his book, can only come about when the retribution has been exacted. He doesn't believe in anyone being sorry, and he certainly never believes that he's in the wrong.'

'And yet he comes to church every Sunday and sits in the front pew, saying the prayers and listening to your sermons ...'

'I doubt if he'll be doing that much longer,' Felix said. 'He's been looking more and more dissatisfied, and he didn't like what I said to him at the wedding. I suspect he's looking for another church to go to.'

'The Methodists, you mean, or the Congregational?' Both had a church in Tavistock. 'But he went to the chapel before – would they be any more in step with what he wants?'

'No, I don't think they would. He wants something much stricter, much more fundamental. The Jehovah's Witnesses, perhaps, or the Plymouth Brethren. I wouldn't be at all surprised if he announced his intention of joining something like that.'

'But they're terribly strict. Wouldn't they want the whole family to join too? And suppose they don't – I've heard that they're not even allowed to eat together.'

'I certainly think it would be hard on Ann. She does seem to get some comfort from our services.' He took another slice of bread and spread it thinly with butter. 'There wouldn't be another pilchard, I suppose?'

'Not without opening another tin. But I will if you want me to.'

'It's all right. I'll survive – as long as there's cake as well.' He looked at her hopefully, and she laughed.

'You know very well there is. You smelled it baking when you came home this afternoon. It's cherry loaf, and I suppose you want a thick slice.'

'Is there any other sort?' he asked innocently. 'And better not leave it out on the table – Bob Pettifer's coming to see me in half an hour, and his legs are even longer and hollower than mine!'

Bob came half an hour later, apologising for his clothes. 'I'm working in the village, so it seemed a bit daft to go home and change first.'

'Of course it would have been. Come in, Bob.' Felix showed him into the study that had been John Berry's when he was vicar here. It still had most of John's furniture in it, since Mrs Berry had passed a lot on to Felix and Stella when she'd gone to live with relatives after her husband's death. 'Sit down. What can I do for you? Is it about your brother?'

'Terry? No – he's all right. And I dare say you know Patsy came over this afternoon to see her mother. I had to dash up quick to let 'em know old man Shillabeer was coming home, mind, or he'd have caught 'em – not that there's any reason why the maid shouldn't be there.' Bob was starting to sound angry, but then recollected himself. 'Anyway, that's not why I came. I wondered – it seems a bit of a cheek now I'm here, but I said I'd ask, so I will, only you mind you say no if you don't want to do it.' He floundered to a halt, while Felix gazed at him, perplexed. 'The thing is, Mr Copley, a few of us over in Burracombe wants to start up a bit of a skiffle group. I dunno if you've heard about skiffle, it's a new sort of music with a washboard and a tea chest – sounds a bit daft when you say it out loud, but Vic says he's got a cousin up near Okehampton that's in a band, and—'

'I know what skiffle is, yes,' Felix said patiently, thankful that he was apparently not being asked to intervene in the Shillabeer family affairs. 'And it sounds a very good idea. But what does it have to do with me?'

'Well ... I know it's a bit of a cheek, but I remembered that when I helped you move into Aggie Madge's a few years back, I noticed you'd got a guitar. And we just wondered—'

'You don't mean you want me to join the group?' Even though he knew it was impossible, Felix felt extraordinarily pleased, and, for a moment or two, rather tempted. 'It's very good of you, but I don't think—'

'Oh no,' Bob said hastily. 'No, none of us thought of that. We just wondered – well, if we could sort of *borrow* it.'

'Oh.' Felix felt deflated. Then he pulled himself together and said, 'Of course you could. I hardly ever play it now. I'd be delighted to lend it to you. Who will be playing it?'

'Reg. He hasn't got an instrument yet. Roy'll be on the washboard – his mum's just got a new one and hasn't thrown the old one out yet – and Vic's going to make a double bass out of a tea chest, if Creber's will let him have one, and I've got my mouth organ and the spoons, only they'm not really skiffle. But I don't reckon that'll matter. And if we get a lot of practice, we might be in the Christmas show in the village hall.'

'Goodness,' Felix said, thinking of Joyce Warren's rather high standards. 'Has Mrs Warren heard you yet?'

'No, she don't know nothing about it, and anyway, us haven't started yet. But we got plenty of time between now and Christmas.'

'What about a singer?' Felix asked, wondering if it would be fitting for a vicar to appear with a skiffle group. 'You'll need a singer as well, won't you?'

Bob nodded. 'We thought of asking Brenda Culliford,' he said, dashing Felix's hopes once more. 'She's not all that bad-looking now she's growing up a bit, and she's got quite a good voice, and us thought it would be good for her.'

'I'm sure it would. You'd have to look after her, mind. She's very young.'

'Oh, she wouldn't come to no harm with us,' Bob assured him, and Felix looked at his honest face and believed him.

'Tell Reg to come over sometime soon,' he said, 'and I'll give him a lesson. And I'll tell you what – I've got an old ukulele as well.

136

Brenda could use that. The singer needs an instrument as well.'

'A ukulele!' Bob said, his eyes shining. 'That'd be master grand, Mr Copley. We were thinking of trying to knock up a banjo for her out of an old clock, but a proper ukulele ...'

'I don't know what sort of condition it's in,' Felix warned him, but Bob just grinned and said that didn't matter, they were all pretty handy, and he'd tell Reg to come over the very next day, and Felix would get free tickets to their first concert. He departed then, clumping through the hall and out of the front door with a cheery goodbye to Stella, and marched off down the front path, whistling.

'Whatever was all that about?' Stella asked as Felix shut the door.

'A skiffle group,' he said, smiling a little ruefully. 'He and some of the other boys are starting one up and they want to borrow my guitar. D'you know, for a few minutes I wished I could join them, and then I realised – apart from being too busy – they'd probably think I was too old.' He looked down at her with exaggerated sadness in his face. 'Too old! And it's true. I'm getting positively middle-aged.'

'You?' she said, giving his arm a shake. 'You'll never be middle-aged. You've hardly progressed beyond early childhood yet.'

Chapter Eighteen

Hilary had slipped into the habit of confiding regularly in Charles Latimer. She did not go to his surgery, but he came over to play chess with her father at least one, often two evenings a week, and usually found an opportunity for a few minutes alone with her as he left. Not that she ever found anything new to say.

'We seem to be treading water in the same old spot instead of swimming to get somewhere,' she said. 'Either that, or the tide's sweeping us in directions we don't want to go.'

'When all you really want to do is enjoy the beach,' he said with a kindly smile. 'It's very difficult for you, but you know, things *will* change, even if it doesn't seem very likely at present.'

'It doesn't seem likely at all,' she said gloomily. 'I don't know how we ever thought it would. We're so far apart, Charles, and I don't see any prospect of getting any nearer. David can't abandon his father and I can't abandon mine. He has the practice, I have the estate. We're both just too tied up.'

Charles regarded her thoughtfully. 'Haven't you told me that your father's always been keen for you to marry?'

'Of course he has. Always on about it.'

'Well, you'd have had to leave the estate then, and with his blessing. He would have managed somehow. You've got Travis, after all.'

'I suppose so. But it seems different now. Perhaps because it wouldn't be with his blessing.'

'You don't know that.'

'I do! His daughter, marry a doctor? He wants "someone like *us*" – with a country house and some land. Someone who understands our way of life.'

'I think,' Charles said gently, 'that what he really wants is to see you happy.'

Hilary opened her mouth and then closed it slowly, thinking about it. She hadn't exactly been about to refute the doctor's words, but her immediate response had been that the estate was her father's first priority. She felt ashamed, knowing that this wasn't true. It might have been once, but her father's illness, together with the upheaval caused by his half-French grandson Rob, had changed him. He no longer seemed quite so single-minded, and he'd only a little while ago told her very definitely to take her own happiness if she found it.

'It's not that easy, though, is it?' she said slowly. 'I know he's pretty well over his heart attacks now, but you've told me it could happen again and be worse next time. How can I leave him? How will he manage? And it's not just that, it's the estate. What happens when Dad's not here any more? I know we have Travis and I trust him absolutely, but he can't make all the decisions. It's not his land. And then there's the house. It's a big place – I can't leave Father to rattle about it on his own. It's always been his dream to have his family grow up here – not just me and Stephen, but his grandchildren too. And Stephen really doesn't want it. He's not cut out to be squire.'

'And are you, Hilary?'

'Yes, I think I am. I've been here all my life, apart from during the war. I manage the estate now – and that took some persuasion; you know Dad wasn't at all keen on the idea to start with – and I love doing it. I love visiting the farms and going round the village knowing that Napiers have been a part of it all for generations. Making sure it's kept and looked after as it should be – making sure the people are all right. It's a responsibility, but it's one I'm happy to have and one I can't just throw aside.'

'No,' he said. 'I can see that.'

'And it's the same for David. He finished his training, became a GP and has worked with his father ever since. They've looked after families they've known all their lives, people they brought into the world and people they're seeing out of it. How can I ask him to leave all that?'

'I think it will come right for you, Hilary,' he said. 'You're positive and determined, and although you feel you're floundering at present, somewhere deep inside you're thinking it all through. You'll come to your own conclusion soon, I feel sure.'

He departed, and Hilary stood watching him walk down the drive in the early moonlight. If only he could be right, she thought. He sounded very sure, but how could anyone know the future? And how could anyone be sure that her future and David's would be a part of each other?

With a sigh, she closed the door and went to make her father's cocoa.

'I've got to make a decision soon,' Luke said restlessly. They had sat up late into the night, talking round and round the subject and always coming to the same conclusions. Neither wanted to be the one to force the other, but at the same time neither wanted to give way. 'Tell me honestly, Val – would you absolutely hate it in London?'

'I don't know. Probably not absolutely *hate* it, no. I'd make the best of it. There are lots of interesting things to do and things for Chris to learn about as he grows up. And if we lived near a park, so that we could see green grass and trees ...' Her voice wobbled a little. 'It's just the thought of city streets instead of village lanes – bricks and stone everywhere, hardly any birds except pigeons and sparrows, no rabbits or squirrels, no cows or sheep or wild ponies. And not knowing our neighbours.'

'You'd soon make friends.'

'But how? Who with? People in those streets don't even know the person next door. I know they talk about the community spirit in the East End and all that, but we wouldn't be living there, and anyway, it's all different now. So many of those places were bombed and the people are living elsewhere. I don't think there is any community spirit now – not like there is in Burracombe. Can you see the people in a London street rallying round to help someone like Maggie Culliford? Taking her rock buns and scones, scrubbing the walls and painting them, digging over the garden and putting a bit of grass down for the children to play on? I can't.'

'I'm not sure you're being fair. We don't *know* that people in London wouldn't do those things. They're people like us, not an alien race.'

'I know that,' Val said irritably. 'But everyone knows that people in cities don't know each other like we do.'

'I think it's more likely that cities are just made up of a lot of villages pushed together,' Luke said.

There was a short silence. After a moment, Val said, 'Well, all right. I've said I wouldn't absolutely hate it. And I don't suppose Chris will either. He'll just be used to it – to growing up a city boy.' Her voice shook again.

Luke sighed. 'He can come back here in the holidays and stay on the farm. You both can – we all will. And when he's big enough, he can come on his own. Although he might have a brother or sister or two by then, I hope.'

'I'm not sure about that. I don't think I'd like to have another baby so far away from home. Suppose the same thing happened to me as happened before? I wasn't allowed out of bed for months. How would we manage then?'

The silence was longer this time. At last Luke took in a long, deep breath. 'That settles it, then. If it's going to affect whether we can have more children, I don't have any option. I'll tell Richard the gallery can look for someone else.'

Val stared at him. 'Luke, I didn't mean—'

'You didn't mean to force me. I know.' He took her hands, looking down at them intently. 'But it's what it comes down to. I love you and Chris, darling, and I'll love any other children we have. But I quite see that you can't risk having them in a strange place, with nobody near to help if you develop eclampsia again. *I* can't risk it either. If I thought there was a real chance of that, I wouldn't even suggest any more babies.'

'It probably wouldn't happen again,' she said.

'But the chance is there, and you have to be within reach of help if it does.' He stroked her fingers. 'I think we've talked about this long enough. Maybe it's just me that needs to make the decision. I'll say no.'

Val said nothing for a minute or two. Then she shook her head.

'You can't do that. Not now. This is something that affects all

141

three of us, whether we go to London or not. If we stay here and you're miserable, it'll be as bad as if we go to London and I'm miserable. We've got to find a way that suits us both.'

'And Chris,' he said. 'Neither of us wants him to be miserable. Whatever we do, we'll put Chris first – but we won't pretend it all depends on him. After all, I grew up in London and I don't think I'm warped for life!'

Val smiled a little. 'Well, not completely anyway.' She stood up. 'I'm going to have to go to bed. I'm so tired, I could sleep standing up. We've talked and talked and I still don't think we've come to any real conclusion.'

'We've moved a bit further along the path, though,' he said. 'We must have.' But as he switched the lights off and followed Val up the narrow cottage staircase, his face was sombre and there was a look in his eyes that would have told her, had she turned in time to see it, that he felt he had lost.

Chapter Nineteen

rances Kemp returned from her holiday at the end of the
first week in August and, as she had promised, took over
some of the day-to-day care of the youngest Culliford
children, taking them for walks and picnics and organising games
on the green with other village children. James Raynor came along
to help.

'It's like a permanent playtime,' she observed as they made their
way back to the school house for a cup of tea at the end of the first
afternoon. 'I'm thinking of setting up some lessons!'

'Ever the teacher,' he grinned. 'But why not? Something different from our normal lessons – the sort of thing we don't often get
the chance to teach.'

'What do you suggest?'

'Well, we've got a spell of nice weather, so let's take advantage
of it. Nature walks are all very fine, but how about learning to live
with the land? The kind of things they do in Boy Scouts.'

'Camping, you mean? I'm not sure—'

'Not camping overnight. I don't think I'm that dedicated! But
I've got an old army tent and we could set up camp in one of the
fields during the day, and teach them how to make an open fire
and cook a few things. Woodcraft, too – how to recognise trees and
know which are best for fires, and how to be careful with fire, so that
they respect it and don't risk accidents. That spot on the brook, just
above the ford, would be ideal – a nice little grassy plateau by the
water, with the woods close at hand.'

Miss Kemp unfastened her garden gate. 'But they're just small children. Jeanie and Freddy are no more than babies.'

'They're old enough to collect wood, and Billy's of an age to learn to be sensible, and young Joe's quite a handy little chap for six. I don't know Betty and Shirley so well, since they're both in your class now, but I'm sure they'll enjoy frying bacon and sausages over a fire.'

'I'm sure they will, since they probably seldom get bacon at home,' Miss Kemp agreed drily. 'It's just as well meat is off ration at last.'

'What about the older two – Jimmy and Brenda? Would they come too?'

Miss Kemp shook her head and opened the back door, leading him into her small kitchen. 'Unlikely. Jimmy's just left St Rumon's, and I believe he's starting work for a builder in Tavistock. He's hoping for an apprenticeship. And Brenda's working for Mrs Warren in the house, as well as helping with the children. The family must be glad of a little extra income, so we mustn't interfere with that.'

'No, indeed. Anyway, I think you and I should be able to manage half a dozen small children.'

'That's if it stays at half a dozen,' she said ruefully. 'I rather think we'll have the rest of the school descending on us once they see what's happening.'

'That's all right. We'll organise them properly.'

Frances Kemp regarded him for a moment. 'You do realise what we're taking on, don't you? A field milling with children, over whom we have no real authority during the holidays?'

'We'll have the authority if they want to join us,' he said firmly. 'Don't forget, I'm an ex-army officer. And I've taught at a boys' prep school, too, where we were always devising ways of wearing the little blighters out by bedtime. I don't think we'll have too many problems.'

'I hope you're right.' She filled the kettle and set it on her small spirit stove. 'Now, I think I've got some biscuits somewhere ...'

Later, as they sat in the garden, they discussed what activities they might do and Frances found her enthusiasm growing. 'We did a lot of those things when I was a Girl Guide. I was one of the first, you know – they started in 1910 and I joined a year later, as soon as

I was eleven. I loved the freedom of it, the hiking and camping – we only went three or four miles away for a night or two, but it felt like an expedition. Girls had never been able to do those kinds of things before. I suppose it prepared us for what was to come, too,' she added thoughtfully.

'I'm sure it did. I feel the same about scouting. Being started by a soldier with so much experience of bushcraft, it was bound to be organised along those lines, I suppose. Baden-Powell was a very far-seeing man.' He sighed. 'I always felt rather guilty that I'd escaped that war when so many of my age had been called up. I would have gone as soon as I left school, of course, but it was over by then. That's why I was so keen to get into the next one.'

'Keen to go to war?' Frances said with a shudder, and he shook his head.

'Not keen on the idea of war itself, no, but keen to do my bit. What about you? Did you go to university after it was all over? I see you at Girton somehow!'

'A bluestocking, you mean.' She smiled slightly. 'No, I didn't. I *had* expected to go to Girton, as it happens, but the war ... changed things for me. I went to a teacher training college instead.' She lifted the lid of the teapot and peered inside. 'Not much left, I'm afraid. Would you like another cup?'

'No, I must go.' He began to get up. The stiffness of his artificial leg was only really noticeable when he sat down or stood up again. 'I meant to tell you, I've heard of a cottage for rent about a mile away, near the ford. I want to go and have a look at it.'

'Really? Which cottage is that?' Frances began to gather up the tea things.

'The one that stands by itself, not far from the river. In fact, I think there's a stream running through the garden. It sounds like just what I want.'

'And it's in the village, too. I know the one you mean – it could be ideal for you. But don't you want to buy?'

'If I'm appointed permanently, yes,' he said with a smile. 'But I'm still on probation, aren't I! I know it was meant to be just until the end of the summer term, but that wasn't really long enough for the governors to be able to make a firm decision.'

Frances stared at him. 'Goodness, I suppose you are. I'd quite forgotten. I'm sure everyone is happy with you, or they'd have said. Somehow it seems – well, almost as if you've always been here.' She made a mental note to remind Basil. 'I can't think why nobody has confirmed it.'

'I feel that too,' he said quietly. 'Burracombe seems to have become my home as no other place has ever done – not since the war, at any rate. And as far as the cottage goes, it may actually be for sale. The owner's in no hurry to decide, though, and has agreed to rent it to me for a few months. If it's suitable, and if I'm still here at the end of that time, I'll have the option to buy.'

'Well.' Frances stood by the garden table, the tray in her hands, and looked at him. She felt suddenly unsure of herself, although why she should feel that, she did not know. She took refuge in politeness. 'That all seems very satisfactory. I hope it works well for you. For us all.'

James smiled again. 'I think it will,' he said. 'I really think it will.'

The Culliford camp, as it came to be known, was a success for the entire village. Once the children it was intended for had been seen helping to erect Mr Raynor's old bell tent on the grassy plateau by the stream that ran into the Burra Brook on the outskirts of the village, others arrived to ask if anybody could join, and neither of the two teachers had the heart to say no. Before the first day was out, their numbers had swelled to fifteen. Micky Coker and Henry Bennetts, at a loose end during the long school holiday and keen to avoid being roped in to help at the forge, were among the most enthusiastic.

'My dad's got a tent,' Henry volunteered, back from helping Micky to dig trenches for latrines. 'Shall I lend it off him and bring it along tomorrow?'

'*Borrow*, Henry,' Miss Kemp said a little wearily, adding to Mr Raynor, 'I honestly wonder why I bother. I try for six years to get the children to say borrow instead of lend, and it seems to go in one ear and out the other. I wouldn't mind, but Henry and Micky are at the grammar school now!'

'They're bright lads,' he said, accepting Henry's offer. 'And as long as they and whoever they're talking to know what they mean, perhaps it doesn't matter all that much.'

'Not *matter*?' she exclaimed, scandalised. 'And you a teacher! Of course it matters! English grammar serves a purpose, and if it's not used accurately, communication becomes a minefield. Not matter indeed!'

He grinned and handed her a frying pan. 'Let's get the kitchen set up. Betty and Shirley are desperate to make sure everyone knows they're in charge.'

'It *is* meant to be their camp, after all,' Miss Kemp agreed, surveying the busy scene.

As soon as he had realised how many children were keen to join in, James had formed them into a semicircle, sitting on the grass, and had laid down a few rules about safety, about strict obedience and about remembering why they were here. 'Mrs Culliford is in hospital and naturally the children are worried about her, so I expect you all to be as kind and helpful as you can. Now, this is going to be a proper camp, not a home for savages, and Miss Kemp and I are in charge. I'm the commander-in-chief – you can call me Chief, if you like – and Miss Kemp is my lieutenant. Henry and Micky are the oldest boys here, so they will be my aides.'

Micky nudged his friend. 'I'll be first aid.'

'Very funny, ha ha,' Henry said.

James divided the children into teams, one each for himself, Miss Kemp, Henry and Micky. He and the headmistress set about organising the tent and kitchen, while the rest were sent to collect buckets of water from the brook and kindling from the wood. By twelve o'clock the camp looked as orderly as any Scout camp – or indeed, as James observed, any army camp – the fire lit and a can of water already boiling. Two of the girls had been dispatched to the village for supplies and returned with bacon and sausages from Bert Foster, potatoes and tomatoes from Edie Pettifer and eggs from Alice Tozer. Joey and Billy Culliford had been sent back to Joyce Warren's to collect a few early Worcester Pearmains from the orchard, and some of the others were picking blackberries from nearby hedges.

After that first day, the Culliford camp became a way of life. Children came and went as some were taken away on holiday, to visit relatives, help on the farms or, in the case of those moving up to 'big school', to go on shopping trips for school uniforms. And many of the adults came, to see what was going on and to offer a helping hand. They brought provisions, too – milk, vegetables, bread and buns for the children's tea. The fine weather continued and the children ran in and out of the brook, climbed trees, made little dens and camps of their own in the wood or along the banks, and turned as brown as nuts. They worshipped James, who told them stories of life in Africa and taught them songs to sing around the fire. They went home at tea time but begged to be allowed to sleep there all night, until at last Frances, who had quite forgotten that she was a headmistress, gave in and agreed that some of the older children would be allowed to do so.

'That's not fair, miss,' Betty Culliford said at once. 'It's our camp, us ought to be allowed to sleep here.'

'That's true,' Frances acknowledged. 'Well, all your family can sleep here one night, if your father agrees, and then we'll let some of the others do it another night. But not the younger ones, and only if their parents say they can.'

'We'd better both be here as well,' James said. 'It's a good thing Henry borrowed his father's tent. We can have that for you and the girls, and mine for me and the boys.'

Sleeping in camp meant more organisation and more equipment. Some of the fathers found they had sleeping bags left over from the war, and old blankets and pillows were carried down to the field. Jimmy and Brenda Culliford brought nearly all the family's bedding and said they wanted to stay too, for which Frances was very grateful. More provisions were needed for breakfast and more kindling for the fire. The gatherers were having to forage deeper and deeper into the wood.

At last all the Cullifords were rolled up in their blankets like a row of Bert Foster's sausages, only their heads peeping out. Jeanie and Freddy, the smallest ones, were inclined to be a little tearful at first, but were soothed by their big sister Brenda and after a few more minutes all was quiet.

The two teachers sat in the twilight by the dying fire, gazing into the embers. James took out his pipe and began to smoke, the sweet scent of the tobacco filling the air and keeping away the midges. Frances watched him absently, thinking how strong his profile looked against the deepening indigo of the sky. His square face with its corrugated forehead was in shadow, but a few silver glints showed like stardust in his crinkled black hair. We're almost the same age, she thought, remembering their conversation a few days earlier, yet he's had so much more experience than I. He's been to Oxford, worked in London, joined the army and served in several different countries, been badly wounded and lost his wife, whom he obviously adored. And after all that, he started a new life as a teacher and ended up here in Burracombe.

And yet was her own story any less strange? So few of the villagers knew or remembered now that she had been a frequent visitor here in her youth, that she too had suffered tragedy and that she had come back to fulfil a vow. She thought of the photograph in her bedroom, the one she still touched and wished good night to every evening, and the familiar pang of grief caught at her heart. Dear, sweet love, she thought sadly. My dear, dear sweet love …

Chapter Twenty

Maggie Culliford came home at last in the first week of August, the day after the Bank Holiday. The village fair had been held on the Monday, and bunting was still strung in welcome from tree to fence post to telegraph pole. More bunting was festooned over the cottage door, and the bit of turf that Jacob had put down in the front garden was cut close and neat. Jimmy was posted at the far end of the street, watching out for the doctor's car, and as soon as it appeared, he dashed through the village shouting at the top of his lungs that they were coming. By the time the car pulled up, the whole family was lined up just outside the gate waving the Union flags the school had had for the Coronation, for all the world as if it were the Queen herself arriving.

'Oh, the dear of them!' Maggie cried, almost knocked over in the rush as she got out of the car. 'Oh, I've missed you so bad! Come here and give your mother a hug. Betty – Shirley – Jeanie – Joe – Billy – Freddy – Jimmy, you've growed another six inches since I been away. And where's our Brenda?'

'In here, making you some tea,' the girl said, appearing at the door. 'The kettle whistled just as you got here. Oh, *Mum* ...' She wrapped her arms around her mother, tears brimming over. 'I'm so pleased you'm back. The house don't seem the same when you're not here.'

'I'm glad to be back too. I never thought for a minute I'd be away all that time. A month and more! But you've all been looked after while I been away, so I hear.'

'We've been staying with Mrs Warren,' Betty said. 'She let us play in her orchard and she says we can go up there any time we like now Billy knows not to carve things on the trees with his penknife. We can pick apples, too, when they'm ripe. And Miss Kemp and the new teacher, Mr Raynor, took us out on nature walks and picnics and then we had our camp up above the ford. And Mrs Tozer let us help collect eggs from her hens and keep some to bring home for Dad's breakfast. And—'

'You can tell your mother all that later on,' Arthur interrupted. 'Dr Latimer wants to get back home once us've got her settled in. And I dare say her's gasping for that tea Brenda made before it gets too stewed. Come on, let's get through the door.'

Without too much fuss and commotion, they got Maggie settled in the old rocking chair in the back room, and she leaned against a pile of cushions and closed her eyes.

'I thought I was all right after all that time idling my time away in the convalescent home, but I feel as tired as if I done a day's heavy scrubbing.'

'You will feel that at first,' the doctor said. 'But it will soon wear off. You'll be on your feet in no time.' He surveyed the children and nodded at Arthur. 'I'll leave you now. Let me know if you're at all worried, but I don't think you will be. She's quite recovered now.'

Arthur held out a big calloused hand. 'I got to say thank you, Doctor. If it hadn't been for you ...'

'No need for thanks. I'm glad to have been able to help as much as I could. Now, take care of each other.' He smiled at the children. 'That means all of you too, you know! Yes, even little Freddy. I'm sure he can do something.'

'He can sit on my lap,' Maggie said, drawing the toddler close. 'I've been starving for someone little to cuddle.'

Charles Latimer looked down at her, feeling a sudden rush of sympathy. By now, she should be cuddling her twin babies; instead, Freddy was the last baby she would ever have. Plenty of people would say this was a good thing, but as he'd grown to know Maggie and Arthur over the past few weeks, his respect for both of them had grown. Faults they most certainly had, but what was an element of fecklessness when compared with the love these two clearly felt for each other and their family? Responsibility could be taught – and both of them showed signs of learning it now – but true, heartfelt love could only come naturally. The greatest wonder was that the village had never recognised it before.

We should all learn from this, he thought as he returned to his own home. Maggie and Arthur have lived here all their lives and been dismissed as of no account. But now they're part of this big family we call a village and they'll never be neglected again and in a strange way, Burracombe is all the richer for their presence.

'So what's all this about a skiffle group? What is skiffle anyway?'

'It's music,' Brenda said. They were all sitting round the kitchen table eating beans on toast, and there was a plate piled with Dottie's rock buns in the middle. 'Anyone can play it because you don't need real instruments. Roy Nethercott's going to use his mother's old washboard and Vic's going to get a tea chest from Creber's, to make a double bass.'

Maggie stared at her. 'You mean they make musical instruments out of old rubbish? They want to come round here, then. Us got enough for a full orchestra.'

'Not any more us haven't,' Arthur said. 'Me and some of the village chaps sorted it all out and took a lot of stuff down the tip. You mean to say you hadn't noticed?'

'I did think it all looked pretty tidy, but I thought you'd just shoved a lot of stuff into the cupboards like us did when Mr Napier or Miss Hilary came round. Anyway, you go on about this skiffle group, Brenda. What sort of instrument are you going to play? A couple of saucepan lids?'

'Mr Copley's lending me his ukulele. What do you think of that?' Her face flushed and her eyes shone with delight.

'What, like George Formby plays, you mean? But you don't know how to play a ukulele. And I don't want you singing no dirty songs, mind, like that one about cleaning windows.'

'Is that dirty?' Brenda asked. 'I can't see how. Anyway, Mr Copley's going to lend Reg his guitar too and he said he'll teach us to play them. We'm going over to the vicarage in Little Burracombe tomorrow night.'

'But why do they want you in it?' Maggie asked, a little suspiciously. 'They're all years older than you.'

'Only a few. Anyway, they want a singer – a girl – and they reckon I got the right sort of voice. I *can* do it, can't I?' she asked, suddenly anxious. 'It's only two nights a week rehearsing, and we might put on a bit of a show at Christmas. Or we could be asked to play at village dances. And now I've got a proper job with Mrs Warren, I'll be bringing a bit of money home, like our Jim does. I'll still be able to help you here, though,' she added hastily.

Maggie looked at her husband. 'I don't see anything against it, do you, Art?'

'Not so long as they treats her with proper respect,' he said. 'I'll have a word with young Bob and make sure he knows what's what. Us don't want you going the same way as his brother and young Patsy Shillabeer.'

'Dad!' Brenda turned scarlet and Maggie laughed.

'You'm embarrassing the poor maid. It's all right, my bird, you can be in this old skiffle group if that's what you wants to do. I dare say it'll only be a flash in the pan anyway. And what about the rest of you? How's my Billy looking forward to going back to school after the holidays, and what's this new teacher like?'

Brenda met Reg Dodd next evening under the great old oak that spread its branches over the village green, and they set off together along the lane that led behind the Bell Inn to the narrow footbridge that crossed the Burra Brook. The wild profusion of honeysuckle, campion, ragged robin and foamy cow parsley had tired now and given way to a softer green, yellowing in places and dusted with seed heads. Blackberries were now thick on the hedges, and they paused now and then to pick a handful and cram them into their mouths.

'Better not get too mucky,' Brenda said, looking at her purple-stained fingers. 'Or Mr Copley won't lend us the instruments.'

'Us'll ask to wash our hands when us gets there,' Reg said. 'He'll probably ask us if us wants to anyway. Posh people always do.'

'Why? Their sort of visitors don't get dirty on the way, do they?'

'It's not that. What they really mean is, do they want the lav. Because they always wash their hands after they've been, see?'

Brenda gazed at him. Like many of the cottages in Burracombe, the Cullifords' had no indoor plumbing. It didn't even have the benefit of a cesspit, let alone anything as sophisticated as a septic tank. The lavatory was in a small, smelly hut at the bottom of the garden, and the contents were emptied into a tank by the night-soil man and taken somewhere away from the village. You might well need to wash your hands after a visit, but by the time you got back indoors again on a cold, wet day, you'd probably forgotten all about it.

'I'll wash them in the river,' she said, climbing down the bank by the Clam and dunking her hands in the swift, clear water. The stains came off with a bit of rubbing, and Reg followed her example. 'We'd better not pick any more now. We can get some on the way back.'

Relatively clean, they presented themselves at the vicarage door and Stella welcomed them in. 'So you're starting a skiffle group. Felix and I are coming to your first public performance!'

Reg looked startled. 'Us haven't even started practising yet. Might never be good enough for that.'

'Of course you will be.' She led them into Felix's cluttered study. 'I can tell you, Felix is wildly jealous. He'd love to be in it himself.' She caught Reg's look of alarm and laughed. 'It's all right, he's not going to ask you. He's far too busy learning to be a vicar.'

'Don't he already know that?' Reg asked, even more bewildered, but before Stella could answer, the man himself came through the door, struggling with two unwieldy wooden cases.

'Hello, you two! I'm so glad you came. Here they are.' He dumped the cases across a desk already piled with papers, half of which immediately slid to the floor. 'Oh Lord, there goes next week's sermon. I'll never get the pages in order now.'

'You ought to number them as you write them,' Stella said, bending to pick them up and almost cracking her head against Reg's as he did the same thing. 'Not that it will make the slightest difference to your parishioners what order they come in. Half of them are wishing you were still available to marry, and the other half are asleep.'

'That's a dastardly slur,' Felix began, and noticed Brenda's look of shock. 'It's all right, Brenda, I said *dastardly*, not ... well, never mind. It just means it's not true. And Stella was only joking anyway.'

'Don't you be too sure,' she warned him, and turned to go. 'I'll bring some lemonade in in a minute. Would either of you like to wash your hands first?'

Brenda felt a giggle begin in her lower chest, and turned away to help Felix with the fastenings on the cases. 'No thank you, Mrs Copley,' she managed, and heard Reg mutter the same. The door closed and Felix opened the first case and took out a guitar.

'And here's the ukulele.' He held them up, one in each hand. 'Now, who's playing which?'

'Oh, they're proper handsome.' Brenda reached for the ukulele and cradled it lovingly, while Reg took up the stance he believed to be right for a guitarist and strummed a few notes.

'You're an expert already,' Felix told him. 'But hold it this way, you'll find it more comfortable.' He looped the strap over Reg's neck and showed him how to rest the instrument on his thigh. 'Now, cradle the neck in your palm so that all your fingers and thumb curl round and you can reach the strings. We'll just get you used to feeling the strings with your fingertips and then I'll show you how to tune it. Do you know the names of the keys?'

Reg stared at him. 'What keys? Bob never mentioned no keys.'

'Well, perhaps just basic strumming is all you need,' Felix said diplomatically. 'It's more important to have an ear for it. You have a little go on your own and I'll show Brenda the ukulele. It's not so very different really,' he added, seeing that she was looking nervous, 'and in a skiffle group it's mostly a case of all strumming along in harmony together. The tea chest and washboard aren't going to be exactly tuned in any way. Do you have any songs yet?'

'Us wants to write our own,' Reg said. 'But we know us got to use proper ones to start with.'

'Yes, that's probably a good idea.' Felix glanced round with relief as Stella came in bearing a tray of glasses and a tall jug of lemonade. 'Well, why not try a few of the hillbilly songs that most people already know? I've got some records if you'd like to hear them. Come into the sitting room.'

He led them through to a large room furnished with sofas and armchairs, and went over to a cupboard on top of which stood a Dansette record player. 'Stella gave me this for my birthday,' he said proudly. 'And my records are in the cupboard underneath.'

He bent and extracted a dozen or so 78 rpm records and sorted through them. 'Here we are. A couple of Hank Williams songs – "Your Cheatin' Heart" and "Hey Good Lookin'". They'd make a good start for you.'

He put the first record on and they all listened. When it came to an end, Reg said, 'I'm not sure I'm up to that. And it's a man singing – we really want girls' songs.'

'Girls can sing it too. Let's listen to it again.' He reached out for the guitar and played along with the record. The next time, Brenda joined in with the ukulele and Felix grinned at her and began to sing. Reg, not to be outdone, thumped his hands on the arms of his chair and Brenda joined Felix in his singing. Their confidence growing, they were all hard at it when the door opened to admit Olivia Lydiard.

Olivia was one of Felix's most attentive parishioners. Married to a retired naval commander, she had seemed to be forever at the vicarage when Felix had first come here, while Stella was in hospital after her accident. It had seemed to him then that he could barely move without tripping over one or another of the ladies of the parish, vying with each other as they bore gifts of cakes or casseroles into his kitchen – and if it wasn't them, it was Tessa Latimer, the doctor's daughter, who had for some time had an eye for Felix. Luckily, Charles was well aware of this and had made sure she wasn't a nuisance, while Olivia, being safely married, had been no real threat. But since Stella's recovery and their marriage, most of these attentions had died down, and now Olivia seldom arrived unannounced.

'Good heavens,' she exclaimed, stopping short in the doorway. Stella could be seen hovering apologetically behind her. 'I thought there must be something wrong with your gramophone! Whatever are you doing?' She surveyed Reg and Brenda, her finely drawn eyebrows raised.

'We're practising skiffle,' Felix explained.

Olivia glanced at him dubiously, not sure whether he was serious, and Stella came to the rescue.

'Felix is lending the group his guitar and ukulele. He got them when he was an undergraduate and hasn't played them for years, have you, darling?'

'No, although now that I see them again, I feel I'd rather like to. I might use them during one of my sermons. That would make the congregation sit up.'

'It would make them stand up and walk out,' Stella retorted. 'Mrs Lydiard, do sit down. I'm sure Felix won't be long now. Had you forgotten you had an appointment this evening?' she asked him, frowning behind Olivia's back to hint that he should say no.

'An appointment? With Olivia? Of course I hadn't forgotten.' What on earth had she come about? he wondered wildly, convinced that no such arrangement had been made. 'I think we've done enough for one evening,' he said to the two skifflers. 'You've made a really good start. Why don't you come over again next week? Do some practice in between and we'll try a few of my other records.'

Beaming self-consciously, the budding musicians packed away their instruments and carried them proudly from the room. Felix winked as they passed him and Brenda very nearly got the giggles again. Stella opened the front door and smiled away their thanks.

'It's been no trouble at all. I'm glad you've got the instruments – it means there's no danger of Felix taking them to church.' She said goodbye and shut the door, returning in time to hear Olivia Lydiard's rather reproachful voice.

'The harvest supper, Vicar. We haven't had one since before poor Mr Berry was taken ill, and the village did so enjoy them. I know we're only in August, but it's not too soon to start planning – you know how time flies. As we have an official meeting next week, I thought I'd just call in and run over a few points with you ...'

So it hadn't been arranged after all, Stella thought. She just wanted me to think it had because she wanted to get in ahead of the rest of the parochial church council. Well, I won't fall for *that* little trick again!

157

Chapter Twenty-One

Jennifer Kellaway's baby was born as sweetly and easily as if Jennifer had had a dozen already, instead of this being her first. The midwife didn't even need to call Dr Latimer, but he came anyway, arriving with the birdsong, his shoes dampened by the sparkle of an overnight shower on the grass. The leaves of the trees surrounding Wood Cottage were freshened by the same shimmer, and already a mist of heat was rising from the ground, so that at first sight the cottage seemed to be floating above a soft cloud of faintest grey.

The path leading to the front door was bordered with the flowers Jennifer had planted there – the pink and white naked ladies of a late dicentra, a billow of flame-coloured montbretia, the starry white faces of marguerites and the clear bright yellow and red cushions of dahlia blooms. The smooth curving lawn led to a cluster of hydrangeas with their huge blue globes and azaleas now past their flowering, before the woodland itself took over and there was only an increasing depth of green and brown shadows.

The cottage door stood open, and as Charles approached, Jacob Prout came out, his face so wreathed in smiles that every seam and wrinkle formed a network of delight. He beamed at the doctor and held out a big horny hand to be shaken.

'There you are. Not that she have any need of attention, mind – had the little dear as easy as shelling peas, so Lucy Dodd tells me. But 'tis main good of you to come so early. Travis is upstairs with them now.'

Charles followed him up the steep cottage stairs. The bedroom door was open and the pale flowered curtains were drawn back to let the early sunlight flood through a window flung wide to admit the summer air and the scent of Jennifer's garden. Jennifer was in bed, propped against a cloud of pillows and covered by a white quilt, with the baby in her arms wrapped in a shawl of soft old lace. Travis was beside her, and as Charles entered, they both looked round, their faces glowing equally, and Travis moved aside so that he could come nearer.

'A very fine baby,' Charles said, looking down at the creamy face touched with rose pink, the head fuzzed with pale gold and the eyes tightly closed. 'And not at all crumpled and wizened as most new babies are!'

'Of course she isn't,' Travis said. 'She's *our* baby. Is either of us crumpled or wizened?'

Charles laughed. 'No, and I can see a definite resemblance to her mother, if not her father. You must both be very proud.'

'Almost as proud as Jacob,' Jennifer said, turning her head as the old man appeared in the doorway. 'He's been here all night – Travis knocked on his door when he went for Mrs Dodd, and he came straight away. Travis says he's been like a cat on hot bricks.'

'I come to be a support to him,' Jacob said with dignity, and Travis laughed.

'More like the other way about! And now you'd better go home and get some rest. The hedges and ditches of Burracombe will have to manage without you today. I'll take you in the Land Rover. You'll need to be at the Bell tonight to give all the villagers the first-hand news.'

'And wet the baby's head.' Jacob nodded, and came over to the bed. He reached down and touched the baby's cheek gently with a fingertip. 'The dear of her. I'm your grandad,' he said to the sleeping child. 'Maybe not strictly your proper grandad, but as near as maybe. And you'm always going to be a granddaughter to me.'

'I'll take you back to the village,' Charles said. 'Travis needs some rest too. Not to mention the proud mother.' He smiled at Jennifer. 'Have you chosen a name yet?'

'Mary,' she said. 'We both like it – a good, sensible name and with a lovely warm feel to it. And Susan, after both our mothers

159

– Travis's mother had it as a second name. It's a pretty combination, isn't it?'

'Mary Susan. Very pretty. Well, I'll call in again tomorrow, unless you need me sooner, which I doubt, and of course Lucy will let me know if she thinks there are any problems. It doesn't look as if there will be, though. I've seldom seen such a contented newborn baby, or such a composed mother. It's as if you've been waiting for each other all your lives.'

'That's exactly how I feel too,' Jennifer said, and handed the baby to Travis, who laid her gently in the wooden cradle he had made for her. 'And now I think I'll go to sleep.'

As the doctor drove Jacob back to the village, the old man drew in a deep sigh of satisfaction.

'What you said was right, Doctor. But it ain't just Jennifer that's been waiting for her babby all her life. It's me and Travis as well. It's like us just needed that little dear to make everything complete. Like it's come round full circle for me; like her's filled a gap that's been there ever since I lost my Susan – Jennifer's mother. It's nice that they've give her that name, isn't it? And such a pretty little thing, too. A real princess.'

Charles Latimer smiled. Like many of the villagers, he had come to know the story of Jacob's love for Jennifer's mother Susan, who had lived in Burracombe as a girl, and the feud that had arisen over her between him and his friend Jed Fisher. For some time, when she first came to the village to seek her real father, Jennifer had thought it might be Jacob, but she had finally discovered that it had been Jed, with a sudden loss of control while Jacob had been away during the First World War, who had fathered her. Susan's family, deeply ashamed, had sent her away to have the baby and told Jacob that she had died. Instead, she had married and lived in Plymouth until only a few years ago, and after she'd died Jennifer had come to seek him out.

Even though he wasn't her true father, Jacob had always felt himself to be as close as a father could be, and she had often stayed with him when visiting the village, even though Jed had left her the cottage she now rented to Val and Luke. Now, the little family was as close-knit as any family could be – and more than some, Charles reflected. Jacob would indeed be a grandfather to his little princess, and there would be no granddaughter more loved than Mary Susan Kellaway.

It was clear to everyone that the same grandfatherly love would not be extended to Patsy Pettifer's baby. Not by Patsy's father, anyway – Jack Pettifer, although still deeply disapproving of the way the baby had been conceived, would love it in exactly the same way as any other member of his family.

'It'll be our first,' he said to Nancy, lighting his pipe as they sat outside their back door watching the sunset after spending the evening picking blackcurrants in their garden. 'How do you feel about being a granny, then?'

'About the same as you do about being a grandad, I reckon. It's come a bit sudden, and I thought our Bob would be the first to bring us a grandchild, him being the older boy, but nobody can ever tell which way the world will wag. And Patsy's a nice little maid. She'll be a good mother.'

'You're sure you don't mind them stopping with us till Terry's finished his apprenticeship? Not that he'll be bringing home much of a wage even then – hardly enough to keep a wife and kiddy.'

'They can stop with us as long as they like. And if Miss Hilary wants Patsy to go on working up at the Barton, I'll be happy to have her leave the little one with me. Another little tacker round the place will keep us both young, that's the way I see it.'

Jack put his arm round his wife's waist. 'You'm a good woman, Nancy. I knew it when I first set eyes on you, down on the old bridge by the ford that summer evening. That's my girl, I said to myself then, and after that I never even looked at anyone else.'

'But we've known each other since we were five years old!' Nancy said in astonishment.

'I know, but we were just tackers ourselves then. I'm talking about when us was growing up and first noticing boys and girls were different. It was the day before my birthday, that's why I remember it – sixteen next day, and you'd have been fifteen. I made up my mind then that you'd be my wife, and you know that when I make up my mind to a thing, that's what usually happens.'

Nancy smiled. In her recollection, it had been she who'd noticed Jack Pettifer, ugly as he was with the family gargoyle features, seeing his friendly, honest eyes and frank grin. She hadn't made up her mind that very evening – and neither, she thought, had he – but she'd managed to be around quite a lot when he was down at the bridge where all the young folk met of an evening, and it was surprising how often they'd run into each other in the village street. You only had to learn a person's habits and know when they were likely to be sent to the shops for their mother's groceries. Soon enough, they'd paired up at the bridge, and then they'd begun to drift away by themselves for a walk along the banks of the Burra Brook, and before you knew it, they were inviting each other back to their homes for Sunday tea. By the time Nancy was twenty, they were engaged, and they married three years later. Whether it had been her idea or Jack's by then, neither could have said. It had just happened, as naturally as their first kiss.

'It's so different today,' she said, following her thoughts. 'We took our time over it all – a nice steady courtship, three years engaged, it gave us time to know each other properly, and save up for our home. Patsy and our Terry – why, they'm hardly out of the nursery themselves. All this talk about being in love, they don't know what it means. I just worry sometimes ...' She paused and looked down at her fingers, linked together on her lap.

'What? What do you worry, my bird?'

'Well, that they'll fall out of love as quick as they fell in. And them with a babby, too. It's a miserable life, Jack, if you'm tied to someone you can't love. Look at Patsy's mother. Poor Ann must have thought she loved him at the beginning, and look at her now. Frightened of her own shadow and lost her eldest daughter because of his bullying ways.'

Jack was silent for a minute or two. Then he heaved a deep sigh and nodded. 'I know. She has a poor time of it, right enough. But our Terry will never go the way of Patsy's father.' He took his wife's hands and said comfortingly, 'They'll be all right, Nance. It's not what we wanted for them, but they're in a settled home now for their start in life, and that's the way they'll go on when they get their own place. And I agree with you – it'll be good to have a little'n round our feet, to keep us green. There's only one thing I wish for it.' He paused and relit his pipe.

'And what's that?'

'Why, that it don't look too much like its father! It'd be a nice change in this family if one of us don't look like us should be stuck up on the corner of the church tower! I'd like *this* little Pettifer to take after its mother.'

Patsy had slipped over to see her mother again. Once again she chose a Wednesday, when her father would probably be at the Tavistock cattle market, but since Bob wasn't working in Little Burracombe now and able to keep watch for her, she had arranged that her mother would hang a white towel out of the bedroom window as a signal that it was safe. Percy didn't always go to the market, and it was quite possible that he would decide at the last minute to stay on the farm.

This afternoon, the towel was in place and Patsy hurried through the yard to the back door. None of the farm workers was about and the back door stood open, leading into the big cluttered kitchen. Ann was bending over the deep white sink, washing up the dinner things, and the two youngest children were playing in a corner and jumped up when they saw their sister.

'Patsy! Oh, you'm earlier than I expected – I was going to send these two down the fields to pick blackberries.' Ann looked frightened, and Patsy hastened to put her arms around her.

'It's all right, Mother. I saw the towel so I knew he'd not be here. And I wanted to see the little ones. I miss them.'

'It's not that.' Ann dried her hands on a tea towel. 'It's what they might say to him. If he finds out you've been here ...'

Patsy looked at her. 'I thought you'd told him you were still going to see me?'

'Well, I didn't exactly say that. I just told him you'd always be my daughter and he couldn't stop me being your mother. But as for you still coming over ...' She shuddered, and Patsy remembered how her mother had flown about the kitchen, tidying away all the evidence of a visitor the last time she'd been here. Ann looked at the two small children, now hanging on to Patsy's skirts and trying to attract her attention. 'You don't have to say nothing to Daddy about our Patsy being here, mind. You understand that?'

They nodded, wide-eyed, and Patsy gave them both a hug and went over to see the game they had been playing. After a while, they settled down to the old building bricks that Patsy remembered from her own childhood and Patsy went back to her mother, who had made tea and carried it outside into the garden.

'So how are you keeping, my bird?' She glanced at Patsy's figure. 'You're beginning to show. Five months gone now, aren't you? No more sickness?'

'No, that's all gone. I'm feeling really well.'

'I must say, you look proper blooming.' Patsy's skin, usually rather pale, had developed a creamy glow and her hair was glossy. Her slender figure was filling out a little and she seemed to carry an air of restful confidence. 'It's done you good to get away from here.'

Patsy picked up the wistfulness in her mother's voice and said quickly, 'It's not getting away from *you* that's done me good, Mother, you know that. It's getting away from *him*. But mostly it's being with Terry. We really do love each other.'

'I know, my bird, and I hope it all goes well for you. It's good for me to see you looking so well and happy. And what about the Barton? You're not doing too much heavy work, I hope?'

'No, Mrs Curnow is a real angel, and Miss Hilary always asks how I am and tells me I must rest whenever I feel tired. And she've got troubles of her own, too.'

'Have she? What sort of troubles?'

Patsy hesitated. 'Well I don't know exactly, but she looks so sad at times, and sometimes when you speak to her, she looks as if she don't even hear. As if she's somewhere else. And she talks a lot to Dr Latimer when he comes to see the squire.'

'It's probably about him, then. She's had a lot of worries there, with those heart attacks of his.'

'I don't know. He's almost better now, up and about and doing as much as ever.'

'But if the doctor's coming regular ...'

'Oh, he's not coming in that way – he comes to play chess and bridge. But he always has a talk with Miss Hilary and she always looks sad after.'

'Maybe the Squire's worse than they're letting on, then,' Ann said, pouring more tea. 'And how are Jack and Nancy?'

They chatted on about the family and other people they knew, and were cosily engrossed in yet another list of possible names for the baby when a shadow fell suddenly across them. As they looked up, a roar of fury brought them both to their feet in shock.

'What in the name of all God's goodness are *you* doing here?' bellowed Percy. He turned to his wife, shooting out a huge hand to grip her painfully by the shoulder. 'And what are you doing letting her come? You know full well I forbade you ever to let the dirty little minx over the doorstep, and here I find you drinking tea and gossiping like two old biddies. How many times has this happened, eh? Every time I've been out? Every time I've been to Tavi?' He shook Ann roughly, and as Patsy started forward with a cry, his bellow turned to a snarl. 'Don't you dare interfere! Just get out – go on, get *out*, I tell you – and don't you never come here again or you'll be sorry.' Rage was blackening his face, and Ann began to weep with terror. 'You'll *both* be sorry.'

'Stop it!' Patsy faced him, her grey eyes brilliant with anger. 'Let her go! You're nothing but a bully, that's what you are. Leave my mother alone.'

'Oh, so you're giving the orders now, are you? And just what are you going to do if I don't?'

'I'll tell Bert Lillywhite. I'll fetch him now if you don't let her go.'

Percy let out a bark of laughter. 'The village bobby? And what d'you suppose he'll do? The police never interferes between husband and wife, you should know that, and if you don't now, you'll soon find out, once that ugly mug you've tied yourself to shows his true colours.'

'The vicar, then,' Patsy said, not bothering to counter his accusation about Terry. 'He'll soon set you right.'

'He don't have no jurisdiction over me neither. I'm leaving the church and joining the Exclusives.'

The two women stared at him. 'The Exclusives?' Ann quavered. 'But aren't they Jehovah's Witnesses?'

'Plymouth Brethren,' he corrected her. 'I'm going to the meeting in Plymouth next Sunday to find out all about it. And you don't need to think you can come over then, while I'm out of the way,' he told Patsy. 'The door will be locked while I'm gone. There'll be plenty for your mother to do indoors of a Sunday morning. Say her prayers, for a start.'

'You can't lock her up!'

'I can do what I like. I'm her husband, in case you've forgot. And 'tis my duty to turn her from her sinful ways and set her feet—'

'*Her* sinful ways?'

'You heard. And you'd do well to look to your own salvation, that's if you ain't beyond it already.' He had dropped his hand from Ann's shoulder now, but she gazed at him in fear as he ranted, his eyes glittering and his mouth working with passion. 'That's if you ain't *both* beyond it. And things are going to be different around here from now on. I can't live with sin in the house.'

'Sin? What sin – apart from yours?' Patsy demanded. She put out her hand to her mother, but it was immediately slapped away by her father and she cried out in shock.

'You're riddled with sin, all of you, and 'tis my duty to set it right. There'll be no more of it, I tell you. From now on, we walk in the path of God.' He wheeled suddenly and marched into the house. A moment later he emerged carrying the wireless set that had so often been the only friendly voice Ann heard for days. As the two women watched in dismay, he lifted it above his head and threw it savagely to the ground, where it fell with a crash and burst apart in a tangle of cables and smashed valves. Ann burst into tears and Patsy sprang forward and gripped both her father's wrists.

'Why did you do that? You know she loved her wireless. It was her only pleasure. Why smash it up? Why?'

He shook her off like an irritating fly. 'It's the work of the Devil, that's why. Wireless, television, all that sort of thing leads to sin, and I won't live with sin. I won't have it near me.'

'Oh, that's just stupid. And if that's what these Exclusives say, they're as stupid as you. I'll get Mother another wireless, and if you smash that too—'

'You won't,' he stated, glowering at her. 'You won't give her anything. You won't be coming here again.' He turned back to his wife and took her arm in a grip that would surely leave bruises. 'Now get out. And don't come near this place again. Not if you've any thought for your mother at all, for it's she will suffer for it.'

Patsy stared at him. She turned her gaze to her mother's white face, and Ann nodded, her eyes filling again with tears. 'He's right, my bird. You'd better go. He'll be all right once he've had a cup of tea and settled down a bit.'

Patsy doubted that, but the entreaty in her mother's voice persuaded her. Reluctant to leave them all the same, she moved hesitantly towards the gate, but too slowly for her father, who made a threatening move towards her.

'Out! Out! And don't never come near the place again, you and your Devil's spawn.'

'Do as he says, please,' Ann begged, and Patsy turned away. Half blinded by tears, she fumbled for the gate catch and dragged it open. She ran through the yard, ignoring the stare of the stockman bringing the cows in for afternoon milking, and out into the lane, feeling little safer there from her father's rage. For a moment, suddenly breathless with haste and shock, she paused to recover herself.

When she walked on again, it was not directly towards the Clam and Burracombe. Instead, she stopped at the vicarage gate and went up the path to knock on Felix's door.

Chapter Twenty-Two

'**B**ut that's dreadful,' Stella said when Patsy had poured out her story. She had declined Felix's invitation to talk to him alone in his study and asked to sit in their kitchen while Stella made tea and listened too. 'Felix, surely he can't be allowed to act in this way?'

'I'm afraid he can, in law,' Felix said. 'The police won't come between husband and wife. And the wireless set – well, I suppose strictly that's his property, since he's the breadwinner and Mrs Shillabeer has no money of her own.'

'But it was a Christmas present,' Patsy said. 'Us all put our pocket money together and give it to them both, though it was Mother us really meant it for.'

'It would still count as his, then. I'm really sorry, Patsy. I'll talk to him, but I doubt he'll take much notice. He's not approved of my sermons ever since – well, ever since your wedding.'

'But that's the other thing,' Patsy said miserably. 'He says he's leaving your church and joining the Plymouth Brethren – the Exclusives, he calls them.'

'Yes, that's their correct name. Oh dear.' Felix looked dismayed. 'That puts a whole new complexion on things. You're right, he won't even want to speak to me again, let alone listen to anything I have to say to him.'

'But aren't they one of those very strict sects?' Stella asked, and Felix nodded. 'Where will he go for their services? Is there a church in Tavistock?'

'They're not services, they're meetings, and he'll have to go to

Plymouth. It'll take him half the day to get there and back on the bus.'

'That will give your mother a little respite, then. And she'll still be able to go to church. You can talk to her then, Felix – we both can.'

Patsy shook her head. 'She won't be able to go anywhere. He's going to lock her in.'

'*Lock her in?* But why? What does he think she's going to do? Is it to stop you going to see her?'

'It's because he won't have sin in the house. He *says*. I think it's the only time there won't *be* any sin myself.' Patsy's face flushed. 'He says she's full of sin. My mother! She never sinned in her life.'

'That's the way they think,' Felix said. 'They believe they are the only Christians without sin, and that even consorting with other Christians will contaminate them. I'm afraid your mother is in for a difficult time, Patsy. Unless she joins too, he will probably never speak to her again.'

'Well, that won't be any loss,' Patsy said.

'It's not just that. He probably won't eat at the same table with her, or in the same room. He'll demand that the children eat separately too. And living with someone who won't speak isn't easy – especially as it doesn't prevent them from using other forms of persuasion.'

'You mean he'll hit her?' Stella asked in horror. 'Like he did today? Though he didn't actually hit her, Patsy, did he? Just took hold of her?'

'He hurt her. And he's hit her before – I've seen him. We all have. He used to hit me too if he got in a temper. There's nothing Christian about him,' she said to Felix. 'And these people – these Brethren – they're going to make him worse.'

'Well, that's not necessarily their fault,' Felix said, trying to be fair. 'I don't think they advise members to be violent towards each other. But they are very, very strict. There are a lot of things we take for granted that are forbidden to them. The wireless is just one example.' He shook his head and ran his fingers through his fair hair. 'I can't see what we can do about it.'

'There must be something,' Stella said. 'Men surely aren't allowed to knock their wives about. Are you certain that if Patsy went to see Mr Lillywhite he wouldn't be able to do something?'

'I don't think he could. It depends how far it goes, of course – I mean, if she were seriously hurt and ended up in hospital, or if—' He stopped, and Stella stared at him.

'You mean if he killed her,' she said flatly, and Patsy let out a cry of terror. 'I'm sorry, Patsy – I shouldn't have said that. But how far *is* it allowed to go before someone intervenes? It's outrageous.'

'I know. I'll try to find out. And meanwhile,' he said to Patsy, 'you must try not to worry too much. Stella and I will keep an eye on your mother. I might take one or two others into my confidence as well, if you don't mind. We don't want the whole village gossiping – although Percy himself might bring that about – but I'd like to be sure there are a few people watching to make sure things don't go too far. He hasn't actually joined the Brethren yet, has he? They might make him see sense. They might not even admit him.' But his tone as he made those last two suggestions sounded less than hopeful. 'And please come to see us whenever you want to, Patsy. Between us we'll see that your mother is all right.'

Patsy nodded and stood up. 'Thanks, Mr Copley. And you, Mrs Copley. I knew you'd understand. I'd better be getting on back now. Terry will be home for his tea soon and I said I'd get it ready for everyone. Me and Mrs Pettifer takes turns now.'

They went with her to the door. Stella said, 'It's good to see you looking so well now, Patsy. Felix is right, you know – you must try not to worry too much. It's bad for the baby. And things often turn out better than we expect.'

Patsy smiled at her and walked off down the path. They watched her go, and then Stella shut the door and turned to her husband.

'Oh Felix,' she said. 'That poor girl. And her poor mother. And the other children too. What an awful man he is. Is it really possible that nothing can be done about him?'

'*I'd* like to do something about him,' Terry said when Patsy told him about the afternoon's events. 'I'd like to go over there and have it out with him right away.' He began to get up, but Patsy put out her hand to restrain him.

'It's no good, Terry. He's a lot bigger than you and he won't care what he does if you go interfering. It's no use you getting hurt.' She stared despondently at her plate. Although she had cooked the meal – toad in the hole, with fresh runner beans and new potatoes from Jack's garden – she hadn't been able to eat more than a few mouthfuls. 'I just wish I knew what was going on now.'

They were all silent for a few moments, then Terry said, 'There's one thing. I don't reckon you ought to go over there any more.'

Patsy's head came up. 'Not go over there? But I've got to. How am I going to know she's all right? And how's she going to feel if I stop going? She'll think I don't care.'

'She won't think that,' Nancy said quietly. 'She knows you care. But I reckon Terry's right. It could make it even harder for her if he finds out you've been back.'

'I suppose so. But I'm so worried about her. You didn't see him when he smashed that wireless. He looked as if he was going mad. Really mad, I mean, not just in a temper. And if he joins these Brethren and gets even worse ... I don't know what'll happen.' A tear splashed on to her plate.

Nancy reached over and patted her arm. 'Now look, my bird, 'tis no use you making yourself ill over it. That won't help you or your mother, and it certainly won't help your baby. And there's nothing to stop her writing a letter to you, is there? You can get it the same day if she posts it early. But maybe we're all worrying too much anyway. Once he calms down, happen he'll see things differently. And we don't *know* that these Exclusives will be bad for him – going to their meetings and having a bit of a rant might get it out of his system. At least it'll give his poor wife a few hours' peace of a Sunday.'

'Nancy's right,' Jack said. 'Come on, Patsy, eat your supper now. You got to think of your own little one. If I know your mother, she wouldn't want you fretting yourself away when there's good food in front of you.'

Patsy nodded and managed a weak, wavering smile. She picked up her knife and fork and put a few more pieces of sausage and batter into her mouth, then set them down again.

'I can't eat any more, honestly. I think I'll go and lay down on the bed.'

'All right, love,' said Nancy, watching as Terry followed her out of the room. She turned to her husband and shook her head.

'It's a bad do, Jack. I can't see what's to come of it, can you?'

'I can't. I don't know who I feel more sorry for, Patsy or her mother. The maid's going to fret herself away thinking it's all her fault, and poor Ann Shillabeer – well, who knows what she's going through? But I tell you what worries me most.' He paused, and Nancy looked at him.

'What's that?'

'What Patsy said about the look on his face. As if he was going mad – *really* mad. If that's what's happening to Percy Shillabeer, there's no knowing what will happen next. And seemingly not a thing any of us can do to stop it.'

Once it was declared that Jennifer Kellaway was ready to receive visitors, it seemed that the whole of Burracombe beat a path to the door of Wood Cottage. After a steady stream on the first day, Travis decreed that visiting could only be for an hour or two in the morning and again in the afternoon. The baby's feeding hours must be avoided and Jennifer given time to rest.

'She's beautiful,' Hilary said, echoing the words of every single visitor as she peeped at the tiny face that was the only part visible amongst the soft white shawls and blankets. 'I thought all new babies looked like either coconuts or Winston Churchill. Crumpled and squashed, and a bit bruised. But there's not a mark on her. How did you manage that?'

Jennifer laughed. 'I don't know. It was just so quick and easy, she didn't have time to get squashed. I'm not saying it didn't hurt, mind – it did. But not nearly as much as it does some people. I suppose I'm just lucky.'

'You are.' Hilary looked wistfully at the little bundle in the cradle. 'I suppose now you've found how easy it is, you'll be having lots more.'

'I think we need time to get used to this one first. Neither of us has any idea how to look after babies, you know. Mrs Dodd has had to give me lessons in everything – bathing, feeding, putting her nappies on, everything. I'm terrified we'll do something wrong.'

'You won't. Mothers always know how to look after their babies. Well, most of them, anyway. After all, what Lucy has told you are the essentials – feed them and bathe them. The other one you know already.'

'What's that?'

'Love them,' Hilary said quietly and, as everyone had done, touched the baby's face very gently, rejoicing in the almost impossibly soft skin of her cheek. 'And this little darling is going to be very easy to love.'

'She is,' Jennifer agreed, reaching out towards the cradle and rocking it slightly. 'It's so strange – she's only five days old and yet she seems to have been a part of us always. I can't imagine being without her now. It makes you feel different, being a mother. More responsible, somehow. I suddenly realised the other day that she's going to be with me all the time now – I can't just walk out of the door and leave her for a few hours, like I can the dog. I just give Tavy a bit of biscuit and tell her to look after the house, I'll be back soon, and she goes to her basket and sleeps till I come back. I can't do that with a baby!'

'Not very well,' Hilary said with a smile. 'But you knew that before you had her.'

'Oh, I *knew* it. But realising it is different somehow. It's real now – it's come true. It's not that I *mind* – quite the opposite. I feel somehow complete now. As if a part of me that's been missing all my life – all my grown-up life, I mean – has suddenly been found and fitted into place.' She was still looking at the baby and didn't see the expression on Hilary's face. By the time she glanced up again, Hilary had recovered herself and was gathering her bags together.

'I nearly forgot – I brought you both a present.' She took out a package wrapped in tissue paper, and Jennifer took it and shook out a long dress of fine white satin overlaid by net embroidered with tiny flowers. She gasped with delight.

'Hilary, that's absolutely beautiful! It will be perfect for a christening robe.' She laid it on the bed and looked up, her eyes wet. 'And we wanted to ask you ... Will you be her godmother? You and your father have done so much for us both, we'd love it if you would.'

'Of course I will.' Hilary bent over the cradle again, hiding her own sudden tears. 'Just to have a part of this little sweetheart will be lovely. Thank you so much.'

She left soon after that, half joyous and half wistful, and walked back through the woods towards the village, glad of a chance to come to terms with her feelings. The perfection of little Mary Susan had taken her by surprise, and the surge of longing she'd felt then for her own child had shaken her. Jennifer's words had struck at her heart. Would she ever feel the completion that Jennifer had spoken of? Would she ever know what it was to hold her own baby in her arms – her baby and David's – and feel that at last their lives were complete?

At least I shall have a god-daughter, she thought, coming out of the trees and pausing to look at the view of Burracombe spread before her: at the cluster of cottages, some with thatched roofs, some with slate; at the sturdy church tower that had stood at the centre of the village for hundreds of years; and at the roof of her own home, Burracombe Barton. At least I have all this – and now a god-daughter as well.

But would that ever be quite enough?

Chapter Twenty-Three

'You mean you're going to London *now*?' Val exclaimed. 'This week? Without even discussing it with me? I thought we agreed we'd talk it over.'

'But we never have,' Luke said. 'Val, I've tried time and time again, but whenever I open the subject you turn away and talk about something else. We can't go on like that for ever.'

Val sighed. 'I thought you'd decided to stay here and paint in the holidays. You've been round at the charcoal burner's hut almost all the time since term ended. Surely you must have painted enough for an exhibition.'

'It's not just that. I need to be *there*. I thought you understood.'

They stared at each other. Then she said flatly, 'So that's it, then. You're going. Whatever I say.'

'It's only for the rest of the holidays.'

'That's three weeks! Three weeks in London by yourself, leaving me here with Chris. And then what happens when you come back? Will you be giving in your notice to leave the school at Christmas?'

There was a brief moment of silence. The question hung in the air between them. Then Luke said quietly, 'It depends what happens in London. I can't say for—'

'So you might! You're thinking of it. You'll come home at the beginning of September and tell me our lives here are over, that I've got to move to London whether I like it or not, that Chris has got to grow up in a city instead of the countryside where he belongs. I won't have any say at all.'

'Val, we've talked and talked . . .'

'You said just now we hadn't talked enough.'

'And *you* said you wouldn't use Chris as a bargaining tool.'

'Oh ...!' Val turned away. Then she wheeled back. 'Luke, I honestly thought you'd given up on the idea. You said so – more or less, anyway. I'd stopped even thinking about it.'

'You believed what you wanted to believe,' he said quietly. 'All right, I have tried. I've tried to put the idea out of my mind. I've tried to tell myself that teaching and holiday painting are enough for me. I've tried to believe that everything I want is here. And it is,' he said quickly as Val began to protest again. 'You and Chris *are* all that I want – as a normal human being. But I'm not quite normal, am I? I've got this other part of me that wants to do something – paint – and wants it so strongly that I can't just pretend it's not there. I can't push it out of sight. I don't know how else to explain it,' he finished miserably. 'If you can't understand, there's nothing else I can say.'

Val was silent. Then she looked up at him and said hopelessly, 'That's it, then, isn't it? There's nothing I can do. You'll go to London, and if you decide to stay – or go back after Christmas, when you've worked your term's notice – I'll have to go with you.'

'You don't have to,' he said in the same quiet tone.

'Of course I do. We can't afford to live in two places. And a wife has to go where her husband does.'

'Not if she really doesn't want to.'

'She does! We're married, Luke. Of course I have to go with you.'

He looked at her for a moment, then said in a slow, heavy tone, 'You don't. You can decide to stay here. Make your own life.'

Val stared at him. 'You mean – you want us to *separate*? Not be married any more?'

'No, of course I don't want that! I love you, Val, and I love Chris. All I'm saying is that if you really don't want to come to London, you don't have to. I wouldn't force you.'

'No,' she said. 'What you're saying is that your painting matters more to you than Chris and I do. If I won't come with you, you'll go anyway, and then I'll have deserted you and you can divorce me.'

'No!' he cried. 'I'm not saying that at all! Of *course* I don't want that.'

'What, then? It seems to me that that's just what you do want.'

Luke ran his fingers through his dark hair. 'You've taken all this much too far, Val. I love you. I'd never want us to part. It's only if *you* wanted it – if maybe you didn't feel I was worth staying married to, if you'd rather be here than come to London ...' He stopped and looked at her, then said, very slowly, 'Maybe the truth is that Burracombe matters to you more than I do.'

They gazed at each other. Then Christopher cried out upstairs and Val turned swiftly away. She pulled open the staircase door and ran up to the bedroom.

When she came down again a few minutes later, Luke had gone.

Luke left early next morning. He caught the bus to Tavistock and then the train to London. He carried with him a large flat case containing as many paintings as he could fit in, and a rucksack containing a few changes of clothes. Val had watched him pack, helpless to change either what had been said or what seemed to be happening.

'I can't believe you're doing this,' she said in a trembling voice. 'I thought we were happy together. I thought we loved each other.'

'We do. We *are* happy. This is nothing to do with any of that.'

'It feels like it, when I see you packing to leave me and go and live in London.'

Luke fastened the straps of his rucksack and straightened up. 'Val, I am *not* leaving you. I am not going to live in London. Not in the way you're saying it. It's just a sort of exploration, to see whether my paintings would sell. Then we can decide what to do – and we'll decide together.'

Val turned away. 'Like we decided together that you'd go now. I don't remember any discussion about that.'

'Val, we've talked and talked—'

'And come to no conclusion. As far as my memory goes, we left it to be discussed later, and then yesterday you just came in and announced that you were going.'

'I didn't announce it. I said I wanted to go and asked you to come too.'

'You knew I wouldn't be able to.'

'Not able to? Why not?'

'Oh, for goodness' sake!' she exclaimed. 'You *know* why not. It's

– it's Chris, it's Mum and Dad, it's – it's everything. I can't just up sticks and go swanning off to London for heaven knows how long. It's all right for you – all you have to do is walk out of the door, knowing I'll be here to to wash up the breakfast things, make the beds, do the washing, keep things going. But if I go too—'

'Val, stop it. You're grabbing at every excuse you can think of. You could have come with me, and you know it.' He stopped and took a step towards her, lifting his hands. 'You still can. Come on, throw a few things into your suitcase and let's go together. It doesn't matter about the washing-up. We can do that when we come back.'

Val stared at him. 'Throw a few things into a suitcase? Have you any idea what you're saying? What about all of Christopher's stuff? His clothes and his nappies, his cup and plate and spoon, his teddy bear, and that's just the start. He needs a suitcase to himself. You're talking absolute nonsense.'

She turned away. Her throat felt tight and her eyes were burning. She could hear the tremble in her voice and knew that in a moment it would crack completely and the tears would come. She stood very still, her hands clenched tightly at her sides, and then took a deep, shuddering breath.

'Just go, Luke,' she said hoarsely. 'Just go and – and do whatever it is you think you have to do. And come back when you're ready. If you're ever ready.'

Luke took a step towards her. 'Val . . .'

'Go!' she cried, stiffening her back and moving quickly away. 'For goodness' sake – just *go*!'

Luke stopped. He hesitated, reached out a tentative hand, then let it fall. He looked uncertainly at the unresponsive back, then picked up his case, shouldered his rucksack and opened the door.

There was a moment of utter stillness. Luke turned once and looked unhappily towards his wife. For a second or two he seemed about to drop his luggage and go back inside. Then, with one more glance at Val's rigid shoulders, he turned away again and stepped on to the path.

Val heard the door close. She stood quite still, wondering if he had indeed left or if he were still in the room, waiting for her to turn; waiting to tell her he wouldn't be going after all, that their lives could continue as they had been until now.

When she turned at last, Luke was gone, and she knew that by now he would be out of sight along the village road, perhaps already aboard the morning bus. She stared unbelievingly around the room, which seemed suddenly comfortless and bare, and burst into tears.

'He just *went*,' she told her mother later. 'He knew I didn't want him to go but he went anyway. He said he wasn't leaving me, but – but it felt as if he was. It felt as if it was the end of everything.'

Alice gazed at her in consternation. She had dropped in on her way to the village shops to see her daughter and grandson and ask if Val needed anything. Now, it seemed she needed far more than anyone had ever suspected.

Her face was blotched with tears, her eyes so swollen and red that she could barely see. Her voice was thick, as if her nose was blocked, and every few minutes she drew in a deep, shuddering breath. She had obviously been crying ever since Luke had left.

'But why has he gone to London? I don't understand.'

'I've *told* you. He thinks he can make pots and pots of money selling his paintings to rich Londoners. It's that one he sold to the man who came to see him a few weeks ago that started it all. He paid a lot of money for it and it's gone to Luke's head. He thinks he's going to be rich and famous and have his paintings in all the best galleries and – and ...'

'Well, perhaps he is,' Alice said uncertainly. 'I mean, I don't know much about art, but I know that some pictures do cost an awful lot of money. Is Luke really good enough?'

'I don't know. I mean, he's good but it all depends what people want. Look at all the painters who only got famous after they were dead. That's not much good when you've only just turned thirty.'

'I know what your father will say,' Alice said, remembering Ted's doubts about Val's marriage to an artist. 'He was so pleased when Luke got the job in the school. Even that didn't seem like proper work to him, to be honest, teaching kiddies to draw, but at least he got a good wage. He's not going to give that up, is he?' she asked with sudden anxiety.

'That's just it, Mum – he says he is. He'll give in his term's notice the first day back. He doesn't even want to stay that long – if he could, he'd drop it straight away. Do you know, I think he might

179

even ask them if he can. There's another art teacher who might be able to take over, if they'll promote him. And if they do, Luke will want to go straight back to London – and he'll want me and Chris to go with him.' She stared wildly at her mother and ran her fingers through her hair so that it stood up like a bird's nest. 'We'll have to leave Burracombe.'

There was a long silence. They sat in the two armchairs, facing each other across the fireplace. Christopher was in his pram under the old apple tree in the garden, cooing at the shifting pattern of leaves against the blue sky. They heard the clop of a horse's hooves in the village street, probably on the way to Alf Coker's forge to be shod. The voices of children sounded as a cluster of them went by. A few sparrows burst into sudden noisy twittering in the bush that touched its leaves against the open window.

'Well then, it seems to me you'll just have to go with him,' Alice said at last.

Val's mouth opened. She stared wordlessly at her mother. At last she said, in a voice that was a mixture of dismay and indignation, 'What do you mean?'

'What I say, of course. I can see you'm upset about it and I can understand that, but Luke's your husband, and if he thinks his place is in London, then your place is with him. I don't see no question about it.'

Fresh tears trickled down Val's cheeks. 'I thought you'd be on my side.'

Alice moved her hand impatiently. 'My stars, Val, this isn't a question of sides. It's as plain as the nose on your face. You married the man, didn't you?'

'Yes, but—'

'Well there you are, then.' Alice folded her hands in her lap and sat back.

'Mother, it's not as easy as that. I thought when we got married that we were going to stay in Burracombe all our lives. Stay with all of you – with everyone I've always known. Bring up our family here. I thought that was what Luke wanted too. Now he's turned everything upside down and I don't know where I am any more.'

'Are you sure it's him who's turned everything upside down?' Alice asked. 'Seems to me you might have taken too much for granted. Look, Val, if you'd wed a local boy, then perhaps you'd have had a right to expect to stay round here, but Luke came from London, not all that long ago, and if you cast your mind back, you'll remember that he never really meant to stay. He only came because Mr Harvey's his godfather and told him about the charcoal burner's cottage. I know you and he knew each other years ago, during the war, but that wasn't why he came – or so you've told me.'

'No, it wasn't,' Val said, regretting once more that she'd ever confided in her mother the truth about her earlier relationship with Luke. 'It was sheer coincidence. But even if he didn't mean to stay at the beginning, he did when we got married. He was as pleased as I was when Jennifer offered us this cottage.'

Alice sighed. 'Val, I don't know much about artists. Luke's the only one I've ever met in my life. But from what I've heard about them, they're never properly happy if they aren't doing what they're good at – painting or playing music, whatever it is. Do you think Luke's been properly happy?'

'Yes, I do. I thought he'd got everything he wanted. Me, Chris, our home here and time to paint in the holidays. Why can't that be good enough?'

'I don't know, my dear. But then I'm not an artist.'

Val frowned. 'But Luke could still be an artist. He has been. I've never stopped him painting. He's had all the holidays, evenings, weekends. Maybe not as much since Chris was born, but he can't expect that. And now he's gone. It's as if he just doesn't care about us any more.' She burst into tears again.

Alice waited a minute or two, then got up and went over to kneel beside Val's chair. She put her arms around her daughter, and Val turned and wept against her shoulder. They stayed like that until the sobbing began to abate and Val fumbled for a hanky and mopped her face.

'You'm going to make yourself ill if you go on like this,' Alice said quietly. 'Now, just calm down and I'll make us both a cup of tea, and then we'll have a bit more talk.'

She went out to the kitchen, and Val heard her fill the kettle and get cups down from the dresser. After a while, she came back bearing a tray laid with a gingham cloth and holding a teapot, jug, sugar bowl and two cups and saucers. She set it on the side table, poured the tea and handed a cup to Val before taking hers to the other chair.

'Now then,' she said, stirring her tea and taking a sip, 'you got to look at this sensibly. From the way you been carrying on, anyone would think Luke had left you for good.'

'He might have done, if we can't——'

'No, you listen to me. All he's done, from what I can make out, is go to London for a week or two to see if he can make a living from his paintings. Us knows he's sold quite a few already, so maybe he can and I don't see nothing wrong with that. It's what he came to Burracombe for in the first place, after all.'

'But things are different now.'

'Yes, they are, and he's done his best to fit in with what you wanted. He's got a teaching job and painted in his spare time, more like a hobby. But it's not a hobby, is it? Not to Luke.'

'No, but——'

'I don't pretend to know anything about art,' Alice said, overriding Val's interruptions. 'But to me it seems plain enough. Like I just said, he've done his best to fit in with what you want, and maybe now it's time for you to fit in with him.'

Val looked at her. 'You mean you think I should go to London? Leave you and all the family, and everyone I know? And not even be sure that he can make enough money to support us?'

'If Luke had been living in London when you first met him,' Alice said, 'would you have married him and lived there then?'

Val was silent. She gazed into her tea, then said, 'But it's different now.'

'Oh, for pity's sake, stop saying things are different now!' Alice exclaimed in exasperation. 'Things are always different! Life changes all the time. You ought to know that, with all the travelling you did during the war. You've been away from home before, you've been in the forces, you've been to Egypt, and we don't need to talk about what you did there. Why is it such a disaster for you to leave Burracombe now?'

'Because things *are* different now! Because we've got Christopher. Because I thought we were settled.'

'Then perhaps you shouldn't have thought that,' Alice retorted. 'Perhaps you should have thought a bit more about what your husband wanted. And since you don't seem to have done that so far, perhaps you ought to start now. Perhaps you ought to think about what it means to be his wife – to be married at all. Luke wants to look after you and your baby in the way he knows best, and if that means going to London, that's what he must do. And 'tis your duty, as his wife, to go with him.'

'I never thought you'd say that,' Val said in a quavering voice. 'I thought you'd want me to stay here.'

'Well of *course* I'd rather you were here, all three of you. But that's what happens when your children get married. Sometimes they stays nearby and sometimes they moves away. Whatever you and Luke decide to do, it won't be for me and your father to have any say in it.'

'You didn't take that attitude with Jackie.'

'No, because that really is different. Jackie's under twenty-one and still our responsibility. It stands to reason us wouldn't want her to go jaunting off to America, and we'm still not happy about the situation. But you're a grown woman, and a married one too, and you have to make your own life, without our interference.'

'You don't think you're interfering now, then?' Val flashed. 'Taking Luke's side against me. Maybe you'd rather I went away. Maybe you're fed up with having us around Burracombe.'

'Now you'm just being silly,' Alice said coldly. She got up and picked up the shopping basket she had set down inside the door. 'I'll be on my way now, since it seems there's no more to say. But I hope you'll think about what we've been saying. You've got a good man there and you'd be a fool to let this drive a wedge between you.'

She departed, leaving Val sitting in her chair, staring at the empty fireplace. At last the clock struck twelve, and she stirred and went slowly to the kitchen to prepare Christopher's lunch.

Her mother's words rang in her ears. Her duty, as Luke's wife, to go with him. Not just to London, but wherever he chose to go. Anywhere in the world.

It's not simply a case of duty, though, she thought. It's a question of love as well. If I loved Luke, really loved him, with my heart and soul and being, as I believed I did, I wouldn't even hesitate. So what does all this actually mean?

And if he really loved me, with his heart and soul and being, would he even have contemplated doing this? What does it mean for us both?

She felt as if she were gazing down a road that led to their future, a road that had always stretched clear and inviting straight ahead. But now it had twisted suddenly, and what might lie round the corner made her heart sink with dread.

Chapter Twenty-Four

Alice hurried along the village street, her heart thumping. She was by no means as confident of her words as she had given Val to believe, and she knew that Ted's view was likely to be rather different. He had never liked the idea of his daughter being married to an artist, and although Luke had redeemed himself by taking the teacher's job in Tavistock, this latest development would put him right back where he'd started.

She had gone past the village shop before she remembered that she'd come out to buy some groceries. Turning back, she saw Ivy Sweet going in, and her heart sank. She was in no mood to encounter Ivy this morning, but there wasn't time to do anything else now. Minnie was waiting for a block of lard to make pastry for a meat pie, and if she dallied any longer, it would never be ready for the men's dinner.

'Oh, hello, Alice,' Ivy said with a smile as sweet as her name. 'How be you this morning? I saw your Val's man off catching the bus earlier on. Had a big case and a haversack with him. Going on holiday, are they? Only I was surprised not to see her and the baby too. I suppose they'm following on later.'

'No, they're not,' Alice replied tersely. She would have preferred not to answer at all, but with several other people hearing every word, you had to be careful what you said. 'Luke's had to go to London on business. He'll not be away long.'

'Oh, that's good. It would be a shame to see things go wrong for those two, and them with such a lovely little baby, too. So your Val won't be going to live up there, then?'

Alice gasped. How did these rumours get round? She was sure that Val had said nothing to anyone but her, and that only this morning. Maybe someone – Ivy herself, in all probability – had been passing the cottage when Val and Luke were arguing. She remembered that they'd been talking this morning with the windows open. Anyone could have heard what they were saying, especially if they took the trouble to dawdle by the front hedge. She made a mental note to remind Val to be more careful.

'I don't know what their plans are,' she said now. ''Tis their business what they do, and I dare say if they got anything to tell me they'll do it in their own time. I wouldn't dream of interfering.'

'I'm sure you wouldn't,' Ivy said with a nasty smile. 'Us can see that by the way you let your Jackie go gadding all over the world. I'll take a packet of ten Players too, please, Edie,' she added to the woman behind the counter. 'And a box of matches.'

'Dr Latimer was saying the other day how cigarettes are bad for you,' Alice remarked to no one in particular. 'The scientists reckon they might cause a lot of illness. I wouldn't be surprised if it's true. It stands to reason – anything that can turn your fingers that dirty yellow colour can't be good for your insides.'

Ivy flushed and turned to go, picking up her basket. She stalked out of the shop and the other customers laughed.

'You two always put each other's backs up,' Aggie Madge said. 'I reckon it goes back a long way, too. I don't remember a time when you weren't scratching one another's eyes out whenever you met.'

'I wouldn't demean myself,' Alice said with dignity.

Jacob Prout, who had come in for his Woodbines but was now examining his own fingers with some anxiety, said, 'I reckon it's all to do with your Ted, isn't it, Alice? Ivy had an eye for him ever since she were a little'n, and then you come along to work for his mother in the farmhouse and after that he never looked at another girl. I don't reckon her's ever forgive you.'

'That's as maybe,' Alice said. 'And if you've finished your shopping, I need to do mine. Mother's waiting for the lard to make a pie. That's a pound block, please, Edie, and a tin of golden syrup so she can make a treacle tart as well for tomorrow.'

'You should have asked Ivy for a loaf of stale bread for the crumbs,' someone sniggered. The others laughed, but Alice gave them a cold look.

'I've no quarrel with George. He's a good baker and a good man and I reckon he've a lot to put up with. All that hair dye Ivy uses, for one thing!' And she took her groceries from Edie, paid for them and marched out without another word.

Dottie Friend was walking down the street as Alice made her way back to the farm, and the two of them stopped for a chat. In truth, Alice would as soon have gone home without speaking to another soul, but she couldn't ignore Dottie. She was afraid that her old friend's shrewd eyes would notice her agitation, but Dottie had other matters on her mind.

'I had a letter from Maddy today,' she announced, almost before they'd finished wishing each other good morning. 'She says they're settling in wonderful. They've got a nice little apartment, with everything you need, and lots of other young couples all around them from the air station, so they'm making plenty of friends. They go swimming almost every day and it hardly ever seems to rain. It must do sometimes, of course, or it'd be all desert, but so far it's been lovely. She sounds as happy as a lark.'

'That's good,' Alice said, trying to summon up some enthusiasm. 'It's time that maid had some happiness. Her had a bad time when her first young man died so cruel. But she and Mr Stephen will do well together.'

Dottie nodded, her rosy face beaming. 'Maybe by the time they come back they'll have a little bundle of joy to show round the village. But are you all right, Alice? You'm looking a bit peaky, if you don't mind me saying so.'

Alice sighed. 'To tell you the truth, Dottie, I'm worried about our Val. I wouldn't say anything to anyone else, but Luke's gone off to London for a week or two, and she's a bit upset about it. If you ask me, she's making too much of it, but I don't see at the moment how it's going to be sorted out.'

'Oh dear.' Dottie gazed at her. 'There's nothing *really* wrong, is there? I mean, he hasn't gone off in – well, you know – a huff or anything?'

'No, nothing like that. It's to do with his painting. Keep it to yourself, Dottie, if you don't mind, although from what I heard in the shop just now, half the village knew he'd gone before I did anyway.'

She hurried on, and Dottie continued on her way towards the shop, eager to impart her own news. Most of the villagers had known Maddy as a little girl, when she had lived with Dottie during the war, and had seen her grow to a pretty young woman. Since she'd married Stephen Napier, they were even more interested in her, and Edie, who was on her own in the shop now, listened with a broad smile on her face.

'It's good to see a happy ending. It don't happen to everyone.' She gave Dottie a cautious glance. 'You didn't happen to run into Alice Tozer on your way here, I suppose? Her Val seems to be a bit at sixes and sevens just now, from all accounts.'

'Not from Alice's, though,' Dottie replied, consulting her shopping list. 'It don't do any good repeating rumours, Edie, as you and I know, and I'm sure you'll put a stop to any you hear in this shop.'

'Oh, I will, of course I will,' Edie said hastily. There was a look in Dottie's eye that dared her to continue with the subject. 'Was that plain or self-raising flour you wanted?'

'Plain, of course. I never use self-raising, as you should know by now – a teaspoon of tartaric acid and one of bicarbonate for a pound of flour is just as good, and you can alter the amounts to suit what you'm baking. You don't even need that baking powder you got on your shelves then. And some cornflour too, for making parsley sauce. I got Felix and Stella coming over for their dinner today and I'm giving them a bit of fish.'

'And there's another happy ending,' Edie said sentimentally. 'They went through a lot too, before they came to theirs. But you know what they say – the path of true love never did run smooth. Maybe that's why you and me are both still spinsters, Dottie!'

Dottie laughed, forgiving Edie for her attempt to be nosy about Val and Luke. It was natural in a village for folk to want to know each other's business. 'I suppose we both had our chances, but it never panned out right for us somehow. Still, I reckon us have fared well enough just the same, don't you?'

Edie, who had a friendship with Bert Foster that nobody could ever quite figure out, blushed and turned away to fetch the flour down from the shelf. Dottie put it into her basket with the rest of her groceries, then paid and went on her way.

Happy endings, she thought. Did anyone ever really know if they had theirs? Edie and Bert, for instance – why they didn't get married, nobody could understand. And herself and Joe Tozer – two chances she'd had there, one when she was a young girl and then again in the past year when he'd persuaded her to go back with him to America for a visit and wanted her to stay. Maybe that would have been her happy ending, but she'd felt on both occasions that she could never have been happy away from Burracombe. So perhaps she had hers anyway – here and now.

As for Val and Luke, and even Maddy and Stephen, they were still at the beginning of their lives. How could you say it was a happy ending when it had only just begun? Who knew what they might face in the future?

As she pondered, she saw Hilary Napier coming down the street leading her horse, Beau. Now there was someone who really needed a happy ending, she thought, but she seemed to have little chance of finding one.

Hilary waved to Dottie but was relieved when the little woman turned in at her gate without stopping to chat. She was taking Beau to Alf Coker's forge to have new shoes. He had caught one on the fence in his paddock and pulled it off, and he was almost due for a new set anyway. While Alf was working, she would go down to the old bridge by the ford and have a few quiet moments to think.

David had rung that morning and asked her to go to London again to meet him. At first Hilary had hesitated, remembering the frustration of their last meeting, but she had known that she would go. Either they continued to love each other and strive to be together somehow, or they must part and make an end of all hope. She dreaded the pain of doing that, but always in her mind there lurked a fear that this was what it would come to. And when David declined to tell her the reason why he wanted them to meet, she wondered with a stab of anguish if this was what he meant to do.

Sybil's death should have made things easier, she thought as, having delivered Beau to the forge, she leaned over the low parapet of the old stone bridge and gazed into the tumbling waters of the brook. But distance and responsibility seemed to create just as impassable a barrier as the difficult marriage that David had endured. And what had made it worse, she realised, was the fact that he was a doctor. Almost any other profession could have overlooked a divorce, even a scandalous one, but a doctor was especially vulnerable.

The water flowed swiftly below the bridge, its undulating surface as sinuous as a snake as it wound over and around rocks worn smooth by centuries of its constant caressing. On some rocks, large enough to break the surface, it flung itself in a flurry of spray and shimmering droplets, always the same yet always subtly different, while where it ran smooth, it was clear enough to show a gleaming bed of pebbles and the occasional swift flicker of a small fish.

Once, when Hilary had looked over, she had seen the body of a salmon, half eaten and left on one of the bigger rocks. An otter, she supposed, either sated or disturbed at his meal. It was a big fish, on its way up the Burra and probably into the Tavy to spawn. She had walked more times than she could count along the banks of both rivers, all the way up to the wild forgotten glory of Tavy Cleave, hidden between the shoulders of the great tors. For its entire length, from source to estuary, where it met the Tamar, the river Tavy passed only through beauty, and it took the Burra Brook and other small tributaries with it.

Was David about to ask her to leave all this and go and live with him?

Hilary had never been to Derby. Apart from its being a city, she had no idea what it was like, but she knew that it encompassed the Peak District, where there was also wild and beautiful scenery and rivers such as this. She would not be imprisoned in city streets, with no way to reach the countryside that was in her bones. But her daily life would not be in the countryside; it would be in the house where David had grown up, where he worked with his father in a city practice, and she would never walk her horse down the street to have him shod less than a mile from her own front door.

Was she prepared to give all this up to be with him?

You never really know how you will react until the moment comes, she thought. Until a person died, or a baby was born – she had been quite unprepared for the rush of emotion she had felt on seeing Jennifer's baby for the first time – or someone asked you to change your life for them. She might spend hours of each day and each night working through her problems, and even believe she had arrived at an answer, but she could not be absolutely certain until the question had been asked.

She sighed and turned away from the bridge. It was time to go back. She thanked Alf and took Beau's reins in her hand, using the mounting block to swing herself into the saddle. The horse's feet felt firm, his back as comfortable as an armchair. She walked him up the street, and then, instead of going straight back home, swung him up the little lane that would take them to the open moor.

A gallop always did them both good. Even if it did not give her answers, the exhilaration of speed and the rush of air past her cheeks would bring respite to her heart.

Chapter Twenty-Five

Percy Shillabeer had done as he had threatened. On Sunday morning, he locked his wife in the farmhouse and rode his old bike to Tavistock, leaving it at the bus station in Plymouth Road in order to catch the bus. The children were in the house too and gathered round their mother, anxious and fearful as they heard the key turn in the lock.

'Why has Daddy locked us in?' asked Milly, the youngest girl, speaking round the thumb she held firmly in her mouth. 'Us haven't done nothing wrong, have us?'

'No, my bird, it's just to keep us safe till he comes back from church,' Ann said, though her heart was thumping with fear. Percy had been so strange lately, either silent and glowering or ranting about children of sin and quoting passages from the Bible that she had never heard before, all about punishment and retribution. She was half afraid that he had abandoned them for ever and that they would die here, neglected and forgotten.

'But why hasn't he took us to church as well? Us always goes to church on a Sunday morning.'

'Daddy's gone to a new church in Plymouth. I expect he'll take us too when he's sure it's the right place.' Ann had no wish to go to the Exclusives meeting, but she would face that problem when it arose. Her hope was that once Percy had been to a meeting, they would lose their appeal for him and he would return to the village church. Then perhaps Mr Copley would be able to have some influence over him and return him to gentler ways.

Meanwhile, she had plenty to do. Percy would expect his dinner to be ready for him when he returned some time after one o'clock, and Bert Foster over in Burracombe had let her have a nice piece of pork to roast. She had picked the beans and peas to go with it yesterday, and had dug some potatoes and young carrots. The preparations would take most of the morning, and she would make a sponge pudding for afters. Percy liked a sponge pudding with custard, and the children would enjoy it too. A good dinner after his long morning out might put him in a better frame of mind.

She scrubbed the potatoes and carrots and prepared the peas and beans. She had grown the vegetables herself, in the garden where she found her only real pleasure. Seldom going far from the farm, she had felt at peace as she dug and planted, while harvesting the fruits of her labours had given her a deep satisfaction. Percy could not accuse her of being a burden and an encumbrance when she could put food on the table almost entirely grown by herself. Not that that always stopped him.

By eleven, when Percy's meeting would be beginning, she had done all the vegetables and made the sponge pudding. At this time of a Sunday morning she too would usually have been in church with all the family, listening to the gentle notes of the organ begin as the bells stopped pealing, as they had stopped a few moments ago. People would be wondering where the Shillabeer family were, she thought. They never missed church, the whole family washed and brushed and in their best clothes as they filed into their pew. She wished she were there now, sitting quietly with her children, Percy beside her, silent for once except when bellowing out the hymns or joining in the prayers with his loud Amen. As if you needed to shout at God, who could see right into your heart and needed no thundering voice.

What did God see when he looked in Percy's heart?

Percy would not be home for at least two hours. The sun shone outside and the children were restless and fidgety, wanting to be in the fresh air. They were not allowed to play many of their games on a Sunday – no rushing about or shouting – but they were allowed, after church and again in the afternoon, to put on old clothes and go down to the fields where they had set up a small camp out of sight of the house. She would have let them go down there now if the door had been left unlocked.

'Can't us climb out of the window?' begged Ben, the eldest boy. 'We'd be back before dinner. He'd never know.'

Ann hesitated. That would be a deception, and deception was a sin, especially when it involved deceiving your father. But the children had done nothing wrong and didn't deserve to be locked up like this. Wasn't that a sin too? And if she let them go, she could take the sin for herself. Percy would be only too willing to punish her.

'All right,' she said. 'You can go out through the back kitchen window, but make sure you'm back in time to get your hands and faces washed, and don't do anything silly.'

'We won't!' They scrambled out through the window and disappeared through the yard like animals escaping from a zoo. Poor little tackers, she thought, half inclined to climb through after them. It's cruel, caging up little children like that on a fine summer's day. It surely can't be God's will.

Now on her own, she glanced around for something else to do. Percy forbade work on Sundays, apart from the necessary tasks involved in feeding him and the family, and certain gentle pursuits such as needlework, which might include the repair of his clothes or the darning of his socks. But Percy wasn't here and neither was anyone else, and if it was a sin to give the boys' bedroom a good clear-out and the floor a bit of a scrub, she'd talk it over herself with God come Judgement Day, if he didn't have anything better to deal with when that day arrived. With two world wars behind them, not to mention all the other sins of the world Percy was constantly harping on about, she had a feeling that he would.

The task took longer than she had anticipated, but she didn't notice the flying time and had started on the girls' room when she heard a sudden commotion downstairs. Hastily scrambling to her feet, she scurried to the landing to look down at the grandfather clock at the foot of the stairs and realised to her horror that it must have struck not only twelve, but one as well. How had she never heard it? Worse still, the back door stood wide open and the increasing pandemonium was the sound of her husband's voice raised in fury, and the pleas and weeping of the children as they scrambled panic-stricken for the back kitchen window, only to find their father waiting inside to harangue and chastise them for their wickedness.

'Children of sin and spawn of the Devil, that's what you all are,' Percy declaimed as the family stood pale and frightened before him. 'And you'll be punished. It's given to me as your father to punish you and see that you walk in the paths of righteousness from this day.' The phrases rolled from his tongue with relish, and he fingered his belt as if he would enjoy what he did.

Ann shivered, then spoke up. 'You don't need to punish them, Percy. They're just children, and children need to play out in the fresh air. I'll take their punishment, yes, and mine too if you think I warrant it. Though how any of us could sin more than you have, locking us up like prisoners, I don't know!'

Percy wheeled round. 'What's that? You accuse me of sin? Me, who will be accepted into the Exclusive Brethren and—'

'Oh, don't say you've joined them!' Ann exclaimed. 'Percy, whatever be the matter with our own church, that's stood there hundreds of years, and our own nice young vicar? Why can't we go there like us always have?'

'Us haven't always gone there. If you remember, us used to be chapel folk, and 'tis a pity us ever left. But the Exclusives ...' He seemed for the moment to have forgotten talk of punishment, and to her surprise she saw that he was addressing her as a normal human being, someone to be talked to, reasoned with, rather than as the object of labour he generally seemed to consider her. 'They'll show us the path to salvation. Once we'm Exclusives, everyone else will be outsiders, and as long as we stay apart from them, we'll be saved. Everyone else is full of sin, Ann, as the world is full of sin, and though it be a difficult path to follow, as long as we tread the ways of the Lord, we shall be with him in the Kingdom of Heaven.'

'What do you mean – stay apart?' she asked, dread entering her soul as she gazed into his burning eyes.

'Apart, that's what I mean. We must not meet or talk to any person who is not an Exclusive. We must have no dealings with them. We must not listen to the wireless or go to the cinema or theatre' – they never did these things anyway – 'or own a pet or take out life insurance. From now on, we walk the paths of righteousness, knowing only those who know the Lord as we know Him, and salvation will be ours.'

Ann gazed at him. 'You've been told to say these words, Percy. *They've* told you to say them. You can't really believe them. Not listen to the wireless? Not that we can, now you've broke the one we had. Not have a pet? How is that what God wants? And what about our Tommy, that the kiddies had as a kitten and love so much? Do you mean to tell me that God thinks it's wrong to have him?'

'Yes, I do!' he roared, so loudly that they all jumped and the youngest children began to cry again. 'The barn cats, we'll keep they because they keep down the vermin and never come indoors, but that kitten is an abomination and he's going. He's going now!'

He strode across the kitchen, snatched the small ginger cat, only half grown, from its cushion and marched over to the sink. Before Ann realised what he meant to do, he had picked up the bucket of water she had drawn from the well before he went out and plunged the terrified creature inside. Its frightened miaowing was suddenly cut short and the water churned with its struggles.

The children screamed and Ann rushed to her husband's side.

'Percy, no! You can't do that! You can't drown the poor little dear! He've done nothing wrong, and isn't he one of God's creatures too? Let me take him away, find him another home, or let him live in the barn with the other cats, but don't do this – 'tis cruel.'

She tried to drag at his arms, but it was like trying to move a tree and Percy shook her off as easily as if she were a fly. The kitten's struggles were feebler now and in a moment ceased entirely. The water slowly settled down and the only sounds were the crying of the children and Ann's sobs. Percy waited a few moments longer, then lifted out the limp, shrunken body, its fur darkened and bedraggled by the water.

'Oh, Percy,' Ann said, covering her face with her hands. 'Whatever have you done? And in front of our little ones, too.' She turned away and sank on to one of the chairs around the big kitchen table, and held out her arms to the children, who clustered about her, shrinking away from their father. 'How could you be so cruel?'

'Cruel?' he bellowed, planting himself in front of them all and looming over the little group. 'I'm cleansing this house of sin, that's what I'm doing. How can that be cruel?' He tossed the tiny body out of the open window. 'We'll all be the better for it, and so you'll come to understand when you've been saved like I have. When you come to the meeting next week—'

'I'm coming to no meeting!' she flared, leaping to her feet to confront him. 'I don't know what they'm teaching you, Percy, but it's not the ways of God, not the God I've always known and loved, the God our vicar talks about in his sermons. You go if you must, but I won't go with you and neither will our young ones. And I won't stay locked in of a Sunday morning either. I want to go to our own church, same as I always have done. And so I will.'

Percy took a step back. Ann had faced up to him few times, but never like this, shouting into his face as if he were a mile away, and sounding so determined. For a moment he hesitated, then he lunged at her and gripped both shoulders, shaking her like a disobedient puppy. The children cried out and Ben pulled at his father's trousers, but Percy kicked him away. He flung Ann back into her chair and stood over her.

'You're my wife and you'll do as I say. Remember the vows you made in church – to love, honour and obey. *Obey!*'

'And you vowed to love, honour and *cherish*,' Ann retorted, trembling but determined not to give way, the thread of steel that had been buried for so long, but had emerged in Patsy, uncoiling like a thin, toughened snake inside her. 'I've obeyed you ever since that day, but you've never cherished me once, not once ...'

There was a silence. They stared at each other, he with fury in his eyes, she with defiance. The children watched, silent now with fear.

'All right,' he snapped at last, turning away. 'Have it your own way. But remember this – as long as you refuse to come to the meeting with me, you're an outsider. And that means you don't eat with me, you don't share the same table or the same room. I won't speak to you, nor have any kind of contact with you, except that I must and need.' She knew well enough what he meant by that. 'And if I decide you must be locked in for the good of your own soul and salvation, then locked in you will be. You're to speak to nobody outside this family. You're to stay here on the farm and you're to have no visitors. Not the vicar, not your sister, not the doctor nor the schoolteacher. And especially not that hussy you call your daughter, bringing her evil ways and her Devil's spawn here.'

He sat down heavily in his own chair at the head of the table.

'I'll have my dinner now, wife, if you've seen it your duty to cook it for me. The rest of you can eat in the scullery.'

Chapter Twenty-Six

The skiffle group now met two evenings a week in Jack Pettifer's shed. It had to be Tuesdays, because Jack went to the British Legion club in Tavistock then, and Fridays because he would be at ringing practice. Otherwise he liked the use of the shed for himself – for mending the family's shoes, doing a bit of woodwork or other chores – and sometimes Bob did little jobs in there too.

'I don't think much of that song you wrote, Roy,' Vic said disparagingly. 'The lines are all different lengths and it don't even rhyme.'

'It's not meant to. It's a song, not a piece of poetry. It'll sound all right when it's got its own tune.'

'What is the tune, then?' Reg asked, balancing Felix's guitar on his knee in a surprisingly professional pose.

'I don't know, do I! I just wrote the words.'

They gazed at him. 'You mean you think one of us should write the tune?' Bob asked at last.

'Well, of course. All song writers work in pairs. One does the words and the other one does the tune. Like Rodgers and Hart and George and Ira Gershwin.'

'Was she his sister or his wife?' Reg enquired. 'I've always wondered about that.'

Roy stared at him. 'Was who whose sister or wife?'

'Ira Gershwin. Was she George Gershwin's sister or was she—'

'She wasn't either!' Roy snapped in exasperation. 'She wasn't even a she. I mean *he* wasn't even a she – Ira Gershwin is a man. He was George Gershwin's brother. I think,' he added a little doubt-fully.

'Go on, that can't be right. Ira's a girl's name. I mean, who'd call a boy Ira? Can you imagine walking round Burracombe with people shouting out "Ira" at you? You've got that wrong, Roy.'

'I haven't and I'll prove it to you. Anyway, that's not the point. The point is, one person writes the lyrics—'

'The what?'

'The *words*, dumbo. And the other one writes the music and they jiggle it all about a bit until it all fits and then everyone sings it, and if it gets on the wireless you get famous. So I've written the words and now it's up to one of you to make up the tune to fit.'

They looked at each other.

'I don't reckon I could do that,' Reg said. 'I can't even remember the tunes other people have written.'

'Well you're going to be a lot of use in a band, aren't you! What about you, Bob?'

'I might be able to do it on my mouth organ. I do sort of make up tunes on it quite a lot.' He took the instrument from his pocket and began to try out a few notes, his brow furrowed as he studied the words Roy had written. After several false starts and a couple of attempts that went wrong in the middle and were difficult for his listeners to tell apart, he took it from his lips and said in a complain-ing voice, 'I can't do it with you all staring at me.'

'You'll have to do it with people staring at you when we perform in public,' Roy pointed out. 'You might as well get used to it now.'

'I didn't think that last bit sounded too bad,' Reg said, trying to encourage his friend. 'Try it again.'

Bob, who had no idea what he had just played, tried again. He then thought he had a better idea and varied the notes so that the song went from very deep to very high. At that moment, the shed door opened and Brenda walked in.

'My stars, I thought someone was strangling Mrs Pettifer's cat. Whatever are you doing, Bob?'

'He's making up music,' Vic explained. 'To go with this song Roy's written. Here, you have a look, since you'll be singing it.'

Brenda took the paper and scanned it quickly before pushing it back at him. 'You don't really expect me to sing this tosh, do you? I thought we were going to do proper songs.'

'It is a proper song,' Roy said indignantly.

'Well it don't look like one to me. The lines are all different lengths.'

'So they are in proper songs. If you wrote the words of one down, you'd see that. It's the tune that makes them work, but if none of us can write a tune … I suppose you couldn't do it yourself, Brenda? Make it up as you go along, like a jazz singer?'

'No, I couldn't. And I'm not going to try. I've been practising the ukulele all week and I've got some songs I reckon we could sing a lot better than that.' She produced several sheets of paper torn from an exercise book and handed them around. 'Let's try one of these.'

The boys looked at them doubtfully.

'These are Hank Williams songs.'

'That's right. Mr Copley said they'd be good for us, didn't he, Reg? Look, maybe we can try doing our own later on, but let's do these to start with. I like this one – "Your Cheatin' Heart". I've been practising it a bit – singing, I mean. We all know the tune, so why not have a go?'

'I suppose us could,' Bob said doubtfully. He put his mouth organ to his lips again and played a few bars of the song.

'Hey, that's good, Bob!' Vic exclaimed. 'You never said you could play hillbilly.'

Bob rolled his eyes. 'You knew I could play the mouth organ. I can play pretty nearly any tune if you just say the name.'

The others gazed at him with new respect.

'Right, that's it, then,' Vic said, taking charge. 'Bob plays the tune and Brenda accompanies him on the ukulele, since she's been practising it, and she can sing as well. Reg, have you been practising the guitar?'

'I can only strum it,' Reg said anxiously. 'But Mr Copley said that'd be all right.'

'Well, it might be. We'll have to see. I'll be strumming too, on the tea chest.' Vic displayed his instrument with some pride. He plucked at one of the wire strings and it twanged obediently. 'It took a bit of doing, getting them tuned up right, I can tell you, but

I can play a few tunes on it already.' He plucked again and they all recognised 'Three Blind Mice' and then, with a bit of concentration, 'Happy Birthday to You' and the National Anthem.

'They'm not exactly hillbilly, Vic,' Reg remarked.

'They're not meant to be. They were just to show I got the notes there. Let's have a go at this Hank Williams song, then.'

A few minutes later, the shed was resounding to a somewhat tattered version of the country song, and Nancy Pettifer, sitting out in the garden with Patsy as they topped and tailed a bowl of late gooseberries, raised her eyes to heaven.

'Whatever will those young chaps be up to next? Still, I suppose it's better than strangling chickens – even if it do sound just like it!'

Terry could hear the skiffle group too. He was in the bedroom he shared with Patsy, reading up on the latest notes he had made about domestic electricity. He went to night school in Tavistock once a week and had a half-day at the local technical college to get his qualifications as an electrician. He listened to the faltering progress of 'Your Cheatin' Heart' and thought wistfully of the fun his brother and the others were having. No worries or responsibilities, no anxiety about a young wife about to have a baby, enough money to go out for a drink or to the pictures ... Terry wasn't even old enough to go to the pub, yet he felt a hundred years old compared with his elder brother.

It wasn't that he regretted falling in love with Patsy. He still thought she was the loveliest girl in the world, and the only one for him. He wasn't sorry they were married, either – who could be? He wasn't even sorry about the baby, which would bring even more responsibility and care to his shoulders. He just wished it could have all happened two or three years later, when he'd finished his apprenticeship and was earning a living wage. He was miserably aware that at present his parents were supporting his wife more than he was.

I shouldn't have let her talk me into it, he thought for the hundredth time. But I did and so I can't blame her. I was the one who should have stood firm.

He heard a tap on the door and his father's voice. 'Are you in there, Terry?'

'Yes, Dad. It's all right, you can come in.'

Jack Pettifer entered. It was British Legion night and as a rule he would have stayed on for a pint or two before cycling home with the other Legion members from the village. Terry looked at him, wondering why he was back early.

Jack glanced over Terry's shoulder at the work he was doing, then sat down on the end of the bed.

'Glad to see you'm not slacking on your job. You're going to need your qualifications.'

'I know.' Again Terry wondered why his father was here and why he was concerning himself with Terry's work. He knew that he was taking it seriously. 'You don't have to worry, Dad. I'm going to get through the exams all right.'

Jack sighed and rubbed his chin. 'I know that, boy. I never had any worries about you or Bob on that score.' He was silent for a moment, then he said, 'Look, I heard summat at the Legion tonight and I don't like it. It's summat you ought to know.'

Terry gazed at him. He felt a sinking sensation in his chest. Whatever this was, it wasn't going to be good.

'It's Percy Shillabeer,' Jack said at last. 'Some of the chaps from Little Burracombe were at the Legion tonight and there's a lot of talk going round about him. Seems he's left the church and started going into Plymouth to some sort of Sunday meeting. None of the chaps were too sure what it was, but they reckon it might be the Plymouth Brethren.'

Terry felt bemused. 'The who?'

'Plymouth Brethren. One chap thought they might be called the Exclusives, but nobody knows if that's the same lot. Whatever they are, they're very strict.'

'How d'you mean, strict?'

'They take the view that they're the only ones that are going to be saved, as they call it, and all the rest of us will be damned.'

'Oh.' Terry tried to take this in. 'Well, Mr Shillabeer's always been a bit like that. All sort of fire and brimstone. And if he goes off to Plymouth on Sunday mornings, maybe Patsy could slip over to see her mother then. I could go with her.'

Jack shook his head. 'He locked his wife in the house last Sunday when he went to this meeting, and apparently he means to go on

203

doing it. And he makes her eat her food in the kitchen, and she's not allowed off the farm. Ever.'

Terry stared at him. 'How d'you know about this? Has Mr Shillabeer been telling folk?'

'He won't talk to nobody, except when he got to, for farm business and such. It was Ann who got the word out. Her sister Edna from up Mary Tavy went round to see her one day and Ann told her all about it. Luckily Percy was out, but Edna says she was like a cat on hot bricks the whole time in case he came back and found Edna there. Edna's married to George Lillywhite, one of our Legion members, and he was telling us about it.'

'He can't keep that up, surely,' Terry said. 'He'll get tired of it and go back to the church.'

'I dunno,' Jack said. 'Some of these religious people are almost fanatics, and Percy's the sort who could easy go that way. I thought you ought to know, anyway, before Patsy gets to hear about it. It might mean she can't go over to see her mother at all.'

'But Mrs Shillabeer ... How's she going to manage? And what about the rest of the family? He can't stop them going to school.'

'You don't know what a bloke like Percy Shillabeer might do when he gets the bit between his teeth,' Jack said. He sat in silence for a moment or two, and then they heard voices downstairs as his wife and Patsy came in from the garden. The din from the shed had ceased and, looking out of the window, Terry saw Brenda Culliford emerge and set off along the lane, her ukulele case slung on her back. The young men came out after her and walked off in the direction of the inn.

Jack got up and laid his hand on Terry's shoulder.

'Don't worry too much about it, son,' he advised. 'I dare say it'll all come out in the wash. You're probably right, he'll get tired of it or have a row with them and stop all this malarkey, but I thought you ought to know what's going on, for Patsy's sake.'

'Thanks.' Terry stared out of the window. Twilight – the 'dimpsy light' – was casting its shadows across the garden, and the blackbird that had been competing with the skiffle group (and would have won hands down, Terry thought, if there'd been a competition) had fallen silent. His mother would be getting a bit of supper ready down in the kitchen and Patsy would be helping, unless she'd been ordered to sit down and take it easy. In a minute, he and his father would be called down to eat cheese on toast and drink cocoa.

'I don't see as he ought to be allowed to go on like that, all the same,' he said at last. 'Somebody ought to do summat about it. I tell you what, Dad, if he upsets my Patsy any more, I'm going to go over there and give him what for.'

Chapter Twenty-Seven

'It's my father,' David said. They were in a small restaurant off the Strand, driven indoors by heavy rain. Their main course had arrived and they were picking their way through a lamb casserole.

Hilary paused with her fork halfway to her mouth. 'He's not ill, is he?'

'No – no, he's fine. Both my parents are as fit as fleas. But Sybil's death seems to have hit him harder than I'd thought. Odd, really, when you think how much death we doctors see during the course of our work, but when it happens to someone close … well, we're just like anyone else.'

Hilary looked at him. 'Was he especially fond of her, then? I didn't think …'

'No, not particularly. I don't think he or my mother ever liked her all that much. But she was my wife, part of the family. They knew what she was like, in the end. The past couple of years – she hadn't made much secret of it. But she was still too young to die like that, and it seems to have made Dad think.'

'About what?'

'About how we spend our lives,' David said. 'About not wasting them. He asked me to go out with him for a long walk the other day. We went up to the Peak District and walked from Edale to Kinder Scout and back. Remember the song that Ewan MacColl wrote for the mass trespass back in the thirties, "I've sunbathed on Kinder, been burnt to a cinder"? It's a great area – quite a tough walk, but we had a good day for it and hardly saw another soul. We had plenty of time to talk.'

Hilary took another forkful of lamb and mashed potato. 'What did you talk about? Sybil?'

'Partly, but the upshot is that he doesn't think we ought to waste what time we've got. We should make the most of it.'

'And?'

'He doesn't think I've been doing that. Well, it's obvious I haven't – he and Mum have known for some time that I wasn't happy in my marriage. He thinks that although Sybil's death was a tragedy for her, it doesn't mean I can't make up for what I've lost over the past few years.' David paused. 'He knows about you.'

'About me? You told him?'

'Not to begin with. But he says that he and Mum both noticed something different about me in the past year. They knew something had happened and it didn't take much to figure out what. They knew there was someone. So yes, I told him. There didn't seem to be any reason not to.'

Hilary lowered her fork to her plate and said tensely, 'How did he react?'

'Much as I'd have expected. He doesn't judge, my father. He's seen too much life to do that. He just nodded and patted my shoulder and didn't say very much at all for a while. But then he went on to tell me what he and Mum have decided to do about their own lives. For a start, he wants to retire.'

'*Retire?*'

'He *is* sixty years old,' David said with faint amusement.

Hilary gazed at him. 'I suppose he must be. I just never thought about it. But you said "for a start". What else does he want to do?'

'Travel. Go abroad. They used to go walking in Germany before the war, but they've always wanted to visit America. Mum's got some relatives there and they're planning to go and stay with them and then maybe travel about a bit. Not immediately – there's a lot to be sorted out first.'

'The practice,' Hilary said, light dawning. 'He'll expect you to carry on, won't he?'

'That's why I needed to see you,' David said. He finished the last of his casserole and laid down his knife and fork. 'We have to talk about it.'

The waiter came and cleared away their plates. He asked if they wanted dessert and they said yes, more so that they could stay here, in this quiet corner away from the pouring rain, than because they actually wanted anything else to eat. Until it arrived, they remained silent, each considering what to say next.

That's the end of Burracombe for me, Hilary thought. Or else the end of David and me. I can't have both. I'm going to have to choose. She had thought she knew what her choice would be, and if she had been able to make it a few years ago, it would have been simple. Before her father was ill, before she had become so involved with running the estate, before Stephen had finally rejected any possibility of taking over ... Her father's health had improved now, and of course there was Travis, but even so, although she still wanted to make that choice, it was all much more complicated.

'I don't have to carry on the practice, Hilary.'

'But of course you do! You've been there ever since you left the army. You've always worked with your father. It's like a family business.'

'It is, in a way. But family businesses can change hands. They can be sold.'

'Would he want you to do that? What about your patients? They've been with you for years too. All their lives, some of them.'

'Yes, and they'll miss us for a while. But they'll have other doctors. They're going to lose Dad anyway. A lot of them have never been my patients and never will be. If I did stay, I'd have to take on a partner. What's the difference between one new doctor and two?'

Hilary shook her head. 'It seems too casual. Just to say you're handing over to strangers. I suppose I'm used to a different attitude. In my world, farmers pass their farms on to their sons and grandsons, and people like my father will do almost anything to keep their estates intact. Nobody I know would just sell up and move on.'

'But my father has a right to retire,' David said gently. 'Nobody would argue with that.'

'No, of course not ... But doesn't he *want* you to carry on the practice? Wouldn't he be disappointed if you moved away? And where would you move *to*?' she asked a little desperately. 'I've been trying to come to terms with moving to Derby and now – now I don't know what's going to happen. What are you going to do, David, if you don't stay there?'

'Well, I could move to Devon.'

'To *Devon*?' she echoed, as if she'd never heard of the place before. 'You mean you'd find a practice to join down there? In Plymouth or Exeter or somewhere?'

'It's a possibility, isn't it? Then you could stay on in Burracombe. We both could. As long as it was near enough for me to drive to, I could work anywhere. There must be someone who wants a new partner!'

'I suppose there might be,' she agreed. 'Would you really want to do that?'

'Why not? As for whether Dad wants me to carry on in Derby – I told you, he's more concerned that we make the most of our chances. He knows I've a shot at happiness at last, with you, and he wants me to do whatever I can to achieve that.'

Hilary felt the sudden heat of tears in her eyes. 'He hasn't even met me. How does he know I'm right for you?'

'He knows me, and he knows what I've told him about you.' David smiled and reached across the table for her hand. 'Believe me, I've left him in no doubt about that.'

'Oh, *David* ...' Hilary laid down her spoon. 'Do you really think it's going to turn out right for us after all this time? After all that's happened?'

He tightened his hand on hers. 'I really do. And I don't just think it – I *believe* it. You must do that too, Hilary my darling. Believe it, because it's going to happen. I told you, we can make it happen. Somehow or other we're going to be together, and we'll be together in Burracombe.'

Luke too was in London that day.

He had been there for nearly two weeks now. He had gone home at the weekend, but things had been stiff and awkward between him and Val, and he thought that she was as relieved as he was when he left again on Monday morning. He had felt depressed and anxious as he walked away with his rucksack and some more paintings. He began to wonder again if it was all worth it.

I can't seem to find my way through to her, he thought. It all used to be so easy between us – we didn't even have to say what we were thinking, we just knew. Or maybe we only thought we knew.

Perhaps all this time, we've been thinking and wanting different things and only imagining that the other felt the same way.

No, he could not believe that. Val and he *had* wanted the same thing – a happy home together with their baby and any other children they might have. The difference was that Val was firmly rooted in Burracombe and thought that home should be there, whereas Luke, although loving the village, knew he could live anywhere as long as it was with Val and as long as he could paint.

And that was the crux of the matter – he had to be able to paint. He could paint in Burracombe, of course – he had done his best work there and he wanted to continue, to capture the moor in all its moods. But he also wanted to paint portraits, and that was less easy to do in a remote west Devon village. A portrait painter needed to be where people could see him and his work, where they would be willing to sit for him. And portraits were what earned most money.

You had to be in London, at least some of the time. You had to have a studio there. You had to *live* there.

It seemed, Luke thought, as he hurried down the Strand in the pouring rain, to be a choice between a real opportunity as a painter, as was being held out to him now, or a return to teaching art in a rural grammar school and resigning himself to painting in his spare time.

Or, to put it rather more cruelly, a choice between painting and his family. Painting – or Chris and Val.

He scurried into the shelter of Charing Cross underground station and shook the drops off his raincoat. I can't choose painting over them, he thought. But I can't give it up either. Surely there has to be another way.

He bought a ticket for Bond Street, where the gallery was that was to put on his exhibition, and went towards the escalator, just missing Hilary and David as they took their turn at the window to buy tickets for Paddington, where Hilary was to catch her train home.

'Good heavens!' Hilary said. 'That was Luke.'

'Luke?'

'My friend Val's husband. You remember Val, in Egypt.'

'Oh yes, of course. He's the painter, isn't he?'

Hilary nodded. 'He's up in London arranging an exhibition. Val's not too happy about it.'

David glanced at her in surprise. 'Not happy about it? Surely that's a huge feather in his cap. An exhibition in London could be a tremendous boost for him.'

'I know. It's not that that troubles her. It's that he wants her to move to London and she doesn't want to leave Burracombe. They've got a baby, too. She wants him to grow up in the country.'

'Well, he probably could. Even if they moved here now, they needn't stay. Not if Luke does well with his painting.'

'I don't know,' Hilary sighed. 'It's not as easy as that, is it? You never know how things will turn out.'

David nodded. 'It seems they're in much the same position as us – wanting to be together but not seeing how to manage it. But at least they're married.'

'Yes,' Hilary said, and fell silent. It struck her that David had never actually asked her to marry him. It had become taken for granted – but could she really assume it? She felt herself blush as she wondered what to say next, and then a man pushed against her and she realised they were holding up the queue.

The crowd swirled about them and for a moment she lost sight of David. Then she saw his head above a knot of travellers a few feet away, and thrust her way through to reach him.

'I thought I'd lost you.'

He grasped her arm and looked down intently into her face. 'You'll never do that, never. Darling, this isn't the right place, but it's been bothering me that I've never proposed to you. I couldn't while Sybil was alive – not properly – but now I'm free ... I've had a sudden panic, wondering if you really do still feel the same way. I need to hear you say it!' His look, half laughing, became suddenly urgent. 'Hilary, sweetheart, will you marry me? Please say yes. I'll do it romantically next time, on bended knee with roses and champagne and everything, but please – before you go home today – please say yes.'

Hilary's heart jumped and banged against her ribcage. She caught her breath so sharply it was almost a sob, then as more people swarmed into the station she fell against him and he pulled her into his arms.

'Yes,' she said breathlessly. 'Yes, yes, yes. And I don't need roses or champagne, or bended knees. This is romantic enough for me. In fact' – she looked around the dinginess of the underground station – 'I think this is the most romantic place in the world!'

Chapter Twenty-Eight

S chool started again at the beginning of September. The Culliford camp had been dismantled a week or so earlier, at Frances Kemp's insistence – 'Mr Raynor and I must have some time to ourselves, to prepare for the new term' – and nobody now questioned the new teacher's fitness for the job. The governors met, more as a formality than for any other reason, to confirm his permanent appointment, and once the business was over, Basil produced a bottle of sherry and Gilbert Napier a bottle of whisky and it turned into a party – even more so when Grace came through the door bearing a tray laden with sausage rolls and small savoury biscuits spread with cream cheese and Gentleman's Relish, with tiny pickled onions perched on top.

'Basil hinted that we might have cause to celebrate,' she smiled, handing them round. 'I'm very pleased to add my welcome to Burracombe, Mr Raynor. Though it seems rather strange to be doing that now, since you've already made yourself so much a part of the village.'

'Thank the Cullifords for that,' he said, taking a sausage roll and accepting a whisky from Gilbert. 'If it hadn't been for the Culliford camp, I'd have been at a loose end all summer and nobody would have known my face.'

'Not all newcomers would have gone to so much trouble to help a local family through hard times,' Basil said. 'And the village camp was a stroke of genius. You've gone far beyond the call of duty – especially as you didn't even know if your appointment would be permanent.'

'I've enjoyed it. And I've a suspicion that the village camp, as you call it, might become a tradition. More than one child has asked if they can do it again next year, and the parents think Christmas came early.'

'Well, it won't go on for so long if it does happen again,' Frances Kemp said firmly. 'A week will be quite long enough. I hardly know what the inside of my house looks like any more.'

They laughed, and at that moment the doorbell rang. Grace went to answer it and Felix and Stella walked in.

'Stella, my dear, how good to see you!' Frances exclaimed. 'You're looking so well, too. Did you know we'd be here?'

'Basil told us,' Stella said. 'And you know what Felix is like, he'll go anywhere for a sausage roll. Two, that's all,' she told her husband. 'And not too much sherry. I don't want you falling into the Burra Brook on the way home.'

'I shan't drink any sherry at all,' Felix said righteously, his eyes on the whisky bottle.

Constance Bellamy, who also preferred whisky, turned to James. 'How are you settling into Brookside?'

'Very well, thank you. I'm renting it until Christmas, but now that I know I'll be staying, I'll probably buy it, if we can agree a price. It's a delightful place – a decent-sized living room and kitchen, a room I can use for a study and three bedrooms upstairs. Well, two and a half – the third is tiny. Once it's mine, I'll put in a bathroom.'

'That will be a lot of work. You'll have to have all the plumbing done.'

'Yes, but it's worth it. I can't continue to take my early-morning baths in the brook outside. Not in winter.'

Constance looked at him searchingly, but his face remained perfectly grave.

'I know very well you're pulling my leg,' she said at last. 'People always make the mistake of keeping too straight a face when they're telling whoppers. But I'll expect to be invited to the housewarming when it's all done. And now I must be off. Thank you for a delightful end to the meeting, Basil, and thank you, Grace, for the refreshments. Most welcome.' She stumped out and Basil hastened to open the front door for her. As she made her way to the gate, Basil turned to find Gilbert Napier and the two teachers close behind.

'We're going too,' Frances said. 'We've both got a lot to do to prepare for the first day of term. Thank you so much, Basil and Grace.'

James Raynor nodded and shook the vicar's hand. 'I'm really delighted to know I'm to be a permanent fixture in Burracombe. I think I'll find everything I ever wanted here.'

Gilbert shook hands too and they all left. Basil closed the door and went back to the living room, where he found Grace and Stella gathering up glasses and plates.

'Another whisky, Felix? The Colonel insisted on leaving it here.'

'A small one, thank you.' Felix held out his glass. 'As a matter of fact, Basil, there's something I want to discuss with you. I'd like a piece of advice.' He stared pensively into the glowing liquid for a moment, then said, 'What do you know about the Exclusive Brethren?'

'The Exclusives? Well, much the same as you do, I imagine. But why do you ask?'

'Because a member of my congregation seems to have gone over to them,' Felix said gloomily. 'Normally I'd consider that his right. But it's affecting other members too – his own family, who want to continue to attend my services but are prevented from doing so.' He looked up at the older man and drew in a deep sigh. 'Not only that, I believe he is physically cruel to his wife and thinks nothing of giving her a black eye. As you know, the police won't intervene unless she agrees to prefer charges, but I can't just stand by and see this happen without doing something about it. She's still one of my parishioners and would still like to be a member of my congregation, and I have a duty to care for her. But I just don't know what to do.'

Basil stared at him. 'But that's appalling. I know these things happen, of course, and I've had to call a man to order more than once when I've seen him behaving in this manner, but if this man has left your congregation, you have no authority over him. His wife, though ... Who is it, Felix? Can you tell me?'

'Oh, I can certainly tell you. It's all round Little Burracombe and will be here soon enough. It's Percy Shillabeer.'

'Percy Shillabeer.' Basil pursed his lips thoughtfully. 'Yes ... I'm not surprised, to tell you the truth. You know his story, of course?'

Felix frowned slightly. 'His story? I'm not sure ...'

Basil poured a little more whisky into Felix's glass and added some to his own. He sat down in his armchair and looked serious.

'It's a sad tale, I'm afraid, and explains much about Percy as he is now. It was like this ...'

'A very pleasant evening,' James said as he and Frances strolled back through the village.

'It was. And it shows how pleased everyone is that you're going to be staying here. Gilbert Napier doesn't shower bottles of whisky about indiscriminately.'

James laughed. 'I don't suppose he does. He's invited me to the Barton one evening, incidentally, to play chess.'

'Really? You are honoured. He normally plays with Charles Latimer.'

'He asked me if I played bridge, too. I do, of course, but I'm a little rusty – I haven't played since I was at the prep school, and we were always liable to be interrupted by some small crisis. Do you play?'

'I do. Miss Bellamy sometimes asks me to make up a four, but she's terrifyingly good. She seems to be able to see right through the back of the cards to know what you've got in your hand. I'm only a moderate player.' She hesitated. 'I could get up a four sometime, if you'd like to start again.'

'Thank you. I would. And now that I'm settled into Brookside and we've given up camping for the summer, I'd like to invite you to supper with me one evening. In a week or so, perhaps, when term is fairly under way. I'm not a bad cook,' he added with a smile. 'I won't poison you.'

'I have to admit I was worried for a moment – I thought you might be after my job! Yes, I'd like to come. I'll look forward to it.'

They had arrived at her gate and paused for a moment, looking at each other in the fading light. Then both started to speak at once, stopped, laughed and started again. James put out his hand and she shook it, feeling the warmth of his palm. He opened the gate for her and she went into the tiny front garden.

'Still a few roses left on the hedge,' she remarked. 'The scent's so lovely in the evening air, isn't it?'

'Yes,' he said quietly. 'It is. Good night, Frances.'

He watched as she went to her front door, and then he turned and limped away along the village street.

School was about to start for Luke, too.

He had come home the week before, knowing that a decision had to be made, and found Val on edge and inclined to snap. Christopher was teething and grizzly, and on the first night back he kept them awake with a continual miserable whining. Their reunion was not what Luke had been hoping for, and as they sat at breakfast next morning, he felt heavy-eyed and had a nagging headache.

'You needn't look like that,' Val said crossly as she spread lime marmalade on her toast. 'You've had almost a whole fortnight off. I've been dealing with this for the past week or more.'

'I'm sorry. I know he can't help it and I ought to have been here to take my turn with him. But I'm back now.'

'Yes, but how long for? When are you going back to London? You haven't told me a thing.'

'I haven't had much chance. We need to talk properly, Val, when we can be sure of not being interrupted.'

'By Christopher, you mean? He's just a nuisance to you now, isn't he?'

'No!' Luke stared at her angrily. 'Of course he's not! You've no right to say that. But you know as well as I do that we can't talk if one or other of us is attending to him every few minutes.'

'All right, then. He's asleep now – so talk.'

Luke sighed and rested his head on one hand, his elbow on the table. 'We need to be in the right mood.'

'Oh for goodness' sake!' Val slapped her knife down. 'There's always some excuse, isn't there! Last night you were tired after the journey, then you just wanted a quiet evening settling back in, then Chris was awake half the night, and now that he's asleep, you're not in the mood. What will it be next?'

'I said *we* need to be in the right mood. It doesn't strike me that you're any more ready for it than I am just at present.'

'Ready for what? Ready to be told I've got to pack up and move to London?'

'I didn't say that.'

'It's what you mean, though, isn't it? That's what you're going to say. We're going to up sticks and leave Burracombe, and I'm not going to get any say in it at all. Because you're my *husband* and I promised to *obey* you and even my own mother says that's what I should do!' She burst into tears and covered her face with both hands.

Luke stared at her in shock. He pushed her plate aside and leaned across the table, then got up and came round to stand behind her, his hands on her shoulders.

'Val, don't. It's not like that at all. All I want—' But he was interrupted by the fretful wail of the baby, and Val shook his hands away and pushed back her chair. Luke stepped back hastily. He started towards the stairs, but Val shoved him out of the way.

'I'll go! After all, he hardly knows you now.'

'*Val!*'

But she was gone, leaving Luke alone in the kitchen.

Chapter Twenty-Nine

'I always think,' Joyce Warren said to Basil as he came into the church while she was arranging swathes of Michaelmas daisies on the altar, 'that September should be the start of the new year, not January.'

'Do you?' Basil asked in surprise. 'Most people think it should be spring.'

'Well, there are things to be said for that too,' she conceded. 'New growth and births and all that. Yes, I can certainly see their point of view. But September is when we start new things. New school terms, new years for organisations, from bridge clubs to drama groups, all kinds of new beginnings. It's as if we naturally look on autumn as such a time.'

'And what are you going to begin?' he asked, knowing that Mrs Warren was nearly always about to embark on some new project. He waited in slight trepidation for her answer.

'It's funny you should ask that, Basil,' she said, confirming his fears. 'Because I've been thinking' – his heart sank a little lower – 'and I'm sure you'll agree with me that it's high time we started seriously to raise money for the repairs to the church organ. We've been talking about it long enough, in all conscience.'

'We certainly have,' Basil concurred, knowing that it had been on his conscience too. 'I was planning to discuss it at the parochial church council meeting next week.'

'There, you see!' she exclaimed, tweaking a straggling daisy into place. 'Another new beginning. I'm glad you're going to raise it, because I've had a few ideas. For one thing—'

'Shall we leave them until the meeting?' he asked, a little desperately. 'I only popped in for some papers I left in the vestry – I've got the rural dean coming in half an hour and I've any amount of things to do before he arrives. I don't want to keep him waiting.'

'Of course not,' she agreed, thinking that he looked more like Lewis Carroll's White Rabbit than ever, with his halo of fuzzy white hair and anxious pink face. At any moment he might exclaim 'Oh, my paws and whiskers!' and dive down the nearest hole. In fact, although she would never know it, this was exactly what Basil would have liked to do on many of the occasions when he met her. 'But I will just tell you that I'm planning a special Christmas extravaganza this year, rather than a pantomime, and all the profits will be going to the organ fund.'

'But we haven't even set up an organ fund yet,' he said, halfway to the vestry.

'No, but we will, won't we?' she said serenely, tucking in the last daisy and standing back to admire the effect. 'That will be one of the main considerations at the meeting. By this time next week, it will be well under way!'

'A Christmas extravaganza?' Alf Coker said dubiously, finishing the last shoe on Tessa Latimer's mare. 'And what be that, exactly?'

'A Christmas show, of course,' Joyce said impatiently. 'A variety show. I want everyone in the village who has any talent at all to take part. You'll be singing, of course. You have such a fine bass voice, Mr Coker.'

Alf gave her a sideways look. 'You wouldn't be trying to get round me, by any chance?'

'Now would I do that? But you really would be the mainstay of the whole production, Mr Coker. You see, we'll need an MC – a master of ceremonies – and I can't think of anyone better than you.'

'I thought you wanted me to sing.'

'I do, of course. At least two songs – more if you can manage it. But I'd also like you to run the whole evening – introduce the acts, you know. Would you?' She gave him her most winning smile.

Joyce Warren's winning smiles made most men quail, but Alf Coker was made of sterner stuff. However, the idea of being an MC, like on *Variety Bandbox* on the wireless, was quite appealing.

And if he could sing a few songs as well – 'Friend of Mine', and 'This Was Our Lovely Day', which were two he was particularly fond of – it could be something to look forward to in the long dark winter evenings. He stroked his chin and said, 'I'll think about it. Can't say more than that straight away.' It didn't do to let Mrs Warren know you were giving in too easy.

'That's wonderful.' She seemed to be taking this for assent anyway. 'All profits are to go to the organ repair fund – a very worthy cause, I'm sure you'll agree.'

'I didn't even know there was one.'

'Well, there isn't yet, but there will be quite soon. But that's just between ourselves, Mr Coker.' She smiled at him a little roguishly, and he blinked. 'And now I must go. Lots to do, you know.'

She marched away and Alf watched her go, scratching the back of his neck. He felt as if he'd agreed to something without even knowing what it was he was agreeing to.

Still, a Christmas show, with himself as MC and singing a few songs. It didn't sound a bad idea at that.

'I'll have to go and see her,' Felix said. He was sitting at the kitchen table, finishing the shepherd's pie Stella had made for lunch. He watched gloomily as she removed the enamel pie dish and replaced it with a Pyrex bowl of stewed blackberries and apples. 'I can't just let this go on in my own congregation and do nothing about it.'

'But didn't Basil say there's nothing anyone can do, unless Ann asks for help herself?'

'He said there's nothing the *police* can do. And obviously if Percy really has left my congregation there's nothing I can say to him. But as far as I know, Ann *is* still one of my congregation – or wants to be – and it's my duty, if nothing else, to visit her. Besides,' he added, 'I want to. I want to make sure she's all right and offer whatever comfort I can.'

'Would you like me to come too?'

Felix shook his head. 'Not this time, thanks, although I'm sure she'd welcome a visit from you. I really need to see what the situation is first. In a way, it doesn't make it any easier that Basil told me about Percy's background. A child with a violent parent, locked in a dog kennel at night as a punishment and beaten for the smallest misdemeanour, doesn't have much chance to grow up normal. And it seems as though Percy was never quite the same as other children in the first place. The story Basil told me about his trying to drown another child, when he was barely six years old, was quite horrifying.'

'I don't believe a child of six understands quite what they're doing,' Stella said. 'He can't have known the other child might die.'

'It's not normal behaviour, even so. Children seem to me to have an innate understanding of how far they can go. Pinching seems to be their favourite method of inflicting hurt, or biting, but even that's less common by that age. But you'd know more about it than I would.'

'I think you're right, in general. But Percy seems to have grown up in a very strange family, where normal rules didn't apply. And if he had a temper anyway ...'

'Quite.' Felix poured custard over his fruit. 'A childish temper that was never properly corrected. A child who is treated as cruelly as Percy seems to have been treated will either grow up in a permanent state of fear or become a bully. Which is what seems to have happened to him.'

'I wonder if it's as simple as that,' she said thoughtfully. 'It's the way he turned to religion that's so curious. You'd think he might find comfort in it, and learn compassion and love, as you teach. But instead ...'

'He's gone to the Old Testament,' Felix said. 'Fire and brimstone and eternal wrath. And punishment. He seems addicted to punishment. You know, I think that's an interesting point, Stella. It's as if he has decided it's his duty to punish others, on behalf of God.'

'Perhaps because he's afraid that if he doesn't, he'll be the one to be punished,' Stella said. 'Somewhere deep inside he may still be that terrified little boy locked in a dog kennel, knowing that when he's let out at last he'll be beaten again.'

They sat silent for a few moments, thinking it over. Then Felix drew in a deep sigh and got to his feet.

'Whatever the reason, it's the situation now that we have to deal with. Percy Shillabeer seems to be losing his reason, and his wife is in desperate need of help. And it's up to me to see what, if any, can be given.'

'Percy's not home,' Ann Shillabeer said when Felix knocked on the farmhouse door. She peered out nervously, her fingers picking at her lips. 'He won't be back till tea time. He won't talk to you, though.'

'I know.' Felix looked at her kindly. 'It's not him I've come to see, Mrs Shillabeer. It's you.'

'Me?' She looked frightened. 'I'm sorry I haven't been to church the past few weeks. Only Percy goes to his meeting on Sunday mornings, and – and ...' She faltered, clearly unwilling to tell him the truth of what happened on Sunday mornings.

Felix spoke quickly. 'It's all right, Mrs Shillabeer. I haven't come to reproach you. I know it's not always possible to get to church. I just wanted to see you and make sure that everything's all right. That *you're* all right.'

'Oh yes,' she said. 'I'm all right, Vicar. There's nothing wrong with me, nor the children. Nor Percy, neither. It's just a busy time of year, and what with him going to his meeting of a Sunday, well ...' Again her voice trailed off, and she gazed at him as if not knowing what to say.

'Mrs Shillabeer,' Felix said, 'may I come in? I think we should have a little talk.'

It was unusual for him to be kept standing on the doorstep. As a rule, parishioners would invite him in at once and insist that he have a cup of tea. Sometimes, after a round of visits, Felix would arrive home declaring that he never wanted to see another teapot in his life. But Ann Shillabeer had not even fully opened the door. He was beginning to feel like an unwelcome salesman.

Ann hesitated, and he wished he had not asked. He had clearly put her in a difficult position – she didn't want to invite him in, but she didn't want to refuse either. After a moment of obvious mental struggle, she stepped back and opened the door a little wider.

'Come in, Vicar. I'm sorry to have been rude – it's just that I didn't expect any visitors. Us don't get many these days.'

Because Percy has put them off, Felix thought, stepping into the kitchen. It was clean and tidy, with the table clear of the pile of papers that often cluttered farmhouse kitchen tables. There was one place laid with cutlery and a glass. Ann saw him looking at

223

it and said quickly, 'That's for Percy's tea. He don't take strong drink, only water.'

'That's all right, Mrs Shillabeer. I was just wondering where the places are for you and the children.'

'They has their dinner at school. The youngest is over at my sister's for the afternoon.'

'I see. But you? You'll be eating with your husband? And the children will have something too?' He spoke gently, knowing the truth but needing to hear it from her own lips. Yet he could not ask her outright, for that would embarrass and upset her even more.

'Us don't eat in here these days,' she said in a mutter. 'It's better for us to eat in the back kitchen.' She turned towards the door that led to the scullery and he followed her in, gazing in dismay around the dank little room. And this was where Ann and her children were forced to eat! 'The little ones drop their food sometimes and it's easier to clear up.' She avoided his eyes and he felt immensely sorry for her.

'Mrs Shillabeer,' he said quietly. 'Ann ... is there something you'd like to talk about?'

There was a moment of complete silence. She turned away and he could see that her back was shaking as she brought her hands up to cover her eyes. He stood quite still, then laid his hand lightly on her shoulder. She gave a stifled sob, and began to turn towards him.

'What in God's name is going on here?' The sudden roar filled the air, and they both jumped violently. 'Who let this messenger from Satan into the house? Who told you to come bothering decent folk, soiling my own home with your false witness?'

Felix turned swiftly. Percy Shillabeer's huge bulk filled the doorway, blocking out the light. He felt a flame of rage lick through him and faced the angry farmer.

'You'll take back those words, Mr Shillabeer. If Satan has a place here, it's not because I brought him. Neither did your wife invite me in. I asked to come.'

'So that you could poke your nose into our affairs and seduce her back to your church. Outsiders, that's what you are, and not fit to consort with the chosen ones.' His hot, angry eyes raked Felix's face and then turned to his wife, who was shrinking back against the rough table where her own and her children's places were laid.

'You – you might still be saved. There's hope yet, though little sign I've seen of it. But you, calling yourself a vicar, a man of God – you've come straight from the Devil and you've soiled the whole house with your evil. Get out – now. *Now!*'

'Please, Vicar,' Ann begged, her eyes wet and frightened. 'Please do as he says. You don't know what he'm like.'

Felix hesitated. He thought of Basil's story about this man's childhood and what his father had done to the young Percy and his mother. How could he leave this poor woman at the mercy of such a man, with the example that had been set him? Yet what else could he do? He turned to her, trying to ignore the fury of the man who loomed over them both.

'Ann,' he said rapidly, 'remember this. I'm your friend, and so is my wife. Everyone in the village wishes you well. If you need help, all you have to do is ask. Ask anyone. We are all here, ready for you.'

She nodded, but she was shaking so violently, he could not be sure how much she understood. He looked again at Percy, standing now with knotted fists and glittering eyes. The man's mad, he thought with sudden certainty, he's completely mad; and he wondered if a doctor would help.

'Please go,' Ann whispered, and he touched her arm, gave the enraged man one more look, and passed him by to leave the house.

At the kitchen door, he turned again and spoke directly to the farmer, who had shifted his bulk to watch him go.

'You'll not hurt your wife, Mr Shillabeer,' he said firmly. 'You'll not touch a hair of her head. Because if you do, you'll have me to answer to – me and my God. And my God may be very much more compassionate than yours, but he will have no mercy on a man who strikes an innocent woman. No mercy at all.'

225

Chapter Thirty

'**H**e's asleep,' Val said, coming downstairs and sinking into her chair by the fireplace. 'So if you want to talk ...'

Luke looked at her sympathetically. 'Darling, you look exhausted.'

'I am. He's been like this for days now. I shall be thankful when this tooth's through. It seems so unfair that little babies should suffer like this.'

'It prepares them for life, I suppose,' Luke said wryly. 'Val, I really am sorry I left you to manage on your own. I should have been here more.'

Val glanced at him but said nothing. After a minute or two, she shrugged. 'If you'd been in the navy or something, you'd have been away even more, so I suppose I shouldn't grumble. One of my friends from Egypt married a sailor and he went away the day their baby was born – only a few hours before, so he didn't even see it – and didn't come home till a week before its first birthday. And even then he wasn't back for long...'

'Yes, but she knew that sort of thing would happen when she married him. You didn't expect me to suddenly go off and leave you.' He paused. 'Do you feel up to talking now? I mean, you must be so tired ... wouldn't you rather just have a quiet evening and we can discuss it tomorrow?'

'And have it still hanging over us with Chris crying all day again? No thanks. Let's get it over with now. Tell me the worst.'

Luke sighed. 'I don't know why you assume it's the worst.'

'Don't you?' Already her tone was hostile. He turned and pulled a dining chair from the table and drew it up beside her, sitting close so that he could lay one arm around her shoulders. With his free hand he stroked her wrist and then curled his fingers around hers.

'Perhaps I do,' he said quietly. 'I haven't given you much cause to think otherwise. Sweetheart, listen to me. I've had time to think while I've been in London – time to think about what really matters to me.'

'I know what matters to you,' she said tiredly. 'Your painting.'

'Yes, my painting matters to me, it matters a lot. But not as much as you and Chris do. You are the most important part of my life. You and Chris. And our lives together.' He paused. 'Here in Burracombe.'

Val turned her head and looked up at him. Her eyes were shadowed and weary. She said, 'What are you saying, Luke?'

'I've got two suggestions to make,' he said. 'Whichever you choose, that's what we'll do. But—'

'But they're still *your* suggestions. Made without talking to me first.'

'Yes, but they're not the only options. If you don't like either of them, then we'll do whatever you want to do. I think I know already what that will be, and if that's what you decide, there'll be no more argument.'

She eyed him uncertainly. 'Go on, then.'

'First,' he said, 'you should know that the exhibition was a success.' He didn't say that he was hurt at her not asking about it. This wasn't a game of scoring points over who was most hurt. 'I sold quite a lot of paintings. Even more importantly, I got several commissions – if I want them.'

'And of course, you do.'

'Yes, I do. I'd be a fool not to. You can't expect me not to be pleased about that, Val.'

'No,' she said after a moment, 'I can't. So what are you going to do?'

'I haven't told you my ideas first.' He squeezed her fingers. 'One is that I leave the school, we move to London and I go on painting – and concentrate on portraits, since that's where most of the money is.'

'Is that what you really want? To become a society painter?

Turning out portraits of sweet little debutantes in their expensive dresses and earning lots and lots of money?' Her lip curled a little. 'I thought better of you than that, Luke.'

'Thank you,' he said gravely. 'I'm glad of that, because it is most definitely *not* what I want. But it's one of the possibilities that's been offered to me and it's only right that you should know about it. Don't you think so?'

'I suppose so,' she said a little grudgingly. 'Well, what's the other one?'

'This one is what I really want,' he said. 'But it's for you to say yes or no. I really mean that, Val.' He paused again. 'What I thought of was that I could give in my notice—'

'So you *are* going to leave the school! You do want to move to London!'

'Yes and no. Yes to the first, no to the second. Val, the paintings sold for more than I ever expected. People really do like my work – the portraits *and* the landscapes. It will be quite possible for me to stay here and take my work to London. The gallery say I can have a permanent spot on their walls. I'll always be seen. I can paint portraits as well, but I don't need to be there all the time.' His voice grew more enthusiastic, the words coming quickly. 'One week a month would be enough.' Now he was gripping both her hands in his, the chair pulled round to face her as he leaned forward. 'I could stay here in Burracombe, using the charcoal burner's hut as my studio just as I have been doing, painting full time and going to London for just one week at a time. It would work, Val, and I could earn enough money to keep us. More than enough. Much more than my teacher's salary. What do you say?'

She stared at him. His eyes were burning and she realised suddenly that this was the old Luke, the Luke she had first fallen in love with, the Luke who had been gradually disappearing over the past few months without either of them noticing it. Or without *me* noticing it, she thought guiltily. Luke had known. He had known and tried to ignore it, but in the end he couldn't.

'One week a month,' she said thoughtfully. 'Would it really be enough?'

'If I were painting full time, yes. But I can't do it if I have to teach as well.' He looked at her a little uncertainly. 'It drains me, you see.

I'm good enough at teaching, and I enjoy it – but by the end of the day all my *painting* energy has gone. I *can* paint, of course – but there's no fire in it. No life. And there doesn't seem to be much life in me either, somehow.'

'No,' she said. 'There isn't. You're still my dear, sweet, funny Luke – but the fire's gone. At least, it had.' She looked into those burning eyes. 'It's come back now, though, hasn't it?'

There was a long silence, and then Luke looked down at their entwined hands. Val looked down as well and suddenly lifted them, four hands clasped, and pressed them to her lips.

'Let's do that, then,' she said in a shaking voice. 'One week a month. I think Chris and I will be able to manage that.'

Luke stared at her. 'Do you mean it? Really mean it? Val ...'

'Yes,' she said. 'I really mean it.' And she leaned closer and kissed him.

For the first time for over a week, Christopher slept right through the night. When he woke next morning, his tooth had finally broken through and he was his old sunny self again. The whole family went into Tavistock for Luke to give in his term's notice, the day before school started again, and then they caught the Okehampton bus and took a picnic up to Widgery Cross, high on the moor. There was a small pool at the foot of the hill, just deep enough to wade into, and they stripped off Christopher's clothes and bounced him in the water, chuckling with him as the tiny waterfall splashed his naked body.

'This is better than anything London has to offer,' Luke said afterwards as they lay on the grass in the warm September sunshine. He leaned up on one elbow and narrowed his eyes as he gazed at the stretching moorland and the tumble of rocky tors.

'Don't tell me!' Val said, laughing at him. 'You're painting! In your mind, you're painting. And this is supposed to be *our* day.'

He turned and grinned down at her. 'You'd better think of a way to stop me, then.'

Val glanced sideways to where Christopher was lying on a rug, sprawled in blissful sleep under the old umbrella they'd brought to protect him from the sun. She glinted a wicked look at her husband and pulled him down beside her.

'I've thought of one already,' she said.

As Joyce Warren had observed, the autumn brought many beginnings. But there were endings too, and the most important of them were the harvests. Good or bad, according to the weather, they brought barns filled with wheat, straw for winter bedding, apples for making cider and gluts of monster-sized marrows and other vegetables from the village kitchen gardens.

On the evening of the first Thursday in October, Basil held his annual harvest festival service and the church was packed with produce. The font was surrounded by pyramids of gleaming apples, boxes of hazel nuts and mushrooms gathered from the hedgerows and fields, and trays of tomatoes smelling of fresh, rain-wet earth. More were ranged along the windowsill, together with vases of chrysanthemums and Michaelmas daisies, and at the altar steps lay two of the most enormous marrows Basil had ever seen. There were turnips and parsnips, just touched by the first autumn frost and scrubbed until they glowed with their own pearly light, onions of rich bronze and bunches of carrots the colour of sunset. The vegetables and fruit that had come and gone during the summer were represented by jars of pickles and chutney or jewel-coloured pots of jam, and there was a sheaf of corn standing proudly at either end of the altar itself, with a huge loaf of bread, baked by George Sweet in the shape of a third sheaf, propped up in the middle.

The congregation packed the church. It was one of those occasions, like Christmas and Easter, when almost everyone came, and Basil welcomed them all, never implying the slightest hint of reproach that they did not come more often. He was simply glad to see them now. They sang all their favourite hymns – 'Come, ye faithful people, come, Raise the song of harvest home', and 'We plough the fields and scatter, The good seed on the land' – and Basil preached a sermon, as he always did, about thankfulness for what was provided. It was always the same theme – it had to be – but he always managed to invest it with the mention of some local celebration or joy over the past year. He could not let this one pass without a reminder of Felix and Stella's wedding, held in this very church only four months ago, or the joyous birth of Travis and Jennifer's baby. Harvest, he said, was not only about the gathering-in of food and sustenance for the coming winter; it was about the fulfilment of human life, a fruition of joy to be shared by everyone present.

Afterwards, a few went home but most continued on to the village hall, where Alice Tozer and some of the other women had set out tables laden with ham salad, pasties and cider, followed by apple pie and custard. The meal went on for a good hour, with the cider jugs being continually replenished, and by the time it was over and the auction of the produce, carried down from the church, began, it was not only the villagers' tongues that had been loosened, but their wallets too. Andrew Kelly, the auctioneer from the cattle market in Tavistock, who performed this duty every year and knew his audience well, took up his gavel and looked around with narrowed eyes.

'You all know that the profits from the auction tonight are going to the organ fund, so I hope you'll bid generously. You were all at the service, so you know just how badly the organ needs these repairs. In fact, when I heard all those wheezes and squeals during the hymns, I thought someone had brought a pig for the harvest.' Without waiting for the laughter to diminish, he lifted his gavel. 'We've a lot to get through, so let's make a start. What do I have for this box of apples? Two shillings? Anyone offer two shillings? One shilling? Someone had better bid, for I won't go lower. All right, sixpence. Sixpence bid. A shilling. One and sixpence – now we're moving. Two shillings in the corner. Is that a bid, madam, or are you just winking at someone else's husband? Two shillings and threepence. Half a crown ... Sold to the lady who winks at strange men. Now, what do I have for this bag of potatoes ...?'

Driven by his rapid delivery, the sale was under way. Boxes of apples, plums, nuts and mushrooms were bid for with huge enthusiasm, chutneys, pickles and jams were taken home by people whose cupboards were probably already stuffed with jars of their own making, and Bernie Nethercott bought one of the two big marrows to display on his bar. Basil kept the other for the church, where the flowers were also to remain, along with the two sheaves of corn and the wheat-shaped loaf.

Only one item remained: the huge jar of pickled onions that was traditionally always kept till the end. Although many would bid at the start, they would all gradually fall away until only two contestants remained – Bernie and Jacob Prout. Up and up their bids went, watched with enjoyment by the rest, until they reached heights that everyone knew were quite ridiculous. Ten shillings. Twelve and sixpence. Fifteen shillings. Who would pay fifteen shillings for a jar of pickled onions, they asked each other, and what was Jacob going to do with it if he won? But Jacob had no intention of winning. At a pound, he dropped out and let Bernie have them, and everyone knew that they would next appear on the bar of the Bell Inn, to be sold at a penny or two each.

'I love harvest festival,' Hilary said as she and her father walked home together afterwards. Gilbert was fully fit now, although he had been warned that he must never overexert himself. But gentle exercise was good for him, and where he would once have driven down to the village, now he was content to walk. You saw more that way, he said, and Hilary hid a smile as she reflected that it had taken him a lifetime to discover this. 'It's such a warm occasion, and the auction is always fun. Mind you, we should have brought the car really, to carry home those boxes of apples and plums you insisted on buying.'

'Have to pull our weight,' he said. 'You can collect them in the morning. I noticed Travis didn't stay for the supper.'

'He wanted to get home to Jennifer and the baby. It's the christening on Sunday.'

'So it is. How old will she be?'

'Ten weeks. And she's the happiest little thing – laughing and smiling all the time.' Gilbert had seen the baby when Jennifer had brought her, then just two weeks old, to the Barton. He'd found little to say other than a gruffly muttered few words of congratulation, and had pressed a gold sovereign into the tiny curled palm. Jennifer had protested, but he'd brushed her aside, saying that he'd kept a few for special occasions and there were plenty left for his own grandchildren, when they came along. He hadn't looked at Hilary when he said this, but she'd felt a sharp pain all the same, knowing that it was far more likely to be Stephen who produced the next grandchild than she herself.

'And you're to be godmother. Who are the other godparents?'

'One of Jennifer's sisters, and Travis's brother Leonard. You met him in the summer when he came to stay for a few days. Nice man.'

'I remember. Bit younger than Travis. Lives over near Bridport.'

'That's right.' Travis came from Dorset, and most of his family still lived there. 'The whole family is coming. Wood Cottage is going to be bursting with people.'

'And half the village in the church, I dare say.'

'I don't think so. Christenings are usually just family affairs, aren't they? A nice quiet, private little service in the afternoon with tea and cake afterwards. You will be coming too, won't you, Father?'

'Of course I will. Pleased to be invited. It'll be interesting to meet Travis's family, and I dare say there'll be people to talk to. Charles mentioned that he and Grace will be there.'

Hilary nodded. She hadn't bumped into Charles Latimer much lately – not since she'd spoken to him at a sherry party not long after her last visit to London, when she'd told him that David's father was considering retirement. Even then, there'd been little time to talk, as the telephone had rung and he'd been summoned to a patient with suspected appendicitis. And in the past few weeks she'd spent a good deal of time at Wood Cottage with Jennifer, getting to know her prospective god-daughter, and had been out when Charles came to see her father.

Mary Susan wasn't, of course, the first baby that Hilary had known, but she was the first she had had much to do with. Under Jennifer's tuition, she had learned to change a nappy, bath and dress her, and even give her a bottle filled with water. The baby knew her and laughed, waving her arms and legs, when Hilary appeared, and had started to hold out her arms to be picked up. Jennifer said that she mustn't be spoilt by being given in to, but Hilary was quite unable to resist and lifted her from her pram or cot every time, to cuddle the firm little body against her and nuzzle the soft creases of her neck.

She was looking forward to the christening as one of the few bright spots in her life at present. Events in Derby still seemed to be moving with maddening slowness. It seemed that it wasn't a simple matter for a doctor to retire, and the sale of Dr Hunter's practice would not be complete until at least January and possibly even later than that. David seemed unable to make any decision about his own future until that was settled, and once again Hilary felt in limbo. Life was ticking by, she thought despondently, and everyone else was moving on – Val and Luke had settled their differences and were looking forward to their new regime once Luke had left his teaching job at Christmas; Stephen and Maddy were enjoying married life in Cyprus; Jennifer and Travis had taken to parenthood as easily and proudly as a pair of swans with a new cygnet, and Stella and Felix looked almost nauseatingly happy. I'm in danger of becoming envious, Hilary told herself sternly. Envious and bitter – it won't do.

She dressed carefully for the christening in a new dress and jacket in deep lilac. In the church, she took the baby in her arms while Basil read the first words of the short service, and then handed Mary Susan over to be baptised. The baby, dressed in her long white gown, was wide awake and gazed up trustingly into the vicar's face until he trickled water over her forehead, after which a look of astonished indignation spread across her features and she opened her mouth to an almost perfect square and howled with fury. Everyone smiled, and Basil, who was quite accustomed to this, finished what he was saying and then handed her back to Hilary.

'They say that's the Devil being driven out,' remarked Jacob as they went out into the churchyard. By now the baby had stopped crying and was back in her mother's arms. 'Though how an innocent little dear like Mary Susan could ever come to have the Devil in her, I've never understood. 'Tis all a tale, if you ask me.'

'I rather agree.' They stood at the church door while Felix organised them for a photograph. It was a mild afternoon, almost as warm as summer. The wooded valley was touched with autumn colour, the trees turning to flame and auburn and shimmering gold. The few blackberries left in the hedges were either wizened or overripe and in either case not worth picking – and the Devil had had his wicked way with them too, Hilary thought, for on the last night of September he was said to go round spitting on them, and who wanted to eat a blackberry the Devil had spat on? You'd think he'd have something better to do. Or, given who he was, something worse ...

'There you are, my dear.' She turned to find Charles Latimer behind her. 'I've been hoping to have a word with you, but you've been remarkably elusive lately.'

'Just busy. And I've been at Wood Cottage a lot. What do you think of my god-daughter? Isn't she gorgeous?'

'She is. And going to take after her mother, I think. Jennifer's a striking-looking woman, and little Mary seems to have her eyes.'

'They're so lucky,' Hilary said wistfully, watching as Travis helped settle his wife and baby in the Land Rover, scrubbed and polished for the occasion. 'Jennifer must have wondered sometimes if she'd ever have a family. And to come to Burracombe looking for her father, and find a husband – it's really quite romantic when you think about it.'

'Everyone's story is romantic when you think about it,' Charles observed. 'And a surprising number have happy endings. As I'm sure yours will, Hilary.'

'Are you?' She turned and looked into his kindly face. 'I don't know ... It all seems to be dragging on so long, I wonder if we'll ever come to any conclusion. Whenever it seems we can take a step forward, something happens to push us two steps back.'

'I don't think it's really that bad,' he said quietly. 'Let's have a talk. I may be able—' He broke off as Jacob came up to them. He looked as proud as if he were the baby's father instead of an adopted grandfather, his face creased with beaming smiles.

'Isn't she a proper little princess, and that yell her let out – that would have frightened the Devil away if anything would, the dear of her. I don't think she'll have no trouble with he.'

'She's the loveliest baby I've ever seen,' Hilary told him. 'You must be so happy.'

'I am. It were a good day for me when my Jennifer come to Burracombe, even though that old Jed had to get his oar in first. But there, 'tis all in the past now and he'm no long with us, so mustn't speak ill of the dead – even when they're old curmudgeons like Jed Fisher. And speaking of curmudgeons, have you heard the latest about Percy Shillabeer? Talking of selling up the farm, he be.'

'No!' Hilary stared at him in dismay. 'But why? What does he mean to do?'

'Go into business with one of they Exclusives, down in Plymouth. They'm not supposed to do business with what they call outsiders, so they has to work together. It's bad luck on poor Ann, though.'

'That's terrible,' Hilary said. 'Do you mean she'll have to give up her home and move to Plymouth? She'll have no friends or relatives there – she'll just wither away.'

235

'She'll have the children,' Jacob said. 'But 'tis going to be hard for her, especially if she holds firm about not joining them herself.'

Hilary turned in distress to Charles, who shook his head.

'You know I can't intervene. She's my patient – I can't even discuss her.'

'But we can't stand by and let him uproot the whole family and make them go to live in Plymouth! And what about Patsy? She'll never see her mother at all if that happens.'

'She don't see much of her now,' Jacob said. 'Bob Pettifer's been working over that way and he says Percy's threatened to set the dogs on anyone who comes near the farm without his say-so – and that includes Patsy.'

'But they'd never attack Patsy – they know her.'

'The old sheepdogs do,' Jacob said tersely. 'But not that new one he've got. Looks more like a wolf, if you ask me, and Ann's scared to walk near it herself.'

'Someone's got to do something,' Hilary said resolutely, but at that moment the rest of the group in the churchyard began to move off in the direction of Wood Cottage and she was compelled to go with them.

She frowned, thinking of the sadness of the whole situation, and forgetting, for a little while, her own problems with David. She also forgot that Charles had suggested they have a talk about David and had been interrupted before he could say any more.

Chapter Thirty-One

I t had come as a considerable surprise to Felix to walk into church that morning and see Ann Shillabeer sitting in her usual pew with her children beside her.

He had almost stopped short, but he had schooled himself neither to show surprise nor to acknowledge any parishioner personally during his services. Afterwards, he would give each one his full attention, but while leading worship, he must treat them as one body.

Try as he might, though, he could not help his gaze wandering to the pale woman sitting three rows back with her silent family. They all looked so subdued, even cowed. He felt his anger rise up against the man who had brought them to this, and had difficulty turning his mind and heart to forgiveness, even with knowledge of Percy's bitter childhood. Percy had turned to God, but somehow he had created a god that Felix did not recognise, a god of vengefulness and hate. Why could he not have found the God of love and compassion?

At last the service was over. Felix felt he had delivered a poor sermon, a mechanical repetition of words that had seemed when he had written them to contain wisdom and guidance. Now, as the congregation said its final prayer, he walked down the aisle so as to be at the door to greet them, and felt that Ann would have received scant comfort from his words.

She came to the door amidst a flurry of children, cleanly though poorly dressed, and would have slipped by if he had not put out his hand. Hesitantly she stopped and gave him hers, and he was aware of the curious eyes of other people. The whole village knew what Percy had done and no one had expected to see her in church.

'I'm very glad to see you, Mrs Shillabeer. We've missed you.'

'I've missed coming, Vicar,' she said, so softly he barely heard her. 'But Percy ...' She glanced around, ducked her head and pulled her hand away. 'I'll have to go now.'

'Has he gone to his meeting?' Felix had no right to ask, but he couldn't let the poor woman go like this. 'Will he be home soon?'

'Yes. Just after one o'clock. He'll be wanting his dinner.' There was panic in her eyes now, and he realised that Percy didn't know she was here and that she was afraid of his finding out. Perhaps he had forgotten to lock the door. In any case, Felix could not detain her any longer. He put his hand on her arm and smiled at her, giving what comfort he could and miserably aware that it was far too little.

'Go along then. You mustn't be late. But come to church again, won't you? And if you need me, at any time ... You're not forgotten, Ann.'

It was not the first time he had used her Christian name, but he did so now quite deliberately, wanting to draw her closer to the family of the church that he knew she belonged to in her heart. He saw the flicker of warmth in her eyes and then she turned away, gathered the children to her and hurried down the path. The rest of the congregation watched her go.

'Poor bird,' one said compassionately. 'And her was such a pretty, lively little maid before her married Percy Shillabeer. He's half killed her with his crazy ways, and that's the truth.'

'And he looks set fair to finish the job, the way he's carrying on,' said another, and when Felix turned to him in horror, added quickly, 'I don't really mean that, Vicar. 'Tis just a figure of speech, like. Men don't really kill their wives, do they – not in places like Little Burracombe.'

Felix was still thinking about this as he followed the others from the Burracombe church to Wood Cottage. He and Stella had walked across the Clam, pausing to watch the swirling waters below, and would go home after tea, while it was still light, to be back in time for Evensong. He walked pensively, the joy of the baptism ceremony receding in his anxiety over the Shillabeers. The words that farm worker had spoken this morning echoed disturbingly in his mind: *Men don't really kill their wives, do they – not in places like Little Burracombe ...*

But men did kill their wives, and in all sorts of places – city streets, great houses, small idyllic villages. Hate could seethe beneath the surface anywhere, and where madness lurked, anything was possible.

Felix was as certain as he could be that Percy Shillabeer was mad. His madness did not come from the Exclusives, nor from Patsy's actions, nor from anything that Ann had done or not done. It may have come from the brutal childhood he had suffered, or it may have been deep in his blood since he was born, inherited from his violent father.

The important thing now was not why he had tipped into madness, but what was going to happen next, and what Felix, or anyone else, might do about it. I can't just turn a blind eye, Felix thought. One of my parishioners is in danger. Maybe those children are in danger too. Percy has removed himself from me, but I still have a duty towards the rest of the family, and I have a human duty towards him too. If anything happens and I've not even tried, I will carry that on my conscience for the rest of my life.

'Felix?' Stella asked, and he started. He'd almost forgotten she was there, and indeed why they were walking along the track towards Wood Cottage. 'You don't seem very happy. What are you worrying about?'

He stopped and turned towards her. 'I'm sorry, darling. I was just thinking.'

'About the Shillabeers?' Stella had been in church that morning too, and noticed the family. She had left as soon as the service was over to go home and prepare their Sunday dinner, so hadn't seen Ann stop at the door, and Felix hadn't mentioned her. But she had known from his unusually subdued manner that he was anxious, and waited for him to tell her, if he wanted to. 'You're upset about them, aren't you?'

'It's a nasty situation,' he said sombrely. 'I'm afraid for her, Stella, I really am.'

'Do you think he'd harm her? I know he's a bully, but ...'

'I don't know what he might do. But I feel I should try to do something about it. I wonder if Charles could help. Percy's a sick man, Stella, I'm sure of it – a very sick man.'

'You mean he's mad?'

'I can't say that. I'm not a doctor. But ...'

'But you think he is,' she said quietly.

Felix rubbed the back of his neck. 'I don't like to think it – it's too appalling. But I can't see any other reason for his behaviour. I honestly can't.'

'The Exclusives are very strict,' Stella said thoughtfully. 'I've been reading about them. They do say exactly what Percy does – that members mustn't eat with outsiders, or do business with them, or have any contact at all that isn't absolutely necessary. It sounds out of all reason to us, but it doesn't mean they're all mad. They don't kill each other. They don't even hurt each other. That's Percy.'

'And that's just it,' he said. 'It's *Percy*. One of my own congregation, until a few weeks ago. And Ann and the children still are – whatever he likes to think. I can't just ignore it.'

'No, you can't.' She took his hand and looked up into his eyes. 'I think you need to talk to someone else about it. To Charles or Basil, or maybe the Bishop. What about your father, or one of your uncles? One of them must have come across this sort of situation before.'

'Yes,' he said. 'That's a good idea. I'll do that. But since I can't do anything about it now, I'll try to put it aside and enjoy this afternoon. It's an occasion for joy, after all – a new soul brought into the church. Especially as one seems to have been lost to us.'

They walked on and at the next turn came into view of Wood Cottage. Other people were there already and the doors stood wide open, allowing guests to wander out through the French windows on to the lawn, where Travis had set up some tables and chairs borrowed from the village hall. Laughter floated in the air and they could see the star of the show, little Mary Susan, being handed from one to another like a bouquet of flowers.

'It's a happy day, Felix,' Stella said as they stood watching for a moment. 'A celebration. Don't let's allow Percy Shillabeer to spoil it.'

Yet neither of them could quite forget Ann Shillabeer, and what was happening in the farmhouse across the river.

'A very nice way to spend Sunday afternoon,' Charles Latimer commented as he came upon Hilary standing alone at the end of the garden, gazing reflectively into the dappled woods. Sunshine fell in glittering coins of gold and auburn on the fallen leaves of beech and oak, although there were still plenty still clinging on to the branches as if reluctant to fall, and the light that speared between them brightened the green of summer and turned it to bronze as it merged with the colours of autumn. There was a scent of woodsmoke in the air, drifting across from the remains of a bonfire Travis had lit the day before, and it merged with the fragrance of the roses Jennifer had planted when she had first come here to live, blowsy in their late flowering. 'It was a very nice service and Jennifer has provided a sumptuous tea.'

'I think Dottie helped,' Hilary said, turning to smile at him. 'But then there are very few occasions in Burracombe when Dottie doesn't help. It's a good job she didn't decide to marry Joe Tozer and stay in America.'

'Yes,' he said. 'We don't want to lose too many people from the village.' He paused and looked at her intently. 'Which brings me to what I wanted to talk to you about.'

Hilary sighed and looked away. 'There doesn't seem to be anything to talk about just at present, Charles. These things take so long, and Sybil's only been gone four months. David's had such a lot to sort out – she had money of her own, you see, and he didn't even know about some of her bank accounts or shares. He just had to work through it all. He had an accountant and solicitor to help, of course, but he still had to do a lot himself. And her will was complicated. So what with that and his father's announcement about retiring ...'

'Yes. That's what I want to talk to you about. Let's sit down, over here. I don't think we'll be interrupted.' He led her to a bench in the corner, tucked behind a cluster of azaleas. 'The thing is, Hilary, I've been thinking of retiring myself.' He saw her look of astonishment and laughed. 'It's not so surprising – James Hunter and I are the same age, after all. We trained together. It's only natural we should come to retirement age at the same time.'

'Well – yes, I suppose it is. I just never thought of you that way.' She stared at the ground for a moment. A small beetle was working busily at a blade of grass. 'We shall miss you dreadfully. Father will be most upset.'

'I'm not thinking of retiring entirely,' he said. 'I don't feel quite ready for that and Grace agrees with me that we can carry on for a few more years. But I'd like to step back a little – keep some of my oldest patients, like you and your father – and take on a partner. Then, in a few years, I can hand over completely and the village will have had time to get used to their new doctor.'

'A partner? You'll need to be awfully careful who you take.'

'Yes,' he said, 'and that's why I wanted to talk to you. I thought, you see, that it might be ideal for your David.'

Hilary's head snapped up. She stared at him, her eyes wide. '*David?*'

'Of course. Why not? It could be the ideal solution for all of us.'

'Why, yes,' she stammered. 'It could. But – how can you know he'd be right for you? You've never even met him.'

'That can easily be put right,' he said, amused. 'And of course I would need to meet him. I couldn't appoint anyone, even David, without being very sure. But remember, I knew his father well, and if David's anything like him ...'

'I don't know. I've never met his father.' She pushed back her hair. 'Charles, do you really mean this? You'd take David on as a partner, and maybe let him take over completely in a few years? I can't believe it.'

'Please do believe it,' he said seriously, and took both her hands in his. 'It would be a favour to me too. Grace and I want some time together – a doctor's life is a very busy one, for both him and his wife, as you'll find out, my dear – and semi-retirement would be ideal for us. But finding the right person could be very difficult. If David is indeed like his father, as I have every confidence that he is, I'm sure he would be the right man. I could hand on the baton to him without the slightest qualm.'

'But what about Felicity? She's qualified now. Wouldn't you like to hand it on to your own daughter?'

242

He shook his head. 'Felicity doesn't want to be a GP. She's decided to specialise in psychology. She'll be staying in London, at one of the big teaching hospitals.'

'I see.' Hilary stared down again. Her thoughts were whirling. 'I can't quite take it in.'

Charles patted her hand. 'Think it over, my dear. There's no great hurry. As you say, these things take time, and both you and David need to be very sure. If he does accept my offer – supposing I make it, when he's been here and we've had time to get to know each other and to talk – then he would be here for a very long time. It could be a little awkward if ...' He paused.

'If things don't work out between us,' Hilary supplied in a steady voice. She lifted her glance and met his eyes. 'I believe they will, but I know you're right. We all have to be very sure.' She thought for a moment and then said, 'How do you want to approach this, Charles? Do you want to write to David yourself to make the suggestion, or may I say something to him myself?'

'I think that would be best. You need to discuss it between you. A proposal coming from me, out of the blue, might seem rather odd. Talk to him, and if he's agreeable, he could come down here and see the lie of the land – have a look at the practice and the general area. It will be very different from the city practice he's accustomed to.'

'Yes, I suppose it will. He might not even like it – I'd never thought of that. Perhaps he'd rather work in Plymouth or Exeter than out here in the sticks.' She looked at him again. 'I don't want him to take it just because of me. It's got to be what he wants – he's got to be happy with his work.'

Charles nodded. 'You're quite right. This is a major decision for you both, Hilary, and it has to be right. It's for you two alone to make that decision – but my own feeling is that it could be very, very right for you.'

'I feel that too,' she said, and felt the realisation of what might happen course slowly through her blood, warming her heart. 'Oh Charles, thank you *so* much.' And she leaned closer and kissed his cheek.

'So here you both are!' cried a cheerful voice. 'Canoodling behind the bushes! Charles, you ought to be ashamed of yourself – does

Grace know about this?' And Felix, his blue eyes laughing, came into view with Stella close behind.

'Caught!' Charles said wryly. 'Hilary, I'm afraid our secret is out. We'd better go back and face the music.'

Hilary laughed. She felt suddenly so light with happiness that she might at any moment float. She jumped up. 'I'd better go and see what Father's up to anyway. I hope he's not had too much of that champagne Travis was handing round when I came outside.'

'Only a bottle or two,' Felix said gravely. He looked at Charles. 'Actually, I was looking for you. There's something I want to talk to you about.'

Stella hooked her arm through Hilary's. 'Let's go back and leave them to it. I want to see that baby again – it's at least half an hour since I had a cuddle.' She slanted a look at Hilary. 'To tell you the truth, she's making me feel quite broody.'

Chapter Thirty-Two

'Come to Burracombe?' David echoed. 'Come and *work* in Burracombe? Be the village doctor?'

'Yes!' Hilary tried hard to contain the delight in her voice. *He might not want to*, she'd been telling herself all evening as she waited impatiently for her father to go to bed so that she could use the telephone. *It's too good to be true. It might never happen.* But she could not prevent the tremor of excitement and anxiety. *Please let him say yes, please let it be all right ...*

'Say it again,' he ordered. 'Tell me exactly what he said to you.'

Hilary took a deep breath. 'He said he was thinking of retiring, just like your father – they trained together, I told you that some time ago, so they're the same age – but he doesn't want to retire completely, he wants to find a partner who might take on the whole practice later on, when he does decide to finish. And he thought of you because I'd told him your father was retiring but you didn't want to stay in Derby, and he asked me if – if you might consider ... David, *would* you? It would be so marvellous. It would solve everything. We could be together here, you would still have your work and I'd still be in Burracombe ... we could live here at the Barton – I can't think of anything better!' Somewhat belatedly, she remembered her vow not to try to persuade him. 'Only if you want to, of course,' she added rather lamely. 'It's got to be what you want.'

'What I want? Of course it would be what I want! I can't think of anything better either.'

Her heart leapt. 'But you still need to come and see for yourself. You need to talk to Charles.'

'And he needs to see me. He might not like me at all.'

'He says he will, if you're anything like your father.' She remembered again that she had never met David's father. '*Are* you like him, David?'

'No, I'm like Great-Uncle Willie, the black sheep of the family.' He laughed. 'Only joking. Yes, I am quite a bit like Dad but I'm *not* him. Dr Latimer and I still might not get on. I think I'd better come down and see him. And you too, my darling.' He paused. 'I was feeling really down until you rang. Everything seemed so complicated and difficult – and now it's as if a dark curtain has been suddenly lifted aside. I'm beginning to see a way ahead at last.'

Patsy could see very little way ahead. With her baby due within a month, she had stopped working at the Barton and Brenda Culliford had taken her place. Joyce Warren had suggested this herself to Hilary, saying that she'd only kept Brenda on until a permanent place was found, and this seemed a good solution all round. The two girls could even work together at the Barton once Patsy's baby was born, for the new mother would be unlikely to want to work full time.

Patsy, now large and cumbersome, moved awkwardly about the Pettifers' cottage, feeling incessantly tired. She suffered from the burning pain of heartburn in her chest, the stabbing pain of sciatica in her right hip and thigh, and a constant vigorous thumping in her stomach that told her that the baby was alive and well, but impatient to be born. 'At least when he'm here I can put him in the pram and wheel him round the village,' she said to Terry. 'Or I can hand him over to you, and get a bit of rest that way.'

What she most wanted during these last tedious weeks was to see her mother, but that had become almost impossible now. It wasn't just that Ann was more or less trapped in the farmhouse and unable even to go to Tavistock for a morning's shopping; it was also that Patsy herself couldn't go far. The walk down to the river and across the Clam and up the other side to the Shillabeer farm, and then back again an hour or so later, was just too much for her. Norman Tozer offered to take her round in Ted's pickup truck, and Felix suggested coming over in the Baby Austin to collect her, but she dared not accept either offer. Percy was always around; you never knew when he might show up at the farm, and she dared not risk it.

'He do seem to have settled down a bit,' Jack Pettifer said at supper one evening. 'He still won't let Ann off the farm, but she've been in church once or twice by all accounts and her don't look too bad. If you want to know what I think, she's better off now he won't eat with her and the little'ns. They can have their food in peace without him watching them like a hawk all the time and calling them to order. As long as she puts his dinner on the table and does his washing and keeps the place as it should be, he seems to leave her alone.'

'As long as she behaves like his servant, you mean,' Nancy said sharply. 'Slave too, more like, if he won't let her out. You might think it's all right, Jack, but to my mind 'tis a crying shame. A disgrace.'

Jack looked abashed. 'I didn't mean it like that, Nance. I didn't say it was *right*, did I?'

'What about the farm?' Patsy asked. 'Is he still selling it?'

'I haven't heard anything more about that. He still goes to those meetings in Plymouth on Sunday mornings, though, so if he means to carry on with they Brethren I suppose he'll have to.'

'And then they'll all go to Plymouth and I'll never see them again,' Patsy said miserably. 'And Mother will never see her little grandchild.'

They ate their sausages in silence for a while, then Terry said, 'I'm going to go over there and see him.'

Patsy dropped her fork. 'You're not! Terry, he'll kill you!'

'He won't. I'm pretty near as big as he is now.' This wasn't anywhere near true. Terry was probably as tall as Percy, but he was a string bean to Percy's marrow. 'And I'm a lot younger. Anyway, I don't reckon he'll try anything on. Bert Lillywhite'll be on to him straight away and have him up in court.'

'And what good will that do my mother?' Patsy asked. 'Don't go, Terry. You'll only make things worse.'

Terry said nothing more, but he thought his own thoughts. He wasn't going to take this lying down. Not any more. He was a husband and soon to be a father, and it was time he took matters into his own hands.

*

Bob hadn't been at supper with the rest of the family. He'd been with the skiffle group, rehearsing for the extravaganza. It wasn't really a Christmas show now, as there was so much on in December that Joyce had decided to bring it forward and had booked the hall for the second Saturday in November. With only two or three weeks to go, the group needed as much practice as it could get.

'Mrs Warren's coming to hear us tonight, don't forget,' Bob told them as they gathered with the rest of the performers in the village hall. 'It's a sort of dress rehearsal and audition all rolled into one. And she's getting Luke Ferris doing posters to put round the village.'

'With our names on?' Reg asked. 'Here, didn't we ought to make up our minds what to call ourselves?'

'It needs to have a country sound,' Vic said. 'It's country sort of music, isn't it? Something blue and hillbilly.'

'What about the Blue Hillbillies, then?' Bob suggested, but Brenda shook her head.

'Doesn't sound right. The Blue Billies would be better.'

Roy gave a snort of laughter. 'Everyone will call us the Blue Willies! Think of something else, Bren.'

Brenda gave him a withering look. 'The Burracombe Billies, then, what about that? Or the Burracombe Hillbillies?'

'That's not bad,' Reg said thoughtfully. 'It tells everybody a bit about what sort of music to expect, and where we come from. After all, we might get some bookings after this, to play in other villages.'

The others roared with laughter. 'Bookings? You reckon?'

'Why not? There's plenty of villages have Christmas shows and might want a bit of music. Or we might get asked to play at parties. Weddings, even.' At this, the laughter drowned his voice completely. 'Well, anyway, it's a good name and I vote that's what we call ourselves. The Burracombe Hillbillies.'

By now, they had three songs by heart, with Brenda singing the verse and the boys playing and joining in with the chorus. Brenda had turned out to have a good touch on the ukulele and could play and sing at the same time, something Reg was never able to master with his guitar, despite all Felix's coaching, and they'd achieved a passable harmony as well. Roy had written a song that they all thought wasn't at all bad and Vic had put it to a tune, although the tune seemed to owe rather a lot to another of Hank Williams' songs.

'It's all right if you change a few of the notes,' he'd defended himself. 'There's only eight of them after all – they must be running out of tunes by now, some of them are bound to sound the same. Anyway, it's the words that matter and these are all about Burracombe in the old days, when they were mining hereabouts, so folk will like that. I bet everyone will be singing it the next day.'

For the dress rehearsal, they were all wearing the clothes they'd chosen for their band costume. The four boys had check shirts in blue and red which they'd bought at Tavistock Goosey Fair, while Brenda's blouse was of white broderie anglaise and her skirt very nearly matched the dark blue corduroy of the boys' trousers. They looked clean, smart and country-ish, and when Joyce Warren saw them, she was pleasantly surprised.

'Very professional. You've certainly made an effort with your dress. Let's hope your musical accomplishments are as impressive.'

'I wouldn't call 'em accomplishments, exactly,' Roy said, but Joyce had already turned away and was clapping her hands for attention.

'Now then,' she said when they were all quiet at last. 'It's amazing how much people find to talk about … Anyway, thank you for coming. You've all told me what you can do and I've put together a rough programme, so what I'd like to do is have a run-through now and see if it needs a little tweaking. We've got two weeks before we open, and we may need to do quite a bit of rehearsing before then, so let's not waste any time.' She consulted her programme. 'I'd like to open with Alfred Coker singing a medley of old songs, just to get things going. And I'm very pleased to say that our new schoolteacher, Mr Raynor, has agreed to play the piano for us.'

There was a spattering of applause, during which the blacksmith made his way to the stage, which was erected when needed from a collection of pallets with sheets of hardboard laid over them. James Raynor opened his music, glanced at the blacksmith to see that he was ready, and struck the first note of 'Glorious Devon'.

'That was very good, Mr Coker,' Joyce said as he finished his second song, 'Ol' Man River'. 'And we'll be hearing more of this fine voice later in the evening.' Clearly she had decided to take the master of ceremonies role herself. 'Now, there's nothing like a good laugh …'

'And this is going to be nothing like a good laugh,' Roy muttered as Norman Tozer climbed up beside her.

'. . . so we're going to have some comedy from Mr Norman Tozer.'

Joyce stepped aside and Norman laboured through the same jokes that he told every time there was a performance such as this. Everyone laughed politely, because after all, as Jacob said, you couldn't hurt the man's feelings, and Norman climbed down again, grinning from ear to ear at his own wit.

'Those jokes are so old they ought to be put out of their misery,' Vic said behind his hand, and the skiffle group laughed, then pulled themselves to attention as they heard their name called out.

'. . . something entirely new,' Joyce was saying. 'But I'm sure we're all going to enjoy our very own skiffle band – the Burracombe Hillbillies.' She raised her voice encouragingly and the band straggled self-consciously on to the stage, clutching their instruments and wondering suddenly how they'd ever got themselves into this.

Bob began the announcement, his voice unaccountably squeaky. He stopped, lowered it to a growl, and started again while the others sorted themselves into their agreed positions.

'I dunno if any of you have heard of skiffle,' he said, seeing from the audience's faces that most of them hadn't, 'but it's a new sort of country music. You might think,' he went on, warming to his task of educating his listeners, 'that we've just made our instruments up out of old rubbish, but that's what skiffle's all about.' Someone gave a snort of laughter and there were a few giggles. Bob blushed to the roots of his hair. 'It's not rubbish, though. It's proper music that anyone can play and these are the proper instruments. Anyway, us have been practising for weeks now . . .'

'And don't us know it!' observed Norman Tozer, who lived near enough to hear the sounds emanating from Jack Pettifer's shed, and who had also heard Roy's comment as he went on stage. 'Thought someone was being murdered, us did.'

'. . . and this is what we'm going to play for you tonight,' Bob finished, and the band launched into their very own version of 'Your Cheatin' Heart'.

When they finished, it was to a round of surprised and enthusiastic applause. Norman, who was not ungenerous, turned to his neighbour and said in a loud whisper that it wasn't half as bad as he'd expected, and Joyce, who lived far enough away to have missed the rehearsals, beamed at them.

'That was really very good, boys. And Brenda, you have a very nice little voice. Well done.' She looked out at the audience. 'We'll be hearing more from the Burracombe Hillbillies in the second half. Now we're going to hear one of those wonderful Jan Stewer stories, read to us by Ted Tozer. Ted ...'

Ted dragged a chair on to the stage and sat down. He opened up his book of Jan Stewer stories, written by A. J. Coles, and as they all settled back for a genuinely good laugh, he began in a Devon dialect as rich as clotted cream: 'This is the story of Jan and the census ...'

Chapter Thirty-Three

I t was arranged that David should come to Burracombe in early November. He would arrive on Thursday, stay with the Latimers and spend a day with Charles, attending his surgery and accompanying him on his rounds. On the Friday evening, they would all come to dinner at the Barton. He could then spend most of Saturday with Charles, discussing the practice, and have Sunday with Hilary before returning to Derby on Monday.

'Are you happy with that arrangement?' Charles asked her. 'I know you'll want to spend some time together, but we will need a good day or two for him to get an idea of what a country practice involves.'

'It's fine,' she assured him. 'And much better that he should stay with you. He could have come to the Barton – I've already told Father that I know him – but ...'

'Better not – this time anyway,' he agreed. 'There'll be no need for any awkwardness or embarrassment, you know. People – including your father – will soon accept that you knew each other before, and if romance seems to blossom once he's here, nobody will be anything but pleased. Everyone in the village wants to see you happy. And to know that the estate is in safe hands too, of course.'

'It's a lot for David to take on,' she said thoughtfully. 'A wife who runs a big estate, and having to live in the family home. Not all men would be happy with that.'

'And that's another reason why you need to take it slowly for a while,' he said. 'Both your lives are going to be very different, and sometimes a big change like that can alter a relationship.'

'I know.' But not ours, she thought. Please, not ours.

Or if it did, only for the better.

'It seems to me,' Felix said to Stella, 'that the whole situation is like a pot about to boil over. Or a volcano about to erupt.'

'I thought it had improved,' Stella said. 'Ann comes to church every Sunday now.'

'Yes, but I'm not sure Percy knows that. As long as she has his dinner on the table when he comes back, and the children are playing quietly at whatever games he allows on a Sunday – no running about outside, no board games such as ludo, which count as gambling apparently – he says nothing.'

Stella thought about this. They were in the sitting room of the vicarage. The curtains were drawn and the fire crackled in the hearth. Felix was working on some parish papers and Stella was mending socks. She said, 'It's a strange way to live. I can't see how they can keep it up for ever.'

'Exactly. Something is going to give one day, and I'm very much afraid it will be Percy. He probably suspects what's going on, and although he allows it by pretending he doesn't know, that so-called conscience of his is eventually going to explode. And God knows what will happen then.'

'Do you think he'll hurt her?' she asked anxiously, and Felix sighed.

'Even if he doesn't hurt her physically, she's suffering in other ways. I talked about it with Charles Latimer, you know. He can't say much because she's his patient – and so is Percy, come to that – but he says that in cases like this, there's very little anyone can do. The people concerned have to ask for help themselves – nobody can interfere. If she went to him, he'd be able to find out more about her life with Percy, but she never goes near the surgery. She struggles on alone.'

'And Patsy can't do much either,' Stella said, biting off a length of darning wool. 'She's very near her time now. Bob told me she's persuaded Terry not to go and have it out with Percy. He desperately wants to, but they think it would only make matters worse. Felix, you don't happen to have seen my scissors, do you?'

'They're here,' he said guiltily, handing them over. 'I was cutting up some paper. Sorry.'

'For goodness' sake! How often have I asked you not to cut paper with them? It ruins the blades. Oh, I meant to tell you – Hilary's invited us to dinner on Friday week. Apparently a friend of hers is staying with the Latimers. He's a doctor – did you know Charles was thinking of taking on a partner?'

Felix nodded. 'He mentioned it at the Kellaways' baptism party. He wants to take it a bit easier. Who else will be there?'

'Basil and Grace, the Latimers and us. I think that's all. I'm not quite sure if we're being shown to this doctor friend of Hilary's or he's being shown to us. It will be interesting to meet him, though, and we always have a good time at the Barton, especially if Colonel Napier's on form.'

They spent the rest of the evening listening to the radio and then turned to the Home Service for the nine o'clock news. Mostly they listened to music, but tonight they also heard the first of a new comedy series – *Hancock's Half Hour* – which had them both laughing until tears ran down their cheeks. They'd heard Tony Hancock before, in *Educating Archie*, in which he'd played one of the numerous tutors employed to teach the schoolboy ventriloquist's dummy, and as Felix remarked, he'd been funny then but now he seemed to have come into his own.

'We must make sure we hear it next week,' he said. 'It's different from the other comedies we've heard, like *Take It From Here* and *Stand Easy*. They're like variety shows, with sketches and songs, but this was more like a short play.'

They went to bed. Stella lay for a while thinking of Ann Shillabeer and her family, whose wireless had been smashed as the work of the Devil, and felt sad that they could no longer enjoy such innocent pleasures as music from London's great concert halls, or comedy to lighten their days.

More important, though, was Felix's fear that the situation in the Shillabeer household was like a simmering volcano. Was he right? And if so, what would happen next?

Friday was Guy Fawkes Night, and for the past few days the children of the village had been making guys out of straw, cardboard and old clothes, and vying with each other for the best pitches outside the village shops for the collection of pennies. Nobody could go shopping during the hour or so after school had finished and before darkness fell, without running the gauntlet of a series of unsightly images dressed in jackets and trousers that wouldn't have been accepted into a jumble sale, each accompanied by several protectors demanding money.

'Penny for the guy?' Billy Madge entreated as Ivy Sweet tried to get into her own husband's shop. 'It's for a good cause.'

'And what cause is that, apart from stopping people going about their business?' she demanded.

'Fireworks,' Billy replied with a cheeky grin. 'Us wants a big rocket.'

'You wants a big rocket all right! Now get away from my doorway. We don't want guys cluttering up the street and making it look untidy.'

'I bet you'll buy fireworks for your Barry,' he grumbled.

'That's my business. He won't have to go out begging for them, anyway.'

Billy opened his mouth and then closed it again. He quite liked Barry Sweet, and he didn't think it was necessary to tell Ivy that her precious son was actually standing with another guy outside Edie Pettifer's shop. He'd probably hidden when he'd seen his mother come along the street. There was quite a lot Barry did that his mother didn't know about.

'Go on,' Ivy said crossly. 'Get away from here.'

George Sweet came out. 'What's the matter, Ivy? They're not doing any harm.'

'I don't like them here. It gives the bakery a bad name.'

'Come on,' he said. 'It's only once a year, and the tackers like to think they've paid for the fireworks theirselves. It's tradition.'

'Tradition!' Ivy snorted. 'It's rubbish, that's what it is. Look at the rags they've used to make the horrible thing.' She peered closer. 'Here, isn't that your old shirt that I was going to use for a polishing cloth? How did they get hold of that?'

'I gave it to them. It was wore out. I didn't know you wanted it.'

'You know I always use old things. It was in the rag bag. You didn't have no right—'

'No right? It was *my* shirt! Paid for out of what I earn here in this bakery.'

'No it wasn't. I give it to you for Christmas five years ago. Had to use my own clothing coupons to get it, too.'

'Well, that wouldn't have mattered much, since clothes came off ration soon after that anyway. Doesn't matter who paid for it; it was my shirt and no reason why I shouldn't give it away if I wanted to.'

Ivy drew in an angry breath, and then noticed Billy and his friends listening with interest to the exchange. She tossed her head.

'I don't have time to stand here argy-bargying. I came round for that pie for your supper. You kept one back, I hope? I don't have time to cook before I go off to work.'

'It's on the shelf. Help yourself.' George watched her go inside, then winked at the boys. 'You'd better make yourselves scarce for quarter of an hour. Time you went home for your tea anyway. Here . . .' He fished inside his pocket and took out a threepenny bit. 'Take this and don't come back till tomorrow.'

'Thanks, Mr Sweet.' The boys gathered up their cap of pennies and seized the little wooden cart they'd made out of a few bits of wood and two pram wheels, dragging it along the street. George watched them, grinning. He remembered doing exactly the same thing himself as a young boy, and he remembered Ivy tagging along behind, whining to be allowed to bring her own guy dressed as a girl in an old cotton frock. She'd never really understood why they wouldn't let her.

I don't reckon she's ever got over that, he thought as he went back into the shop where Ivy was wrapping her pie in yesterday's *Daily Sketch*. It wouldn't do to remind her, though. It wouldn't do at all.

Hilary had seen the various guys positioned around the village and given them each a few pennies. She knew that on Friday evening the gardens would be smoky with bonfires built of sticks gathered from the woods over the past week, with the precious guys balanced precariously on top, and the sky bright with fireworks for about an hour after tea, and then it would be all over for another year. As she walked back to the Barton with a basket of shopping, she met Miss Kemp coming the other way.

'You'll be glad when Bonfire Night's done with,' she said with a smile. 'It must be quite a distraction for the children – the boys especially.'

'There's always something to distract them,' the teacher said wryly. 'It's been conkers for the past few weeks, but they've had their day now until next autumn. In the spring and summer, when it's warm enough to sit in the playground, it's fivestones and guessing games. In winter, it's chasing and hunting, to keep warm.'

'I remember those games,' Hilary said, smiling. 'They come round in their seasons, the same ones each year.'

'The children hand them on to each other – we never have to teach them. Some of them are so mysterious you can watch for hours and never really understand, but the children know all the rules and stick by them rigorously. It's a pity they don't apply the same principles to the rules *we* try to teach!'

Hilary laughed. 'How is the new teacher getting along?' she asked. 'He's been up to play chess with my father two or three times now. They seem to get along very well.'

'He's a nice man,' Frances Kemp agreed. 'And very keen to be part of village life. Mrs Warren has dragooned him into playing the piano for the extravaganza next Saturday. You'll be coming, I hope?'

'I certainly will. I'll be bringing a friend, too – a doctor. He's staying with the Latimers – Charles and his father trained together.' She hesitated. David's reason for coming wasn't yet general knowledge, since Charles didn't want to announce his plans until they were more certain. 'They haven't seen each other for years, but since David was going to be down this way ...'

'That'll be nice,' Frances said comfortably. She didn't ask how Hilary also came to know the Latimers' guest. Perhaps it really was going to be as easy as that, Hilary thought. 'Does he live in the country?'

'Not really. He works in his father's practice in Derby.'

'Well I hope he's prepared for village entertainments,' Frances said with a laugh. 'James – Mr Raynor – says it's going to be quite an eye-opener. The skiffle group has to be seen to be believed.'

They parted and went their separate ways. Frances was on her way to buy two pork chops for the supper she was cooking for James. Since his invitation to her a few weeks ago, they had developed a habit of inviting each other for supper once a week, to discuss school affairs or to listen to music. It was a loose, comfortable arrangement and they knew each other well enough now to feel easy in each other's company. Often they talked about other things – their lives, their experiences, holidays they had both enjoyed. Both had travelled before the war, and hoped to do so again, when it became easier and you could take more money than the current limit of fifty pounds.

'Walking in Germany,' James said later that evening, as they ate the chops she had grilled. 'I used to enjoy that. But now there are other places I'd like to visit – Switzerland, the Pyrenees, Spain. There's so much world out there, and so little time!'

Frances laughed. 'I've always wanted to visit Australia, or New Zealand. But it takes such a long time to get there – six weeks each way. It's impossible until I retire.'

'You'll probably be able to fly there by then. You might even be able to now, by taking lots of planes. It would be quite an adventure to try.'

'And still take too long, even in the summer holidays. And suppose you got stranded and couldn't get back?' She shook her head. 'It will have to remain a dream, I'm afraid.'

'Have you ever thought of emigrating?' he asked. 'The Australian government is very keen to encourage that. They offer a very cheap fare out – "Ten Pound Poms" they call Britons who take advantage of it. You have to stay two years or pay the whole cost if you return early, but the aim is to get people to move there for good.'

Frances shook her head. 'I'd never consider leaving England. It's my home, whatever its difficulties. It would seem very disloyal to stay here all through the war and then abandon the country when it's struggling to get back on its feet afterwards.'

'I feel that too,' he said thoughtfully. 'We had no choice during the war, of course, but we do have one now and I agree – if we loved England enough to fight for her, we should love her enough to stay. But everyone has a right to make their own choice.'

They followed the chops with stewed plums and custard, then washed up together companionably. On the first few occasions when they had eaten together, they had each insisted on leaving the washing-up to be done later, but now they did it together and were almost as familiar with each other's kitchens as with their own. As James put away the last of the pudding bowls, Frances made tea and they took it into her small sitting room.

'A very pleasant evening,' James said, sitting on the sofa and stretching out his legs. 'Thank you.'

There was a small silence. For the first time that evening, Frances felt slightly uncomfortable. It was at this moment, when they had finished eating and were sharing a pot of tea or mugs of cocoa, that conversation lapsed, as if there were something more that needed to be said but neither knew how to say it. I don't even know what it is, she thought, gazing at the fire. I don't know what I want to say, or what he wants to say to me.

James opened his mouth, and she was invaded by a sudden sense of trepidation. She got up quickly.

'Shall we have some music?' Her voice was, she knew, unnaturally bright. 'I've got a surprise for you – the whole three-LP recording of *Porgy and Bess*! I've been saving it.'

She opened her gramophone and took the three big long-playing records from the shelf. James came across and looked at the sleeves, handling them reverently. He gave her back the first and she put it on the turntable.

The awkward moment passed as they listened to the first strains of 'Summertime', and when James took his leave an hour or so later, they had regained their previous comfortable companionship.

Chapter Thirty-Four

That last week before David arrived in Burracombe seemed to Hilary to be the longest of her life. She roamed the estate on foot, in the Land Rover or on Beau, taking him for long gallops across the moor and standing for hours on the ridge above the village, staring out across the bleak, dead bracken towards the faraway glitter of Plymouth Sound. She tidied the office to within an inch of its life, so that Travis complained he couldn't find a thing any more, and she paced the house until her father called her a cat on hot bricks and asked her what on earth was the matter.

'Nothing, Father. Just winter coming on. You know how I hate these dark evenings, and we'll have to start thinking about Christmas soon.' Christmas. Where would she and David be at Christmas? Could this be the first they'd celebrate together? But she shook her head. Whatever happened between him and Charles Latimer, he would have to be in Derby until sometime next year. Maybe Easter ...

'... Rob over again,' she heard her father say, and looked at him in bewilderment.

'Rob?'

'Yes, of course. At Christmas. Wasn't that what you were talking about? And Marianne too, if she wants to come, but he's old enough to travel by himself now.'

'He's still only thirteen.'

'Is he? Good Lord. But of course you're right – he was born in March 1941. He seems older than that. Anyway, it's time we saw him here again. I missed him during the summer holidays.'

'Yes.' Hilary had missed her nephew too, with his striking resemblance to her dead brother Baden, and his delicately polite ways. She remembered the day he had run away from school and tried to make his way back to France, and how David had come to the rescue. Her father had written to David and thanked him, thus unwittingly setting off a train of further calamity when Sybil saw his letter and deduced that David was meeting another woman – Hilary herself. 'You know it's David Hunter who's coming to dinner on Friday evening, don't you? The man who found Rob in London and put him on the train back here?'

'Is it? I didn't realise that. Seems a decent enough chap, from what Charles tells me.'

'Charles hasn't met him yet, but he is. I knew him in Egypt.' She had told her father this before, keeping the information to a minimum, but it seemed to be enough, since her father merely nodded and said, 'Looking forward to meeting him. I can thank him in person then. Charles tells me he's considering him as a partner – seems a bit odd, since he's never met the man either.'

'He knew David's father. They trained together.'

'So I understand. He hopes it'll be like father, like son, I suppose. Well, sometimes it is and sometimes it's not.' He frowned, and she guessed he was thinking of Baden, who would have followed so closely in his footsteps, and Stephen, who resolutely declined to do so. And daughters are still only second best, she thought with resignation, but that's Father and his generation and there's nothing to be done about it. At least he's finally accepted that I'm competent enough to run the estate – with Travis's help, of course.

She wondered how her father would take to the new changes that were about to happen. If Charles and David got on ... if David accepted the offer she was sure Charles would make, and came to live and work in Burracombe ... if she and David were able to at last be open about their relationship ... if they married and she became Mrs David Hunter ...

The thought gave her a little thrill. But she knew that their difficulties might not be over even then. There would be fresh hurdles to face, and her father's reaction might well be the highest of them all.

*

Thursday finally arrived, and Charles went to meet David at Tavistock railway station. He took Hilary with him and waited discreetly outside while they greeted each other.

'David! I thought you'd never get here.'

'So did I. I swear the driver slowed down deliberately after Exeter. I almost looked out once or twice to see if there was a man walking in front with a red flag.' He held her tightly. 'Oh Hilary, to think we're going to be together for a whole weekend in your own home!'

'Well, not exactly. You'll be staying with Charles and Mary, and spending most of your time with them.'

'It'll feel like being with you,' he declared. 'I'll be in Burracombe and you'll be there too. That's a start. And I'll see you tomorrow evening, and again on Sunday.'

They came out of the station and Hilary led him towards Charles's car. Charles got out and Hilary introduced them. They shook hands, assessing each other with their eyes, and Charles smiled.

'You're very like your father.'

'So people tell me. I can see it myself, in photographs. Not so much now.'

'He's old and grey like me, I suppose.'

'Silver, I'd say,' David said. 'And neither of you looks old. Distinguished, perhaps.'

Charles laughed and turned to Hilary. 'You didn't say he was a flatterer!'

They got into the car and Charles drove them through Tavistock towards the moorland road leading to Burracombe. David looked about with interest as Hilary pointed out the local landmarks – the big church that was almost all that was left of the ancient abbey dominating the square, the bridge over the tumbling river, the rows of tiny cottages that the Duke of Bedford had built for his workers. The statue of the Duke himself, standing outside the tiny, ancient guildhall; the courthouse, and the police station that was one of the oldest in the country and faced straight down Plymouth Road to the other statue – that of the most famous of local boys, Sir Francis Drake, proud and arrogant on his stone plinth, less than a mile from his birthplace.

'Drake was born just down the road from here,' Hilary said. 'He did a lot for the area when he retired from the sea and he developed Plymouth's first water system from Dartmoor.'

She wished David could sit in the back with her, so that they could touch each other, hold hands, but it would have looked odd for Charles to arrive in the village sitting alone in the front, like a chauffeur. Gossip didn't need much fuel in Burracombe, where the mere sight of her and David in the back of the car would have had them paired off even before they got out. Not that gossip would be far wrong in this case, she thought, but if David were to become the local doctor, he must be untainted.

They got out at the Latimers' house and went inside. Mary welcomed David and took him upstairs to show him his room and the bathroom, and then came down to make the tea. She brought it into the sitting room on a trolley and they sat round the fire, toasting crumpets. David arrived just as Hilary was beginning to butter them.

'Crumpets! Just the thing for a cold November afternoon.' He sat beside Hilary on the sofa and she felt the warmth of his arm against hers. It seemed impossible that he was actually here, beside her. She stole a glance at him, to assure herself that it was true, and he glanced sideways at the same moment as if doing the same thing. They smiled and then laughed, although neither of them could have said what was funny, and then Mary began to ask about his journey and they all relaxed into a welcome banality.

'It's so strange,' Hilary said later, when tea was over and the Latimers had left them alone by the fire. 'I've imagined you coming to Burracombe so many times, and it was never like this. I always pictured you walking down the street, or knocking at our door, or sitting in our drawing room, or just being with me in the fields and the woods. I never thought it would be here, in Charles Latimer's house, coming to be our doctor.'

'We don't know yet that I will be,' he said. 'But I hope so … I've imagined it too, all the things you've just said, even though I didn't know what any of those places looked like. And every time I imagined it, I felt as if I would be coming home.'

'And do you feel that now you're here?'

He turned his head and smiled at her. 'I will do, when I see them. Anywhere I can be with you is going to be home.'

After she had taken a reluctant farewell and gone home, Hilary did not see David again until the next evening. She was busy all Friday preparing for the evening. They were to have roast beef, with roast potatoes, Yorkshire pudding, carrots, parsnips and cauliflower, followed by apple pie and clotted cream – a traditional meal and one that was guaranteed to put her father in a good mood. It was important, she thought, that he should be so, because this would be the first time he met David, and she needed it to be an occasion he would enjoy.

Mrs Curnow and Brenda worked hard too, making sure the house was at its best, and fires were lit in all the downstairs rooms. Brenda brought coal and wood into each one, so that they could be easily replenished during the evening. She was still rather overawed by the Barton, and the idea of having more than one fire in the house was clearly something she had found hard to understand. At five o'clock, she came to Hilary and asked if she could go home now.

'Only 'tis the last night before the extravaganza,' she said, twisting her hands together in her apron. 'And me and the boys wants to have a run-through before we go to the village hall for rehearsal.'

'Of course you can go, Brenda. There's nothing else for you to do here. And don't worry about tomorrow – everything will go well, I know. We're all looking forward to it.'

'I almost wish us wasn't doing it at all!' the girl burst out. 'I dunno why I ever let them talk me into it, really I don't!'

'Now don't be silly. You know you've enjoyed rehearsing, and you'll enjoy tomorrow even more. Run along now and have a nice evening, and get a good sleep tonight. You'll be the stars of the show.'

'Us won't be that. Mr Coker'll be that. He always is. Or Mr Tozer, reading his Jan Stewer stories. Or—'

'You'll be a great success – all of you.' Hilary propelled her towards the door. 'Now go along, do. I've got to get ready myself soon. We'll see you tomorrow.'

She watched the girl pull on her coat and let herself out into the night, and almost wished she were going with her. I feel every bit as nervous, she thought, though for very different reasons. This evening is important for us both.

For the first time since the reunion when they had met again, she and David would be together in the company of other people – people who were going to have influence over their lives. If – she dared not yet say 'when' – David came to Burracombe to live and work, these were the people they would have most contact with – her father, the Latimers, her friends Stella and Felix, Basil and Mary. She had no doubt that they would like David, but she felt a sudden terror of seeing him on her home ground. She recalled a friend from her youth who had told her once in despair that whenever she took a young man home, they stopped liking each other. They seemed to see a different aspect of each other and the attraction disappeared. The kiss of death, she'd called it. Could that happen to herself and David?

No. Of course it couldn't. They were mature people in their thirties, not impressionable youngsters. They had made their own lives, known powerful love, thought each other lost and come together again. Simply meeting now in her own home wasn't going to change their feelings for each other.

All the same, her heart seemed to tremble as she waited for the doorbell to ring. She had spent half an hour in panic, trying to decide what to wear – this woollen dress, that skirt and blouse – and finally settled for a dress in fine needlecord, of dark brown and golden checks, with a scooped neck and tight waist billowing into a full skirt. She had bought it in London and only worn it once or twice, and her father looked at it with approval.

'Suits you, Hilary. And that amber necklace looks very effective with it. You look very handsome.'

Handsome? she thought. Not, perhaps, the adjective she would have chosen, but a compliment from her father. She smiled at him, and then the doorbell rang, startling her so much that she almost knocked over the vase of chrysanthemums she had been adjusting on the hall table.

'Good God, girl, have a care. Anyone would think we weren't expecting visitors!' He waited while she opened the door. 'Ah, Charles. Good to see you. And Mary – come in out of the cold.'

'It's getting foggy,' Charles Latimer said, following his wife through the door. He pulled off his thick gloves and shook Gilbert's hand while Mary kissed Hilary's cheek. 'Let me introduce you to our visitor. Gilbert, this is Dr David Hunter – David, this is our squire, Colonel Napier.'

David and Gilbert shook hands, and then David turned to Hilary. She had braced herself for this moment, but when she met his eyes, her fears melted. He was apparently quite at ease, and his hand was warm and firm as he shook hers. She felt the reassurance he was offering her and relaxed. They smiled at each other.

'I expect Hilary's told you that we've already met,' he said to Gilbert. 'Years ago, in Egypt, and again at the reunion. We've kept in touch since then.'

'And you were responsible for rescuing my young grandson when he ran away,' Gilbert said. 'Owe you a debt of gratitude for that. No knowing what might have happened to him if Hilary hadn't been able to contact you.'

'It was a pleasure. He's a nice young fellow. Back in France now, I understand.'

'Yes, it seemed best for him to be with his mother. French ways are different from ours and you can't transplant a half-grown tree. I hope he'll spend more time with us here when he's older. But why are we standing around in the hall? If Hilary's seen to your coats, let's go into the drawing room and have a drink. Basil and Grace will be here any minute, but you know Basil – always a little late.'

'Always *afraid* of being late,' Hilary said as the doorbell rang again. 'He usually does manage to arrive on time.' She opened the door again to reveal their four remaining guests. 'Come in. Charles says it's getting foggy – we thought you might have got lost.'

'Cheek!' Felix said cheerfully, stamping his feet on the mat. 'Stella and I could find our way across the Clam blindfold. Not that we came that way this evening. Stella said her new frock wasn't suitable for walking in.'

'It's very pretty,' Hilary said, admiring Stella's slender figure in the deep blue dress. 'Give me your coats and then go into the drawing room. Father's handing round sherry, or whisky if you'd prefer. I just need to go and attend to things in the oven.'

She escaped and stood for a moment in the quiet kitchen, collecting herself. So far, so good, she thought. The moment of arrival and greeting was over and her father was at his most expansive. David's help with Rob and the fact that he had been in the army and served in Egypt counted in his favour. Charles and Mary seemed happy with their visitor, and Felix would lighten the atmosphere if there were any awkward moments. She felt herself relax a little more.

There was little to attend to. The beef was on the table, resting under a wire canopy and two tea towels. The potatoes were roasting, the vegetables simmering and the Yorkshire pudding was ready to slide into the oven as she made the gravy. She had just time for a quick sherry with her guests.

'So there you are.'

Hilary gasped and whirled round. She was in David's arms instantly, lifting her face to be kissed. He let her go and they stared into each other's eyes.

'I've been waiting for this all day,' he murmured. 'And yesterday, having to be circumspect and polite – it was almost unbearable.'

'I know. Charles and Mary were so understanding, leaving us alone at tea time, but all the same ... And we don't have time now, David. How did you find me?'

'I followed the smell of roast beef! I'm supposed to be washing my hands. Are you coming back?'

'Yes, just for a few minutes. Stella will come out and help me then.' She held him tightly. 'I can't believe you're really here.'

'Neither can I, quite.' He kissed her again. 'Come on. We don't want your father sending out a search party.' He looked into her eyes, grave again. 'And don't worry. I have a feeling everything is going to turn out right for us.'

'However much bigger am I going to get?' Patsy asked. She stirred uncomfortably in Jack's big armchair, which he'd given over to her during the past few weeks, when her bulk seemed to make every other chair in the house too small. 'I'm like the side of a house. I don't feel as if I'll ever be thin again.'

'You will, sweetheart.' Terry stroked her cheek. He was sitting on an upright chair beside her, his arm around her shoulders. 'You'm not fat – 'tis only the baby taking up all that room.'

'It's like being old,' she said. 'Slow and clumsy, not being able to bend or do things easy. I don't know how anybody goes in for more than one baby.'

'Mum says they forget what it was like. Or they like the baby so much when it comes they wants another just like it.'

'Or else it happens by accident. I reckon that's more likely.' She shifted again. 'I dunno what's the matter with me tonight. I don't feel right, somehow. You don't think it could be starting, do you?' She looked at him with frightened eyes.

Terry was nonplussed. He had never known a pregnant woman before, not as close family. He'd seen Joanna Tozer when she was carrying her twins, of course, but he didn't know her well and he hadn't taken much notice. And Val Ferris had spent a lot of her time in bed while she was waiting for Christopher, and nearly died of it. The thought gave his heart a clutch of fear. Suppose something like that happened to Patsy ...

'I don't know, love. Didn't Mrs Dodd say there'd be signs?'

'Yes, but they don't all happen. There's waters breaking, but that's not always first, and then there's pains. I haven't got those either. I feel a bit sort of tight sometimes, but I don't call that a pain. I think it's my skin – like wearing a shirt that's too small. Terry, you don't think I'll burst, do you?'

'Crikey, I hope not! I've never heard of it happening, anyway. D'you want me to call her? Or the doctor?'

Patsy thought for a moment, then shook her head. 'No, not yet. The baby's not due till the end of next week anyway. It's just me being daft. I'm fed up with it, that's what it is. I just want it to be over and for us to have our babby.'

'I know. But if you want me to get them – or anyone else ... It's a pity Mum and Dad have gone into Tavi to that whist drive.'

'It's my own mother I want really,' she said wistfully. 'Yours has been ever so good to me, Terry, and so's your dad, but it's weeks now since I saw her and I really do miss her.' She began to cry quietly, and Terry tightened his arm around her shoulders. 'If I could just see her for a few minutes, and know she's all right ...'

Terry made up his mind. 'I'm going over there. I know you talked me out of it before, but a maid needs her mother at a time like this and I'm going to fetch her here, whatever your dad says. He can't keep her a prisoner. It's not right.'

Patsy clutched at his hand. 'Terry, you can't! You can't leave me here all by myself. Your mum and dad won't be back till eleven, and Bob's out at his skiffle practice for tomorrow ... 'Tis too late anyway, and foggy. It'll be pitch dark down by the Clam. You could fall in and drown, and then what would I do?'

Terry freed his hand so that he could hold her with both arms. 'I didn't mean straight away, my bird. I wouldn't leave you on your own. I'll nip over tomorrow. I've got to work in the morning – me and Bob are still working at that house over to Peter Tavy – but I'll go in the afternoon, straight after dinner. You'll have your mother here then, don't you fret. Look, why don't you go to bed? You'll be more comfortable laying down than trying to sit in this chair. I'll come up with you.'

For the past week or so, Patsy had had the double bed to herself and Terry had been sleeping downstairs on an old mattress, but he always went upstairs to be with her for a while until she fell asleep. She didn't stay asleep all night, he knew – she spent half the time rolling awkwardly from side to side in an effort to get comfortable – but when she dropped off for the first time, he would slide quietly away and go downstairs to get his mattress from against the wall and lay it on the floor. At first he'd been afraid that Patsy would need him in the night, but Jack had given her one of the thumbsticks he'd made from the branches he layered in the hawthorn hedges, and told her to thump hard on the floor if she wanted help.

'I'm like an old woman,' she said again, slowly climbing the stairs with Terry's hand on her back to help her. 'Lumbering about like an elephant. I'll be all right now, Terry. You go down and listen to the wireless. It's *Top of the Town*, with Stanley Black, you like that. I'm just going to go to sleep.'

'I'll look in after about half an hour,' he said, helping her to take off the voluminous smock that Val Ferris had lent her. 'Here's your nightie. D'you want a hot-water bottle?'

Patsy shook her head. 'I'm boiling. The baby's keeping me warm. Go on, love. Good night.'

'Good night,' he said, and kissed her. They clung awkwardly together for a few moments, then he helped her into bed and covered her up. He kissed her again and went downstairs.

Tomorrow, he thought, I'm going over to Little Burracombe whatever anyone says. It's all wrong, what old man Shillabeer's doing. It's all very well for Patsy to say she agreed to what he said,

269

but he never ought to have said it in the first place. Call himself a Christian? He don't know the meaning of the word. And I'm going to tell him – see if I don't.

Chapter Thirty-Five

The second Saturday in November was a busy one in Burracombe. Joyce and her minions were in the village hall early in the morning, sweeping it clean (although it was clean enough already, in most people's view) and setting out chairs. The pallet stage was erected, with a good deal of muttered cursing as legs were banged by the corners, and the big sheets of hardboard laid on top, with an old carpet (donated by Basil Harvey when he and Grace had bought a new one for their living room) over that to deaden the thuds. Tea, coffee, milk and sugar were set out in the tiny kitchen, with the motley collection of glasses, cups and saucers collected over the years and several large plates ready for the home-made biscuits Dottie had baked on Friday. George Sweet was busy making pasties, which would be cooked later and brought hot to the hall for the interval, and Bernie Nethercott was sorting out a barrel of cider to be trundled down in Jacob Prout's wheelbarrow.

'That's if he don't drink it all before he gets there,' Bernie said slanderously to Rose. 'Us better send someone down after an hour or so to make sure he'm not sleeping it off under a hedge.'

Val Ferris was filling jugs with orange squash for the children and non-cider drinkers when Maggie Culliford, wearing an old mac and headscarf, put her head round the door. 'Do you need any help, Val? Only with my Brenda being in it tonight, I thought I ought to offer.'

'Thanks, Maggie. I think we're pretty well finished now. Are you coming to see the show?'

'I'd like to, but it's the little'ns. I can't leave them by theirselves. It's either me or Arthur – one of us has got to stop home.'

'It's the same with me and Luke. What we want is someone who can look after all the children at once. Actually, we could do with it all the time, not just tonight!'

'Like a sort of nursery school,' Maggie said. 'There's one in Tavi. Takes kiddies from babies up to school, for people that goes out to work.'

'I don't think I'd want to do that, but two or three days a week would be a help.' Val filled another jug. 'But couldn't you bring your children to the show? They're old enough to enjoy it, surely.'

Maggie looked dubious. 'I don't think my Freddy could sit still that long. I'd probably have to take him out before it was half over. Anyway, I can't afford it, not at sixpence for me and Arthur and threepence each for all them.'

'Oh, I think the littlest ones could come for nothing,' Val promised recklessly. 'Then it won't be quite so bad if you have to take them out. I'll make sure it's all right with Mrs Warren.'

'Under-fives free?' Joyce said doubtfully when Val approached her. 'I don't know ... It's not a children's show, after all.'

'I'm sure they'll be all right. And Maggie says if not, she'll take them out. It would be a help to us all – I could bring Chris, so Luke can come as well, and Joanna could bring Robin. I expect she'll be leaving Heather with old Mrs Tozer.'

'Well, all right, but it must be understood that they can't be allowed to disrupt the show. And no running about during the interval.'

Val promised and sent Micky Coker, who had been helping with the stage, to take a message to Maggie. 'And you could call up at the farm as well, and tell Joanna. I know Robin would like to see his father on stage.' Tom was competing with Norman Tozer for the title of Burracombe's favourite stand-up comedian and was likely, Val thought, to win hands down. She thought it was only right that the children should be there to see their brothers, sisters and fathers perform.

Micky took the bike he had been given for passing the examination for the grammar school and cycled round with his messages. Then he went back to the hall, where he and Henry Bennetts were still practising the magic tricks they were to do. Micky had borrowed a top hat that his father intended to wear during some of his songs, and a toy rabbit from Jeanie Culliford. He wanted to use a real rabbit but Joyce had forbidden it. He and Henry, who kept white rabbits and had a fine buck who fitted the hat perfectly, were aggrieved about this but had a healthy respect for Joyce. All the same ... They whispered and giggled together in a corner, causing several people to look at them with suspicion. You never knew what those two would get up to.

The skiffle group, having also helped with the stage and the chairs, went back to Jack Pettifer's shed for a final run-through. Unfortunately, two of the strings on Brenda's ukulele broke halfway through and they could find nothing amongst Jack's shoe boxes and old biscuit tins that would make the same note. Brenda was in despair.

'I'll go over on me bike and see if Mr Copley's got any spares,' Reg offered at last. 'It won't take me more than half an hour or so.'

'That's if he's got one and can find it,' Brenda said despondently. 'And 'tis raining cats and dogs, Reg. You'll get drenched.'

'Go on, I got me old cycling cape, and I'm not made of sugar.' He grinned cheerfully. 'Got to keep our lead singer happy!'

He set off. The rain, which had been threatening on and off all morning, had now settled down to a steady downpour. The path down to the Clam was slick with mud, and the river had risen rapidly and boiled along beneath the narrow bridge. He got off his bike and pushed it across. Falling in off a greasy pole at the Coronation party on a June afternoon was one thing – toppling in on a cold November afternoon with the river in flood would be something else. People had drowned here before, and Reg Dodd didn't intend to add to their number.

On the way into the village, he overtook Terry, clad in an old waxed jacket and thick waterproof hat, marching along the lane as if he were off to war. Reg slowed down beside him.

'You look as if you'm meaning to punch someone on the nose!'

'I might, too,' Terry growled. 'I'm going to see old man Shillabeer. My Patsy's getting near her time and she wants her mother, and I don't see why she shouldn't have her.'

'So you'm going to beard the lion in his den. I hope he don't eat you for his dinner, Terry.'

'If he does, I'll give him a stomach ache he'll never forget,' Terry promised, and marched on.

He meant it too, he thought grimly as Reg cycled away towards the vicarage. Patsy's increasing distress had upset him badly and he had lain awake for much of the night, seething with anger at the way Percy Shillabeer treated those he was supposed to love and cherish. Terry had read the wedding vows before he married Patsy, and took them very seriously, and he believed that Percy had broken every one. Well, almost every one. He'd probably 'kept himself only unto her' but who else would have wanted him anyway? Terry very much doubted if even the Devil himself would have thought it worthwhile putting that particular temptation in his way. But he'd been downright cruel to his wife and daughter, and that was something Terry intended to stop.

A mother ought to be on hand at a time like this, he thought as he approached the farm, and a daughter had every right to see her. Patsy had never expected to feel like this when they'd embarked on this course – she'd been too young to look ahead and understand, and so had he – but wrong though they might have been, this was the time to put things right. He'd go softly to start with, give the farmer the chance to make amends, but if he wouldn't – and Terry felt pretty sure that would be the case – then Terry would do whatever he had to, to make him see reason.

The voice, when he heard it, came like the roar of a bull deprived of his cows.

'And what be you doing here?'

Terry jumped violently. He turned and saw Percy Shillabeer on the other side of a field gate, gripping the top bar with knotted fists. Rain dripped off the brim of his hat and lodged in his eyebrows, making them seem even larger and shaggier than usual, and his face was like thunder.

'I've told you before – you'm not wanted here. Get out!'

Terry stopped and faced him. 'I've come to tell you about Patsy. She's—'

'I don't know no Patsy!'

'Mr Shillabeer, she's your *daughter*. You can't say you don't know her.'

'I got no daughter name of Patsy. Now be off.'

'Please, Mr Shillabeer. She's near her time and she needs her mother.'

274

'Her mother don't want no more of her.'

'That's not true! Of course she do. Mr Shillabeer, Patsy's having a baby, your grandchild – you can't turn away from her now. Please let her mother come to see her. *Please*.'

There was a silence. They stared at each other across the gate, and then, slowly and deliberately, Percy Shillabeer began to open it. He came through, his hard black eyes fixed on Terry's face, and Terry quailed but stood his ground. He felt rain trickle like thin ice down the back of his neck, and shivered a little.

'I got only one thing to say to you,' Percy began in an ominous tone. 'And that's *get out of here*. Get out, before I takes me stick to you.' He raised a stick with a knotted top that turned it into a cudgel. 'Get out before I takes me *gun* to you.' And to his horror, Terry saw that he had a shotgun slung over his shoulder and was lifting it slowly, menacingly, as if about to take aim.

'You can't do that,' he said as firmly as his quivering voice would allow. 'You can't go round shooting people. Patsy – your daughter – is having a baby. She might even have it tonight. It'll be your grandchild, Mr Shillabeer, flesh of your flesh, blood of your blood. You can't shoot the father of your own grandchild.'

'I told you,' Shillabeer said in the same harsh, grating voice, 'I got no daughter named Patsy and I'll have no grandchild from her neither. Now – get back where you belong.' And he raised the gun to his shoulder and fired.

Reg Dodd heard the shot as he knocked on the vicarage door, and Felix, who had seen him cycling up the path, heard it as he opened it. They looked at each other uncertainly.

'Just someone out shooting pigeons, I dare say,' Reg said.

'I expect so. It sounded a bit near the road, though. Come in, Reg. Take off that cape, it's streaming with water. It doesn't matter about the puddles on the floor. What can I do for you?'

'It's Brenda's ukulele,' Reg said, stepping over the threshold and shrugging off the yellow cape. 'Well, your ukulele really. Two of the strings have broke and we got the extravaganza tonight so I come over to see if you got any spares.'

'I have, as it happens.' Felix led the way into his study and started to root about in the drawers of his desk. 'I came across some the other day and put them in here, meaning to bring them over to Burracombe with me, but every time I've been over there, I've forgotten ... Ah, here they are. Strings, ukulele, for the use of.' He handed over the box. 'How have the rehearsals been going? All ready for the big night?'

'As ready as us'll ever be, I reckon. To be honest, I think Brenda was hoping you wouldn't have any strings and her wouldn't have to play.'

'What nonsense,' Felix said cheerfully. 'She plays really well, and you can tell her I said so. Stella and I are looking forward to it – she can't let us down.'

'It were a shambles at the dress rehearsal. Norman Tozer fell off the stage and Tom forgot the best line of one of his jokes – the one about Nellie Dunn – and the piano keys got stuck and Mr Raynor could only play the black notes. Honestly, Mr Copley, you've never heard nothing like it.'

Felix roared with laughter. 'I wish I'd been there. It sounds better than the performance itself.' He caught sight of Reg's woebegone face and pulled himself together. 'It'll be fine, Reg, believe me. A bad dress rehearsal always means a good performance.' Well, sometimes it does, he added silently, remembering pantomimes he'd been involved in when a bad dress rehearsal had meant an even worse performance. 'And the skiffle group will take everyone by storm. I've heard you and I know you're good.' He spoke sincerely, still hankering after a part in it himself. 'And if anyone drops out, you've got me as an understudy.'

Reg grinned and thanked him. He pulled the cape over his head again and went outside. The rain seemed to be easing off a little, but the clouds were ominously low. He got on his bike and rode back towards the Clam.

There were no more gunshots, and he saw no sign of Terry.

'Percy! In heaven's name, what have you done?'

'Nothing that didn't need doing,' he growled, staring at the crumpled figure on the ground. 'And what be you doing out here? Get back in the house.'

'I won't. You've gone too far this time, Percy. You can't go round firing off your gun at people. Who is it, anyway?' Ann Shillabeer bent and lifted the thick waxed hat to reveal the white face beneath. 'Terry! It's young Terry!'

'Who else d'you think it would be? Coming over here, telling me my daughter's near her time and needs her mother with her ... I told him, I have no daughter, not by the name of Patsy, and I'll have no grandchild by him neither. Spawn of the devil—'

'Percy, stop it! I won't hear any more of your ranting! You've shot this poor boy, you might even have killed him, and you'll have to shoot me too if you want me to leave him here in the road to die. You're mad, that's what you are – *mad*!' She turned her back on him and touched Terry's face again. 'Well, he's not dead, you should be glad to know, or you'd be a murderer as well as a fool. And I don't think he's badly hurt – I can't see no blood.' She looked at the hat. 'It's torn, see? Got little holes ripped in it. I reckon the shot just grazed along the side. You've been very lucky, Percy.'

Terry was stirring now and opened his eyes. He stared at Ann for a moment, bewildered, and then past her at Percy, and his eyes widened as he drew in a sharp breath.

'It's all right, Terry,' she said soothingly. 'It's all right. He'll not do it again ... Were you hit? Does it hurt anywhere?'

He moved cautiously. 'I don't think so. My head stings a bit.'

Ann lifted the hat away. ''Tis a bit grazed, that's all.' She turned back to her husband. 'You'm a stupid fool, Percy Shillabeer, and I've been a fool for letting you bully me. Now unload that gun and take it back to the house. I don't want to see you out here no more.'

Percy stared at her. He looked as dazed as Terry. 'But 'tis milking time ...'

'Then go and do the milking. That should keep you out of mischief for a couple of hours. And then you can stop here on your own, because I'm going over to see my daughter. The others are with my sister so you don't need to bother about them.'

Percy made a final effort to regain control. 'I told you, wife, that girl is no daughter of ours. We gave her a choice and she made it. Now she got to stick by it, and so have you.'

Ann rose to her feet and faced him, tilting her head back to meet his wild eyes. 'She made the choice you forced her to make. That don't count. And I made a choice too, years ago, when I was as young and foolish as she, but I made it of my own free will so

277

it do count and I'll stick by it. I'm your wife for better or worse, Percy Shillabeer, and even though it's turned out worse than I ever thought it could be, I'll stick by my vows. But I won't desert my own daughter, and nothing you can say will make me. I'm going back with Terry now, and I'll be home in my own good time. Now get and do your work.'

Terry was on his feet too now. He was still shocked, but he knew he was unhurt. He watched Ann with awe as she faced her tyrant of a husband, and then took her arm.

'Are you sure, Mrs Shillabeer?'

'Of course I'm sure!' she snapped. 'If Patsy's as near her time as you say, we don't want to hang about. And you can stop calling me Mrs Shillabeer. I'm your mother-in-law now and you can call me Mother, or Ma if you like. Now, you can walk me back to Burracombe.'

She shrugged her old mac closer round her shoulders and stalked away down the lane. Terry cast a quick glance at the big man, standing bewildered and defeated in the middle of the track, and hurried after her.

Percy Shillabeer watched them go. His mind was hazy and stunned. He could think of nothing now but the girl who had defied him, and all that had happened since that night when she'd told him of her sin. His shame and the rage that had come from that shame. His sense of betrayal by the church and by Felix, who had spoken as if he – *he*, Percy Shillabeer – were the sinner. His discovery of the Exclusives, who had seemed to confirm all that he believed, who had taught him how to manage his home and family, encouraged him to treat them as the outsiders they were. His increasing fury against his daughter and his wife, and most of all against Terry Pettifer. And now this: his own wife, defying him and treating him like an animal.

He turned and stumbled back through the rain to the farm. The cows were gathered in the yard, lowing to be let into the milking parlour so that their aching udders could be relieved. He dropped the gun at the door and went inside.

Chapter Thirty-Six

'So what's the verdict?' Hilary asked as she and David strolled beside the river in Tavistock during a brief respite from the rain. 'How do you like our village?'

He smiled at her. They had come into Tavistock after Charles had conducted his morning surgery and had had lunch at the Bedford Hotel. Hilary had shown him the sights of the little market town and now they were enjoying the local park, known to all as the Meadows. It was bordered on one side by the river Tavy and on the other by the canal that ran four miles from Tavistock to the derelict mining village of Morwellham.

'I like it very much. I like the whole area. I like the people, too – one person in particular.' He smiled at her. 'It's so good to be here with you, darling.'

'It's good to have you here. It makes everything feel ... complete.'

'I know. I feel that too.' They paused to look down at the river. The broad path was eight or nine feet above the rushing stream. A cluster of mallard ducks sat on the rocks, splashing into the water every now and then and upending themselves in quiet eddies. A grey wagtail flickered its tail on a small patch of shingle under the opposite bank.

'The river's high today,' Hilary remarked. 'It's all that rain. It's usually a good four feet lower than that. If you fell in now, you'd be in Plymouth Sound before you could shout for help!'

'It's beautiful. Tavistock's a nice little town,' David remarked. 'And Burracombe is exactly as I imagined it. I believe I could be very happy here.'

'Really? You mean it? And what about the work – Charles's practice? Would you be happy doing that too?'

'Yes. Charles and I get along very well. We've had some long talks and I've sat in on his surgeries, so I've met quite a few of the locals. That young girl you employed for a while came in – Patsy Pettifer. Nice little thing.'

'She is, but she and Terry have had a difficult start in life. Her baby's due any time now.'

He nodded. 'She should be all right – no complications as far as I could see, just feeling rather uncomfortable. I have to admit, I don't find their dialect easy to understand – the rich Devon brogue is very different from the flat Derbyshire vowels – but that will come. It's a very attractive accent.'

Hilary turned away slightly and gazed down the river. The great trees overhanging the water were at their best now, tinted as brilliantly as the flames of last week's bonfires, gold and crimson and deep shimmering bronze. Many of the leaves had fallen and lay like a glowing carpet at their feet. A few children came by, laughing as they scuffed them into a flying kaleidoscope of colour.

'So are you going to accept Charles's offer?' she asked after a pause.

'On certain conditions, yes.'

She turned quickly. 'What conditions?'

David put his hands on her shoulders. The children had gone and the mist was gathering again as dusk fell. Apart from the clamour of the river and the soft quacking of the ducks as they settled for the long night, there was little sound. There was just enough light now to see each other's eyes.

'I couldn't live here unless I was with you,' he said quietly. 'To be near you and yet not part of your life – that would be a worse torment than these past months have been. It would be intolerable. And I know we've said all this before, but sometimes feelings change when people see each other on the home ground of one. There can be a shift. So I am asking you again, my darling. Will you marry me?'

Hilary met his gaze. Her heart was beating hard against her ribs. All that had gone before was as nothing compared with this moment, the moment when above all others they would make their real commitment.

'Could you live with me at the Barton?' she asked. 'It's not a condition. If you don't want to, we could find another house. But I will have to go on running the estate. Can you accept that?'

There was a beat of silence, and then he said, 'It's a part of who you are, Hilary. Of course I can accept it. And yes – I will live with you at the Barton. Provided your father is happy with that.'

'Oh, he will be,' she exclaimed joyously. 'He likes you. And I suspect he already knows anyway – I saw the look in his eyes as he watched us on Friday evening. So yes, David – please. I will marry you.'

David drew her close against him, and as the November fog closed around them and the ducks ceased their murmuring, he bent his head to hers and kissed her lips. For a long moment they stood very close, breathing in each other's scent, and the smell of rushing water and cold winter damp and rain-soaked earth. And then David lifted his head and said, 'Damn!'

'What? What's the matter?'

'I promised that I would propose to you properly, on bended knee, with flowers and champagne. I've even got them, back at the Latimers' house, waiting for the right moment. I meant to do it this evening. And now I've gone and done it again!'

Hilary laughed. 'Maybe we're not meant to be the world's most romantic couple after all. We'll have the champagne another time. We couldn't do it this evening anyway – we're going to the extravaganza. You've got to see that before you can really know the awful truth about Burracombe!'

The rain didn't ease in Burracombe until six in the evening. When Terry and Ann Shillabeer arrived at the Pettifers' cottage, it was still teeming down, and Nancy, opening the door to find two bedraggled creatures standing outside, pulled them in without ceremony.

'Look at the two of you! Soaked through to the bone! And Terry, you're covered in mud. What in the world have you been doing? Go upstairs and get out of those filthy wet things straight away. Ann, my dear, 'tis good to see you, but didn't you have no better coat and shoes than that to walk all this way in?'

'I didn't know I was coming,' Ann said, her teeth beginning to chatter. 'I just ran out of the house when I heard Percy shouting ... Terry says Patsy's started her labour – is that true?'

'It might be. We'm not sure entirely. Lucy Dodd's been in and says it could be a false labour like happens sometimes a week or two beforehand. She've been having a few pains but nothing much, just feels uncomfortable, you know how it is. But her'll be master glad to see you.'

'Where is she?'

'Upstairs having a lay-down on the bed. You can see her as soon as we've got you into some dry clothes. You'll catch your death of cold else, and I don't want another invalid on my hands.' She bustled Ann upstairs and into her and Jack's room, where she handed over a large towel and looked out some of her own clothes while Ann stripped off her wet things. 'My frocks are going to look like tents on you, but you can't keep they wet things on. Here – this skirt's got a belt you can tie up, and this jumper's nice and warm. Now, you go and see your Patsy and I'll bring you both up a hot cup of tea.'

Ann pulled on the clothes. As Nancy had said, they almost swamped her, but they were warm and comforting, like wrapping herself in a blanket. She tapped on the door Nancy indicated, in case Terry was still dressing, and went in.

Patsy was on the bed. She had grown considerably bigger since Ann had last seen her, though her face was thin and her grey eyes looked like enormous pools of rainwater. Her face lit up when she saw her mother, and at the same moment her eyes filled with tears and her mouth trembled.

'Oh, *Mum*!'

'Patsy, my little bird!' Ann crossed the narrow space to the bed in less than three steps. She threw her arms around her daughter's shoulders and they hugged. Both were crying, and Terry, who had been on the other side of the bed, slipped round and went downstairs.

Ann drew back at last and Patsy mopped her face with one of Terry's hankies. 'Oh Mum, it *is* good to see you. I've been wanting you so bad.'

'I know, my dear. Every young woman wants her mother by her when she has her first. And how have you been?'

'Not too bad. Heartburn and nasty pains down my leg, but Mrs Dodd says they'm to be expected.' Patsy looked at her mother. 'I didn't know it would be like this.'

282

'You've seen me this way often enough.'

'I know, but our Jacky's nearly three – I was only just fourteen when he was born and I didn't notice much. And maybe 'twas easier for you.'

Ann smiled. 'Not for my first, and that was you, my bird. But never mind that. I'm here now, and from what Terry says, you could be on your way. By this time tomorrow, you could be the mother of a fine little babby and it'll all be over. Are you having any pains?'

'I was, but they seem to have gone off.' Patsy looked at her. 'How did you persuade him to let you come? I didn't think I was ever going to see you again.'

'I didn't persuade him. I told him. He saw I wasn't going to take no for an answer and he gave in.' Patsy didn't need to know all that had happened, she thought. If Terry chose to tell her that her father had fired a gun at him, that was his business, but why worry the poor maid, especially just now? 'Now, let's make sure you'm comfortable. The size you are, I dare say you feel awkward whichever way you sit.'

'I do. I might get up in a minute and come downstairs. I feel so restless – I'll be better moving about. I wish I could go out for a walk, but it's so wet outside.'

'It's cold, too. You stay indoors.' The door opened and Terry came in with two cups of tea and a plate of biscuits on a tin tray with a picture of kittens on it. 'Now, that's just what we need. Thank you, my handsome.'

Terry put the tea on the chest of drawers and went downstairs. He felt suddenly in the way. Patsy had her mother and didn't seem to want him any more. He stood by the kitchen window, staring at the rain streaming down the glass, his hands in his pockets.

'It's no use standing around like a spare part,' Nancy said, rolling pastry on the table. 'Find yourself something to do.'

'I don't know what to do. It's like waiting for Christmas, only worse. You want it to happen but you can't make it happen quickly.'

'So the best thing is to find something to do, like I said. Go down the shed. Your father'll give you a job.'

'The skiffle group's there. Can't you hear them?'

'I've had the wireless on. Do some of your studying, then. You've got your exams soon.'

'I can't put my mind to it. If it wasn't for this rain, I'd go out and chop some wood.'

Nancy glanced at him. She felt sorry for him. He was too young for this – he and Patsy both were – but there was no getting out of it now. My stars, she thought suddenly, he's making me a grandmother, and he could be a grandfather himself by the time he's thirty-five! It's all happening too soon. It's too much for them. They're still children themselves.

'You could chop wood in the rain. Put on your father's big waterproof. It'll do you good to be outside.'

Terry nodded and did as he was told. Swathed in his father's big waxed coat, with a wide-brimmed hat to keep the rain from his face, he went out to the woodshed and got the axe. He found a few logs that Jack had brought back from some tree felling he'd done, and began work.

As he chopped, he remembered Percy Shillabeer's fury, and the attack the farmer had made on him that afternoon. He had told his parents nothing about it. Jack would want to go over and confront him, and Nancy would want to call the police, and Terry couldn't face that, not with Patsy the way she was.

But something would have to be done soon, he told himself. He's mad. He's out of his mind. And he felt a chill of fear as he wondered what the farmer, half crazed by his rage, might do next.

Chapter Thirty-Seven

The village hall filled up early. People always arrived in good time, partly to make sure of a good seat and partly because it was a chance to catch up with each other, have a gossip and freshen up the grapevine. Tonight, they arrived in macs and wellingtons, carrying umbrellas, because although the rain had stopped its relentless downpour, there was no saying it wouldn't have started again by the time they went home. As it was, the fog had descended again and you could barely see your hand in front of your face.

Hilary and her father joined the Latimers and David about four rows from the front. Ted and Alice Tozer came in and sat behind them, and Hilary introduced them to David. They were saving seats for Joanna and Robin, since Tom would be in the front row with the other performers. Val and Luke arrived, rather breathless, just before Terry's cousin Cyril, who was in charge of the lights, plunged the hall into complete darkness and then fumbled for the switch for the stage lights, turning on one row after another until he found the right ones.

'Where are Nancy and Jack?' Alice asked in a whisper as Joyce Warren mounted the stage.

'I saw Jack come in just before the lights went down,' Hilary murmured back, 'but I think Nancy's probably stayed with Patsy and Terry. Patsy's very near her time now, you know.'

'The dear of her,' Alice said. 'I hope everything's all right for them, foolish though they have been.'

Joyce called for silence, and gradually the chatter ceased. She explained the programme for the evening and the arrangements for refreshments. 'The pasties and drinks will be brought to you in your seats, so that you don't have to queue, so please stay where you are when the lights go up. Yes, of course you are,' she added sternly to one of the Crocker twins, who had asked cheekily if they were allowed to go to the lav. 'You know perfectly well what I mean, Edward. And don't say you're George, because I happen to be able to tell you apart.'

This was greeted by a shocked silence, and then everyone laughed. Whether or not she was speaking the truth nobody really knew, but she had obviously got it right, and the twins were seen to spend most of the evening examining themselves to see what small difference she had noticed. It was, thought James Raynor as he sat at the piano, the most effective way of silencing them that anyone had discovered so far.

Joyce announced Alf Coker, who climbed the two steps made out of apple boxes and took his place on the stage. He surveyed his audience, who gazed back at him in happy anticipation of their evening's entertainment, then, as James struck the first deep note, launched into 'Glorious Devon'.

'Oh!' Patsy gave a sudden squeal and grabbed convulsively for Terry's hand. 'Oh, that hurt!'

The two women were on their feet at once. 'What is it? Where do it hurt?'

'In my back,' she panted. 'It's sort of gripping me all the way round. Oh. *Oh* ...'

Nancy glanced at Ann. 'That's a bit more like a proper labour pain,' she muttered. 'What do you think?'

Ann looked at the clock on the mantelpiece. 'Wait for the next one and count how long it is between them. I usually reckon to call Lucy when it's about ten minutes, but with the first, you can usually wait a bit longer. It depends how regular they are.'

They waited. Patsy moaned, and Terry looked wildly at the two mothers. 'Isn't there anything us can do? It's hurting her real bad.'

'It'll get worse than that before it gets better,' Ann told him. 'You men ought to think of that before you has your fun.' Then she bit her lip. 'All right, boy, forget I said that. I know 'twasn't you at fault.' She turned to her daughter. 'Is that another pain?'

'No. I don't think so. It's just an ache, that's all, and a tight sort of feeling round my tummy. Oh Terry. *Terry.* Don't go away. Don't leave me.'

'I won't, sweetheart. I'm here. I won't leave you.'

'You'll have to in a minute,' Nancy said. 'Someone's going to have to go for Lucy Dodd, and there's nobody else here.'

'Is Lucy going to this extravagant do in the village hall?' Ann asked.

'Extravaganza. I don't know. I expect so. I reckon pretty well everyone's going.' Patsy cried out and Nancy made up her mind. 'You'd better go now, son. Better safe than sorry,'

'Sorry?' He was on his feet, alarmed, and Nancy shook her head at him.

'It was just a figure of speech. Better sooner than later, I should have said. Oh, go on with you! Tell her Patsy's having pains every seven minutes and us reckons her ought to get here quick. And put your coat on – us don't want you going down with pneumonia on top of everything.'

Terry snatched his coat from the hook on the wall and dashed out. He tore along the village street towards the hall, where he could hear the first strains of the skiffle group playing 'Your Cheatin' Heart'. Oblivious of the whispered entreaties to be quiet, he wrenched open the door and stumbled into the darkness, almost falling over Val Ferris, who had been stationed there to repel latecomers.

'What on earth's the matter?' Val whispered, righting her chair. 'Terry, it's you. Is it Patsy? Has she started?'

'Yes. I've got to get Mrs Dodd. Where's she sitting?'

'She's not here. She was called out to someone over in Little Burracombe. I thought it was a false labour?'

'Well, it's not. Mother and Mrs Shillabeer are both with her and they say to tell her it's every seven minutes and coming quicker. Oh my dear God, what am I going to do?' He remembered that Val had been a nurse. 'Could you come?'

'The doctor's here. I'll tell him.' Val tiptoed down the side of the hall and leaned across to Charles. 'It's Patsy, Dr Latimer. Terry's here and says she's having pains every seven minutes. Nancy and

Ann Shillabeer are with her, but Lucy Dodd's gone over the river to someone else. Could you go?'

'Of course.' Charles was on his feet at once, squeezing past his wife to reach the aisle. 'No, you stay here, David. Enjoy the show.'

He slipped out behind Val, and the skiffle group, somewhat distracted, started on their version of a song nobody else had ever heard of, called 'Jelly Baby Stomp'. Charles, hearing the sounds of the washboard, tea-chest double bass and comb-and-paper kazoo, smiled to himself and wondered what David Hunter, city doctor, was making of this bucolic entertainment. He got into his car, checked that his bag was in place, and drove swiftly the short distance to Jack and Nancy Pettifer's house.

Percy Shillabeer went back after milking to a cold, empty kitchen. He had spent the past two hours with his cows, washing their udders and sitting by each one in turn to draw the milk from them. They soothed him with their warmth and their big mild eyes, and their unquestioning acquiescence. That's how a family ought to be too, he thought. People could learn a lot from cows.

To begin with, he could feel his anger swirling inside him, a violent maelstrom of bitterness and rage. But the cows would not let down their milk to fingers that were taut with fury, and gradually he allowed their placidity to calm him. By the time he was halfway through, he was lost in the only world where he had ever found peace, but it was an uncertain peace, more a heaviness that had settled upon him like the dark stillness that preceded a thunderstorm. He could feel the black clouds gathering within him, a threat that he barely understood but knew could drag him into a terrifying abyss. He had experienced it before and fought his way clear with temper and fury, but as he finished his work and the cows ambled back to the yard, he felt it wrap around him like a heavy greatcoat, its pockets filled with stones, and knew that it was almost beyond him now to battle his way free.

He stood at the barn door, staring across the yard to his darkened house. There was something wrong, but he couldn't put his finger on it. Something had happened ... something that was so bad he couldn't get a hold on it, couldn't bring it to mind. Something that afternoon, before milking ... His wife and someone else ...

Something that had filled his breast and his heart almost to bursting point, something that he could not endure.

Slowly he stumbled across the yard and through the open door. He looked into the kitchen, illuminated dimly by the lamp that had been lit early that dark, foggy afternoon. The range had gone out and he remembered hazily that the children were at their aunt's house, where they spent more and more time these days. He stood on the cold flagstones and stared around, vaguely bewildered. Where was his wife? Where was his tea?

He walked into the back kitchen, where he had decreed that his family, all outsiders, should eat their meals. The table there was bare too. The sink was still piled with dishes from their dinner. What had they had for dinner? He remembered liver and bacon, mashed potatoes, cabbage. Whatever her faults, his wife put on a good table, always had. Where was she now? Where was his tea?

He went back to the main kitchen and sat down heavily in his chair at the head of the table. Once, before all this started, he'd had a family around him, children sitting on each side of the table waiting for him to be served before their mother gave them their plates, an elder daughter who was quiet and submissive, a help to her mother, and a wife at the other end ladling out plates of stew, bowls of soup she'd made from leftovers, or heaps of cottage pie. Or on a Sunday, after church, he would be carving a joint and there would be a bowl piled with golden roast potatoes and others filled with sprouts, cauliflower, peas or beans.

Where had it all gone?

He remembered that life as an orderly one, as he thought life should be. A man in charge of his own home, his own work, of life itself. A woman who had vowed to obey him and had never gone back on that vow. Children who looked up to their father, feared him as children should, and always did his bidding. A house kept as a house should be, the floors swept and a clean shirt always ready for church. A woman in his bed to satisfy the God-given needs of a man.

And then it had all gone wrong, collapsed around him a like a pack of cards. Patsy had been the cause – Patsy, defying him, taking her disobedience to the most sinful lengths so that he was forced to disown her. It had been his duty to do that. He could not have such sin in his house. And the vicar, still wet behind the ears, with no more understanding than a fly about the true path to God, forcing him to look elsewhere for guidance. And the Exclusives ...

They had been his salvation, he thought. Without them he would have been a lost soul indeed, floundering in the wilderness. But they had shown him the way, believed in him when nobody else did. They had shown him that his wife and family were outsiders, cast in sin, and that contact with them tainted his own soul. It was right that they should be made to eat apart, right that he should have smashed their wireless set, right that Patsy should be cast out and Ann turned away from his bed, save for the nights when he needed relief. All these things were right, and what he was going through now was no more than the suffering he must endure to be saved. The path to redemption was not easy. It never could be.

After a long time, he got up and stumbled out of the kitchen into the dark, foggy night. He knew where Ann was. He remembered now – she'd gone with that ugly mug of a Pettifer boy, the one who'd defiled his daughter and robbed him of her. She was over the river, with the pair who had brought all this misery upon him, and it was now his duty to bring her back. And he would deal with the man who had planted his sinful seed in his daughter's body, and this time he would not miss.

Percy fumbled in the murky darkness for the shotgun and found it where he had dropped it, at the door of the milking parlour. He slung it over his shoulder and set off along the lane towards the old sunken track that led down through the trees to the Clam.

'It hurts so bad. Oh Mum – Terry ...' Patsy lay on the bed, reaching out in desperation. 'Oh, I can't – I can't ...'

'Yes you can, Patsy.' Dr Latimer was in the room beside her, pushing Terry gently out of the way and placing a big, warm palm comfortingly on her forehead. 'It's all right. Everything's going well. You'll have your baby soon.' He took his hand away and opened his bag. 'I'll need to examine you. Terry, would you go downstairs, please, and put the kettle on?'

'Go on, Terry,' his mother urged him as he hesitated. 'We'll want lots of hot water soon, and Patsy could do with a cup of tea.'

Terry left the room, which still felt crowded with the two women

290

and the doctor there. Charles Latimer was used to working in confined spaces, however, and completed his examination swiftly. He smiled down at the girl's face as it twisted with pain.

'You're doing very well, my dear. I think this baby is going to come quite quickly. You were right to call me,' he said to Nancy.

'I thought Lucy Dodd would be coming. Her was here this afternoon.'

'She's gone over to Little Burracombe. Betty Hayman, probably. She's a week overdue.'

'Oh dear. And were you hoping for a quiet evening with your visitor? Patsy told me he was in your surgery today.'

'That's right. A very good doctor.' Charles had not mentioned his retirement plans in the village and had no intention of doing so now, but Nancy was only making conversation anyway. Her attention, like Ann's, was on the girl on the bed, with her white, frightened face.

She's only a kiddy herself, Nancy thought. However did she come to this so soon? If that father of hers had let her and our Terry meet and go out together like boys and girls should, they'd be at the village hall together now, laughing and singing with the rest of them, and years to go before they thought of being parents.

Still, it was no good thinking like that. They were here now, and had to deal with the situation as it was. Patsy and Terry seemed to love each other and understand what marriage meant, and that was more than you could say for some people.

Percy Shillabeer, for instance.

Percy stumbled several times on his way down the uneven track to the Clam. It was an ancient way, used over so many thousands of years that it had been worn down to bedrock between high banks. In wet weather it ran with tiny streams, and as soil was washed down the banks, the rocks became slimy with a thin layer of mud. Percy knew it well, and his feet seemed to find each safe foothold, but even so, he slithered several times and almost fell.

The near accidents increased his anger. He shouldn't have to be doing this. He should be at home now, warm and properly fed, with his wife and family around him. He thought of the picture he had carried in his mind for so many years, of a warm farmhouse with comfortable chairs and a table spread with good food, a loving wife and a quiverful of children all looking up to him with deference and respect, obedient to his will.

It had never been quite like that. He had thought Ann would be the wife he wanted, giving him the love he craved. She had been obedient, yes, she had never refused his needs, but he had never, after those early days, felt she loved him. And the children – they'd been obedient too, but had their obedience come from respect, or from something else? He'd known for many years that there was another expression in their eyes when they looked at him across the kitchen table, but it was not for a long time that he'd begun to wonder if it could be fear.

And yet, wasn't it right that children should fear their father? As God's children must fear their Father? Didn't the Bible say that?

Percy shook his head and cursed as he slipped again. The shotgun bumped against his hip, reminding him of his anger. It had all gone wrong when that girl, his eldest, who was meant to be a help to her parents, had defied him and turned to the Devil's ways. It was all due to her and that gargoyle of a boy she'd taken up with. Terry Pettifer. Her fault, and his. And Jack and Nancy Pettifer too, aiding and abetting them, taking her in when she should have been turned away by any decent soul.

The blame didn't end with them. Hilary Napier, who had turned a blind eye when the two of them had met under her roof. The housekeeper, who had encouraged them. Even Colonel Napier, who ought to have known what was going on in his own house. The Vicar, who had married them and had the nerve to tell Percy off for doing what he knew to be right. They were all to blame, all of them.

Percy had reached the Clam now and paused, breathing heavily from the exertion. He laid his hand on the wooden rail and stared through the darkness and the fog at the turbulent water below. The weight of his responsibility seemed about to crush him. All those people, all with the burden of guilt on their shoulders, and only he to repair the damage they had done. Only he, with his shotgun slung over his shoulder and the righteous anger in his heart . . .

Chapter Thirty-Eight

Felix and Stella had been halfway out of the house when the telephone rang. They looked at each other and hesitated. Felix twisted his mouth ruefully.

'I'll have to answer it.'

'I know.' She closed the door on the clammy darkness and came back into the hall while Felix went into the study and picked up the receiver. He came out looking worried.

'It was Ann Shillabeer's sister. She's got the children with her and she says either Ann or Percy should have fetched them home by now but she's not seen or heard a thing from either of them. She's tried telephoning them but nobody's answering. She doesn't know what to do – her husband's in bed with flu and she doesn't want to get him out to drive her over there.'

'Oh dear,' Stella said in concern. 'We'd better go and see if anything's wrong.'

'I'm sorry,' he said. 'You were looking forward to this evening.'

'So were you. But we can't just leave it. The children need to be home – and where are Percy and Ann? It's an awful night to be out.'

They picked up a torch each and went outside to where the little Austin was standing, ready to take them round to the bigger village. 'We'd better drive there, I think,' Felix said. 'It isn't far to the farm, but we may need ...' He didn't finish, but Stella nodded, a cold fear clutching at her heart. You heard such awful things sometimes, and Percy had been very strange. She hoped desperately that nothing terrible had happened.

When they reached the farm, the house was dark except for one light shining from the kitchen window. Felix drove into the deserted yard and stopped. They looked at the uncurtained window in silence for a moment. There was no movement from within.

'I'll go and look,' he said at last. 'You stay here, darling.'

But Stella got out and followed him. Together they went to the door and Felix knocked. After a moment he knocked again, more loudly, and then he pushed open the door and they went inside.

'Nobody,' he said, looking round the cold kitchen. 'No meal laid, no sign of either Percy or Ann.'

'What about the other rooms?'

Slowly, uneasily, they moved through the house. The back kitchen, where Ann and the children ate their meals. The big living room, with its large battered sofa and two armchairs and a fire laid in the grate, ready to be lit. But it was nearly seven o'clock in the evening. Where was the family?

'Do you think we should look upstairs?' Stella asked at last.

'I think we'll have to. It may all be quite innocent, of course.' A sudden thought struck him. 'Do you suppose they've gone to the extravaganza? That would explain everything.'

'It wouldn't. It wouldn't explain why Ann's sister still has the children. She'd know if they planned to be out all evening, surely. Anyway, can you see Percy even considering such a thing, in his present state of mind? He'd think it was sinful.'

In his present state of mind … They looked at each other again, with dread, and then Stella took his hand.

'Come on.'

They mounted the steep, narrow stairs. Felix went ahead, prepared to shield his wife from whatever hideous sight they might see. But there was nothing. The beds had been made, the rooms were tidy. It looked as if nobody had been in them since morning.

'I don't know,' Felix said when they were downstairs again. 'I don't know what to do. Perhaps we ought to search the barns, but we've only got this small torch.' He looked gravely at her. 'I think we should go to the police.'

'Bert Lillywhite? Oh, *Felix* … But it's still quite early. They might come back any minute.'

'We don't know how long they've been gone,' he said. 'I suppose

Percy must have milked the cows – but it could have been one of the stockmen. They might have been gone for hours.'

Stella gripped his hand. 'Felix, one of the parishioners told me they'd seen Terry Pettifer coming up from the Clam this afternoon. Perhaps Patsy's having her baby. Perhaps they've gone over to see her.'

Felix hesitated. 'But Percy would never—'

'He might have had a change of heart, knowing it was his grand-child being born. Don't you think so? Don't you think it's worth a try, before we do anything drastic?'

'We can't take it for granted that everything's all right. It's pos-sible they've gone to Burracombe, but I really can't believe Percy would have changed just like that. I think we have to go to Bert.'

'They could have had an accident,' Stella said. 'If they tried to cross the Clam … You know how much the river's risen with all this rain. And now it's so foggy. Suppose—'

'We can't suppose any more,' he said firmly. 'We've got to do something. Look, you go and fetch Bert. I'll stay nearby in case they come back. We don't know what sort of a state Percy might be in – I don't want you facing him on your own. It's not far to the police house.'

Stella ran off into the darkness. Felix waited until the pinprick of torchlight had disappeared, then turned and began to walk down the track to the river. He had been disturbed to hear that Terry had come over to the farm that afternoon. He did not believe that Percy would have had a change of heart towards his daughter, but he thought it quite likely that Terry's visit might have triggered a final breakdown in the farmer's unstable state of mind. I'll just go down as far as the river, he thought. I'll just make sure …

All those people, Percy thought. All that wickedness and sin. It oppressed his heart. And since he had joined the Exclusives, it had grown even worse. There was sin everywhere, on every side. How could one man defeat it? Even the one man who had been sent for that very purpose had not been able to do that. What hope could Percy Shillabeer have?

He had tried so hard, and it had collapsed in ruins about him.

And yet ... could he be to blame too? We're all sinners, he thought. Every last one of us. And there *is* no hope.

A misery darker than any he had felt before descended on him as the thought entered his mind like a sliver of burning ice. I've failed, he thought. All the plans I had for a family, for the life I've always wanted – the life other children had when I had nothing to go home to but misery – they've all gone for nothing. I got the wife, I got the children, but it's never been right. I've failed.

He lifted his eyes as if to search the blanket of the night sky for answers, but there were none. Why, when he had tried so hard, when he had done his best all his life to walk in God's ways, had he been so abandoned? Why, when he had tried to teach and lead his children, had they turned from him? Why had his own wife deserted him this day? How could this God who wanted so much from him ever be appeased?

Percy lifted both arms in supplication. He stretched towards the blackness of the sky, feeling despair sweep across his body like a huge creature of the night, crushing him with its vast, suffocating wings. He cringed away from it, backing along the narrow bridge to the rocky track. As his foot slipped, he cried out, and then he fell, tumbling down the steep muddy bank.

The chill of his desolation seemed to merge with the water that tore at his body, thrusting him beneath the surface, holding him under as he scrabbled for a branch, a root, a rock, anything that would save him. But there was no air to breathe, only water that sucked into his lungs and a vicious pressure in his chest, a searing pain that streamed through his blood to his brain, and then when he knew he could tolerate no more, a vicious explosion of red and black that threatened to burst his skull apart ...

And then, nothing. His clawing hands ceased to scrabble. The chaotic water eddied him into a tiny inlet, where his body caught in a trailing branch and hung there, buffeted this way and that by the relentless current.

It was there that Felix found him, but by then he was cold and completely lifeless.

Chapter Thirty-Nine

Patsy's baby was born just before midnight.

The birth had been quick and she soon recovered. By the time Terry was allowed in to see her, she was sitting up in bed, pale and tired but radiant, the baby held in the crook of her arm and her grey eyes almost lighting the room with their glow.

'She's here, Terry. She's *here*.'

'A little girl.' He stared down in wonder. He had never seen a newborn baby before and scarcely dared touch her. 'She's so tiny ...'

'Six pounds four ounces, Mrs Dodd says.' The midwife had arrived not long after the birth, in time to deliver the placenta and tidy Patsy up. 'And look how pretty she is! Like a rose just coming into flower.'

'She is. She'm just like a rose.' He looked at the small face, crumpled and deep pink, like a bud unfurling its petals. 'Can we call her that, Patsy? Can we call her Rose?'

'I thought you wanted Dorothy.'

'Rose is prettier. And it's like her. It's what she is.' He touched the baby's cheek. 'Rosebud. My little rosebud. Oh, *Patsy* ...'

He bent and cradled them both in his arms, holding them gingerly as if they might break, and felt a swell of love within him, bright and shining like a sunrise, taking him completely by surprise.

'I never expected to feel like this,' he said. 'I thought – I thought I'd just feel ordinary. Pleased, of course, but – I dunno how to say it. Patsy, I do love you. I love you both.'

'I love you too,' she said. 'And it wasn't wrong, was it? To do what we did? Not if it turns out like this.'

'I don't see how it could be.'

They sat for a while gazing at the baby they had brought into the world, marvelling at the tiny fingers and toes, the minute nails, the fuzz of pale hair.

'She's going to look like you,' Terry said. 'That's a relief. Dad was hoping she would.'

Patsy laughed. 'I don't think you'm ugly, Terry!'

'You're the only one, then.'

Nancy Pettifer came in then, with Jack close behind her. 'Your father wants to see his new granddaughter, and then we'm all going to bed. Ann's asleep already on the settee, worn out she was. Oh, and Bob's here too. Five minutes, that's all. Patsy needs to go to sleep.'

Jack and Bob came in, grinning self-consciously. Patsy pulled the baby's shawl aside to display her face, while Terry stood proudly by. Then she asked, 'How did the extravaganza go? Did folk like the skiffle group?'

'They thought we were the bee's knees,' Bob said. 'We'm playing at a dance over to Sampford the week after next.'

'You're not! That's really good, Bob. I wish I'd been there.'

'No you don't,' Nancy said. 'Because if you had, you'd still be waiting for this little dear, and I reckon you'd had enough of waiting. And so had she. Now – out, all of you. It's another day tomorrow.'

Terry stayed beside his wife. He could not bear to leave her now. 'We'm a family,' he whispered when they were alone again. 'We'm a real little family ...'

It would be another day for all of them, and although Terry, Patsy and Ann did not yet realise it, it would be a different world.

The Burracombe Hillbillies had just ended their final song, to surprisingly enthusiastic applause, when Bernie Nethercott had pushed open the door of the village hall, almost knocking Val Ferris over for the second time that evening.

'Bernie! Whatever are you doing? Don't you have any customers in the pub tonight?'

'They'm all here by the look of it,' he muttered under cover of the clapping. 'But that's not why I'm here. I've had a phone call from Bert Lillywhite, over to Little Burracombe. Say's there've been an accident down at the Clam and they needs the doctor there.'

'An accident?' Val exclaimed. 'But he's not here – he's gone to see Patsy Pettifer. How bad is it?'

'Bad enough, from what Bert says. What about that other doctor – the one that's staying there? They came into the Bell at dinner time. Is he here?'

'Yes – he's sitting with Hilary. I'll go and tell him.' Val made her way between the seats and bent to speak to David. Hilary listened too.

'Of course I'll go,' David said. 'Can someone show me the way?'

'I will,' Hilary began, but Jacob Prout, who had been sitting in front of David and turned his head to hear the exchange, broke in. 'I'll do that. Nobody knows that old track better than I do, and 'tis no night for a lady to be out in.' He was on his feet, pushing his way out with David close behind him. 'Have you got your doctor's bag with you? Sounds like us might need it.'

'It's in Colonel Napier's car. Can we drive there?'

Jacob snorted. 'The first few hundred yards, to the track going down, but after that 'tis Shanks's pony. 'Tis a rough old track, rocky and steep too in places, down to the river, and the water'll be up after all this rain. Someone fell in, Bernie, is that what it is?'

'I reckon so,' the innkeeper panted as they hurried along the lane to where Hilary had parked her car. 'Bert didn't say too much, just that there'd been an accident and they wanted a doctor. God knows who would have been down there on a night like this.'

They stopped at the car. Hilary had left it unlocked and the keys were inside. To David's query, she had laughed and told him this was Burracombe, not Derby, and he was thankful for this as he and Jacob got in and he drove at Jacob's direction towards the sunken track leading to the old bridge, while Bernie returned to the inn.

'Stop here,' Jacob ordered, and David pulled in to the side of the lane. The two men got out into the streaming rain. ''Tis down this way.'

'Good Lord,' David gasped as they picked their way down the rough metalled track. 'You mean to say this is the only way across the river?'

'Unless you goes three miles round by the main road. Been used for hundreds of years, this old road. But only a fool or a madman would try to get across on a night like this.'

'I wonder which I am,' David said wryly, stumbling behind him. 'A fool or a madman!'

And then, as he came down to the depth of the steep little valley by the glimmer of Jacob's torch and the answering lights of the little cluster of men on the far side of the old wooden bridge, he knew that he was neither. He was a doctor, called to his first emergency in Burracombe, and he had come home.

'Percy Shillabeer?' Jack Pettifer, woken from a too-brief sleep after the excitement of the night, stared at the two men, slowly taking in the gravity of their faces. 'Are you telling me he's drowned?'

David Hunter glanced at Felix and nodded. 'I'm afraid so.'

There was a short silence in the Pettifers' kitchen. Jack rubbed his hand over his face. 'I dunno what to say.'

'We'll have to tell Ann. And Patsy,' Felix said. 'I'm very sorry, Jack. I know it's a bad time. We waited till six thirty, but we couldn't leave it any later.'

'But I don't understand ... How did he come to be in the river? Where was he? Who found him?' He stared at David. 'Are you police?'

'No.' Felix stepped forward. 'I should have introduced you. This is Dr Hunter. He's staying with Dr Latimer for a few days.'

'I was called away from the village hall,' David added. 'Charles – Dr Latimer – was already here with your daughter-in-law, so they asked me to go. One of the village men – Jacob Prout – showed me the way down to the river. It seems that Mr Shillabeer fell into the water, by the little footbridge.'

'The Clam, you mean? Fell in?'

'It looks like it. I think he must have slipped and not been able to climb out. The water's running very high and swift just there.'

'It do,' Jack said, still bemused. 'And there's whirlpools too. There was a little tacker and his dad drowned there a few years back. But Percy ... He ought to have known every step of the way blindfold. And what was he doing down there? What sort of time did it happen, d'you reckon?'

'Probably sometime between milking and half past seven, when I found him,' Felix said. 'But he was cold then, so I think he'd been dead for a while. I thought he must have been coming over here. In fact, we were afraid Ann might have been with him. They've had the Tavistock firemen down there, searching the riverbanks. It was only when David – Dr Hunter – arrived that we discovered that she was here already.' He remembered his deep relief that the farmer's wife was safe. For Patsy to have lost her mother as well would have been tragic beyond words. 'He must have been on his way here,' he repeated.

'Over *here*? Well, if he were, it would have been to cause trouble!' Jack gave the young clergyman a quick look. 'I'm sorry, Vicar, I know us shouldn't speak ill of the dead, but you know the situation. If Percy Shillabeer was coming over to Burracombe, it wasn't for a game of darts and a few jokes.'

'But if he knew that Patsy's confinement had started, and Ann was already here ...'

Jack shook his head. 'Leopards don't change their spots, Vicar. Percy wasn't coming to congratulate her. You know how he felt about that. You're sure it was an accident?'

Felix looked shocked. 'Of course I'm sure!'

'I'm not. Percy been getting more and more funny in the head these past few months. I wouldn't be surprised if he'd gone completely off his rocker. When our Terry went over there this afternoon to ask Ann to come, the mad fool chased him off with a shotgun. *Fired* at him an' all. Ann Shillabeer told us that herself.'

'Oh my God ...' Felix said. He glanced at David. 'He had it with him – it was still slung on his shoulder, caught up in some branches.'

The three men were silent. Felix was thinking of the pitiable tragedy of it all, while David was looking ahead to the inevitable inquest. Jack was still rubbing the back of his neck, trying to take it all in.

As they stood there, Nancy came down the stairs, an old dressing gown wrapped around her, her hair over her face.

'What's going on, Jack? It's only just seven o'clock.'

'It's trouble, Nance. Bad trouble.' He indicated the two men behind him. 'Percy Shillabeer's had an accident.'

'An accident?' Ann was at the door now, coming out of the front room where she had spent the night. 'What do you mean, an accident? What's happened? Where's my Percy?' Her voice rose shrilly. 'He's not hurt, is he?'

Felix stepped forward. 'Hold on, Ann,' he said gently, and laid his hands on her arms. 'I'm afraid it's bad news. Percy fell in the river last night. I found him myself some time after it happened.' He paused, framing the next sentence, but Ann forestalled him.

'He's dead, isn't he? My Percy's dead. Drowned. That's what you'm telling me, isn't it?'

'I'm very sorry,' Felix said quietly.

Ann stared at him. She swayed a little and David caught her. Between them they got her back into the front parlour and laid her on the settee where she had spent the few hours of the night. Nancy, almost as shaken, hurried back to the kitchen and found the little bottle of brandy they kept for medicinal purposes. She came back and poured some into a small glass.

'Drink this, Ann. It'll help you.'

The bewildered woman sipped and choked. She looked up at the little cluster of faces surrounding her. 'What happened?'

'We think he was on his way over here,' Felix said quietly. 'Did he know you were here?'

'I came with Terry. Yes, he knew. He tried to stop me.' She met Felix's eyes. 'I told him I wouldn't be stopped. I came anyway.'

Felix said, 'Jack told me that Percy had fired on Terry that afternoon.'

'He did,' she replied dully. 'And would have done it again too if I hadn't stopped him, and Terry laying there in all that mud ... I thought he'd killed the boy, I did really. And you reckon he was on his way here?' She shivered. 'It's God's blessing he never arrived.'

'Ann!' Nancy exclaimed in shock. 'You mustn't say such things.'

'It's true. I tell you, I've been frightened for my life many a time these past weeks, and frightened for the little ones too. I've even wondered if he was going mad. That's why I been sending them over to our Edna so much. Here' – her eyes widened and she began to struggle up from the settee – 'where are they? The children? He's not touched—'

'No, no, they're all right.' Felix pressed her gently back against

302

the cushions. 'They're still at your sister's. It was she who alerted us, wondering where you were. Stella and I went to the farm and found nobody there, and we were worried. In the end, Stella went for Mr Lillywhite and I walked down towards the Clam, wondering if he'd gone down there. That's when I found him.' He paused. 'I was afraid you were with him too, but thank God Dr Hunter knew you were here.'

Ann turned her eyes on the stranger, puzzled. 'How did you know? Who ...?'

'This is Dr Hunter,' Felix said hastily. 'He came because Dr Latimer was here with Patsy.'

'Dr Hunter saw Patsy yesterday at the surgery,' Nancy said. 'She told us.'

There was a short pause. Ann put her hand to her head. 'I feel a bit funny.'

'It's shock,' David said, moving to lay her down again. 'Just rest for a while, Mrs Shillabeer. Perhaps someone could make some tea.'

Nancy nodded. 'I reckon we could all do with a cup. And then someone's got to tell Patsy. Poor little bird ...'

'I'll do that,' said Terry's voice, and they all turned quickly. 'It's all right – I've been here long enough to get an idea what's happened.' He looked at Ann. 'I reckon you'm right, Ma. He's been going mad for months. A lot of people thought so.'

'And nobody seemed able to do a thing about it,' Felix said sadly. 'We tried. I talked to Bert Lillywhite about him, I talked to Charles, but there didn't seem to be any action we could take. Thank God it wasn't any worse.' He thought of the shotgun Percy had been carrying and the fact that he'd fired at Terry earlier. Who could tell what might have happened if he'd reached the Pettifers' cottage with such rage fermenting inside him?

And, he thought then, what had driven him to such desperation? Who could tell what had turned the farmer's tortured mind? A childhood that had been lived in the shadow of fear and violence; a life that had never given him the comfort he must have sought, because no life ever could. The defiance of his child and then his wife. Perhaps it had always been inevitable that Percy's damaged life would end in tragedy; perhaps there had never been anything anyone could have done.

303

When Nancy came back with the tea, he asked them all to join him in a short prayer for the peace of Percy's soul and for the family he had left behind. Then Terry went upstairs to his wife and baby, and the rest of them waited, coming slowly to terms with the situation, until the new young family should need them.

Chapter Forty

'And do you think you'll still enjoy living in Burracombe after such an introduction?' Hilary asked when David arrived at last at the Barton, after Charles had insisted he have a few hours' sleep. 'We don't usually have such turmoil.'

'It has been rather more eventful than I expected,' he admitted. 'But that's life, isn't it? A death and a birth – tragedy and joy. Two sides of the same coin. It doesn't matter where we are, these are the things that are going to happen.'

'You're right. But in a village we're all so much more deeply involved with each other. Patsy used to work for me in the house – that's where she met Terry, when he came with Bob to do some electrical wiring. Felix used be the curate here, and Stella was the schoolteacher, and they're both friends of mine. Even Jacob Prout, who showed you the way to the Clam, is well known in Burracombe – you'll run into him everywhere, digging graves, clearing ditches, cutting hedges and so on. It's like a network of its own. Which is why the grapevine is so efficient,' she added wryly. 'You'll soon find how hard it is to keep secrets around here!'

'I hope we won't have too many to keep,' David said. He took her hand as they strolled through the wood beside the river. The rain had stopped and the fog had dispersed at last. A weak winter sun straggled down through the almost bare branches and glittered on the water, which had receded a little but still ran swiftly over the stones as it hurried on its way to the sea. It was hard to believe that this small river, less than fifteen feet wide, had killed a man last night. 'We won't have to wait too long now, will we, darling?'

305

'You're definitely coming to work with Charles?'

'Definitely,' he said. 'We get on very well and he seems happy for me to take over part of the practice now and the whole thing later on. In two or three years, probably. And are you happy to be married to a country doctor?'

'Oh yes, it will be very useful,' she said demurely, and then laughed at him. 'Of course I am! And when I see how happy Charles and Mary are together – well, I think I'm a very lucky woman. I think that anyway,' she added more seriously. 'You know, there have been times when I thought nothing would ever come right for us. I still can't believe it's turned out so well.'

'There's still a little way to go yet. My father's arrangements are almost complete – he's just been waiting for me to make my final decision – but Charles and I have a lot to sort out. But with fair weather and a following wind, I think I could be here by January, if only as his assistant to start with. And then you and I ...'

'Not too quickly,' she said. 'Not that I wouldn't like to walk round to the church and marry you this very minute, but I do think we need time to let everyone get used to the idea. There'll only be gossip if we spring it on them too suddenly, and even in a place like Burracombe, the local doctor needs to be above gossip.'

'All right,' he said. 'Supposing I'm here in January, what do you say to an engagement at Easter and then a wedding, say, six months after that? That wouldn't be too sudden, would it?'

Hilary stopped and turned to him. She put her hand up to his face and traced the planes of his cheek with her fingers, moving them slowly down to his mouth. He parted his lips and took her fingers into his mouth, biting them gently, and then with sudden roughness pulled her into his arms and kissed her.

'Oh, Hilary,' he murmured, cupping the back of her head with his hand and twining his fingers in her hair. 'Oh, *Hilary* ...'

'No,' she whispered when he let her go at last. 'No, I don't think that would be too sudden at all.'

The verdict of the inquest into Percy Shillabeer's death was accidental drowning. The state of his mind that day – the fact that he was carrying a shotgun and had actually fired it at Terry earlier that afternoon – was taken into consideration, but the coroner took the view that nobody knew what he was thinking or feeling that evening. Perhaps he had indeed been on his way to make amends with his daughter. And plenty of farmers carried a shotgun almost as part of their day's work. Sometimes, the coroner said reprovingly, they seemed to have forgotten they were there, as you might get so used to carrying a stick or a dog whistle that it became part of your normal dress. It might be a good thing if more guns were left at home unless there was a real purpose in taking them.

Felix conducted the funeral a few days later. It was well attended, for Ann and her children's sake more than for Percy's, but he was well known locally and it was only right that respects should be paid. Not many tears were shed, though. Ann, looking white and drawn, wept as she followed the coffin into the church, accompanied by Terry and her eldest son, with the rest of the family following, but she and the other women and children did not attend the burial. They went back to the house, where the big dining table, so seldom used, was laden with a baked ham, relishes and a few of George Sweet's crusty loaves. Jack and Nancy passed round sherry or glasses of squash, and later on Ann and her sister made tea. And then it was all over and there were just a few of them left to clear away.

'You take the weight off your feet now,' Nancy said to Ann. 'We'll do this. You and Patsy sit and have a rest. I'm sure it's time that little dear was fed, anyway.'

She left them in the sitting room, by the fire. Patsy unbuttoned her blouse and lifted the baby to her breast. The curtains had already been drawn against the dark winter afternoon, and the room was very quiet.

'I had two of they Exclusives round here,' Ann said after a few minutes. 'Wanting to know what I meant to do with your father's body. I told them, he'll be buried here in the village where he grew up, and take his place in the churchyard with the rest of the Shillabeers. They started to tell me what I ought to do, and I said they could mind their own business. He was never theirs, not really. They just caught him at a bad time, filling his head with rubbish, and it was that that sent him to his grave. He'd have come round in the end if he hadn't fallen in with them. And I told them me and the family was outsiders anyway, and from what I'd heard they didn't ought to be even talking to me. And then I shut the door in their faces.'

Patsy stared at her admiringly. 'Go on! I didn't know you had it in you.'

'Nor did I, till that afternoon when he went for Terry with his gun. I saw red then, Patsy, I don't mind telling you. Pity I didn't do it a lot sooner.'

'You tried,' Patsy said, thinking of the times when her mother had stood up to Percy and suffered for it. 'You did your best. And we're free of him now, sad though his end was.'

Ann was silent for a moment. Then she said quietly, 'He were different when he were a young man, Patsy. He was hurt bad as a little boy. Us all knew that. I could see he just needed the right kind of loving, that was all. It was a shame I never seemed to be able to give it to him.'

'Perhaps nobody could have given it to him,' Patsy said. 'But you did your best, Mother. You gave him all you could. And I reckon he knew it, too. I reckon, just in those last few minutes, he knew it.'

David returned to Derby, and just before Christmas, Hilary travelled up there to meet his parents. She saw the house where he had lived with Sybil, about to be sold now to a dentist and his wife and four young children, and knew that from now on it would be a happy home. She came away feeling that part of their story was now complete. A few days after Christmas, David left Derby and joined her in Burracombe.

'Charles and Mary have asked me to stay with them for as long as I like,' he told her. 'I'll start work with him in January. I dare say most people know me – or know of me – now, after what happened to Percy Shillabeer, so it shouldn't be too difficult to settle in.'

'They'll be beating a path to your doorway to have a look for themselves,' she told him. 'Expect to be diagnosing a lot of minor ailments for the first few weeks!'

'And now that I'm officially here,' he said, 'can I officially be your friend? Can we start what Wilfred Pickles calls "coorting"?'

'I shall be very disappointed if we don't! But before that, I want to take you over to see Felix and Stella. They've asked us over for tea on New Year's Eve, before the village celebrations, when we all gather round the tree holding hands at midnight and wait for the bells to ring.'

'Do we? I can see I'm going to be constantly surprised by Burracombe traditions!'

They drove round to the other village. Neither wanted to cross the Clam or negotiate that twisting, slippery track at night. Hilary would take David there one day, when the sun was shining and the ghost of Percy Shillabeer could be laid, but for this last day of the year they wanted simple normality, which Felix and Stella would be able to provide.

'And here they are!' Felix exclaimed, throwing wide the door. 'Come in out of the cold and tell us all your news.'

They followed him through the hallway into the big sitting room, smiling at the gigantic Christmas tree standing in one corner and the decorations that festooned the room.

'I told Felix it was rather too much, but he would put up every single decoration we owned,' Stella said, wheeling in a trolley laden with sandwiches, scones and cakes. 'And as it's our first Christmas here, I rather agreed with him. Neither of us has ever had a home of our own before, and we just couldn't resist it.'

She shook hands with David and they settled down to tea. Felix, as usual, wolfed several sandwiches, most of the scones and a large piece of Christmas cake. 'I never seem to feel full,' he explained apologetically to David. 'Do you think there's something wrong with me?'

'Don't answer that!' Stella advised. 'It would take you too long, and even then I could add a few more things to your list. Hilary, how's your father? I thought he looked very well at Mrs Warren's sherry party.'

'He is. He's better than he's been for years. He even went to the midnight service on Christmas Eve.'

'I'd like to have been there,' Stella said. 'The Little Burracombe church is lovely and I'm beginning to feel much more at home here, but I do miss going to the Burracombe services over Christmas. I hope you'll be here for next Christmas,' she added to David, passing him the last scone. 'Do eat this before Felix does. I'm always afraid he'll burst.'

David smiled and took it. He glanced at Hilary and said, 'I think it's pretty certain I'll be here next Christmas.'

'Are you?' Stella looked from one to the other, her eyes full of questions. 'Is there something you're going to tell us?'

Hilary laughed and said, 'All right – but don't let anyone else know just yet. Only the chosen few – you two, Luke and Val and one or two others. We're thinking we'll probably get engaged at Easter and then married sometime in the autumn.'

'Really? That's wonderful!' Stella jumped up and kissed them both. Felix joined in the congratulations, kissing Hilary and shaking hands with David.

'We must toast your future happiness. Tea's no good –I'll find the sherry.' He departed and came back a moment later with two bottles of sherry and four glasses on a silver tray. He looked enquiringly at Stella, who shook her head. 'I'll stay with tea, thanks, darling.'

Hilary turned to look at her. 'And why is that, pray? Do *you* have something you want to tell *us*?'

'I knew we couldn't keep it quiet for long,' Stella said with a laugh. 'All right – you've guessed it. We're having a baby! It's not for ages yet – not till late August. So don't get married then, please, because I'll either be like a barrage balloon or too busy washing nappies! And we don't want everyone to know for at least another month, preferably two.'

'A baby,' Hilary said softly. 'I am so, so pleased for you both. A double celebration. We ought to be drinking champagne, not sherry.'

'That's what Burracombe is all about,' Stella said as they clinked their glasses against her teacup. 'There will always be some sadness, and even tragedy. Things will go wrong. But there will always be good things too. There'll always be things to celebrate in Burracombe.'

'I'll drink to that,' Felix said, and he held his glass high. 'To the year that has passed, with all its tragedies and joys. To the year that is to come. And, most of all, to celebrations.'

'To celebrations,' they echoed. 'Celebrations in Burracombe.'